P9-DNO-694

HIGH PRAISE FOR BRIAN KEENE AND *THE RISING*!

"[Brian Keene's] first novel, *The Rising*, is a postapocalyptic narrative that revels in its blunt and visceral descriptions of the undead."

—*The New York Times Book Review*

"[*The Rising* is] the most brilliant and scariest book ever written. Brian Keene is the next Stephen King."

—*The Horror Review*

"*The Rising* is more terrifying than anything currently on the shelf or screen."

—*Rue Morgue*

"*The Rising* is chock-full of gore and violence...an apocalyptic epic."

—*Fangoria*

"*The Rising* by master wordsmith and storyteller Brian Keene is a gruesome and macabre tale of horrific madness sweeping across the civilized world."

—*Midwest Book Review*

"An apocalyptic epic packed with violence, gore, scares and moral dilemmas. Brian Keene has given zombies their next upgrade."

—*Cemetery Dance*

"Hoping for a good night's sleep? Stay away from *The Rising*. It'll keep you awake, then fill your dreams with lurching, hungry corpses wanting to eat you."

—Richard Laymon, author of *Resurrection Dreams*

"More power to Brian Keene. He reminds us that horror fiction can deal with fear, not just indulge it."

—Ramsey Campbell, author of *The Overnight*

MORE PRAISE FOR BRIAN KEENE AND *THE RISING*!

"Quite simply, the first great horror novel of the new millennium!"

—*Dark Fluidity*

"Brian Keene is one of the best new writers in the horror genre. Period."

—Edward Lee, author of *Flesh Gothic*

"With *The Rising*, Brian Keene has forever raised the bar for extreme horror; this novel is not only gloriously grotesque, it's also smart, literate, exceptionally written, and filled with fully-realized characters that readers can actually care about. It doesn't get much better than this."

—Gary A. Braunbeck, author of *In Silent Graves*

"With Keene at the wheel, horror will never be the same."

—*Hellnotes*

"Stephen King meets Brian Lumley. Keene will keep you turning the pages to the very end."

—*Terror Tales*

"Different, unique and cool—this one doesn't disappoint!"

—*Domain of the Dead*

"Definitely transcends your basic run-of-the-mill horror."

—*The Haunted*

"A must-read for fans of the living dead. Fresh, innovative and full of suspense!"

—*All Things Zombie*

CITY OF THE DEAD

BRIAN KEENE

LEISURE BOOKS  NEW YORK CITY

For Devon. Thanks for making your Uncle Brian believe again...you saved my life and only you and I know it.

A LEISURE BOOK®

June 2005

Published by

Dorchester Publishing Co., Inc.
200 Madison Avenue
New York, NY 10016

If you purchased this book without a cover you should be aware that this book is stolen property. It was reported as "unsold and destroyed" to the publisher and neither the author nor the publisher has received any payment for this "stripped book."

Copyright © 2005 by Brian Keene

This work is a work of fiction. Names, characters, places and incidents are either a product of the author's imagination or are used fictitiously. Any resemblance to actual events, locales or persons, living or dead, is entirely coincidental.

"Our Dream," lyrics by Tony d'Mattia. Copyright © 2003 by Fiz. Used by permission.

All rights reserved. No part of this book may be reproduced or transmitted in any form or by any electronic or mechanical means, including photocopying, recording or by any information storage and retrieval system, without the written permission of the publisher, except where permitted by law.

ISBN 0-8439-5415-9

The name "Leisure Books" and the stylized "L" with design are trademarks of Dorchester Publishing Co., Inc.

Printed in the United States of America.

Visit us on the web at www.dorchesterpub.com.

ACKNOWLEDGMENTS

Special thanks to: Cassandra; Shane Staley; Don D'Auria; the Cabal; my fellow Necrophobiacs Mike, John and Brett; my overworked bodyguard Big Joe; Mark, Matt and Deena for once again being my eyes and ears; John, Shane and Chris of Drop of Water Productions; Greg Nicotero and Chad Savage (they know why); Ken Foree; Gary Klar; Reggie Bannister; Fiz, for the use of his lyrics; Alan Clark; Lisa, Ron and Kevin, winners of the fan club contest; Rich and Tim, who know what time it is; Jon Merz and Sean Terwilliger for their technical assistance; Ryan Harding for a really cool idea; and finally, to all the fans who read *The Rising* and wrote to me about how much the ending pissed them off...

Other *Leisure* books by Brian Keene:
THE RISING

AUTHOR'S NOTE

Although New York City and New Jersey are real, I have taken fictional liberties with them. So if you live there, don't look for your house or your favorite coffee shop. You won't find it, and probably wouldn't want to know what lives there now.

"What is best of all is beyond your reach forever; not to be born, not to be, to be nothing. But the second best for you—is quickly to die."

—Silenus

"During those days men will seek death, but will not find it; they will long to die, but death will elude them."

—*Book of Revelation*, Chapter 9, Verse 6

"I know that we will rise."

—Fiz, "Our Dream"

"And the city of nations fell…for the plague was exceedingly great."

—*Book of Revelation*, Chapter 16, Verse 19

ONE

Standing next to their battered Humvee, Jim, Martin, and Frankie stared into the distance. A cemetery stretched off to the horizon along both sides of New Jersey's Garden State Parkway, and the highway cut right through the graveyard's center. Thousands of tombstones thrust upward to the sky, surrounded by tenements and overgrown vacant lots. Tombs and crypts also dotted the landscape, but the sheer number of gravestones almost overwhelmed them.

Jim said, "I remember this place. It used to freak me out every time I drove up here to pick up Danny or drop him off. Creepy, isn't it?"

"It's something all right," Frankie gasped. "I've never seen so many tombstones in one place. It's fucking huge!"

The old preacher whispered something beneath his breath.

"What'd you say, Martin?"

He stared across the sea of marble and granite.

"I said that this is our world now. Surrounded on all sides by the dead."

Frankie nodded in agreement. "As far as the eye can see."

"How long after all these buildings crumble," Martin sighed, "will these tombstones remain standing? How long after we're gone will the dead remain?"

Martin shook his head sadly. They finished examining the Humvee for any damage suffered during their last battle with the dead, at a government research facility in Hellertown, Pennsylvania. It was an experiment at this facility that had led to the dead coming back to life in the first place. Jim and the others had been attacked outside the facility and barely escaped, and now they were back on their journey to save Jim's young son, Danny.

Satisfied that the Humvee hadn't suffered major damage, they continued on their way.

As the sun began to set, its last, faint rays shone upon the sign in front of them.

BLOOMINGTON—NEXT EXIT

Jim began to hyperventilate.

"Take that exit."

Martin turned around, concerned.

"Are you okay, Jim? What is it?"

Jim clenched the seat, gasping for air. He felt nauseous. His pulse pounded in his chest and his skin grew cold.

"I'm scared," he whispered. "Martin, I'm just so scared. I don't know what's going to happen."

Frankie cruised down the exit ramp and flicked on the headlights. The tollbooths stood empty, and she breathed a sigh of relief.

"Which way?"

Jim didn't answer, and they were unsure whether he'd even heard her. His eyes were squeezed shut, and he'd begun to tremble.

"Hey," Frankie shouted from the front seat, "you

want to see your kid again? Snap the fuck out of it and get your shit together. Now which way?"

Jim opened his eyes. "Sorry, you're right. Go to the bottom of the ramp and make a left at the light. Go up three blocks and then make a right onto Chestnut. There's a big church and a video store on the corner."

Jim exhaled, long and deep, and began to move again. He sat the rifles aside and double-checked the pistol, shoving it back into the holster after he was satisfied. He pressed himself into the seat and waited, while his son's neighborhood flashed by outside.

A zombie wearing a tattered delivery uniform jumped out from behind a cluster of bushes. It clutched a baseball bat in its grimy hands.

"There's one." Martin rolled down the window enough to squeeze off a shot.

"No," Frankie said, stopping him. "Don't shoot at them unless they directly threaten us or look like they're following."

"But that one will tell others," he protested. "The last thing we need to do is attract more!"

"Which is exactly why you don't need to be shooting at it, preacher. By the time it tells its rotten little friends that the lunch wagon is here, we can grab his boy and get the fuck out. You start shooting and every zombie in this town is gonna know we're here and where to come find us!"

"You're right." Martin nodded, and rolled the window back up. "Good thinking."

An obese zombie waddled by, dressed in a kimono and pulling a child's red wagon behind her. Another one sat perched in the wagon, its lower half missing and few remaining entrails and yellow curds of fat spilling out around it. Both creatures grew agitated as they sped by, and the fat zombie loped along behind them, fists raised in anger.

Frankie slammed on the brake, slammed the Humvee into reverse, and backed up, crushing both the zombies and the wagon under the wheels. The vehicle rocked from the jolt.

She grinned at Martin. "Now wasn't that much quieter than a gunshot?"

The preacher shuddered. Jim barely noticed either of his companions. His pulse continued to race, but the nausea was gone, replaced with a hollow emptiness.

How many times had he driven down this same suburban street, either to pick Danny up or to take him home? Dozens, but never suspecting that one day he'd do so armed to the teeth and riding in a hijacked military vehicle with a preacher and an ex-hooker. He remembered the first time, right after his first complete summer with Danny. Danny started crying when Jim turned onto Chestnut, not wanting his father to leave. The big tears rolled down his little face when they pulled into the driveway, and were still flowing when Jim reluctantly drove away. He'd watched Danny through the rear-view mirror and waited until he was out of sight before he pulled over and broke down himself.

He thought of Danny's birth. The doctor placed him in his arms for the first time. He'd been so small and tiny, his pink skin still wet. His infant son crying then too, and when Jim cooed to him, Danny opened his eyes and smiled. The doctors and Tammy insisted it wasn't a smile, that babies couldn't smile; but deep down inside, Jim had known better.

He thought of the summers that he and his second wife, Carrie, spent with Danny. The three of them had played Uno, and Danny and Carrie caught him cheating, hiding Draw Four cards under the table in his lap. They'd wrestled him to the floor, tickling him till he admitted the deception. Later, they sat on the couch together, eating popcorn and watching Godzilla and Mecha-Godzilla trash Tokyo.

The message that Danny had left on his cell phone a week ago echoed through his mind as they turned a corner.

"I'm on Chestnut," Frankie reported. "Now what?"

"I'm scared, Daddy. I know we shouldn't leave the attic, but Mommy's sick and I don't know how to make her better. I hear things outside the house. Sometimes they just go by and other times I think they're trying to get in. I think Rick is with them."

"Jim? JIM!"

Jim's voice was quiet and far away. "Past O'Rourke and Fischer, then make a left onto Platt Street. It's the last house on the left."

In his head, Danny was crying.

"Daddy, you promised to call me! I'm scared and I don't know what to do . . ."

"Platt Street," Frankie announced and made the turn. She drove past the houses, each lined up in neat rows, each one identical to the next, save for the color of their shutters or the curtains hanging in the vacant windows. "We're here."

She put the Humvee in park and left the engine running.

". . . and I love you more than Spider-Man and more than Pikachu and more than Michael Jordan and more than 'finity, Daddy. I love you more than infinity."

The phrase had haunted him over the last few days, resonating with double meaning. It had been a game he and Danny had shared, something to ease the pain of long-distance phone calls from West Virginia to New Jersey. But one of the zombie's he'd faced during the trip had also used the phrase.

"We are many. Our number is greater than the stars. We are more than infinity."

Jim opened his eyes.

"More than infinity, Danny. Daddy loves you more than infinity."

He opened the door and Martin followed. Jim placed a hand on his shoulder, pushing the old man back into the seat.

"No," he said firmly, shaking his head, "you stay with Frankie. I need you to watch our backs out here. Make sure we've got a clear shot at escape. I'm going to leave the rifles here with you guys—just in case."

He paused, and still squeezing Martin's shoulder, raised his head and sniffed the breeze.

"This town is alive with the dead, Martin. Can you smell them?"

"I can," the preacher admitted, "but you'll need help. That buckshot wound in your shoulder ain't getting better. What if—"

"I appreciate everything you've done for me and Danny, but this is something I have to do alone."

"I'm afraid of what you might find."

"So am I. That's why I need to do this by myself. Okay?"

Martin was reluctant. "Okay. We'll wait here for both of you."

Frankie leaned over the seat and pulled one of the M-16s to the front. She placed it between her legs and checked the rear-view mirror.

"Coast is clear," she said. "Better get going."

Jim nodded.

Martin sighed. "Good luck, Jim. We'll be right here."

"Thank you. Thank you both."

He took a deep breath, turned away, and crossed the street. His feet felt leaden, his hands numb. Gripping the pistol, he shook it off and clenched his jaw.

"More than infinity, Danny . . ."

He broke into a run, his boots pounding on the sidewalk as he sprinted for the house. He turned into the yard, dashed onto the porch and drew the pistol from its holster. Hand trembling, he reached out and tried the doorknob. It was unlocked.

Slowly, Jim turned it. Calling his son's name, he went inside the house.

They waited in the darkness.

Martin hadn't realized he was holding his breath until Jim vanished through the front door.

Frankie checked the street for movement again. "What now?"

"We wait," he told her. "We wait and we watch for them to come out."

The night air turned chilly, and it whistled through the hole in the ruined windshield. Frankie shivered. Jim had been right. There was something foul on the breeze.

"So how old is Danny, anyway?"

"Six," Martin answered. "He was—I mean is—a cute kid. Looks like Jim."

"You saw a picture?"

He nodded.

"How long you two been traveling together?"

"Since West Virginia. Jim got attacked outside my church. I saved him and then promised to help him find his son."

Frankie was quiet for a moment. Then she spoke again.

"Tell me something, preacher-man. Do you *really* think his son is alive in there?"

Martin watched the house. "I hope so, Frankie. I hope."

"Me too. I think that . . ." Her voice trailed off and she checked the street and surrounding yards again. Carefully, she hefted the rifle.

The stench was getting stronger.

"What is it?" Martin asked.

"Can't you smell them? They're coming."

Martin cracked his window and sniffed the air, his nose wrinkling in disgust.

"I reckon they know we're here, somewhere. They're hunting for us."

"What should we do?"

"Like I said, we wait. Not much else we can do. Just be ready."

They grew quiet again and watched the silent houses around them. Martin turned back to Danny's house. His jittery legs bounced up and down and he cracked his leathery knuckles in the dark. His arthritis was acting up and he doubted he'd find any medicine lying around for it soon.

"Stop fidgeting."

"Sorry."

Random Bible verses ran through his head and Martin focused on them so that he would not have to wonder what was going on inside the house. *Blessed are the peacemakers . . . Jesus saves . . . For God so loved the world that He gave his only begotten son, that whosoever believes in Him, shall not perish, but have eternal life . . . And on the third day, he arose from the dead . . .*

Martin glanced back at the house again, fighting the urge to get out of the Humvee and run toward it. He thought of the father and son who had saved them from cannibals in Virginia. The father had been mortally wounded and before he could turn into a zombie, the son shot him and then turned the gun on himself.

He gave his only begotten son, that whosoever believes in Him, shall not perish, but have eternal life . . . And on the third day, he arose from the dead . . .

. . . His only begotten son . . . he arose from the dead . . .

. . . His only son . . . arose from the dead . . .

Martin froze.

"Frankie, I—"

A gunshot suddenly rang out, shattering the stillness. It was followed by a scream. Silence returned and then a second gunshot followed.

Both had come from inside the house.

"Frankie, that was Jim screaming!"

"Are you sure? It didn't sound human to me."

"It was him! I'm sure of it."

"What do we do now?"

"I don't know. I don't know!"

Martin's mind whirled.

He shot Danny and then himself! He got in there, and Danny was a zombie. His only begotten son arose from the dead!

Frankie shook him.

"Fuck this shit! Come on, Reverend!"

They jumped out of the Humvee, weapons at the ready, as the first cries of the undead drifted to them on the night wind. The zombies appeared at the end of the street and the doors to the houses began to open at the same time. The undead poured forth.

Martin's voice cracked. "It—it was a trap. L-look at all of them . . ."

"Shit."

Frankie raised the M-16, aimed and fired three shots in quick succession. One corpse dropped and five more took its place. With a horrendous cry, the zombies charged.

Martin turned back to the Humvee, but Frankie grabbed his arm.

"Move your ass, preacher-man!"

They ran toward the house, to see what had become of their friend. More gunshots echoed from inside as they approached.

Above them, the newly risen moon shined down upon the world, staring at a mirror image of its cold, dead self.

TWO

The house was silent.

"Danny?"

Jim crept forward, his heart still pounding in his chest. The floorboards creaked under his feet, and he held his breath. The living room was empty. Danny's movies were stacked neatly on a shelf, next to a row of video games. A thin layer of dust covered the coffee table and end tables. One of the sofa cushions had a crusty, reddish-brown stain in the middle and flies crawled over it.

"Danny! It's Daddy! Where are you?"

He walked into the kitchen and the smell hit him. Whatever was inside the garbage can was long since spoiled. Flies swarmed over its surface. They crawled on the refrigerator, trying to get inside the airtight appliance as well. The incessant buzzing seemed loud in the silence. Jim gagged. Holding his hand over his nose and mouth, he backed out of the room and into the hallway.

He tilted his head from side to side and listened.

There was a sound above him, like something being dragged across the floor.

He went to the stairs.

"Danny? Are you there? Come on out, son! It's me!"

Only a week before (though it now seemed like a year), Jim had had a particularly vivid nightmare about this moment. In the dream, he'd reached the top of the stairs, and limped toward Danny's room. The bedroom door creaked open and his son stepped out to greet him. A zombie.

At that point, Jim had screamed himself awake.

He wouldn't be able to do that this time.

If . . .

The top of the stairs lay hidden in shadows. The noise was not repeated.

Jim limped up each step, his second wind almost gone.

When they'd crossed the border between Pennsylvania and New Jersey, Frankie had asked him a question. Now the conversation ran through his mind.

"Have you thought about what you'll do if we get there and Danny's one of them?"

"I don't know."

But he did know.

If . . .

Pausing halfway up, Jim slid the magazine out of the pistol and checked his shots. Only a few left. But he had enough. Enough for Danny—and for himself.

If . . .

He continued upward, the stairs creaking with every step. The sound came again. A footstep? He stopped, listening. A hallway with four doors waited at the top of the stairs. Two of the doors led to the bedrooms; one belonged to Danny and the other Rick and Tammy. The third door led to the bathroom. The fourth led to the attic.

The sounds came from the attic. Unmistakable now,

they were the sounds of hesitant feet. Of someone trying to walk very carefully and quietly.

"Danny, it's your dad! Are you there?"

He reached the top and crept toward the attic door, passing by the bedrooms as he did. His breath hitched in his chest and the blood rushed in his ears. When he called out, his voice cracked.

"It's okay, Danny. You're safe. Everything's all right now. Everything is going to be fine."

The bathroom door burst open, and his dead ex-wife flung herself at him.

Tammy was a grisly sight. Her bathrobe hung open, stained with dried bodily juices. Decay bloomed, spreading across her rancid flesh. Most of her thick, dark hair was gone and the few clumps that remained were matted and greasy. A worm dangled from her gray cheek and another burrowed through her forearm. Brownish-yellow liquid ran from the corners of her eyes and mouth and dripped from the open sores on her body. Her right breast hung down to her belly button, revealing the rancid meat inside. It swayed with each step she took. Something squirmed inside the dark folds of her groin.

"Hello, Jim!"

The corpse's foul breath clung to him. Too close to shoot, Jim smashed her in the face with the pistol butt, shuddering in revulsion as rotted teeth fell out onto the carpet.

He took a step backward as the zombie staggered, swollen legs struggling to support her bulbous weight.

"I'm here for Danny."

"You're too late," the now toothless mouth slurred, "Danny's dead!"

"Shut up! Just shut the fuck up!"

"Danny's dead! Danny's dead!" She danced around

the hallway, arms flailing, and chanted in a singsong voice. "The whelp is dead! Your son is dead!"

"You're lying. Tell me where he is!"

"Poor Jim. Did you come all this way just to rescue your son? Too late! His spirit is in torment, far beyond your reach. He burns in Hell like all your kind. His body has joined us, and now it's your turn! I will send your soul in search of his so that one of our brethren may flee the Void and inhabit you. There are so many of us waiting. So many. More than—"

Jim raised the pistol, but the thing that had been his ex-wife was faster. She lunged at him, grabbing his forearm with both rotted hands. Bony fingers pulled his arm toward the creature's mouth. The zombie's remaining teeth snapped together as he jerked away. Jim punched her in the face. The skin was cold and moist, and his fist sank through the surface of the thing's cheek. He pulled his dripping hand away with a wet, sucking sound.

Locked in a struggle, they grappled back and forth. The days-old gunshot wound in his shoulder burned. He felt blood leaking out around the amateur stitching. The zombie forced him back a step. She took another bite at his arm, narrowly missing. Jim slammed the creature against the wall once, twice, three times. Picture frames fell to the floor, shattering. Something inside Tammy popped, and black liquid erupted from her mouth and nose. The stench was overwhelming.

Freeing his arm, he swept the pistol around and fired, not bothering to aim. One ear disappeared, along with a portion of her scalp, but the zombie simply laughed. Jim's ears rang from the explosion. Tammy lumbered forward again.

"Did you know that she still loved you? Oh yes. I can see it in here." The zombie tapped her forehead. "She planned on leaving Rick so that the three of you could be a family again. But then you got re-married."

Jim screamed. An all-consuming rage swept over him. The veins in his neck and arms throbbed, and his body shook in anger.

"Shut up, you god-damn bitch!"

This time, his aim was true. The bullet left a small hole just above Tammy's eyes. The back of her head splattered across the wallpaper. He fired again and again—and again. His finger kept squeezing till the gun clicked empty. He stood over her corpse, looking down, and the gun slipped from his numb fingers.

"I'm sorry, Tammy. I wish things had ended differently between us. You may have taken Danny from me, but you didn't deserve this."

The hesitant shuffling sound behind the attic door repeated itself. Stepping over Tammy's remains, Jim started toward it.

"Danny?"

The door creaked open.

His son stepped out into the light.

"Danny!"

The tiny figure was silent, and then—

"Daddy? DADDY?"

"Danny! Oh my God . . ."

The six-year old boy's hair had turned white. Not gray or silver, but snow white. There was a strict demarcation halfway down the length of his hair. Midpoint to the end was still brown, but the rest was white.

"Danny . . ."

Danny ran to him and Jim hugged him tight, crushing his son against his chest. Both sobbed uncontrollably. The emotional weight crushed Jim—the disbelief that he'd actually found Danny alive, the overwhelming tidal wave of relieved shudders descending down his spine, and just the sheer feel of his son in his arms.

"Oh, Danny. I can't believe it."

"Daddy, I thought you were dead. I thought you were like Mommy and Rick and—"

"It's okay, son. It's okay now. Daddy's here now, and I'm never leaving you again. It's okay. I promise it's okay. You're safe now. That's all that matters. Shhh."

There were black circles under Danny's eyes, and he'd lost a lot of weight. Jim felt his son's ribs sticking through the thin Spider-Man pajama shirt. He ran his hand through the boy's white hair. What had happened to him?

What happened to my son? What the hell happened here?

Danny pulled away. "Daddy! You're hurt!"

"It's okay. It's not my blood. It's . . ."

Danny looked down at his mother's corpse and then buried his face in Jim's chest. He shuddered.

"You—you shot Mommy?"

"S-she wasn't your mother anymore, Danny. You know that, right?"

"Daddy, I was so scared. The monster-people came, and Mommy and I hid in the attic. Mommy got sick and then Rick came and I hurt him—I hurt him bad with his bowling ball so he wouldn't get Mommy, but Mommy never woke up, and when she did, she was one of the monster-people too, so I locked myself in the attic again and I blocked the door just like on TV, and Mommy kept trying to get in and—Daddy, WHERE WERE YOU? You said you'd always protect me, but you lied! You lied to me, Daddy!"

Jim squeezed him tighter. After a moment, he wiped his nose with his sleeve.

"I was on my way, Danny. I left as soon as I got your

message. I ran into some very bad people, and I got delayed. But that was a very smart thing you did, calling my cell phone. You were very brave, and I'm proud of you."

"Mommy said you wouldn't come. She said you didn't love me."

The familiar old anger surged through him, and for one brief second, he didn't regret shooting her reanimated corpse.

"When, Danny? When did she say that?"

"After she woke up again. When she was trying to get into the attic."

"Well, she was wrong. That wasn't your mother talking. And now that I'm here, nothing is going to ever hurt you again. I'll die first. Some friends of mine are waiting outside. But we've got to hurry, okay?"

Danny's cheeks were wet and puffy.

"I love you, Daddy. I love you more than 'finity."

Fresh tears rolled down Jim's face.

"Me too, buddy. I love you more than infinity, too. You don't know how long I've been waiting to tell you that again."

The door crashed open downstairs. Danny jerked in his arms. Jumping to his feet, Jim pushed his son behind him and reached for the pistol, still lying on the floor where he'd dropped it. Too late, he remembered that he was out of bullets.

"Get behind me, Danny."

A voice called out from below, "Jim?"

"Martin?"

"I'm here, Jim! Where are you?"

"Upstairs."

Then Frankie's voice, "Move it, old-timer! They're coming."

The door slammed shut with a bang.

Danny cowered behind him. Jim knelt down and looked him in the eyes.

"It's okay, Danny. These are the friends of mine that I mentioned. They helped me come find you. Let's go downstairs, and I'll introduce you to them. Okay?"

"Okay." Danny nodded.

They were halfway down the stairs when the zombies' cries reached Jim's ears. Frankie and Martin were dragging the couch toward the front door. As Jim reached the landing and Danny stepped out from behind him, Martin froze, staring at the boy.

"Come on, Preacher! Help me move—" Frankie paused, then followed Martin's stare.

"Hi," Danny stared at his toes, his voice trembling. "I'm Danny."

Both the preacher and the ex-hooker gaped. Then, Martin's warm laughter filled the room. "Well, I guess you must be! You really do look just like your father. Hello there, Danny. I'm Mr. Martin. It's very nice to meet you."

Smiling broadly, he walked over to the stairs and shook Danny's hand. Danny smiled back at him and then glanced at Frankie.

"Hi, kid. I'm Frankie."

"Frankie? That's not a girl's name."

"Well, I'm not a girl," Frankie countered with a wink. "I'm a woman."

"Oh."

Still beaming, Martin hugged Jim. "See? I told you this was God's will. He came through for you. He delivered your son."

"You think maybe God could deliver this fucking couch over to the door, too?" Frankie asked, trying to push the sofa. "Those things are gonna be here in a second."

"We've got company?" Jim fought to keep the alarm out of his voice. He didn't want to upset Danny further.

"Yeah, we've got company," Martin answered. "Lot's of it."

"The whole damn neighborhood is dropping by," Frankie muttered. "It's like an undead welcome wagon out there!"

Jim grabbed the other end of the sofa and helped Frankie position it against the door. His shoulder throbbed as he pushed. Outside, the shouts and cries increased. The stench of rotting flesh enveloped the house like a cloud, making them all gag.

"Little pigs, little pigs, let us come in!"

Danny shivered. "That's Tommy Padrone, the big kid from down the street. He walked around outside every night and hollered that over and over. I stuck my fingers in my ears, but I could still hear him. It was scary."

Jim frowned, wondering what other hells his son had faced while he was dealing with his own nightmarish journey.

"Martin, that thing got a fresh magazine?"

The preacher nodded.

"Good. Give it here."

Martin handed him the rifle. Its weight felt good in his hands.

"Take Danny upstairs. Go to the attic and close the door behind you."

"Daddy, I want to stay here with you!"

"I'll be up in a minute, squirt."

"You promise?" Danny sulked.

"I promise. Cross my heart and hope to die."

"Okay. Come on, Mr. Martin. I'll show you my baseball cards and stuff."

Jim waited until they'd disappeared up the stairs before turning to Frankie.

"So just how many are we dealing with here?"

"Like I said, the whole damn neighborhood. We didn't stick around to count heads. It's not good."

The clamor outside grew louder.

Jim shook his head in frustration. "Why didn't the two of you stay in the Humvee? You would have been safe. Now you've led them to us!"

"Well excuse the fuck out of me! We thought you were in trouble. Martin thought maybe you . . ."

"Maybe I what?"

She shook her head. "Forget it. Okay? We've got more important things to worry about."

"I'm sorry. It's just—he's safe, you know? I can't believe he's safe. And now I'm afraid it was all for nothing. I may have found my son only to watch us all die."

"Well then you'd better give me that M-16 to go along with mine, because I sure as shit intend to put up a fight."

Jim was quiet, appraising her. Then he smiled.

Fists, hammers and crowbars began to batter the door.

Frankie returned his smile.

"Let's do this shit."

Jim positioned himself at the bottom of the stairway. Frankie crouched down behind the recliner. The pounding on the door increased, rattling it in its frame. In the kitchen, a window shattered. Then another. The stench of decay wafted into the house, stronger now. They struggled to keep from retching.

"Remember—" Jim started.

"—Aim for the head," Frankie finished.

The door splintered, and a dozen arms forced themselves through the crack. The couch slid an inch, then two. Glass shattered in the kitchen, and then the living room window exploded. A zombie clambered through it, jagged shards ripping its flesh. Frankie raised her M-16, fired, and the zombie tottered to the floor minus most of its brain. Another one crawled through the opening behind it.

"Throw down your weapons, humans! We will make your deaths quick. You have our word."

"I got a better idea," Frankie shouted. "Why don't you all fuck off?"

"Bitch! We shall rip out your intestines and wear them as a necklace. We will feast on your hearts and livers. We will—"

"Here comes the boom, mother-fuckers!"

Frankie squeezed off another shot at the second zombie in the window. Its head disappeared from the nose up. Glass crunched under booted feet, alerting her to the creatures in the kitchen. Five of them started down the hall toward the living room. Behind them, she heard the kitchen door crash open.

"Shit!"

She turned and fired, choosing aimed, single shots rather than spraying in panic. Rounds tore through the zombies and also into the wall behind them.

At the same time, the sofa blocking the front door slid backward. The creatures swarmed into the house, only to drop under Jim's barrage. More took their place and fell on top of their comrades. Still more replaced them.

"Swarm them!" a zombie shrieked. "We can overrun them with our numbers."

"Better get upstairs!" Frankie shouted, squeezing off another three-round burst toward the kitchen. "They're coming in on all sides now."

"No way. I'm not leaving you here by yourself!"

"Bullshit! That's your son up there! You mean to tell me you came hundreds of miles just to die down here without him?"

Clenching his teeth, Jim aimed at the doorway and emptied his weapon. The rifle grew hot in his hands. The zombies that weren't mowed down jumped back out the door, taking cover behind the hedge.

"Look," Frankie reasoned, "if you've gotta die—and it looks like we're going to—then die with your son, not down here with me."

Jim slammed another magazine into place and glanced at Frankie.

"God damn it. You're right."

"Well then go!"

He ran up the stairs. Crouching, Frankie laid down a burst of cover fire and then duck-walked from the recliner to the foot of the stairway, taking his place. She retreated a few steps upward as more zombies entered the house.

A bullet plowed into the recliner, littering the carpet with tufts of foam stuffing. Another tore through the stairway's wooden railing. Outside, in the darkness, she saw a muzzle flash.

"Shit, they've got guns too."

She waited for the next shot, saw the flash before she heard it, and fired through the open doorway in the shooter's direction. The flash was not repeated.

"One down, eighty or so to go."

More zombies poured in through the kitchen. Suddenly, she felt a pair of clammy hands upon her ankle, clawing at her through the banister. She screamed, jerking her foot away. The zombie's ragged nails scratched her skin.

"Come here, cow!" the zombie taunted.

She swung the M-16 and fired. The headless corpse toppled to the carpet.

Still shooting, Frankie retreated to the top of the stairs.

"Jim, if you've got a plan, now would be a good time to share it!"

The zombies started up the stairs after her.

"And these are my *Yu-Gi-Oh* cards." Danny held the shoebox proudly.

Martin was amazed that Danny was reacting so calmly. He himself felt like hiding in a closet and pissing in his pants. Still marveling at the boy's resilience, he picked up a bright green, heavily muscled action figure from the floor.

"Who's this mean-looking guy? Wait a minute; I know. He's the Hulk, right?"

Danny rolled his eyes. "No, he's Piccolo from *DragonBall Z*."

"Oh," Martin muttered, aware that he'd just gone down on Danny's cool-meter. "I knew that."

He glanced around the room, saddened at the signs of a young boy forced to hole up here for the last week. Dirty bedding, a rumpled pile of clothes, empty water bottles and cookie bags, and scattered toys.

Gunshots rang out below and they both jumped. It was followed in quick succession by several more single shots; then changed over to the roar of automatic fire.

Danny gave the door a worried glance. Martin tried to distract him.

"You know, Danny, your father really missed you."

"I missed him, too. I didn't think he would come. I didn't think I'd ever see him again."

"Oh, he came all right. And he didn't let anything stand in his way, either. Not a thing. Your daddy is one tough cookie. You wouldn't believe what we had to go through to get here."

"Monster people?"

"Yes. But it wasn't just them, Danny. There were other bad people too. But your daddy never stopped. He was determined to find you."

More gunfire exploded downstairs. Martin clutched his pistol and tried to look calm.

"Mr. Martin, if you're my daddy's friend, and you helped him come find me, then how come I never met you when I went to his house in the summers?"

"Well, that's because I just met your father, after all this—well, after he left to come get you."

"Why?"

"Why?" Martin straightened his stiffening legs. The sounds of combat grew louder, and he had to raise his voice. "Well, because that's what God had planned for us. That's what God wanted me to do. Do you know about God, Danny?"

Danny nodded. "A little bit. Mommy and Rick didn't go to church. I know that he lives in Heaven, up in the sky. I thought that's where dead people went, but now I know better. When people die, they don't go to Heaven. They become monster-people."

Martin flinched, not sure how to respond. He picked up the action figure again.

"They still go to Heaven, if they know Jesus. Those

things out there—they aren't people, Danny. They're just shells—kind of like these toys. Like Piccirilli here."

"Piccolo." Danny corrected him.

"Sorry, Piccolo," Martin corrected himself, still trying to distract the boy. He walked over to the attic window and peered outside, trying to judge the distance to the house next door. It was too far to jump, he decided. Zombies swarmed below them, carrying a variety of weapons.

"Do you see anything?" Danny asked.

"Not really," Martin lied. "But I'm not afraid because the Lord is with us. He's always with us, Danny. Always. He lives inside your heart, and he sees everything that you do and knows everything you think. You might think that, with all of the bad things going on outside, He isn't there, but I can assure you that he is. He's always watching over you."

"Like Santa Claus?"

A frantic pounding on the door interrupted Martin's response. He crept down the attic stairs, pistol shaking in his arthritic hands.

"Wh-who is it?"

"It's Jim!"

He opened the door. Jim burst in and slammed it closed behind him.

"Daddy, are you all right?"

"I'm fine, buddy." He scooped Danny into his arms and gave him a hug. But Martin heard the lie in his voice. Everything was far from fine. The sounds of gunfire, both Frankie's and their attackers, was constant now, as were the angry cries of the zombies.

"Where's Frankie?"

"Downstairs. We don't have much time."

"How many are there?"

"Too many."

"What are we going to do?

Jim shook his head. "I don't know, Martin. I don't know. What about that window over there?"

"I checked it already," the preacher answered. "It's too far to jump and the zombies are waiting at the bottom."

"Damn!" Jim slammed his fist into the wall. Danny flinched, staring at his father in concern.

Martin frowned. "We're trapped, aren't we?"

Jim didn't respond.

"Jim? Tell me now, man! Are we trapped?"

Slowly, Jim nodded.

From below, Frankie shouted, "Jim, if you've got a plan, now would be a good time to share it!"

THREE

Laughing, the demon lord Ob looked out through eyes that had once belonged to a scientist named Baker.

Undead carrion birds hovered above him like a dark cloud, blending in with the night sky. The rag-tag paramilitary group was decimated, beaten by Ob's superior forces. The remains of burned-out tank husks and other vehicles littered the blasted landscape. Wisps of curling, oily smoke still rose from a few, the former inhabitants smoldering inside them. Inanimate zombies lay scattered across the ground, each one brought down by some form of head trauma. Dozens more thrashed in the mud; appendages severed, bodies cut in half, destroyed—but still moving. Hordes of the more mobile ones swarmed about the lawn, feasting on the fallen and wounded humans.

Not all the humans were being killed. Ob had ordered several dozen rounded up, stripped of their weapons, and herded inside the complex. They would be questioned as to the location of other survivors and then used for food—livestock. It wasn't that his kind *needed* to eat—at least, not while in spiritual form. They had gotten rid of that flaw eons before. But still, like any other physical life form, they needed energy, and when they took over these empty human shells, that energy was drawn from food. Eating the living served three purposes. It was an affront upon Him, the Creator, the one who had banished them to the Void. It allowed them to convert the flesh to energy while in human form, even without a digestive system, since his kind processed food on a different level. And it served to dispatch the humans' souls, killing them and enabling more of his kind to take over the bodies.

He chuckled. Gnawing on a still screaming human was much more fun than shooting them. But in the end, all the captives—livestock and otherwise—would host one of his brethren.

The battle had been over for several hours now, and the sounds of combat had faded with the vanishing daylight, replaced only by the occasional scream from the living. The dead had inherited the earth, or at least this part of it. The rest would soon follow. If not today, then tomorrow, and if not tomorrow, then soon. Unlike his kind, humans were not immortal. Eventually, they would die. That was all it took. Ob and his brothers had waited millennia to exact their revenge. If necessary, they could wait a little longer. It was less amusing that way, but it could be done.

He sighed, exhaling fetid breath from lungs that no longer served a purpose.

" 'And when Alexander looked out across his kingdom, he wept, for there were no more worlds to conquer.' Or something like that."

The zombie nearest to him had taken the body of a plump housewife. Gasses swelled its horribly distended belly, and the abdomen was slick and shiny. Ob admired the putrescent beauty.

"Who was Alexander?" it rasped.

"He was a human. A warlord for his time—he conquered much of this planet. I met him once when his soul passed through the Void on its way to Hell. On the field of battle, he was a great warrior. Still, in the end, he was just meat. They all are. Nothing but meat. Cattle. Cattle that used to worship us until the One, the Creator, grew jealous and washed the Earth clean with the Deluge."

He approached a pair of captives, a woman and man taken during the assault on the government's research facility. The zombies had lashed them to lampposts in the parking lot. The woman struggled while the man simply stared. Fear had eradicated what remained of his mind. He'd soiled himself. As Ob watched, the man did it again, unaware.

"Speaking of meat . . ." He leaned over and sank his teeth into the man's quivering neck. He burrowed deep, then jerked his head back. Flesh, veins and thick cords of muscle ripped free. He chewed, relishing the violation.

Dying, the man made no sound. Not a scream or a whimper. Flopping on the pole, he continued to stare while his lifeblood gushed from the wound. The woman screamed for him, her shrieks echoing over the cries of the damned, both dead and living.

Ob swallowed, took another bite, and swallowed again. He moved away, allowing several other zombies to eat their share. All living creatures had an aura and already, this human's life-glow had faded, signaling the passage of his soul. Within minutes, another from the Void would inhabit the empty bag of skin and tissue.

Ob considered his new body; that of the scientist named Baker. The flesh was burned black, and his midsection was an empty cavity. The charred, gory hole was the result of a point-blank machine gun barrage. The flesh he'd just eaten fell out at his feet. The limbs were still in good shape, but even so, this body wouldn't last long. Ob had rather enjoyed toying with it.

Ob grinned. It was ironic that Baker's own hand had opened the portal to the Void, had broken down the barriers between the worlds so that the Siqqusim could inhabit this world.

He shuffled over to the woman. Brownish-blond hair. Full figure. Pretty, for a human, and her beauty was accentuated by her fear. Her life-glow was strong. It always gave them away—tagged them as among the living. Earlier, he'd seen a pair of humans cover themselves in blood and entrails, trying to blend in enough to mix among the zombies and escape, unaware that their soul's light gave them away.

He smiled at the still shrieking woman and placed his hand over her mouth. Eyes wide, she squirmed beneath him.

"Stop your mooing, cow!"

"May we eat her, too?" One of the zombies smacked its lips with greedy anticipation.

Ob considered the request.

"Not yet." He brought his face close as if to kiss her. She gagged beneath his palm.

"I am going to remove my hand, because I wish to talk with you. It amuses me to do so. However, if you continue to scream, if you insist on bellowing, I will allow my brethren to cut a hole in your belly, fish out one end of your intestines, and begin to eat you, slowly from the inside out. Would you enjoy that?"

She gave a muffled cry.

"Then silence." He removed his hand.

She gasped. Her eyes darted around. She opened her mouth and inhaled, breasts rising against her bonds. Before she could scream again, Ob held up one finger. The zombie next to him placed a knife against her stomach. She stopped, sagging against the pole.

"Very good. You are learning. Perhaps your kind can be taught tricks, like the canines and felines you domesticate. What is your name?"

"M-my what?"

"Your name? What are you called? Where are you from?"

"L-Lisa. My name is Lisa. I'm from Virginia . . ." Tears streamed down her dirty face.

"Liiiissssaaaa." He rolled it in his mouth, savoring the word. "Do you know who I am, Lisa?"

"Yes. I-I think so. You're that scientist guy. One of the girls in the Meat Wagon told me about you. I-I saw you when we were moving out from Gettysburg."

Ob slapped her hard across the face. She yelped, but did not scream, still conscious of the knife at her belly.

"You are wrong, Lisa. I am wearing his body, but I am not the scientist. His name was Baker. My name is Ob. Ob the Obot. Do you know that name?"

Lisa coughed. A red welt in the shape of a hand covered her cheek.

"Do you know that name?"

"I-I don't—"

His fist smashed into her mouth. Drops of blood flew through the air and this time she did scream, could do nothing but scream. He struck her again. When he pulled his blackened hand away, one of her teeth was embedded in his knuckle.

"OB! DO YOU KNOW THAT NAME? OB! OB! OB!"

"N-no," she sobbed, "I don't know it! Please don't hit me again!"

Ob's shoulders slumped. He turned to the others.

"She does not know of me. Does not know of us. None of them have so far. We are forgotten among them. We are rumors, legends. Nothing more than fairy tales. We are what they used to make their children stay in bed at night. To entertain themselves with in television and film and literature."

He turned back to her.

"We are the Siqqusim, which means 'abominations that speak from the head' in the Hebrew language. You thought us mere spirits of the dead, but we are much more than that. The Sumerians and the Assyrians knew our true origin. Demons, your kind called us. Djinn. Monsters. We are the source of your legends—the reason you still fear the dark in this age of light. We existed long before Michael and Lucifer chose sides with their 'angels.' They were nothing more than inferior versions of us. We were banished long ago, banished to the Void by Him, the cruel one; the one your kind worships still. He lost favor with us, for he loved you better, his final creations."

One of Baker's organs fell out of the empty stomach cavity, dangling by a thread of gristle. Absentmindedly, Ob tore it away, gave it to another zombie to eat and then continued.

"Have you any idea how long we languished there? You cannot fathom it. The Void is cold, so very cold. It is not Heaven, and it is not Hell. It exists between them and does not exist at all. We dwelled there, trapped for eons with our brothers, the Elilum and Teraphim. He sent us there! Banished us to the icy wastes. We watched while you scurried like ants, multiplying and breeding, basking in His frigid love. We waited, for we are patient. We lurked on the threshold, ever observant, waiting for the time of the Oberim, what you call 'the Rising.' The Oberim is the crossing of the border between this world and the Void, and your scientists finally provided us with the ability to do so. Their experiment opened the door, broke down the dimensional barriers. Finally, we are free to walk this earth again, as we did long ago, before your kind. It is the ultimate offense to Him—as your kind dies, we replace you here. We reside in your brain. We are the worm that burrows through his creations, these bags of blood and tissue, this ball of water and dirt! And He can do nothing about it, for it was wrought with your own hands. Your bodies belong to us! We control your flesh. We have been waiting a long time to inhabit you. Many of us are here, and many more await passage. For our number is greater than the stars! We are more than infinity! And He can only watch! Watch and weep!"

Snot ran down her face. "S-so, you're doing all of this just—just to g-get back at God?"

Ob sneered with Baker's lips.

"Indeed. That—and our own self-interest. We longed to be free of the Void, of course."

He paused in his thoughts while Lisa squirmed on the pole. The dead body of her companion started to move again. It looked at her and grinned. Its fellow creatures began to loosen its bonds.

"Welcome, brother," Ob said.

"Thank you, lord. It is good to be free."

Ob turned back to her.

"So tell me, Lisa. If you'll pardon my melodrama, do

you know who we are now? Have you gained an understanding? Did your elders teach you of these things in Sunday school?"

Her only response was a whimper. Ob flung his hands up in exasperation.

"I am attested to seventeen times in the Old Testament! Seventeen! I am Ob of the Obot! I lead the Siqqusim, just as Ab leads the Elilum and Api the Teraphim. *Yidde-oni!* I am Ob! He who speaks from the head! *Engastrimathos du aba paren tares!*"

Cursing, he shoved the zombie with the knife out of the way. Lisa relaxed slightly against her bonds. Ob grabbed a pistol from one of the other zombies and shoved it between her breasts.

Lisa cringed.

"If you do not know of us, do not know of the Void, or of Heaven and Hell, then I will show it to you firsthand!"

She screamed.

"I told you to stop mooing, cow!"

He squeezed the trigger and then squeezed it again. And again. And again until it was empty. Only then did he let the weapon slide from his grasp. It clattered on the blacktop.

"Undo these bonds, so that the one who will soon inhabit her may be free."

He stalked away. Something ruptured inside him and dark, noxious fluid rushed from the open cavity in his abdomen, drenching his feet. Baker's body was disintegrating faster than he'd expected.

When the Rising first began, Ob's original host body had been a black Labrador named Sadie, owned by an elderly widow in Bodega Bay, California. Unable to lead the Siqqusim in such a limited form, he'd run amok, desperately seeking the body's destruction. He'd found it hours later at the hands of a fisherman who dispatched him with several shots to the head after Ob tore out the throats of his wife and children.

As leader of the Siqqusim, Ob returned to the realms of the living before his brethren. He liked to think of it as head-of-the-line privileges. He also reanimated quicker than the others, almost instantaneously. His second body belonged to a network systems analyst in Gardner, Illinois, and had served him well. The host had been in remarkable physical health and died of suffocation, leaving the body in good shape. Ob still regretted the loss of that one. It ended when a human set the entire town on fire. Ob became trapped in the inferno while crawling through a ventilation duct after some prey.

His third body was a homeless man in Coober Pedy, Australia. The man was already rotting before death claimed him. Ob only inhabited that shell for a day before a human snuck up from behind and drove a pickaxe through his brain.

His fourth had been the body of Dr. Timothy Powell, one of the men directly responsible for freeing his kind in the first place. That body had been dispatched during the recent battle. Now, here he stood, in the body of Powell's superior, Professor Baker. The almost contrived irony was not lost on the demon lord, and Ob wondered if some higher force had a hand in the fact that he'd taken possession of two of the men responsible for his release.

He searched through Baker's memories as if riffling through a filing cabinet. He saw the scientist's escape and flight, his capture by Schow's forces, and the interrogation that followed. He learned of Baker's other companions: Jim, the father searching for his son, and Martin, the elderly holy man.

These two, the father and the preacher, were not with them. They weren't among the zombies ordered to scavenge weapons and round up stray humans from the surrounding countryside. He hadn't seen them in the complex either. The possibility that two of his enemy's companions might have escaped gnawed at him. He didn't like loose ends, especially if it meant that they could warn others of his army's might.

He scanned the horizon. Could they still be out there, hiding in the night amongst the hills and trees? How delicious it would be—how poetic to destroy them while wearing the form of their friend.

Still, no matter. If they had survived, they were gone by now, hunted down and dead. Or dying. Humanity's time was over, its number finite. The Siqqusim's numbers were not. And when this world held no more bodies for them—there were other worlds, a multitude of other living beings for them to violate. They would never go back to the Void, and eventually, they would have their revenge on He who had sent them there. Ob would lead the Siqqusim's corruption of the flesh. When the last bit of flesh had been conquered, his brother Ab would then be free to rally his own forces, the Elilum. They would proceed with the destruction of the planet's plant and insect life, possessing them in the same way that the Siqqusim did with flesh. Finally, when all life had been extinguished, they would depart for other planets, while their brother Api burned the planet to ashes with his fellow Teraphim.

But defiling the Creator's beloved creations was just the first step. Storming the gates of His kingdom would be the next. Ob would personally rip Him from the throne.

Smiling at the prospect, Ob went to inspect his army and make plans. There was much to do. He must amass an army and prepare for the arrival of his brothers, Ab and Api. Once their way had been cleared, they would destroy every living organism on the planet, destroy the planet itself—destroy everything the Creator held dear. Only then would they be victorious, satisfied. And that would be just the beginning . . .

"Holy shit, they stink!" Ron coughed.

"Shut up, you idiot!" Kevin whispered back. "You're going to give us away."

"I can't help it. The smell . . ."

"He's right," Mikey said, squirming. "It's fucking hot. We've been in here for hours. My legs are cramping up."

"Both of you shut up now!"

"Fuck off. When we get out of here, you're dead, Kev."

Kevin ground his teeth in frustration. Never in a million years had he imagined that he'd spend the apocalypse hiding in the bed of a Chevy pickup truck with the infamous Lancaster brothers, Ron and Mikey. The three of them were concealed in the back, the bed covered by a black vinyl, snap-on tarp that hid them from the zombies, but restricted their movements and allowed the sun to bake them. The steel beneath their backs grew steadily hotter as the hours passed. Even now, with the sun vanished beneath the horizon, the space was scorching, the day's heat trapped inside. They heard the creatures clambering around outside the truck, and in the moments when the zombies were silent, the stench gave them away.

Before the Rising began, Ron, Mikey, and Kevin ran numbers for a crime family in York, Pennsylvania. When the shit hit the fan, York fell not only to the zombies but to rival gang factions as well. The bangers out of Baltimore and Philadelphia, skinheads out of Red Lion, survivalists from the southern part of the county and northern Maryland—all of them had decided to carve it up for themselves. So Ron, Mikey, and Kevin split.

They made it as far as Gettysburg, and after showing some proficiency with weapons and an extreme lack of conscience, they were allowed to join Colonel Schow's paramilitary forces, assigned to the crucifixion squads. It wasn't bad work; got them out in the fresh air and gave them an opportunity to live amongst a larger group. Safety in numbers. A strong sense of self-preservation allowed them to justify the most heinous things, including nailing fellow humans to crosses and watching from safety as the dead tore them apart.

When the decision to bug out and move to the government facility came down, the three of them piled into the pickup truck. As the convoy made its way north, they passed the time drinking warm beers and taking pot shots at zombies. Mikey had emptied his clip and both spares before they got as far as Harrisburg. Ron's was empty soon after.

By the time the convoy arrived at its destination, they were down to Kevin's 30.06 and a gas gauge firmly on E. When the combat exploded around them, they jumped out of the cab, climbed inside the bed, and shut the tailgate behind them. They'd lain there ever since.

"Christ, I could go for a burger right now," Ron breathed.

"Yo, fuck the burger," Mikey said, "I want a cold beer."

"Shut the fuck up," Kevin hissed.

Mikey and Ron quieted down again, and Kevin tried

to think. How much longer would they have to wait here, trapped and unable to move? He considered taking a peek outside, but immediately decided against it. The reek of rot and decay remained strong, which meant that at least a few of the creatures were still close by.

The pressure in his groin grew worse. He didn't want to hear Ron whining about the smell or Mikey complaining about muscle cramps. He'd had to piss for the last four hours and he wasn't bitching. Yet.

Gotta think, gotta think! Think about something other than pissing!

He ran through a mental checklist. Weapons: the rifle and a hunting knife. Food: none. Water: ditto (and he was getting really thirsty). Location: fucked if he knew. Somewhere near the border of Pennsylvania and New Jersey. Prospects: pretty fucking grim. Maybe he could push up on the tarp, pop the snaps, and as the zombies descended upon them, make a run for it while Ron and Mikey played decoy.

His bladder grew more insistent. In the darkness, he squeezed the head of his penis through his jeans.

"I swear to God I'm gonna puke," Ron whimpered. "Those things stink so bad."

"Shut up!" Mikey and Kevin both hissed.

From outside came the crunch of feet on gravel. All three held their breath as the footsteps drew closer, stopping at the truck. Then—speech, like someone gargling with glass.

"Did your host know how to operate one of these? Mine was too young."

"Mine did, but we need a key. Look inside. It should be in the steering column."

The door opened, and the truck shifted as something crawled inside the cab. The stench was stifling, even though they were separated by steel and glass. Kevin wanted to scream. He pinched the tip of his penis hard.

"There's no key," the voice was muffled. "What do we do now?"

"We'll find one of our brothers who knows how to hot-wire it, or else we'll tow it back to the facility."

The truck rocked as the door slammed shut. The footsteps faded, and moments later, the smell dissipated as well.

They waited another five minutes.

"I think they're gone," Ron whispered.

"Fuck, I hope so," Mikey sighed, stretching his legs. His joints popped in the darkness. "Kevin, you okay?"

"No," he said through clenched teeth. "I am definitely not fucking okay. I've got to piss."

"Let's make a break for it," Ron said. "Get the hell away from here before they come back!"

As if in response, the smell returned. Seconds later, the footsteps followed.

"I can start it. This is an older model. From the Seventies."

"Good. Drive it down to the complex with the others. Ob wants a fleet. Every operational vehicle is to be serviced and made ready for transport."

They waited, listening as it crossed the wires. The zombie was humming, and after a moment, Kevin recognized it as Iron Maiden's "Children of the Damned." He stifled a laugh, and that only increased the pressure on his bladder. He bit his lip, moaning softly as the urgency changed to pain.

The truck's engine roared to life.

"There's not much fuel," the zombie called. "I may have to coast it down the hill."

"That's fine. The complex has several fueling stations. We shall accompany you."

The passenger door opened, and the truck sagged even lower as more piled in. Then the truck began to move.

"Guys," Kevin breathed, so quietly that they had to strain to hear him. "I can't hold it anymore. I'm sorry."

He let go, and immediately a flood of warmth spread across the crotch of his jeans. It ran down his leg and into the bed of the truck, pooling around his companions. The stench, mixed with that of their forward passengers, was overpowering.

"Ohhhh." Kevin shuddered as the pressure left him. Soaked in his own urine, he gasped in pained ecstasy.

The truck picked up speed now, rolling down the hill. The urine followed the law of gravity, running beneath all three of them.

"Oh Jesus," Mikey exploded. "Stop it, Kevin! Fucking stop!"

"Did you hear something?" someone asked from up front.

All three of their hearts skipped a beat at the same time.

"What?"

"I don't know. Thought I heard a human."

"Your body's ears are faulty. Look around. I don't see a life glow anywhere."

"There's Ob. Let us stop and show him our prize. Perhaps he will reward us."

The truck lurched to a stop, and Kevin's bladder squeezed out the last few drops. The three men lay in the darkness; wet, cold, and afraid.

Ob evaluated the line of vehicles pouring into the facility as one of his undead soldiers directed them. Four-wheel drives, sedans, an M-88 tank recovery unit, several sport utility vehicles, a half dozen Humvees, a motorcycle, and a few tractor-trailers. His eyes widened in pleasure when the two Paladin motorized howitzers rolled up. Several tow trucks crested the hill. The vehicles that hadn't been destroyed, but were damaged or not operational, were being towed inside the facility, so the dead could repair them.

"Good. Very good. You have all done well."

He started to turn, but a beat-up old truck coasted toward him and stalled at his feet.

In the bed, buried beneath the tarp, Ron twisted his neck, trying to work out an agonizing kink. His face slid into a puddle of Kevin's waste.

"Where did you find this pile of junk?" Ob asked.

Ron gagged. Kevin and Mikey stiffened beside him.

"Atop that hill, lord. It only needs some gas and then it will be fine."

Ron felt the cough building inside him. Kevin's urine dripped from his nose and chin.

"Hmmmm. Put it with the rest, then."

Ron fought it down and froze, listening.

"Wait," Ob called. "Why does it smell like human urine?"

Ron coughed, loudly. Another one seized him, rustling the tarp over their heads.

"In the back! They're in the back!"

"Shit!" Mikey shouted. "What the fuck do we do?"

Kevin fumbled blindly for the rifle. His fingers closed around the cold barrel and he pulled it toward him, hitting Mikey in the head. Mikey yelped in surprise and pain.

A dozen creatures surrounded the truck and ripped

the tarp away. Some had been children and office workers. One of them looked like a scientist, or maybe a doctor. Others were their fellow mercenaries, killed in the battle and now fighting for the other side.

Two pairs of mottled arms grasped at Ron, dragging him out of the bed. He twisted, broke free, and fell to the ground. His ankle snapped. Immediately the creatures fell upon him, stabbing him with knives, clubbing him with rocks, and clawing his skin with their dead fingers.

Another corpse locked on to Mikey, its teeth seeking the soft flesh of his quivering throat. He groped at the zombie's head and pushed it back up. His fingers slid into the thing's mouth and he struggled, pulling down in an effort to break the jaw. Instead, the teeth snapped shut, severing his digits at the first knuckles. Blood spurted from the stumps. His scream was cut off as the corpse's mouth found his. They locked in a repugnant kiss, and then the zombie pushed him away, his tongue hanging from between its lips. Mikey collapsed, his screams replaced by a high-pitched gargle. Blood poured from his ruined mouth. Another zombie leaped forward and zapped him with a stun gun.

Ob leaned his elbows against the rim of the Chevy's bed and leered at Kevin.

"Hello, meat! What do you have there? A gun? Doing some deer hunting, were you?"

"Oh shit, oh shit, oh shit . . ." Kevin scrambled backward, his back resting against the cab. The zombies surrounded the truck. He glanced around for the Lancaster brothers. Mikey was dead, his eyes glazed over even as the zombie continued to zap him with the stun gun. Ron lay on the ground moaning. His chest and abdomen were an open wound. Kevin saw the knives and rocks come up, and then flash back down. Up. Down. Then Ron's cries ceased.

Kevin stared upward in fear as Ob leaned in, clutching at him.

"Come here!"

Another zombie opened the tailgate, and several of the undead clambered in after him.

"Ohshitohshitohshitohshit . . ."

"Give me that." Ob gripped the 30.06.

Kevin struggled with him, jerking the rifle back and forward. The creatures on the truck grabbed Kevin's legs and pulled him toward them. The rifle barrel landed against Ob's jaw, and the zombie leader flinched.

"Oh shit."

Screaming, Kevin's body convulsed. His fingers squeezed the trigger.

Baker's head disintegrated in an eruption of flesh and blood and bone.

Ob went with it.

FOUR

He ignored the first two shots. They were faint, though he couldn't be sure if it was from distance or because of the thickness of the walls around him. He strained to hear them over Claude Debussy's "Arabesque #2," floating softly from the battery-operated portable stereo. One shot—maybe—followed by a second. Most likely it was zombies hunting their dinner—some unlucky bastard that had the misfortune to wander into the neighborhood. He considered checking, then decided against it.

He lit another candle and returned to his book, John Steinbeck's *Cannery Row*. He'd read it three times since he'd sealed the door. It was the only book inside the room, with the exception of an old issue of *Entertainment Weekly*, a thriller by Andrew Harper (with everything going on outside, that was the last thing he wanted to read), and Myrna's *Chicken Soup* collection. He hated those *Chicken Soup* books. Wondered if there'd ever be a *Chicken Soup for the Undead Soul* book. Probably not.

The muffled gunfire erupted again. This time, it didn't

fade, continuing unabated for a full minute. He heard different explosions, which meant different guns. There was a brief pause and then more.

Don De Santos jumped out of his chair.

"Jesus Christ!"

His voice sounded funny to him. It was the first time he'd spoken aloud in nearly four weeks.

He listened to what sounded like a war breaking out nearby and wondered what to do about it.

Before the Rising began, Don De Santos had been a successful media consultant, one of the thousands for whom New Jersey was simply a bed and breakfast in between the daily treks into Manhattan. He had a lovely wife, Myrna, and a son, Mark, who had just started his first year at UCLA. A house in the suburbs, a dog named Rocky, a silver BMW, black Ford Explorer, and matching his and hers Honda motorcycles. Life was good, and his investment portfolio was even better.

That changed when Rocky got hit by the car. Had it happened two minutes later, he would have been on his way to catch the train and Myrna could have dealt with it. But fate hadn't worked that way. He was just pulling out of the garage; his coffee nestled between his legs and one hand already dialing the cell phone, when he heard the alarming squeal of brakes in the street, followed by a sickening thud.

Rocky had sneaked out of the garage and run into the road, where he'd met the bumper of Mr. Schwartz's Chrysler. Most of his innards had spilled into the street. At least he hadn't suffered.

Myrna dashed across the yard; shrieking like a banshee, robe trailing behind her. Panting, Rocky raised his head, looked at her, and then died. Myrna knelt over him, weeping and clinging to his fur while Schwartz apologized over and over.

"Oh Christ! He ran right out in front of me, Don! I couldn't stop in time!"

"It's all right. There was nothing you could do."

"Not my Rockeeeeee . . ." Myrna wailed.

In the distance, the old air-raid siren at the fire station blurted to life, startling all three of them. Its wail eclipsed Myrna's.

Don sent Schwartz on his way, assuring him that there were no hard feelings or pending lawsuit. Then he grabbed a blanket from the linen closet and gently peeled Myrna from the dead dog's corpse. He rolled Rocky onto the blanket, nose wrinkling in disgust as more of the dog's entrails spilled out, and dragged him into the garage, unsure what to do next. He folded the blanket over the dog. The fire siren blared on, making it hard for him to think. It was answered by what would be the first of many police sirens that day. An ambulance raced down the street, and for one bizarre moment Don thought it was coming for Rocky. Then it sped past.

"I wonder what's going on?" Myrna sniffled.

"I don't know. Go on inside, hon. I guess we'd better call Mark's dorm and let him know about Rocky."

"It's too early out there. Remember, he's in California."

"But it was his dog too. You know how much he loved Rocky."

She began to cry again.

"What will we do with—"

"I'll take care of it."

"I want to cremate him," she replied. "Let me get myself together and I'll go down to the vet's. Can you—can you put him in the Explorer for me?"

He nodded, kneeling down to cover the dog up with the blanket again. For some reason it had slipped off.

A police car flashed by in the ambulance's wake, followed by another. Don opened his mouth to comment and that was when Rocky bit him.

The dog's hair didn't stand on end. There was no warning growl or bark—no sound at all. One minute Rocky was dead, his intestines cooling on the garage's cement floor. The next, he sank his teeth into Don's hand, right between the thumb and forefinger. Screaming, Don tried to jerk his hand away, but Rocky dug in, shaking his head in defiance. The dog's eyes rolled back, showing the whites.

"Oh shit! Myrna, get him off of me!"

Shrieking, she beat at the corpse. Rocky refused to budge. His muzzle was crimson with both Don's blood and his own.

"What's happening, Don? What is this?"

"I don't fucking know! Just get him off me, God damn it! My hand!"

Myrna reeled back, hysterical. Frantic, Don glanced around the garage. A claw hammer lay perched on the tool bench, but he couldn't reach it.

"Myrna!" No response, just more sobbing. "Myrna! God damn it, look at me. Please?"

"I-I . . ."

"Grab my hammer from the tool bench!"

"I-I can't."

"Do it," he roared. "Do it now!"

She ran, arms flailing helplessly, and returned with the hammer. The dog's teeth felt like rows of hot needles. Rocky regarded him while he chewed. For a second, Don thought he saw something reflected in those dead eyes, something dark. Then the dog shook his head again, burrowing deeper. Don was beyond pain now, beyond fear. He focused on the siren, still bleating in the background, as shock enveloped him.

Myrna handed Don the hammer. Slowly, with a sense of calm, he raised it over his head and brought it crashing down. There was a solid crunch as the swing ended between the dog's eyes. Then he raised the hammer back up and hit it again. Rocky let go. Immediately, the dog's jaws snapped at his leg, but Don lurched backward.

Rocky sat back on his haunches, staring at Don with clear contempt. Then the dog opened its mouth and tried to speak. Vocal cords that had never formed words before began to do so now. To Don's eyes and ears, it was like something inside the dog was borrowing the animal's vocal cords for its own purpose.

"Rrrraaarrgghh! Rowwwlll!"

"Jesus . . ."

Rocky seemed to laugh.

Grimacing, Don swung again.

The dog's head collapsed as the hammer sank deep inside.

Rocky died a second time.

That was how it started. They left the dog's bloody corpse lay inside the garage. Later, while Myrna went to the veterinarian's office to make arrangements for disposing of Rocky, Don drove himself to the emergency room to see if he needed stitches and to get a shot, just to be safe. The hospital echoed of chaos—pure, raw anarchy. Waiting and wounded patients whispered of a possible biological or chemical terrorist attack, something that was making people and animals turn crazy. Homicidal dead ducks attacked an old man in the park who fed them every morning. A rapist cut an old woman's throat, only to have her turn the knife back on him minutes later while he was humping her corpse. A bus driver had a heart attack behind the wheel, died—and then purposely sent the bus careening into a crowd of people at the next stop. A woman shot her husband in a domestic dispute and then he rose up and shot her back, along with the cops responding to the call and the paramedics sent to revive him.

When he was finally admitted after many hours of waiting, Don watched a patient in the next trauma room flatline, then start thrashing a few minutes later, grappling with the doctor hovering over him. The EKG showed no heartbeat, even when the man began biting the doctor. Don left the hospital after that, making do with antibiotics and a gauze pad.

Myrna didn't come home that night. Calls placed to the veterinarian's office were met with a busy signal, just like the calls to Mark's dorm. By the time Don decided to look for her, the police were ordering people to stay in their homes, and the National Guard was patrolling the streets. The electricity and the phone lines went out soon after that. He wondered about Mark, and hoped the situation was better in California—but even then, he knew in his heart that it wasn't.

He checked on his next-door neighbors, Rick and Tammy and their son Danny, and made sure they were safe. The neighbors on the other side, the Bouchers, were on vacation in Florida. After checking in with Rick, Tammy and Danny, Don went back to his home, weeping for his wife while praying for her return, and locked himself inside the panic room.

After the fourth terrorist attack on New York City, Don had hired a security company to convert the closet in Mark's now empty bedroom into a panic room, using frame materials that were resistant to forced entry, high winds, and even bullets. He'd spared no expense. The walls, floors and ceilings were all lined with thick plywood for extra strength, and an alarm system, modem, and phone were installed as well. The electromagnetic lock insured "top security with an ability to withstand tremendous forces" (as per the brochure), and could not be picked or pried open. An electronic keypad with a key code allowed entry only by those who knew the combination—Myrna and himself. A solar powered backup battery was installed on the roof, in case the electricity was suddenly cut off. It operated the alarms, the phone, and the keypad.

He had plenty of bottled water and dried food, batteries, matches, candles, a handgun, knife, and fire axe. He could wait out whatever was happening outside.

He'd been asleep when Myrna returned.

The keypad's beeping woke him. Somebody was on the other side, entering the code. There was a mechanical click and then a rush of air as the door slid open. The bedroom beyond was dark, but he could see her silhouette in the doorway.

"Myrna! Oh my God, honey, where have you been? Are you okay?"

"I'm fine, Don."

Don paused. Her speech seemed oddly muffled. Distorted.

"Well, I'm just glad you're home. I've been worried sick. I thought that maybe you were—"

"Dead?"

"Yes." He got up, his joints stiff from sleeping on the floor.

Myrna stepped into the room, into the soft glow of the candlelight.

"I'm afraid she is dead, Don. Just like Rocky and

Mark. It's just me in here now. But you can join them, if you'd like. In fact, I insist!"

"W-who?"

She lurched toward him, the thing that wore his wife's body. One broken leg trailed behind her, and there was a gaping, pink hole where her nose had been.

"Myrna?"

"She was cheating on you. Spreading her legs for Mr. Pabon, the guy who owns the Mexican restaurant. Twice a week and overnight when you were away on business. His dick was bigger. Much bigger."

It looked like his wife, spewed obscenities with her mouth—her voice. It knew about their son and neighbors—but Don realized that the creature wasn't Myrna.

"You lie."

"No, I don't. It's in here." The zombie tapped Myrna's head with one broken fingernail. "It's all in here. She wrapped her legs around him when she came. You could never make her do that."

"I don't know who you are, but you're not my wife!"

"You want to know who I really am? Come here and let me show you."

Don swallowed and then ran for the pistol on the card table. The handgun was a family heirloom. His grandfather had been one of the first Hispanic soldiers to serve in the Philippines during World War Two, and had passed the government-issued Colt .45 with the eight-shot clip down to him. Next to it lay an open box of Cor-Bon ammo.

The zombie lunged for him.

He didn't bother to aim. He didn't have to. Myrna was right on top of him, clawing at his shirt. She pinched his left nipple between her fingers, trying to tear it off with her bare hands. He shoved the gun between her breasts.

"I'm sorry."

Don squeezed the trigger. Myrna jerked backward, then giggled. She twisted his nipple again, pulling on it now. Screaming, he fired another shot. The bullet passed through her shoulder. She paused, and then lurched forward, broken leg still trailing.

"You're starting to piss me off, dear," the creature said.

A low moan escaped Don's lips.

Cackling, her jaws descended on him.

He placed the gun against her forehead and fired again. The entry wound was the size of a thumb, but the back of his dead wife's head splattered across the panic room, spraying the wall with blood, brain tissue, and fragments of bone.

He hadn't heard another gunshot until now.

Don pushed away the memories. Outside, the barrage continued. He wondered who it was. Perhaps the army had finally arrived. Maybe he was saved! Maybe it was over!

He weighed the risks of leaving the panic room. But the firefight blazed on, and he *had* to see what was happening. He reached for the keypad, had a terrible moment where he thought he'd forgotten the code and would remain trapped inside, then remembered it, and entered the sequence. The door slid open.

Immediately, he noticed the stench. The smell of death.

It was risky to go to the ground floor windows. Too much of a chance of being spotted. Instead, he went upstairs to the attic. It would give him the best vantage point.

From there, Don looked out into hell.

Next door, Rick and Tammy's property crawled with zombies. He tried to count them, but there were too many. Most were armed with shotguns and pistols, baseball bats and butcher knives. Many were his neighbors; he spied Schwartz, the Padrone kid from down the street, and Mr. Pabon among them.

Pabon . . .

She was cheating on you. Spreading her legs for Mr. Pabon.

Don smiled grimly.

"Fuck my wife, will you?"

Pabon's corpse was just starting down the strip of lawn between the houses. A fence ran down the center, and on Don's side was a long, narrow swimming pool, specifically designed to fit between the homes for the purpose of swimming laps rather than recreation. A black shape rested at the bottom of the pool but he couldn't discern what it was. Three years earlier, Don had engaged in a private battle with his county's Board of Zoning Appeals regarding their prohibition against pools in the backyards. He'd gotten a lawyer, petitions from neighbors, the whole works, but the county government had ultimately forbidden him. Finally, he realized that there were no laws against pools in the *side* yard, so he'd built one there instead, just to spite them. He and Rick had had a good laugh about it at the time.

Pabon was on the other side of the pool fence, in Rick and Tammy's yard. As quietly as possible, Don slid the attic window open and pointed the Colt .45 at the top of the restraunteur's head. He knew that his grasp on sanity was slipping. He knew that he was throwing caution and his safety to the wind with this shot—that he would alert the creatures to his presence. But he didn't care anymore. All that mattered in that moment was Pabon. He shifted to get a better line of sight, and as he did, the zombie disappeared around the front. Exasperated, Don glanced at his neighbor's house.

He nearly dropped the pistol.

Directly across, only twenty-five feet away, an elderly black man in a minister's collar stared back at him from Rick and Tammy's attic window.

Martin pointed out the window. "Jim, come take a look at this!"

"Damn it, Martin. Get the hell away from there before you get shot!" He knelt and gave his son a reassuring hug.

"No," the preacher insisted. "You don't understand. There's a man! Look!"

Automatically shielding Danny behind him, Jim turned to the window and froze.

"Holy shit . . ."

It was hard to tell in the dark, but the preacher didn't look dead. He pointed in Don's direction. Then the old man moved aside, and Don glimpsed another figure—one that seemed vaguely familiar. White male, middle to late thirties, shoulder length brown hair. His shoulder was bleeding and he looked pretty rough. Rough enough that he could be a zombie, although why he wasn't attacking the preacher, Don had no idea.

Then Danny stepped out from behind the man, spotted his next-door neighbor, and started jumping up and down in excitement. Don gasped. The little boy's hair had gone white at the roots.

Whoever they were, they weren't zombies—of that he was now sure. He motioned for them to open the window and after a moment's hesitation, the old man did.

"Howdy!" The preacher had a southern accent, and Don had to struggle to hear him over the battle below. Zombies smashed the windows and climbed into the kitchen and living room. The night erupted with muzzle flashes, and Don heard muffled gunshots from inside the house as well.

"Who—who the hell are you people?"

"I'm the Reverend Thomas Martin, and this here's Jim Thurmond. Danny tells us you're Mr. De Santos."

Incredulous, Don shook his head. "What are you doing?"

"Well, at the moment, we're panicking. They've got us pinned down in this house. We sure could use some help."

"Danny, are you all right?"

"I'm okay, Mr. De Santos! Can you help us, please?"

"Okay, don't move!" He ducked out of the window, searching the attic. It had been unfinished when they'd bought the house, and Myrna had always been after him to turn it into a sewing room for her. He'd gotten as far as laying down wooden planks over the insulation.

He pulled up one of the long, heavy planks, thankful that he hadn't nailed them down, but determined that it wasn't long enough to fit between the houses. Then he spotted the aluminum extension ladder. Puffing hard, he carried it back to the window and checked for zombies. Most of them now seemed to be concentrated around the front of the other house. So far, none of them had shown up with a ladder or rope. Quickly, he slid the ladder out the window.

"Grab it," he grunted. "Damn thing weighs a ton."

Jim and Martin grabbed the other end, preventing it from tumbling down into the yards or the swimming pool. It barely spanned the chasm, but Don pulled on his end and they did the same, releasing the extension.

"Let's go," Don urged them. "Hurry!"

Frankie's eyes stung. Her ears rang, and her hands and arms were growing numb. Still, she kept up a steady defense, squeezing off short, controlled single shots. The living room and the bottom of the staircase were littered with bodies, three or four deep. But for each one she dropped, two more creatures sprang up to take its place. They kept coming, despite her efforts. Worse, her magazine was almost empty.

A bullet whizzed by, and plaster dust rained down upon her. More shots slammed into the banister. An aluminum arrow, the kind used for target shooting, bounced off the stairs and birdshot peppered the wall next to her head. She retreated upward a few more steps, then crouched and returned fire. Three more fell—and six rushed in to take their place.

She gagged. "God damn, you things reek."

The stench of decaying flesh was thick. Wincing, she tucked her nose against her shoulder and breathed deep, preferring her own stink to that of her enemies. Then she smelled something else.

Gasoline.

A flash of bright orange light flared in the kitchen, and the zombies began to cheer. The air grew hotter and flames crackled in the background, creeping into the living room. The hair on her arms stood up.

"Oh, you motherfuckers. You dirty motherfuckers!"

"Frankie?"

Jim stood at the top of the steps.

"They lit it, Jim. They lit the fucking house on fire!"

"Come on, let's go!"

She raced up the stairs, the first few wisps of smoke following behind her. Somewhere on the first floor, a battery-operated smoke detector began to shriek. She heard the zombies chanting outside.

"The roof, the roof, the roof is on fire! We don't need no water, let these fucking humans burn!"

Jim ran ahead of her. "Into the attic. We've got a way out!"

"Burn, fucking humans! Burn!"

Frankie shook her head in disbelief.

"If they start doing Doug E. Fresh, I'm going to fall over. Talk about old school."

He paused with his hand on the doorknob. "What?"

"Nothing. Forget about it. Flashback to when I was a kid. Some old school shit."

He led her into the attic. The window was open and a man beckoned to them from the house next door. A ladder bridged the gap between them.

"Who's that?" Frankie asked.

"Don De Santos," Jim told her. "He lives next door."

"What?"

"How many more people do you have in there?" De Santos called. "Are Rick and Tammy with you?"

"This is it," Jim yelled back. "Just the four of us. Martin, you go first."

The preacher hesitated.

"What's that smell?"

"They lit the house on fire. Now go. We're out of time."

Martin's eyes widened. Carefully, he crawled out onto the ladder. Gripping the rungs, he began to edge himself across on his hands and knees, silently praying as he did.

He wobbled in the center and all of them gasped, but then he covered the remaining distance. Don clutched at him, hauling him inside.

Jim stared down. So far, they hadn't attracted the creatures' attention. The majority of them were gathered on the front and back lawns. The narrow swimming pool and the small strip of ground between the houses stood empty—for the moment. Jim hoped it would remain that way. He glanced at the black object at the bottom of the pool, but it wasn't moving. Probably leaves or a deflated pool toy. He couldn't be sure in the darkness and the weird shadows cast by the flames.

"Danny, you're next."

"I'm scared, Daddy. I don't want to!"

Jim knelt before him. "I know you don't, son, but you have to. Martin was scared too, but he made it across fine. Just don't look down. Frankie and I will be on this end and Martin and Mr. De Santos are on the other side. You'll be okay."

"But what if I fall? What if the ladder breaks? What if the monster people see me?"

Jim heard zombies on the stairs. He grasped Danny's shoulders.

"Danny, you have to do this. You have to trust me, okay? I know it's scary, but if we stay here, the monster people are going to get us."

Whimpering, Danny peered out the window. Next door, Martin and De Santos quietly urged him on. He turned back to his father.

"I can't. I want you to come with me!"

"Danny, I don't know if that ladder will hold us both at the same time. I need you to be brave for me, okay? Be a big boy."

Smoke seeped under the attic door, and the smoke detector on the second floor wailed in harmony with the other one.

Swallowing hard, Danny inched onto the shaking ladder. He glanced back at Jim, fear shining in his eyes. Jim smiled and nodded in encouragement. Danny turned back to Don and Martin, hunkered down, and began to crawl toward them, carefully edging from rung to rung.

"That's it, Danny. That's it. Don't look down. You can do it!"

The smoke grew thicker. Coughing, Frankie and Jim pulled their shirts up around their mouths and noses.

Halfway across, Danny looked down and froze.

"Daddy, I can't do it! I'm scared!"

He hugged the frame, wrapping his arms and legs around the rungs. He closed his eyes and began to tremble.

"Come on, Danny," Martin urged. "You're almost here!"

Eyes still closed, the boy shook his head.

"Shit." Frankie shoved Jim forward. "Get out there!"

A muffled explosion rocked the lower level, rattling the house on its foundation. The ladder swayed. The crackling flames grew louder and the temperature in the attic continued to rise.

"Danny," Jim called. "Hang on, squirt. I'm coming across!"

He slid out onto the ladder. It groaned beneath his weight. Holding his breath, he crawled as quickly as he could toward his petrified son. He glanced down, relieved to see that the zombies were still clustered on the other sides of the house. Smoke poured from the lower windows.

Below him, the black shape in the pool moved. It disengaged itself from the bottom and floated to the top. A head broke the water and stared upward in surprise. A zombie. And it had been in the water for quite some time, judging by the bloating. Then Jim saw why. Its arms were missing, and there was no way for it to climb out of the pool.

It opened its mouth to sound the alarm, and water and insects gushed out before it sputtered, "Here! They're here!"

"Go!" Frankie screamed, pulling a fresh magazine from her pocket and slamming it into place.

"Come on, Jim." Martin held his arms out, helpless. "Hurry!"

The pool zombie shouted again, and Frankie raised the weapon, trying to draw a bead on it. It ducked below the water before she could fire.

Jim's heart lurched as one of his legs slipped between the rungs. Panic seized him and he slipped farther. The aluminum frame scraped his back. He dangled from the waist down, clutching the rungs. His heart pounded in his throat. Then he pulled himself back up, took a deep breath, and continued across.

As he reached Danny, the creatures began to race around the house, converging below them.

"Danny, let go of the rungs!"

Terrified, the boy shook his head. A bullet whined directly over them, followed by a second.

"Danny! Do what I say. I've got you."

A bullet slammed into the ladder, gouging the aluminum and making their ears ring. Jim grabbed Danny's waistband. With his father's presence reassuring him, Danny opened his eyes and looked back at him. More shots whined over their heads.

Jim breathed a sigh of relief. "Good boy. Now look at

Martin and Mr. De Santos. Don't look down. And go as fast as you can."

Nodding, Danny moved forward. A volley from below whizzed by them, but then Frankie returned fire.

Don pulled Danny inside. Jim raced along behind him. After crawling through the window, he turned back to Frankie.

"Come on!"

Jim and De Santos laid down a burst of cover fire, shooting indiscriminately rather than choosing targets. They alternated between ducking into the attic and then leaning out to shoot. The zombies ducked as well, scrambling for cover. De Santos shot one-handed, helping Martin steady the ladder for Frankie.

Not bothering to crawl, Frankie stepped onto the ladder and walked as carefully and quickly as she could, going from rung to rung. She concentrated, putting one foot in front of the other.

"I'm empty!" De Santos shouted.

Frantically, Jim searched his pockets. "Shit. Me too! Martin, you have any more ammo?"

The old man shook his head.

"Just what's inside my pistol, and that ain't much."

Jim turned back to the window. "Hurry, Frankie!"

The pool zombie continued shouting and then sank beneath the surface once more. More of the creatures were scrambling beneath Frankie now, pointing upward and hollering. A hunting arrow soared past her leg, missing by inches. Another clanged off the ladder.

"Fuck me running," she whispered, and began to walk faster. "One foot in front of the other. One foot in . . ."

There was a loud clang, and the ladder tilted beneath

her feet. Frankie reached out and grabbed the side, but her fingers slipped. Both she and the ladder plummeted downward. Screaming, the others could only watch as she splashed into the odd-shaped pool and sank beneath the surface. Between the darkness and the shadowy fire-light, they could not see her.

Then, the ripples receded and the water was still once more.

Frankie did not resurface.

FIVE

"She's gone," Jim whispered.

"Are you sure?" Martin asked.

"I don't see her. I can't see anything, between the darkness and the smoke. The power is out. But we'd have heard her by now, wouldn't we? She would have to come up for air by now. The fall alone was enough. Or maybe she hit her head on the bottom. And you saw that thing in the pool . . ."

Jim leaned out the window, but another barrage of shots from the ground chased him back inside.

"We don't have time for this," Don warned them. "Those things are still outside."

Martin was insistent. "We need to look for her."

"There's nothing we can do," Jim said. "She must be dead, Martin. We've got to accept it."

"But—"

"There's no way we can go outside."

"You're right." Martin sighed.

Don hurried toward the attic door, looking uneasy. He beckoned for them to follow.

Martin bowed his head in prayer. He struggled for words, and finally found them.

"Lord, we ask that you please accept her soul into your kingdom that she may dwell with thee. Amen."

"Look," Don said. "I'm sorry about your friend. I really am. But if you don't want to join her, I suggest we get moving."

"Where?" Jim asked. "We're fresh out of ideas."

"And places to hide," Martin added.

"My panic room first." Don opened the door and listened. "I've got to reload."

"Your panic room's no good anymore," Jim protested. "They know we're in here now. They'll find a way through. If not, they'll burn this place down as well."

"Exactly. That's why I don't plan on sticking around. It's not safe here anymore."

"Then what?"

"My Explorer is still in the garage. We can all fit in that, easily."

"That's no good," Jim scoffed. "They're all over the place out there. We've seen them rip apart an SUV like it was a can of tuna!"

"I'll take my chances. Especially since helping you has directly impacted my safety here."

Jim bristled. "Listen, you son of a—"

Danny stepped between them and took his father's hand.

"Thank you for helping us, Mr. De Santos, but can you please not fight with my daddy?"

Both men stared at each other for a moment and then softened.

"I'm sorry, Danny." Don patted the boy on the head and then looked back up at Jim. "So you're his real father, then?"

"That's right."

"I think I met you once, briefly, when you were picking him up for the summer."

"Could be. I don't remember. It was—difficult—being here with my ex-wife and her new husband. I usually didn't stick around too long. It's a long drive back to West Virginia."

"West Virginia. I thought you must be from the South." He nodded at Martin. "You too. The accents kind of gave you away. Your friend wasn't, though?"

"Frankie? No, she was from Baltimore. To be honest, we didn't know much about her. She'd lost a child of her own recently, and was helping us find Danny. And now . . ."

"Oh. Well, I'm really sorry. But may I suggest again that we get moving? We shouldn't be standing around here talking. They'll regroup soon."

Jim paused. "I still think it's pretty useless to go outside, Mr. De Santos. But we can't stay here either. So I reckon we'll try this your way."

"Please, call me Don."

"Okay. Don. And I'm Jim."

"Well then, Jim, at the very least, let's go down to the panic room so I can reload."

Another bullet tore splinters from the windowsill as they started down the steps. The taunts of the dead drifted to them on the breeze, along with the smoke from the inferno next door.

"Jim?" Martin's voice trembled.

"What is it?"

"What if we're wrong? What if Frankie's alive?"

Jim didn't reply.

A tear rolled down Martin's lined face.

"Frankie . . ."

* * *

When the ladder gave way beneath her feet, Frankie had time only to gasp before plunging into the swimming pool. The aluminum ladder splashed into the pool next to her a moment later. Smoky air burned inside her lungs as the cold, stagnant water closed over her head.

She sank like a stone—two feet, five feet, ten feet—before her boots struck the bottom. She opened her eyes, but couldn't see much in the murky gloom. A spray of bullets ploughed through the water in slow arcs. She dove deeper, flattening out along the bottom, as the gunfire drew closer.

Her hand flailed, closing on the M-16's shoulder strap. As she pulled the weapon toward her, she saw something moving. Something close. It was black and mottled and rotting, but still mobile. The armless zombie. She'd forgotten about it. It swam toward her, kicking its legs and licking its wrinkled lips in anticipation. Desperately, she kicked again for the surface.

The yard and pool stood out in the darkness, illuminated by the blazing house. Frankie's head popped out of the water and she choked, gasping for breath. Immediately, something like a swarm of angry hornets buzzed over the surface. She heard the gunfire a half second later. She ducked below the surface again.

The water stung her eyes, but she opened them anyway, searching for an escape. The bloated creature walked toward her along the bottom, slowed by the water. Frankie darted aside and swung the butt of her rifle, colliding with the thing's head. Despite the fact that the swing was slowed by the water, the blow cracked the creature's skull. She swung a second time and it split open. The zombie sank to the bottom, the gray-black, curdled remains of its brain floating upward.

Her temples throbbed, and her lungs felt like they would explode. She swam to the side, gliding as close to the bottom as she could. She could hear them above her, their shouts distorted by the water. She hovered near the pool ladder.

From her previous weapons training by one of Schow's soldiers, Frankie knew that the M-16 was fairly watertight, but the weapon relied on a gas-operated ejection system. The first round should fire no problem. But the others . . .

Well, if they didn't, she was dead. Plain and simple. But then, she was probably dead anyway.

Teeth clenched and rifle gripped firmly in one hand, Frankie grabbed the ladder, swung her feet into the rungs and climbed for the surface.

Danny stared at the moldering corpse in horror and put a hand over his nose.

"Is . . . is that?"

Don hung his head, fingers sliding ammunition into his empty clips.

"Yes, Danny," he answered quietly, "that's Mrs. De Santos."

Cringing, Danny stepped away and wrapped his arms around his father's leg, hiding his face in Jim's thigh.

"I'm sorry for your loss," Martin said.

Don shrugged, continuing to reload.

"After I—after *that,*" he nodded to the remains, "I made sure the house was secure. I nailed plywood over the doors and windows and the garage door is chained shut. Won't stop them now, I'm afraid, but it should slow them down long enough for us to equip ourselves."

"You stayed in this room?" Jim asked.

"The whole time. Luckily, they didn't know I was in

here. I still would be I guess, if I hadn't heard you folks come along."

Jim picked Danny up and kissed him on the forehead. This man, Don De Santos, had sat here in relatively comfortable safety while his son had faced endless nights of terror, peril, and hunger alone in the attic next door. He hugged Danny even tighter.

"I missed you, kiddo. I missed you so much."

"I missed you too, Daddy."

"How much?" Jim nuzzled him.

"This much!" Danny squeezed tighter.

"How much is that?"

"More than 'finity."

They both laughed, and Martin turned away to hide the fresh tears that sprang to his eyes.

"Okay." Don pocketed the extra clips. "I'm ready. Wish I had some ammo for your rifles, but I was never much of a hunter."

Jim grinned. "Even if you were, I don't know that you'd have any to fit the M-16s. They're not exactly deer rifles."

"Like I said, I'm a city boy." Don shrugged. "There's a knife there on the table. One of you can have it if you want."

"I'll take it," Martin offered. "That way, you can carry Danny."

Both father and son seemed to like the prospect, judging by the relieved looks on their faces.

"Not that it will do much good, I guess." The preacher sighed, picking up the blade. "Unless I stick it hard enough to go through their skull." He shuddered, remembering that he'd done that very thing earlier in the day, fending off not a zombie, but a fellow human. It seemed like years ago.

"Why is that?" Don asked, shoving bottles of water

into a backpack. "Why does it have to go through the skull?"

"Damaging the brain is the only way to kill them."

"Makes sense, I guess. I figured as much. That was what it finally took—for Myrna."

"I liked her," Danny spoke up. "She always let me play with Rocky, and she used to babysit me when I was littler."

"Well," Jim said quietly, "at least somebody was watching out for you."

"What do you mean, Daddy?"

"Nothing, squirt. It just seems like your mother and Rick didn't think. They should have gotten you out of here as soon as this started."

Danny's face clouded. "I wish you wouldn't talk bad about them. I don't like it."

Jim opened his mouth to reply, but Martin interrupted him.

"Danny, I bet you're thirsty after that ordeal. Why don't you have Mr. De Santos open one of those bottles of water for you?"

Danny shrugged. "Okay."

"That a boy."

"Shouldn't we come up with a plan?" Jim asked. "Those things outside know that we're in here."

"It will only take a second," Martin assured him.

"Make it quick," Don said. "That plywood won't hold them off much longer."

Jim put Danny down and he scampered across the room. Martin motioned for Jim to follow him outside the panic room. They stepped into the bedroom.

Once there, Jim turned to him with a grave expression on his face.

"What's up?"

The old man's whispered tones were harsh. "What's the matter with you, Jim?"

"What do you mean?"

"I mean talking about the boy's mother and stepfather like that."

"Don't you dare start on me, Martin. You have no idea what they put me—us—through."

"Guys," Don called from the panic room, "this isn't the time for family politics. They're getting through!"

Martin put his hand on Jim's shoulder. "I know they took your son from you, and that's a hard thing. That's a very hard thing. But they put a roof over his head and clothes on his back. Danny loves you—I can see it every time he looks at you. But he loved them too. And for you to say that, especially after whatever he's been through, is an even harder thing. I'm guessing that little boy's hair wasn't turning white two months ago. He's seen his mother and stepfather and everyone around him corrupted by those *things*. He's still in shock that you showed up, along with a bunch of strangers he's never met. And now his house is burning down and we just got done making him walk the balance beam two stories above the ground. The fact that he's alive and unharmed is nothing short of God's work. I have traveled up the East Coast to help you find him, and we've been through hell together. But we did it. We saved him. So knock off your bullshit right now and let's make sure this rescue wasn't in vain."

Jim took a step backward, stunned.

"Yeah, I'm sorry. I was out of line."

"Now look what you did." Martin smiled. "You went and made me curse."

Jim chuckled as they returned to the room. He went over to Danny and picked him up again.

"I'm sorry. Daddy's just tired. I didn't mean to say those things about your mom and Rick."

"It's okay." Danny smiled. "They said bad things about you too sometimes, even before they became monster-people."

"You gonna carry him?" Don asked.

"I reckon so."

"Here." He handed Jim a small hatchet. "Better carry this then, too. You can swing it with one arm."

The sound of gunfire broke out again, drifting up from the pool.

"I think that's our cue," Don urged. "We better get going!"

"Listen," Jim held up a hand. "That sounds like an M-16."

Don sighed in frustration. "We're out of time!"

"Is it Frankie?" Martin asked.

Jim shook his head. "Can't be."

"She was almost out of ammo, but it could be her—if she survived the fall."

"Martin—"

"It has to be, Jim."

Don whipped around. "She's alive?"

"Move!" Martin shouted.

"That's what I've been saying," Don snapped.

They ran for the garage.

Frankie stepped out of the shallow end of the pool and opened fire, squeezing off short bursts as she swept the weapon back and forth. When she saw that she was surrounded, she planted her feet, held down the trigger, and allowed the rifle's kick to pull her around in a circle.

"Come on, motherfuckers," she yelled. "I got something for you!"

When she let go, she grinned at the bodies lying prone around her—then started again.

Some of the creatures shouted taunts, but the roar of the M-16 drowned them out. She switched to short bursts again, so that she could re-aim the weapon. The inferno raged a few yards away, as Jim's ex-wife's home was reduced to cinders. The heat from the fire roasted her face. She squinted, her eyes watering. Empty brass jackets littered the yard, and smoke poured from the barrel. She continued firing, shredding everything in her path—afraid the weapon would fall apart, but not caring. Heads exploded, and limbs were mangled and torn. What wasn't destroyed in the first barrage was knocked down by the second sweep. The rifle vibrated, sending shockwaves through her body and growing hot in her hands.

A little girl, shorter than the rest, ducked in below her field of fire and swung a croquet mallet. Frankie stepped back, swept the rifle butt downward, obliterated the child's head, and brought the weapon back up in one fluid motion.

"Come on. What you got for me? Huh? What you got? You ain't got nothing!"

Something punched her leg—hard. She looked down and saw blood. A second bullet stung her arm. Another whizzed by, shattering De Santos's kitchen window. A zombie to her right heaved a brick at her. It landed in the yard, barely missing her. The blood continued to flow down her leg and pooled inside her shoe. The wound burned.

"Shit."

Another object struck the back of her head. A rock, she thought, even as she yelped in pain. Then she saw what it was as it fell to the ground. A white cue ball, now smeared with her blood.

She wondered how much ammunition was left, but pushed the thought from her mind. The magazine held thirty bullets, but in the confusion, she hadn't had time to count her shots. She continued firing, knowing that if she stopped to check now, they'd overrun her. Her leg felt like it was on fire. More heads exploded, their owner's bodies flopping to the ground. One zombie's right arm remained hanging by a thin piece of gristle. It gnawed at the flesh until the arm came free, then clambered after her again, swinging the appendage like a club.

"Double shit."

Frankie's head began to throb and her left knee buckled, growing numb. She looked down to see that her entire pant leg was now scarlet. The severed arm crashed against her cheek, jarring her teeth.

An undead sparrow landed in her hair and tore away a strip of flesh from the wound there. Frankie screamed. Still firing, she beat at the creature with one hand. Immediately, her arc of fire dropped to ground level, sending clots of dirt flying. Arching her back, she readjusted her fire and snatched the bird from her head. She flung it to the ground and crushed it under her bloody boot.

A one-eyed, three-legged German shepherd stalked towards her, teeth bared. Another rock struck her between the shoulder blades. Her leg, arm and head pounded. Her vision turned red.

Frankie aimed at the dog and squeezed the trigger.

The magazine clicked empty.

"Triple shit."

The circle of zombies tightened around her.

They had to shout to be heard above the noise in the garage. Outside, the creatures pounded on the door with sticks and crowbars and fists. Danny clutched Jim's shoulder and Jim winced. The re-opened wound throbbed as Danny pressed harder.

"My God," Martin breathed. "They're all around us!"

"We've got to do this quick." Don reached into his pocket and pulled out his keys. "You guys get in while I unlock the garage door. Be ready."

"Who's driving?" Jim asked.

"I am," Don answered. "You get in the back with Danny."

"If Frankie's alive . . ." Martin began.

Don interrupted him. "Even if she survived that fall, they've got her by now."

"We don't know that."

"Look, do you know how many of those things are outside that door? Get real, man. You can't be sure it's her out there just because you hear an M-16!"

"We've got to look for her," Martin insisted. "She'd do the same for us."

Don sighed. "Okay. When we pull out, if we see her, we'll stop. But let's be clear. If helping your friend is going to get the rest of us killed, then I'm not stopping."

"That's bull!" Martin exploded. "You cold-hearted son of—"

"Fine, Reverend. You go outside and get her yourself. Did you two really travel all the way from West Virginia just to see those things get Danny?

Martin didn't reply.

Don clenched his jaw. "We don't have time to argue."

Jim cleared his throat. "I hate to say it, Martin, but he's making sense. I'm not sacrificing Danny. I'll sacrifice myself before I'll let those things get him."

Martin shrugged.

"Of course. We can't do that. It just seems so . . ."

"I know. It sucks."

Don jangled the keys. "Okay then. Here we go."

He thumbed the remote. The alarm system beeped softly in the darkness as the doors automatically unlocked. Don tossed Martin the keys and then crept to the garage door.

"Don't start it yet," Don whispered to Martin. "We don't need to alert them."

The Explorer had been backed into the garage. Jim buckled Danny into the backseat and sat next to him. Martin got in on the passenger side, slid the key into the ignition and gave Don a nervous glance.

Carefully, Don rotated the knob on the combination lock. Sweat dripped from his forehead, stinging his eyes. It was sweltering inside the garage, and the stench of rotting flesh overpowered the usual smells of motor oil, paint cans and lawn clippings. It took him three tries, but then the lock snicked open. He nodded at Martin and let the chains fall.

Swallowing, Martin turned the key. The vehicle roared to life as the heavy steel chains landed on the cement floor.

"They're inside the garage," a zombie in the driveway shouted. "Here! They're in here! Around front!"

Don sprinted for the driver's side and slammed the door behind him. The garage door rattled on its frame as the zombies hammered against it.

"You guys ready?"

Jim and Martin nodded.

With the press of a button, Don locked the Explorer's doors, sealing them inside the vehicle. He thumbed a second button and the garage door began to rise, the electricity coming from the battery on the roof. Smoke from the burning house next door curled through the crack. As the door rose further, they saw feet, some clad in sneakers or dress shoes, others bare and in various stages of decay. The door continued to rise.

Don flicked on the headlights.

A dozen zombies stood framed in the garage doorway, shoulder to shoulder, blocking their exit. The one in the middle raised a Mossberg pump shotgun and fired.

Danny screamed.

Wet, cold, and trembling with pain and shock, Frankie glanced around in panic. The German shepherd hobbled toward her on three legs. To her right, six human corpses and an undead cat crept closer. One of the zombies wielded a golf club and two others brandished butcher knives. Closing in on her left was a creature dressed in the tattered remains of a paramedic's uniform. Its skin was burned black and peeling off in layers. It clutched a small .22 pistol in one charred hand. Behind it stood another, fresher corpse, brandishing a fireplace poker. Frankie was afraid to turn and see what was behind her.

The stench grew worse as they drew closer. She held her breath. The smoke stung her eyes, making them water. Her head swam, and her wounded leg and arm felt heavy, like they were made of lead.

"It will be easier if you don't resist," the burned zombie rasped. Its voice was like sandpaper. "Not as much fun for us, but easier all the same."

"Fuck you," she choked, trying to sound brave. To her ears, the words sounded anything but.

Another corpse stepped closer. Frankie watched in revulsion as a plump worm dropped from its forearm.

"How many humans were with you?"

Frankie recoiled. Its breath was like an open sewer.

The dog growled, a phlegmatic rumble that lost none of its menace. Black fluid leaked from its eyes and nose.

The burned ghoul grabbed her arm. Its fingers felt like cold, raw sausages.

"We counted four of you, plus one in the other house. Are there more?"

She spat in its face. The act winded her and the thickening smoke made breathing torture.

"No matter." It grinned, revealing blackened, broken teeth. "We'll find out soon enough."

The grip on her arm tightened and the rest of them closed ranks. Frankie tensed.

"I hope that when you eat me, you all catch herpes."

Her hand darted for the burned zombie's face, plunging two fingers into its eyes, blinding it. The creature reared back in surprise and Frankie broke free of its grip. Without pausing, she clubbed its head with the empty rifle.

The dog leaped, white fangs flashing in the darkness. Frankie dropped and rolled. The dog fell sprawling beyond her.

Above the shouts, Frankie heard a motor turn over.

"They're inside the garage! Here! They're in here! Around front!"

The haze thickened, obscuring everything except the zombies surrounding her. Taking advantage of the distraction, Frankie plunged into the smoke.

The first shotgun blast shattered the passenger's side headlight. The zombie jacked the Mossberg's pump again, and Martin watched, transfixed as the empty shell floated through the air in seemingly slow motion.

"Shoot it, Martin!" Jim shouted.

"No." Don grabbed Martin's wrist. "Don't waste your ammunition. We don't know how long it will be before we can get more."

The creature fired again and took out the remaining headlight. Laughing, the other zombies fanned out, completely blocking the doorway.

"De Santos!" Jim punched his shoulder from the backseat. "Drive!"

Don was frozen behind the wheel, his eyes wide. Panic had gripped him, and he wasn't thinking clearly.

Danny whimpered, covering his ears with his hands.

"Well, what are we supposed to do if we're not shooting?" Martin asked.

"This." Don's paralysis snapped, and he stomped on the accelerator.

The zombie's laughter stopped as the SUV shot toward them. The fresher corpses flung themselves aside. Don mowed down the slower ones. The impact jolted the vehicle, and he prayed that the airbags wouldn't deploy. There were more bumps and then they were free, speeding down the driveway.

Thick, black smoke engulfed everything and with no headlights, Don couldn't see more than a few feet ahead. Frightened and still not thinking clearly, he squealed to a stop and glanced into the rear-view mirror. The zombie with the shotgun clambered to its feet.

"Get down!"

Jim shielded Danny with his body. A second later, the rear window shattered, spraying them with chunks of broken glass. Danny screamed again.

"What are you doing?" Martin shouted. "Drive!"

Don gunned the engine.

"You guys hit?" he asked.

"No, we're not hurt," Jim told him and then turned to Danny. "It's going to be okay. Just hang in there."

"I'm scared, Daddy. I want to go home! I want Mommy!"

"I know, squirt. I know . . ."

Don squealed out into the road and the smoke grew thinner. He ran over another zombie. A satisfied thrill shot through him as he felt the crunch beneath his tires.

"You keep doing that and this thing won't make it much further," Martin said.

Ignoring him, Don spun the wheel and aimed at another figure lurching out of the smoke.

"Stop," Jim shouted. "That's Frankie!"

She limped across the yard, her clothing soaked with blood and her head drooping. Weakly, she raised her hands to signal them. A horde of the creatures pursued her.

"Shit!" Don slammed the brakes. The Explorer fishtailed, ramming into the abandoned Humvee. Jim's head cracked against the side window.

Martin rolled down the window and took aim. His hands were shaking.

"Frankie, get down!"

She collapsed, flattening herself out on the grass.

"Lord, guide my hand."

Martin squeezed the trigger and dispatched the lead zombie. He fired again at the remains of a German shepherd, but the shot passed through its breast. Don put the Explorer in park and rolled down the driver's side window. He crawled halfway out and began firing over the hood. The Colt .45's thunderous roar drowned out Martin's smaller pistol.

Jim glanced around. Zombies were converging on them from every direction.

"They're almost on top of us!"

Frankie crawled toward them. Blood streamed down her dirty face. Martin flung open the door and ran toward her.

"Martin," Jim yelled, "what are you doing?"

Don ducked back inside. "I can't get a clear shot. The old man's in the way."

Martin took two steps and fired, three more steps and fired again, steadily closing the distance between himself and the injured woman.

"What the hell are you doing, preacher-man?" Frankie gasped. "Get back in that ride before they get you too."

"I don't think so," Martin said. "You rescued me in Hellertown so now I'm repaying the favor."

Don drove up over the curb and across the yard toward them. The wind picked up, blowing the smoke away from the street. Orange flames licked across the roof of his home. Anger and sadness welled up inside him and he fought for control.

Goodbye, Myrna, he thought. *I love you and I'm sorry. I'm so very sorry . . .*

Grunting with effort, Martin dragged Frankie to her feet. Supporting her with one arm, he sighted on the dog again and squeezed the trigger. The pistol clicked empty.

"What now?" Frankie grunted.

"We've still got this." He pulled out the knife as he dragged her across the grass. Frankie ground her teeth as Martin accidentally brushed against her head wound with his thigh.

Don whipped toward them, but so did the dog. The dog was quicker. Its jaws snapped shut on Frankie's wounded leg. Shrieking, she beat at its head.

The others watched in horror, and Don was reminded of Rocky.

Martin stabbed with the knife. The blade lodged in the dog's skull, right between the ears. Grunting, he tried to free it, but the knife would not budge.

"Get it off me!" Frankie moaned.

"The blade is stuck in its skull."

A bullet plowed into the dirt by his feet. Clenching his false teeth together, Martin tugged at the handle again. The knife stayed put.

"H-hurts . . ." Frankie panted. "Forget about the knife!"

"Come on."

Martin dragged her toward the Explorer. The dog's corpse trailed along behind them, jaws clamped tight on Frankie's leg, even in death.

Don fired again, and the pursuing zombies drew back, seeking cover. More of the creatures emerged from the other houses.

Jim's hand slid to the door handle. "Danny, stay here."

Danny reached out and grabbed his arm.

"Daddy, no. Don't go out there!"

"I have to. They're in trouble."

Hefting the hatchet, Jim opened the door and ran toward them. With four precise swings, he severed the dog's head from its body. Frankie's eyes rolled up as she passed out. Martin and Jim quickly loaded the unconscious woman into the cargo area of the SUV. The dog's head was still attached to her leg like a leech.

Don ducked back inside the vehicle.

"I'm empty!"

"Forget about it," Jim snapped. "Just drive."

They sped away. The zombies faded in the rear-view mirror. The fire became a dull orange glow, and then vanished as Don turned onto a side street.

Martin sighed with relief. "We made it. Thank you, Lord."

"Any ideas where we're going?" Don asked.

"Away from here," Jim said. He probed the dog's teeth, searching for an opening. Frankie's blood seeped out around them. He pulled and the jaws opened, releasing her. The severed head snapped at him instead. A long, scabrous tongue lolled from the dog's mouth.

"Jesus—it's still moving!"

"The blade must not have hit the brain," Martin said.

Grabbing the head by the ears, Jim rolled down the window and tossed it away.

Frankie's eyes flickered. Her breathing became erratic.

"Where's that bitch going with my baby?" she moaned.

"Is she going to be okay, Daddy?"

"I don't know, Danny. I don't know."

More darkened homes and a strip mall flashed by them.

Don slowed down.

"What are you doing?" Martin asked.

"The headlights are shot out. Last thing we need is to run into something."

"True."

"I'm sorry I freaked out, back there in the garage," Don apologized.

"Don't worry about it," Martin assured him. "These things take some getting used to."

Don glanced into the backseat. "How bad is it?"

"She's been shot in the leg," Jim said, "and there's a bad gash on the back of her head. This dog bite is on top of the gunshot wound. She's lost a lot of blood. I reckon she's in shock. You got any clean rags in this thing?"

"There's a blanket underneath the seat. We used to use

it for Rocky, but I guess it's clean enough. Cleaner than the clothes we're wearing at least."

"Who's Rocky?"

"Our—our dog."

Jim opened a bottle of water and washed her wounds. Then he bandaged them as best he could, tearing the thin dog blanket into strips.

To their left, the New York City skyline rose into the night, the buildings resembling giant tombstones. Don shivered. The city was eerie. He'd grown up with a view of the skyline and lived in its shadow his entire adult life. With the exception of a blackout, he had never seen it so utterly dark. The towering skyscrapers were enveloped in blackness.

All but one.

He pointed. "Would you look at that?"

Ramsey Towers, the second highest building in New York City, was lit up like a Christmas tree, the windows flooded with light. A colored strobe pulsed from red to blue on the roof, flashing a beam into the night sky.

Jim whistled softly and a moment later, Danny mimicked him. They grinned at each other.

"Could we make it there?" Martin asked.

"There are easier ways to commit suicide," Don said. "Do you have any idea how many zombies there must be in the five boroughs? New York's population was what, eight million? They didn't evacuate until it was too late, and how many people were killed during the riots and looting? Not to mention all the wildlife; pigeons, rats, cats, and dogs."

"That's a lot of zombies," Jim agreed.

"Besides," Don said, "it's got to be a trap."

"What makes you say that?" Martin asked.

"Think about it, Reverend. If you were in a skyscraper, would you light the building up and let all those creatures know where you were? That's like ringing the dinner bell."

"I reckon." Martin stroked his chin. "So what do you figure it is?"

"Like I said, it has to be a trap. I remember reading how self-sufficient that building was. Supposed to be able to withstand anything. Some of the zombies probably got the power running inside and lit it up, hoping to attract survivors like us."

"Like mosquitoes to a bug light," Jim said from the back. "Look, we've got to get some help for Frankie. We're better off heading out into the country, away from civilization. Even then, we're not safe. But at least it's somewhere other than here."

"There's a hospital nearby," Don said. "They just finished building it a few months ago. We could get what Frankie needs there. Find a doctor that's still alive."

"How populated is the area it's in?"

"Like everywhere else around here. But maybe one of us could sneak inside, steal some supplies at the very least."

Jim shook his head. "Too risky. Let's get out to the country first. Maybe we can find a doctor's office or something. What about these Pine Barrens I'm always hearing about? How far away are they?"

Don laughed. "South. If you want country, the Pine Barrens are about as country as you can get. We've got about a half tank of gas, so we could make it that far. But I don't know how we'll refill the tank once we're empty. None of the pumps will work with the power off."

"God will provide," Martin said. His voice was dreamy, his attention focused on the skyscraper.

"If you say so," Don replied. "But God hasn't done a real good job so far."

"We're alive, aren't we?" Martin tore his eyes away from the mesmerizing light of the lone skyscraper. "He has seen us through. He wouldn't abandon his faithful servants now."

Don glanced into the rear-view mirror and froze.

"Oh no . . ."

"What now?" Jim sighed.

Don's voice was barely a whisper

"You guys left the keys in your Humvee."

"What are you talking about?" Martin asked. "That doesn't matter. We can find another one."

"Don't need to find one. It found us."

Jim and Martin looked out the back window.

Their abandoned Humvee raced toward them, the headlights like the eyes of an onrushing dragon.

"Fuck, who's driving that thing?" Don shouted.

"Who do you think?" Jim scrambled for a weapon. "The zombies!"

More headlights appeared behind them; as cars, trucks, and a motorcycle joined the chase.

Don wiped the sweat from his brow. "It never ends, does it? It never fucking ends."

"Can they catch us?" Martin asked.

"I sure as hell hope not." Don pressed the accelerator to the floor and the Explorer shot forward.

There was a flash in the darkness and a muffled shot rang out behind them.

"Looks like they've reloaded," Jim said. "We'd better do the same."

"I'm empty," Don grunted.

Martin nodded. "Me too. I used it all saving Frankie."

Jim reached into the back and grabbed Frankie's M-16. He checked the magazine and then thumped the seat in frustration.

"She's empty, too."

The Explorer bounced over some railroad tracks. Another explosion made them jump. The shot hit the rear bumper with a loud crack.

"We've still got the hatchet," Don said.

"Oh, well that's just great. What do we do—throw it at them?"

Their pursuers closed the distance. A red Mazda darted out from behind the Humvee and drew alongside. A zombie leaned out the window, holding an aerosol can. With its other hand, the thing held up a lighter.

Don stared in confusion.

"What the fu—"

The creature flicked the lighter and then depressed the button on top of the can. A burst of flame surged toward them, licking at the driver's side window.

"Jesus Christ," Jim shouted. "Who is this guy—McGuyver?"

Startled, Don swerved away. The driver of the Mazda followed, sideswiping the larger vehicle. There was a hideous shriek of metal as the two collided and then the Explorer ripped free.

"A homemade flamethrower," Don gasped. "I know you guys said these things were crafty, but this . . ."

Danny started crying. Jim slid an arm around his shoulders, and tried to brace him and comfort him at the same time.

"It'll be okay. It'll be—"

The Humvee leapt out of the darkness, its headlights looming in the Explorer's rear windshield. The SUV shuddered as the military vehicle rammed it from behind. The Humvee accelerated and slammed into them again.

Martin's head whipped sideways, striking the window. His false teeth rattled. He winced, tasting blood in his mouth.

Don took one hand off the wheel and wiped the sweat from his eyes. "They'll destroy themselves too, if they keep this up."

"So?" Jim held Danny tighter. "They're already dead. They don't care if their bodies get destroyed in the process. They'll just get new ones."

The Humvee crashed into them a third time, tearing their rear bumper loose. Don fought for control and skidded onto another street, lined with tall oak and elm trees that blocked out the moonlight.

"This is no good," he grunted. "I can't see shit."

"Hang on tight." Martin braced against the dash. "Here they come again!"

Danny's tears soaked into Jim's shirt. The approaching headlights filled the interior, blinding them. In the cargo area, Frankie moaned again.

"My baby . . . took my baby . . . let me get a fix . . ."

Like a battering ram, the Humvee impacted with the Explorer, shoving it forward. At the same time, the zombie on the motorcycle raced ahead. Grinning, it pulled in front of them, extended its middle finger and then purposely spilled the bike.

Both motorcycle and rider vanished beneath the Explorer's tires. Steel and rotting flesh met more steel and pavement. A shower of sparks flew into the air. They spun out of control. The Explorer bounced over the curb, clipped a tree, and then rocketed down an embankment toward a glass-partitioned guard shack in front of a parking garage.

Don had time to think. *It's a parking attendant's booth.*

Jim and Danny clutched each other.

Martin's lips moved in prayer.

"Thy will be done. Deliver us again, Lord . . ."

Then they slammed into the booth and knew no more.

SIX

In the darkness, the old man sipped wine and gazed out upon his city. It festered below him like an open sore—swollen with infection, spurting gangrenous pus, filled with cancerous cells that multiplied into infinity. His city, New York City, was dead yet living. It lived not in the shambling, insect-sized mockeries far below, but in those he had saved, now sequestered here in the tower.

His tower.

His flock.

There was a quiet rustling of air behind him. The flame dancing atop the candle flickered, indicating someone had entered the room. He did not turn around, knowing how proud and strong and sympathetic he must look, standing there outlined by New York's decaying skyline. Appearances were important. They were an illusion, and all power was built upon illusion.

Framed in the doorway behind him, Bates cleared his throat.

Smiling, the old man watched his confidant's reflection in the window. Bates had served him well, long before . . . this. He would continue to do so—as long as the old man kept up the illusion of control.

"Mr. Ramsey? Sir?"

Ramsey turned in feigned surprise.

"Ah, Bates. Come in. I wasn't aware you were standing there."

"Yes, sir, you seemed lost in thought."

"Hmmm, yes. Yes, I suppose I was. I was thinking about these creatures. I assume you're aware that we've determined another entity takes possession of the body after death, thus reanimating the corpses?"

Bates nodded. "Yes, sir. Dr. Maynard explained it quite clearly. Doesn't seem possible, does it?"

"Indeed. It seems like something out of an old pulp magazine. But that's what is happening. All one needs for proof is to take a walk outside the tower."

"I think I'll pass on that, sir."

"Oh, come now," Ramsey teased. "A man of your abilities, afraid to walk the city streets for fear of muggers?"

"It's not the muggers we need to be afraid of, sir. It's what they've become."

Ramsey chuckled, taking another sip of wine. He offered a glass to Bates, who declined.

"I'd better not, sir. We've still got a long night ahead."

"I insist. You'd better enjoy it while you can. It will be a long time before we receive French imports again."

His soft laughter echoed over the muted strains of Vivaldi's "Four Seasons." He poured a second glass and handed it to the bodyguard. Bates accepted, sipping dutifully.

"Thank you, sir. Most excellent."

"That it is."

Ramsey studied the bodyguard. Dressed in sartorial

elegance, black ponytail hanging down to the middle of his back, Bates was still an enigma after all this time. Two tours of duty in the Marines with the 24th MAU, followed by a stint with the Navy SEALs. After rejoining the civilian world, Bates had started his own private security firm, boasting dozens of the world's most affluent and popular rock stars, athletes, and actors as clientele. Then Ramsey hired him exclusively. He'd served Ramsey for almost twelve years. He continued to serve him now, as Chief of Security, whipping investment bankers and short-order cooks and legal secretaries into shape, filling the gaps in the security staff's ranks. Bates was loyal, and Ramsey trusted him implicitly with every detail of his empire. After all, his life was in Bates's hands. But as pleasant and courteous as Bates was, there were occasions when Ramsey had the distinct impression that, rather than looking into a man's eyes, he was looking into those of a serpent. Bates had that look now as he sipped the proffered wine and stared out at the night sky.

"Cigar?"

"No thank you, sir."

"Very well. Suit yourself. But I don't imagine that we'll be getting more Cubans, either."

Ramsey lit up, puffed until the end glowed in the darkness, and exhaled a thick cloud of fragrant smoke.

"So," he continued, "we know that they are inhabiting the bodies of the dead, but we can't determine why brain trauma seems to be the only way to destroy them. Why not other injuries or even holy water and crucifixes?"

"That's what you were pondering, sir?"

"Yes. Do you know much about Native American culture, Bates?"

"Not much, sir, other than their warfare tactics."

"You know that many tribes scalped their enemies, yes?"

Bates nodded.

"Do you know why?"

"Trophies?"

"Partly. But also because they believed that a man's spirit resides in his brain. They didn't just take the hair, as portrayed in the movies. They took the top of the skull. They believed the soul resided in the head."

The seemingly lidless eyes stared at him, and Ramsey grew uncomfortable. It was the snake stare again. For a moment, he half expected a forked tongue to slither out from between Bates's lips.

"The head, Bates. Don't you see? Perhaps these creatures directly inhabit the head. Or more specifically, the brain."

"It would make sense, sir." Bates shrugged. "A head shot seems to bring them down permanently. It would also explain why the U.B.R.D. works so well on the birds."

Ramsey nodded, agreeing with Bates's assessment of the Ultrasonic Bird Repelling Device, which they'd obtained from an abandoned air base during a recon patrol. "I'd considered that as well. Birds do have a sensitivity to sound, and the mechanism physically damages them as a result. That was a stroke of luck, obtaining it. Dr. Stern's hypothesis proved correct, it would seem. If their ears were in their wings, then I suppose the device would be no more fatal to them than a rock 'n' roll concert."

He drained his glass and poured another.

"Are you familiar with acupuncture, Bates?"

"Yes, sir. It was very popular when I worked in Hollywood."

"I suppose it would have been. The Oriental physicians found that the various functions of the body could be influenced by pressing upon specific points on the body's surface."

Bates set his glass on the desk. "You're talking about meridians, right? I studied them during my martial arts training."

"Correct. Each meridian is a pathway for specific energies—one of which is the head and brain."

Bates nodded. "An energy pathway. I see."

"Do you? It all comes back to the cranium—the brain." Ramsey pulled out the overstuffed leather chair from behind his desk and sat. He waved a hand at Bates to join him. "So, what's our status?"

Bates took a chair in front of him and checked his clipboard.

"We just finished inventory of our armory. I don't think we'll need to risk a raid on the National Guard or NYPD stockpiles after all. The federal armory raid netted us just over one hundred M-16 assault rifles and approximately one thousand rounds of ammunition apiece, plus magazines."

"I thought you didn't like M-16's?"

Bates nodded. "I don't. Personally, I prefer the M-1 Garand, but beggars can't be choosers. The weapons were kept cleaned and serviced, and they should perform well enough. It doesn't matter what we defend ourselves with, as long as we have the ability to do so."

"I see. Go on."

"We obtained several Tec-9s and other assault weapons, as well as an assortment of shotguns and handguns, including an especially nice Kimber 1911, which I kept for myself. There are six M-60 machine guns, which Forrest is excited about, and ammunition for each one. We found twelve M-203 grenade-launchers that we can install on the M-16's. We also counted five flame-throwers, and several cases of grenades. Add to this the varied weapons our community brought with them upon each person's arrival and the weapons that we've found inside the building's apartments: more handguns and rifles, knives, crossbows, et cetera, and secondary weapons like baseball bats and broom handles—"

"Broom handles?"

"We can make spears and pikes out of them, sir."

"Ah."

"In short, we should be able to withstand any assault for many months to come."

Ramsey smiled. "We can withstand it, and this building can withstand it as well."

He wrapped his leathery knuckles against the desk.

"After all, I built it."

He rose from the desk and walked back to the window.

"After the multiple terrorist attacks that crippled this city, I built a monument to New York—a monument to America. Eight million square feet of office, retail, research, and living space, resting on solid bedrock and extending far below ground. Ninety-seven stories of reinforced steel and shatterproof windows. Hollow support pillars filled with water to keep them cool during a fire, as well as fireproofing in between the floors and pressurized stairwells that are pumped with fresh air. We've got self-contained air- and water-filtration systems and our own power generator. Ramsey Towers is an impregnable fortress—just the way I designed it. It can survive an earthquake, a tornado, a hurricane, a biological or chemical attack, and, according to the engineers, even a direct hit with an airplane."

Ramsey stared out the window. Far below them, pinpricks of light winked in the darkness.

"Look at them. Encamped, circling this building all day and night, yet they cannot get to us. They shoot at the lower level windows—send their birds to attack. Remember when they tried the grenade launcher assault?"

Although Bates didn't respond, Ramsey knew the man remembered all too well. He'd lost four good men in the attack.

"Failed. As has everything else they've tried. Rats from the sewers. Rushing the doors with battering rams. Ladders. Concentrating their fire on one area. It's useless. They can't get in, and we don't need to get out."

Bates drained his wineglass.

"What about a nuclear detonation, sir?"

"What about it?"

"Surely the building couldn't survive that."

"A nuke? Where would they get their hands on one? And even if they did, yes, I believe we could withstand it—unless they detonated it on our doorstep. As long as I remain standing, so does this building."

"What about a truck bomb of some kind, like the one used in Oklahoma City years ago? At the very least, it would breach the exterior."

"Surely you jest."

Bates didn't respond.

Ramsey stubbed the cigar out in the solid gold ashtray on the desk corner and then returned to his seat.

"So, what else have you got for me?"

Bates turned back to the clipboard.

"Maintenance needs to take the air-conditioning offline tonight for routine repairs. It's scheduled for three this morning and should only be out for a half hour, but I imagine the smell from outside will be bad during that time. Branson and Val have been in contact with a group of survivors in the East Village. They're holed up on the second floor of the KGB Bar on 4th Street. They're armed fairly well, and seem to have enough food and water to last them for a few weeks. However, we lost contact with the group sequestered inside Penn Station, so we'll have to assume the worst in their scenario."

"Pity that I couldn't save them." Ramsey sighed. "We must save as many as we can."

Bates glanced back down at the clipboard and continued.

"Dr. Stern says the new family that DiMassi brought in two days ago has tuberculosis. They were quarantined, as always, so there's no risk of them infecting the rest of the building."

"And DiMassi?"

"He had limited contact with anyone else. Arrived back with the family and went straight to his quarters, where he slept for twelve hours. We've quarantined him as well, but so far he shows no signs. The doctors think he'll be fine. Of course, I still had his bed linens and accoutrements destroyed and the helicopter decontaminated, just to be safe."

"Very good. And you've had no further insubordination problems with him?"

"No, sir."

"Excellent. We can't have discord."

"Speaking of the helicopter, we need to find and secure another fueling station for it. Quinn and DiMassi have been using private airfields in Trenton, Brackard's Point, and Head of Harbor, but now all three are overrun with zombies. It's too risky for them to return. The size of the force we'd need to resecure the areas is more than we could transport with the helicopter itself. We'd need to go by land, which is, of course, impossible. Our men wouldn't make it two blocks at this point, let alone out of the city."

"I see." Frowning, Ramsey steepled his fingers together.

Bates shifted in his chair.

"Permission to speak freely, Mr. Ramsey?"

"Of course."

"Sir, perhaps we need to consider our situation more carefully. Things have become—rather precarious."

"Continue."

"Well, we're down to one helicopter, and it's our only way out of here. We can't go outside because those things have us surrounded, and more are showing up every day. The guy with the ham radio in Chatham told us that the zombies have gotten the Dover train running again and are shipping reinforcements into the city via the Morris-Essex line. What possible reason could they have for doing that? Face it, sir. We're under siege. Right now, it's a stalemate, but should they get more organized—should they get a leader, things could go bad very quickly. And if the U.B.R.D. malfunctions, or we lose the helicopter due to a mechanical problem or hostile fire, we'll be completely trapped."

"But we're not trapped, Bates. Indeed, we are safer than anyone else who remains alive out there."

"But for how long, sir? With all due respect, Mr. Ramsey, I don't understand your insistence on sending out regular patrols to bring back survivors. Sure, we have enough food and water now, but for how long? The more people we bring back, the more supplies we consume. There's no telling how long this siege will last. And every time we send the chopper out, we risk losing it."

"We bring them back because I can save them."

Bates clenched his fist and continued. "Then think of the biological hazard. We're surrounded by thousands of dead bodies. Corpses. I'm not a doctor, but I would imagine they're all carrying disease. Things like the bubonic plaque and hepatitis. These zombies are walking petri dishes. Maybe it's time we considered other options."

"So what would you have me do?"

"At the very least, we should shut off the strobe light on the roof. All it does is attract more of these things."

"How will others know where to find us if we don't show them the way?"

"But the other survivors can't get to us on foot, sir. Instead of worrying about others, maybe we need to worry about ourselves. We have to consider the possibility that sooner or later, no matter how well-guarded, those things will breach our defenses."

Ramsey grinned.

"If that happens, which it won't, then I have a contingency plan."

"Good. I can't tell you what a relief that is, sir. May I ask what it is?"

"No. As of now, that information is given out on a need-to-know basis, and quite frankly, you don't need to know."

Bates leaned back in his chair.

"Begging your pardon, Mr. Ramsey, but how am I supposed to protect us if I don't know?"

The old man took another sip of wine.

"Trust me, Bates. If and when the time comes, you'll be the first to know. Now, what about this situation to the south that you apprised me of earlier today? What became of that?"

"The communication center has continued monitoring, sir: citizen's band, short-wave, all civilian, federal, local, military, and maritime channels, as well as cellular and other frequencies. Branson and Val tell me it was a large force, obviously on the move. Possibly remnants of a National Guard unit, judging from some of the transmissions we intercepted. But we've heard nothing for hours."

"And that was in—Hellertown, Pennsylvania, yes?"

"Affirmative—at a government facility. Quinn and Steve are out now, flying over the Garden State Parkway, Interstates 95 and 78 and all the other major highways nearby, just in case there are survivors heading this way. I doubt they'll find anything. Who would be foolish enough to come *into* New York City if they weren't already here?"

"Who indeed," Ramsey chuckled. "Anything else?"

"We need to reconsider our power usage. Keeping the building lit not only excites the zombies, but it's draining our resources. I suggest rolling blackouts. We need to conserve—"

"Out of the question. I told you, we must keep the building lit so that other survivors will find us. The lights are a beacon to their safety. 'While I am in the world, I am the light of the world.' John, 9:5. You should read the Bible sometime. Fascinating book."

Bates fought hard to keep the frustration out of his voice. "As you wish, sir."

"Is that all?"

"There is one other thing. Earlier in the day, I discovered that one of the new arrivals, a little girl of about seven, had a bag of ripe black plums on her person. She was nice enough to share some with me, in gratitude."

"Plums?" Ramsey salivated at the thought. "Most excellent!"

"I'll have one sent up for you at once, sir."

"No." Ramsey waved his hand. "You'd better wait an hour. I wish to masturbate first."

Bates paused, fighting very hard to maintain his composure.

"Very well, sir. I'll leave you then."

He turned and walked out. The door hissed shut behind him.

Darren Ramsey, billionaire industrialist and the man who was New York, unbuckled his pants, letting them fall around his ankles. Then he shuffled to the window and pressed his hardening member against the cold glass.

He threw his head back, closed his eyes and sighed.

" 'While I am in the world, I am the light of the world.' "

As his hand began to stroke, he gazed out upon the skyline again.

If there were a God, he thought, *I bet his view wouldn't be as good as this . . .*

"I am their savior . . ." he moaned.

This building, Ramsey Towers, spanning the 200 block of Madison Avenue, and stretching between 35th and 36th streets, was his world. And he stood at the top of that world, the ruler of all he surveyed.

Fourteen floors below him, an armless, legless torso strapped to an operating table shouted curses in ancient Sumerian.

Bates stood outside the door, listening.

"Bates?"

He whirled, hand automatically going to his pistol.

"Whoa." Forrest threw his hands up in the air. "It's just me."

"What are you doing?" Bates snapped. "You know better than to be on this level without authorization."

The big man stared at the floor.

"You told me to let you know if Steve and Quinn found anything."

"And?"

"They did. Four survivors. Should be here in about fifteen minutes."

"Wonderful. That's all we need—more people."

"I bet Mr. Ramsey will be happy to hear it."

"I'm sure he will," Bates said. "He'll be delighted."

Because the old fucker has lost his mind and has some kind of messiah complex.

The black man stared at the door, listening to the noises drifting out.

"What's he doing in there?"

"None of your concern." Bates lit a cigarette and inhaled deeply. "Did you tell Dr. Stern to prepare for the new arrivals?"

"He was asleep, so I let Doc Maynard know. He . . ."

"What?" Bates asked.

"He—he was doing something with one of the zombies."

"Another experiment?"

"No . . ."

"What then?"

"He—it sounds fucked up. He was having sex with it."

"*What?*"

"Had it strapped down to a gurney and when I walked into the lab, his pants were down around his ankles, and he was humping away at the fucking thing! It was babbling in some kind of language I never heard."

Bates gritted his teeth. "Wake Doc Stern up. I don't want Maynard left alone with the civilians."

"We're gonna have to do something about him, Bates."

"We will. Let Stern check over these new arrivals. Maynard can assist, if he's able. We'll place him under arrest afterward."

They walked down the hall together. While they waited for the elevator, Bates's headache returned. His temples throbbed and his jaw ached.

"I'm getting too old for this shit. Something bad is coming, Forrest. I can feel it."

The big man snickered. "You mean worse than dead folks getting up and eating people?"

"Yes." Bates nodded. "Even worse than that."

Ob awoke seated on a dusty recliner inside a darkened apartment. Plywood covered the windows and doors. There were no life glows in the room or the hallway, so he assumed that he was alone.

He found a mirror and examined the new body. It was good. It was *very* good. Caucasian male, mid-twenties, naked—the arms and chest were a chiseled mass of muscle. No visible wounds. Ob flexed and smiled. He searched through the host's memory, learning that he'd been a weight lifter named Gary, and employed as a law enforcement officer. He'd barricaded himself in the apartment and died of a heart attack in the chair. For all his strength, he'd had a weak heart. The death had occurred only a few minutes ago, while he'd been masturbating to the memory of an ex-girlfriend. Ob glanced down at the bottle of baby oil on the floor and then returned to the host's mind. Ex-military, combat trained and proficient with a variety of weapons. He searched deeper and laughed out loud. His host knew the location of several fully stocked police and National Guard armories.

"Oh, I like this."

He posed some more, admiring the coiled strength and form. He reached down and played with the penis, shaking it at the mirror. Though flaccid, it was well proportioned. Perhaps later he would try it out and learn what was so special about the act of procreation the humans seemed so preoccupied with.

Still nude, he searched the apartment, verifying that there were no other humans. Disappointed by the lack of prey, he walked to the door. He gripped the plywood with both hands, but then paused. This body was in perfect condition. There was no sense in damaging it this early into the possession. Instead of ripping the barricade off with his bare hands, he looked for a hammer. Finding one, he removed the nails and walked out the door.

Severed body parts littered the stairway—congealing piles of viscera and haphazardly strewn limbs. He stepped through the carnage and almost slipped in a half-dried pool of blood. He left red footprints in his wake.

Near the bottom, a head rolled its eyes toward him. The dry, black tongue slithered out of the dirt-caked mouth like a piece of liver, wiggling for his attention. Ob bent over and picked the head up.

"Alas, poor Yorick. I knew you well . . ."

The head's lips moved, but no sound came out.

"Do not try to speak, brother. Your body lacks the necessary equipment. I will release you so that you may try again."

The eyes blinked, and then the head mouthed silent thanks.

"Go and find another body."

Ob slammed the head into the wall, cracking the plaster. He struck it a second time. The skull split, and the brains leaked out. The lips stopped moving.

The lobby doors were chained shut. He'd expected this, seen it in his host's memories. He pulled the fire extinguisher from the wall and smashed out the windows, picking the fragments of glass out of the way so that they wouldn't damage his new form. Then he crawled outside into the night.

The city was alive with the dead—teeming with them. They were like ants, scurrying through the streets and alleys and buildings. New York City once had a population of over eight million people. Now, it was the world's most populated graveyard. Zombies waved from balconies and fire escapes and honked their horns at each other as they drove by in cars and cabs. Humans, rats, pigeons, cats, dogs—the undead represented every life form native to New York. The air was ripe with the smell of rotting corpses and the screams of those few still living. Rotting garbage littered the streets; the former civilization's debris mingled with offal and internal organs. Graffiti covered the wall of a building across from him, dating from both before and after the Siqqusim's arrival: JESUS SAVES and WEST SIDE BOYZ next to I AM LOOKING FOR MY WIFE—DAWN WILLIAMS—I AM AT OUR APARTMENT and the undead response of WE HAVE YOUR WIFE, MEAT!

In the street, fourteen humans had been tied spread-eagled to the hoods of cars, and a group of zombies slowly flayed the skin from their bodies with razors, box-cutters, and butcher's knives. Another human hung from a lamppost, and was being used as a living piñata, his body beaten with spiked clubs until it burst open, showering them with bloody prizes. Other zombies participated in more mundane activities such as exploring buildings, driving cars and lounging on porches. Several used the windows of a decrepit brownstone as target practice and their cheers drowned out the gunfire. Another group played football in the streets—a severed human foot taking the place of the pigskin. Others played jump rope with a grayish-pink string of human intestines. A dead python slithered through the streets, vertebrae poking through its scaly flesh.

When Ob strode into their midst, all activity ceased. The gathered corpses immediately recognized him. The atmosphere became charged.

He raised his arms. "Hello, brethren!"

A thunderous cheer echoed through the concrete canyons. It was picked up and repeated throughout the city in a multitude of languages: English and Chinese, Arabic and Spanish, French and German, Hebrew and Italian. It was chirped from beaks, barked from canine throats, howled from feline mouths, and hissed on the tongues of serpents. But the words were all the same.

"Hail! Hail! Ob has come! *Engastrimathos du aba paren tares!* Hail!"

They ran to him, stroking his unblemished flesh and shouting with joy. They offered him strips of raw, bleeding flesh and still-warm organs, which Ob gratefully accepted. He ate, and crimson dripped from his chin, splattering onto his bare chest. Then, surrounded by the crowd, Ob leaped onto the hood of a delivery van, climbed onto the roof, and held up his hands for silence.

"Siqqusim! Who am I?"

"Ob! Ob! Ob!" The cheers roared into the night, shaking the windows in the buildings.

"Indeed I am. I am I."

This statement was greeted by more cheers.

"Brothers, you have done well here. This shall be our Necropolis. A new Babylon. How many humans still infest this place?"

A zombie in a fraying business suit stepped forward, followed by another covered in third-degree burns.

"Not many, lord," said the suited one. Its right eye socket was an empty pit. "A few scattered survivors. There is one large group, about a hundred, gathered in a building of steel—what they call a skyscraper. It is similar to Babel of old. They call it Ramsey Towers."

Ob frowned. "I know what a skyscraper is, you fool. My host wasn't born yesterday. Tell me, with all your numbers, why have you not taken this New Babel?"

The burned one slurred as it spoke. "We cannot penetrate it, lord. The building is well guarded, and the defenses are impregnable. We lack the weaponry . . ."

"Where is this building?"

"A part of the city known as Manhattan, mighty one."

"And according to my host's memories, we are in the Bronx, correct? There is an armory near here, where the humans stockpiled weapons. Have any of you discovered it yet?"

"No, lord."

"Then come, I will show you. We have much to do. We will see what secrets this armory holds. With its weapons, we can knock this New Babel down, reduce it to dust. There is an army of our brethren camped not four hours' journey from here. I shall find a means to summon them, be it radio, runner or bird. Then, while we learn how to use these weapons, we will await their arrival. We shall study and plan. Then, when all is ready, we shall deal with this tower."

They raised another tumultuous cry, and Ob smiled, knowing that the sound must surely be reaching the Creator's ears. He hoped those ears were bleeding.

He jumped down and hummed a snatch of song from his host's memory.

" 'Start spreading the news . . .' "

SEVEN

The doctor stared down at Frankie from behind his mask and said, "It's going to be okay."

"Like hell it is."

The doctor didn't respond. Impassive, he snapped on a pair of rubber gloves and adjusted the light above her head. Frankie winced, blinded. She tried to turn away and realized that she was strapped down.

"What's going on?"

"Don't you remember? You were in a car wreck. You've also been shot."

"I-I . . ." She paused, struggling against the restraints. "What about the others? Jim and his boy? The preacher-man?"

"I'm afraid it's just you, Frankie. You and the baby."

"Baby?"

"Yes. You're in labor. The baby is all you have left."

"But—"

"You should be thankful," he told her, as a nurse appeared next to him. "Most heroin users have spontaneous abortions. You've been lucky enough to carry your baby to full term. Personally, I think it's a shame. You don't deserve it."

"But I—"

She stopped, a sudden flash of pain cutting off her words. She squirmed on the table and ground her teeth. The contraction coursed through her body.

"Push."

She did. Frankie pushed with everything she had, pushed till her spine felt like it would snap. Something broke. She felt it, even through the pain. The agony built to a crescendo, and then the pressure vanished, all at once, and Frankie was crying.

Frankie cried, but the baby, her baby, did not. It made no noise at all. She craned her head, desperate to see what was wrong, but the nurse whisked it away.

"Hey," she croaked, "where's that bitch going with my baby?"

The doctor placed one gloved hand against her forehead. The latex glistened with her blood.

"He's hungry. We're going to feed him. Your baby is one of us."

"One of who?"

The doctor's voice changed. The flesh peeled away from his face in wet strips. A hypodermic needle appeared in his free hand.

"One of us. There are many of us. More than you can imagine. More than infinity," it hissed.

"No. Keep that away from me."

"Be still, now. This won't hurt a bit. I promise."

Frankie pushed against the restraints, the muscles in her arms and neck bulging as the needle came closer. A bead of fluid formed on the tip.

"Jim! Martin! Help! They've got my baby."

"I said lie still," the zombie doctor snarled. Its stench filled the room, crowding out the smells of antiseptic and latex and blood.

The cord around her arm snapped as Frankie tore free. She ripped the surgical mask from the creature's face. The lips came with it, stretching like taffy.

"Now you've done it," the zombie slurred. The creature's lips fell to the floor, exposing rotten, ulcerating gums and a gray tongue.

"Give me back my baby, you son of a bitch!"

The other straps broke as Frankie rolled off the table and struck her head on the floor. The creature rushed her, brandishing the hypodermic needle like it was a dagger. Frankie sprang to her feet, keeping the table between them.

"This isn't really happening," she spat. "You're not real! My baby was already dead. It died back in Baltimore."

"Yes, it did. And now you're all alone. Poor Frankie. Frankie the junkie. Frankie the whore. All alone. Still dying for a fix, whether you want to admit it to yourself or not. Dying for it. Dying alone in a dead world."

She sprinted for the door. The zombie ran after her. As it lurched into the hall, Frankie shoved a gurney into it. The zombie fell backward onto the delivery room's linoleum floor. Frankie ran down the hall, darting from one twisting corridor to another.

Finally, she stopped to catch her breath. Shivering, she crossed her arms beneath her breasts. The hospital was cold, and she could see her breath under the fluorescent lights. She glanced around, trying to get her bearings. The hallway was silent except for her footsteps.

She stopped in front of a set of double doors and ran her fingers over a sign hanging on the wall.

MATERNITY WARD

She'd been here before.

"Just a dream. This is just another fucking dream. Any minute now, the preacher's gonna wake me up."

The doors swung open. She stepped through and sniffed the air. Something had spoiled inside.

"Come on, Martin. Wake my ass up!"

She looked through a glass observation window. Dozens of little white bassinets were lined up in neat, orderly rows. Each crib was occupied. Tiny fists pumped the air, and tufts of downy hair peeked over several of the rims.

"I've seen this before," she said aloud. "Where's mine? Show me my baby."

As if in answer, a pair of mottled, pale, blue-veined arms gripped the side of a bassinette. Her baby pulled itself upright. Standing on diminutive legs, it climbed down to the floor and scampered over to its nearest neighbor. The zombie infant wriggled into the bassinette and fell upon the other newborn.

The other babies began to scream.

Frankie could hear the chewing sounds, even over the cries of the other babies, even through the thick glass partition.

Even over her screams.

"Just a dream . . . Just a dream . . ."

The feasting grew louder, and her baby began to speak in a language Frankie had never heard before.

"*Enga keeriost mathos du abapan rentare* . . ."

"Somebody wake me up. Wake me up!"

The baby clambered out of the bassinette and crawled toward the window.

It began to chant. "Ob . . . Ob . . . Ob . . ."

"Martin?" Frankie backed away from the glass. "Jim? Somebody help me!"

The baby drew nearer. Frankie shut her eyes.

Her baby's voice changed again.

"Mommy?"

It sounded like Danny.

From behind her, Martin said, "Frankie, wake up."

Pain. Then—darkness and more pain.

"Daddy?"

A voice. Small and afraid. Disembodied.

"D-Daddy? Dad?"

Urgent. Louder.

"Dad. The monster people are coming! Get up!"

Panic. The voice was Danny's.

"Daddy! Please, Daddy, you've got to wake up. Please?"

It all came rushing back to him—the rescue, the pursuit, the motorcycle crashing in front of them on purpose, and then—nothing.

Jim opened his eyes and saw red. There was no sign of Danny, or any of their companions. In fact, there was no sign of anything. He couldn't see. It was as if a scarlet curtain had been drawn over the world.

"Daddy, what's wrong?"

"I—I'm blind . . ."

A guard shack—the kind used at parking garages. He remembered that.

"They're here. Come on!"

He felt Danny tugging at his arm, heard the trembling in his voice. From somewhere to his left came a groan. Martin? De Santos? Frankie?

He smelled gas.

Then he smelled *them.*

Zombies.

"Danny? It's okay. I'm awake. I just can't see."

"You're hurt, Daddy. You've got blood in your eyes."

The pain stabbed again. Red. The world was red. Hesitantly, Jim touched his face and forehead. They were sticky. He probed at his scalp and winced at the sudden flash of agony.

"Danny, where are the others?"

There was no response.

"Danny?"

Jim heard harsh, ragged breathing and realized that it was coming from his son. Danny's voice was barely a whisper.

"Daddy, they're here . . ."

"Hey kid, want a nice piece of candy?" a zombie growled.

Jim heard the door wrenched open and then Danny shrieked.

"DADDY!"

"Come here, you little fuck!"

Jim's paralysis snapped. He wiped the blood from his eyes—seeing again—and screamed with rage as a pair of mottled arms dragged Danny from the backseat. His son struggled, kicking his legs and beating at the zombie with his fists. Another pair of leathery hands grappled with Danny's seatbelt release.

Jim grabbed the cold hand clutching his son's arm. The zombie's grip was like a vice. Jim pried at the fingers, tugging hard as adrenalin coursed through his veins. The finger tore loose and the creature laughed. Jim tossed the severed digit aside.

Desperate, he looked for the hatchet. The SUV's interior was a mess. Maps and soda cans, Styrofoam coffee cups and empty bullet casings, cigarette butts and shattered glass—all of it knocked loose and scattered on impact. Behind him, Frankie lay unmoving, buried beneath a pile of blankets, tennis rackets, and a cooler. In the front seat, Don sat slumped over the wheel, a white airbag enveloping him. A thin trickle of blood leaked from his gaping mouth. His eyes were shut. And Martin—

Martin was gone. The airbag had deployed, but there was no sign of the old man. Instead, there was a hole in the windshield; the edges matted with blood, hair, and pieces of pink, glistening flesh.

"Daddy, help me!"

Jim punched uselessly at the creature's face.

"Get off him! Get your god-damned hands off my son!"

He beat at the zombies, but could gain no leverage in the cramped backseat. His pulse throbbed as Danny's seatbelt came undone. The zombies dragged Danny out.

"No!"

"*Yes!*"

They jerked Danny into the darkness. The little boy's screams became one long, drawn out wail as the larger zombie's rotten mouth descended upon him. Frantically, Jim grabbed Danny's legs and pulled him backward. The zombies tugged harder.

"What's your fucking problem, pal? Let the kid go. He's just an appetizer. You can be the main course."

Jim was beyond words, beyond thought. The pain in his head and shoulder were forgotten. Martin was forgotten. Frankie and De Santos were forgotten. His entire world consisted of his son and the two undead attackers. Growling, he braced his feet against the console and pulled harder. The smaller zombie, the one who had undone the seatbelt, lost its grip, and Danny slid another inch toward Jim.

"Fuck this," it grunted. "Just kill the little shit so we can get to the adult. More meat on him anyway."

Nodding in agreement, the other creature's mouth fell upon Danny again.

"DAAAAAAAAADDDDDDDDYYYYYYYYYYYYY!"

"Leave him alone, you son of a bitch!"

The zombie's teeth ripped through Danny's shirt, right between his neck and shoulder. The powerful jaws clenched, preparing to bite through the skin, and then—

—Frankie sat up and buried the hatchet in its head, cleaving the skull in two. Gore splashed Danny and Jim.

"Eat that, motherfuckers," Frankie growled.

The decaying hands fell away as the zombie toppled backward. Jim pulled the hysterical boy back inside.

"You're okay, Danny," Jim reassured him. "You're okay now. They're not gonna get you."

"Cheer up, kiddo," Frankie said, "you're rescued."

She sank back down, her eyes fluttering closed. She did not move again.

"Shit. Frankie, wake up." Jim shook her gently, afraid of hurting the unconscious woman any worse than she already was.

"Is she dead, Daddy?"

"I don't think so, squirt. Are you okay?"

Danny nodded.

"Frankie?" Jim tried again. When she didn't respond, he shook De Santos.

"Don. Don, get up!"

"Huzzat . . ."

"Come on. God damn it, De Santos, wake up now!"

"Five more minutes, Myrna . . ."

The second zombie stepped forward and yanked the bloody hatchet from its fallen comrade's head. It was dressed in the tattered remains of a Bob Marley shirt. One ear and half its cheek had been torn away, and dreadlocks hung from its skull in filthy, matted ropes.

"Look what you did to my brother! That wasn't very nice. That wasn't nice at all."

Don stirred.

"Jim?"

"Wake up, Don. We've got go!"

Jim opened the door.

"Where do you think you're going?" the zombie snarled.

Clutching his son, Jim opened the door on the side away from the zombie, and tumbled out of the Explorer onto the cold pavement. He let go of Danny, sprang to his feet, and yanked Don's door open. Don stumbled out of the vehicle.

"Jesus, my chest . . ."

"Can you walk?"

"I-I think so. Just . . . hard to catch . . . my breath."

The zombie slid into the backseat from the other side. A plump, white maggot fell from its nose and lay wriggling on the floor mat. Jim gagged, and Don coughed blood from his nose and mouth.

Jim put a hand on Don's shoulder to steady him.

"Are you okay?"

"My chest," Don wheezed. "Steering wheel hit it. Fucking airbags were worthless. I should sue the manufacturer."

Jim turned back to the wrecked vehicle. "We've got to get Frankie out of there and find Martin."

The zombie crawled across the seat toward them, reaching for the open door. Jim slammed it in the creature's face.

"Danny, stay here with Mr. De Santos."

"No, Daddy, I want to stay with you!"

"I've got to get Frankie out of there, Danny. I don't have time to argue."

He turned to Don.

"When I tell you, open this door."

The corpse beat at the window with its fist, leaving a greasy smudge. Then it turned away from them.

"You want me to do *what?*"

"You heard me."

Inside the Explorer, the zombie pawed through the blankets surrounding Frankie. Jim dashed around to the other side and picked up a large rock.

"Now, Don!"

"Get behind me, Danny. I think your father may have lost his mind."

Swallowing, Don yanked the back door open. Immediately, the zombie turned and swung at him with the bloody hatchet.

Jim was quicker.

Grabbing it by the feet, he pulled it out of the backseat and onto the ground. The axe flew from its clutches and the zombie scrambled for it. Jim jumped onto its back, forcing it down again. The zombie pushed upward, struggling to dislodge him.

Enraged, Jim brought the rock crashing down on the creature's head, punctuating each blow with a snarl.

"I—told—you—to—leave—my—son—ALONE!"

There the skull split open with a loud crack. Pink, foul-smelling liquid spilled from the wound. The zombie bellowed, then finally lay still. Jim continued pounding it with the rock until the head was obliterated.

Panting, covered in blood and drenched in sweat, he looked up to see Danny staring at him. The boy's expression was horrified.

"Daddy . . ."

"It's okay, Danny. He can't hurt you now."

His son continued to stare, eyes wide and mouth open. Still clutching the rock, Jim slid off the corpse's back and walked toward him, drenched in gore.

Don eased Frankie out of the wrecked vehicle's rear, supporting her as she tried to stand.

"Where did the other zombies get to?" Don looked around for the rest of their pursuers.

"I don't know," Jim replied. "Maybe we lost them. How is she?"

"I'm fine," Frankie answered weakly. "Not dead yet, at least."

"Can you walk?"

"Gonna have to. Where's the preacher-man?"

"Oh God—Martin!"

In his concern for Danny, Jim had forgotten all about the old man.

He ran around to the front of the vehicle and searched the area. He found Martin's crumpled form at the base of a tree. The preacher wasn't moving.

"No no no no no . . ."

He stumbled toward his friend, and when he reached him . . .

Jim hoped that Martin had died with a prayer on his lips.

He turned his head and vomited.

"Daddy?"

"Don't look, Danny. Stay over there."

Martin lay on his stomach, but his head was twisted around backwards. The old man's bulging, sightless eyes gaped at him. Deep lacerations split his face, and one arm had been severed halfway between the elbow and the shoulder.

"Oh Martin . . ."

Frankie hung her head. "Is he?"

Jim swallowed hard.

"Yeah. Yeah, he is."

"God damn it . . ."

Kneeling, Jim gripped his rock tighter. The rough surface cut into the calluses on his palm.

"I'm sorry, my friend. I'm so sorry."

"Jim?" Don shifted uneasily.

"What?"

"You—you know what you have to do, right?"

Jim didn't respond.

"He'd want you to. He wouldn't want to—to end up like that." Don cocked his head toward the pulped remains of the zombie.

"I hate to say it, but he's right," Frankie agreed. "You've got to finish it, Jim. We can't let this happen to Martin. Not like that."

Jim closed his eyes and sighed.

"He'd want a prayer first," he said. "We owe him that, at least. Is there time?"

"I don't hear any zombies," Don said. "Maybe we lost the others."

Jim closed the preacher's eyes. Then he reached into Martin's breast pocket and pulled out his pocket-sized New Testament. After a brief pause, he held it to his heart and bowed his head. A second later, Danny did the same, followed by Don. Frankie watched the body.

"Lord," Jim began, "I—I still don't understand why you let all of this happen, why you did this to us, but I know that Martin never stopped believing in you. Not even when things got really bad. He was convinced that you wanted him to help me. He said that you would lead us to Danny. I reckon he was right. Even when his own life was in danger, he helped me because he believed in you. God, we ask—"

Martin's eyes opened. "There is no God."

Jim smashed him in the face with the rock. The zombie jittered.

"I'm sorry, Martin."

He swung again, and something cracked.

Frankie and Don flinched. Danny squeezed his eyes shut.

Jim swung a third time, and Martin's corpse was still. Jim stuffed the Bible in his back pocket.

A horn blared.

"What the hell?"

Headlights speared them, turning night to day as the Humvee crested the hill and roared toward them.

"Here they come!" Don shouted.

"Run!" Throwing the rock aside, Jim picked up Danny and cradled him in his arms. "Can you carry Frankie?"

"I can try," Don gasped.

He hefted her and suddenly collapsed, wincing in pain.

Frankie bit down a scream as fresh agony ripped through her body.

"I can't," Don breathed. "My chest . . ."

Jim shoved Danny toward them.

"Head for that parking garage. I'll lead them away from here and double back."

"You're insane."

"Go!"

"Daddy?"

Jim gave him a quick hug, kissed him on the forehead, and then looked up at De Santos.

"Please—go."

"Daddy?"

The Humvee bore down on them. More vehicles crested the hill behind it. Above them, Jim heard the dry, rustling flutter of wings.

"Daddy!"

"I love you, Danny."

Jim charged toward the Humvee.

"Daddy, no! Come back!"

"Let's go, Danny." Don led the crying boy toward the garage. Frankie limped along behind them, casting one last glance over her shoulder at the ruined flesh that had been the Reverend Thomas Martin.

"Rest easy, preacher-man."

"Come on, you sacks of shit. Over here!"

Jim waved his arms over his head, running directly toward the onrushing vehicles. The zombies obliged, swerving in his direction and spearing him with their headlights. The Humvee's engine roared hungrily.

Something buzzed by his ear. Jim felt a fresh burst of pain as a razored beak slashed his palm. He lashed out, but the bird darted away and circled around again. He spared a quick glance upward and saw more bearing down on him.

"Come and get it! Supper time!"

Bullets dug into the earth at his feet.

He ran, praying that De Santos and Frankie could get Danny to safety, praying that safety itself existed. A carrion crow pecked at his hand. In the distance, over the gunshots, he heard a rumble. Thunder? A helicopter? He didn't know and realized that he didn't care.

Let the sky weep.

He knew how it felt.

The entrance to the parking garage yawned before them like a gaping, ravenous mouth. The interior was pitch-black, and all three of them froze in front of it. Danny squirmed in Don's grip, desperately shouting for his father.

"Danny, stop it," Frankie said. "You'll lead them to us."

"I don't care. I want my daddy!"

Don took a step toward the entrance and paused.

"You think it's safe?"

"There's nowhere on Earth that's safe anymore," Frankie told him.

They walked inside. The parking garage was silent. Frankie heard Don rustling through his pocket, and a moment later, the telltale click of a cigarette lighter. The darkness seemed to surround the flame, as if trying to extinguish it. From far off, they heard gunshots and the roar of motors. Danny cast a glance behind him.

Despite her pain, Frankie knelt down and looked him in the eyes.

"I know you want your daddy, kiddo. I want him to come back too. But right now, he's doing something very brave to help us all. So that means you have to be brave too, okay?"

"But I don't feel very brave."

"That's okay." Frankie winked. "Neither do I. In fact, I feel like I've been run over by a truck."

She stood up and ruffled his hair, but suddenly her knees buckled. Her vision swam. She reached out and caught herself on Don's shoulder, shaking her head and breathing heavy.

"You okay?" he asked, concerned.

"I will be. Blood loss and shock, I think. Just a little dizzy."

"We'll find a spot to rest."

He raised the lighter higher and peered into the darkness.

"Can't see shit," Don muttered, "but maybe that means they can't see us either."

"Don't count on it. I've seen these things hunt in a pitch-black sewer. Don't know how. Maybe they can smell us or see something we can't. Our auras, maybe. But if they're in here, they can see us."

"Thanks. That's really comforting."

"Oh, I'm sorry. Get us out of here and maybe I'll tell you a bedtime story instead. How about it, Danny? What's your favorite bedtime story?"

"Teeny Tiny Tale," he whispered, suddenly shy and timid. "Daddy used to read it to me when I'd visit him."

Frankie smiled, lost in one of the few childhood memories that heroin hadn't erased.

"The dog says, 'Give me my bone. Give me my bone.' Is that the one?"

Danny smiled. "That's it."

Then his smile faded. Despite Frankie's best efforts to distract him, Danny was still terrified for his father. He looked over his shoulder again as another muffled gunshot rang out.

They walked deeper into the garage. Don almost tripped over an orange traffic cone. They smelled oil and gasoline, dust and urine. The silence beat at them, and the ghosts of their footsteps followed along behind. A discarded fast-food wrapper rustled under Frankie's foot. They inched forward, comforted by the flickering flame.

Frankie pointed. "There's the stairway to the roof. Let's make for that. Hide inside until Jim gets back."

"Why not just try the roof instead?" Don asked.

"Birds."

"Birds?"

She nodded. "Zombie birds."

"Oh." His laughter was uncertain. "That's kind of silly, isn't it?"

"Sounds like it—until you've seen them strip the flesh off a body in minutes."

Don frowned.

Beside them, Danny repeated the line from the children's book like a mantra: "When all of a sudden, the teeny-tiny woman heard a voice that said, 'Give me my bone. Give me my bone.' "

His voice trembled with a coming sob, and Frankie's heart broke.

In the darkness, a car door creaked open.

"Give me my bone . . ." something answered.

Don dropped the lighter, and the darkness engulfed them.

Branches whipped Jim's face and arms as he shoved his way through a row of bushes. A dead bird pecked at his scalp, drawing blood. Another darted for his eyes. He threw up a hand in defense, and the bird shrieked its displeasure.

Behind him, the vehicles skidded to a stop. Car doors slammed, and gunfire ripped the night. Rounds streaked toward him, and bullets kicked up dirt at his heels. Panting, Jim broke cover and dashed for a narrow strip of woods between the parking garage and a warehouse. The zombies chased him on foot and wing.

He crashed through the trees and slid down a steep embankment. At the bottom, a drainage pipe trickled water into a thin stream. Jim splashed through it, gasping as its coldness soaked through his boots. He spied a rusty pole and snatched it up without breaking stride.

Tree limbs rustled above him. He looked up just as something small and brown and furry detached from a limb—a dead squirrel, missing its tail and a rear leg—launched itself toward him. Sidestepping, Jim swung the pipe like a batter, and the squirrel careened into the ditch.

A cheer went up from the zombies as they started down the embankment after him. It was a game to them, Jim realized. Nothing more than sport. This was a fox-hunt, and he was the fox.

He ducked between two towering oaks and sprinted back up the hill, coming out behind the parking garage. An iron fire escape ladder hung down from the roof, with access points at the second and third levels. Jim leaned against the wall, catching his breath. He clutched a ladder rung with one hand. A reeking garbage Dumpster stood next to him, but Jim could still smell the zombies over the stink of rotting trash. He heard the rumbling sound again, closer now. Not thunder.

A helicopter.

"Oh Christ—the zombies have a helicopter?"

He closed his eyes. What was the point? In movies, the zombies were slow and stupid, but in real life, they were something quite different. In real life, the zombies had helicopters. Already, the dead outnumbered the living, and their numbers increased every day. Humans.

Animals. No place was safe. Not the suburbs of New Jersey or the remote mountains of West Virginia.

Then he thought of Danny.

There was another explosion. Dropping his makeshift club, Jim started up the ladder.

Bullets peppered the concrete wall, and more of the creatures raced toward him.

"Once upon a time, there was a teeny-tiny woman . . ."

Danny squeezed Frankie's hand as she led him toward the stairwell. They moved as fast as they could without giving away their position.

"She lived in a teeny-tiny town in a teeny-tiny house with her teeny-tiny dog."

They heard it chasing them—wet, dragging sounds. Definitely not teeny-tiny.

"Can you see it?" Don hissed, listening to the zombie approach them.

"No," Frankie answered, "but I can smell the son of a bitch."

Headlights appeared in the garage entrance. The Mazda's engine rumbled, reverberating off the cement columns as the car cruised down the rows, hunting for them.

Fumbling in the dark, Don picked up the lighter and flicked it.

"Put that fucking thing out," Frankie snapped. "What's wrong with you?"

The flame vanished, and the darkness surrounded them again. The zombie's stench grew stronger.

"Go!" Frankie urged. They broke cover and stumbled for the stairwell door.

Don pushed it open, ducking back in case anything

leapt out at them, but the stairway was abandoned. Frankie limped inside, pulling Danny along with her. Don quickly followed, and eased the door shut behind them.

The Mazda's tires squealed. Through the window in the door, Don caught a momentary glimpse of the zombie crawling after them, illuminated by the red glow of the Mazda's brake lights. It was a female, her lower half missing.

"Up the stairs," Frankie whispered. "Don't make a sound."

Quietly as possible, they hurried up the darkened stairway.

"Here," the creature on the other side of the door shrieked. "They're going to the second level!"

Tires screeched again as the car sped up the ramp. Behind them, the legless zombie clawed at the door. More roaring engines drowned out its cries, and above them, Frankie heard a distant rumbling noise.

"Listen—you hear that?"

"It's a helicopter." Don shrugged. "Is that good or bad?"

"Probably bad. I've only seen two things fly helicopters—zombies and soldiers."

She took another step upward.

"And I don't like either of them."

Don panted for breath. "In the movies, people always escape zombies by flying away in a helicopter."

"This ain't a movie."

They reached the second-floor landing, and already the Mazda was racing for the stairwell. Below them, the door banged open.

"Give me my bone," the zombie tittered.

"I'll give you a bone, bitch." Don looked down at Danny and then apologized under his breath.

"That's okay, Mr. De Santos."

"Maybe the roof ain't such a bad idea after all," Frankie muttered.

"But what about the birds?" Don asked.

She lowered her voice. "At this point, I don't think it much matters. Whatever we do, we're pretty much fucked."

As one, the rotting flock banked toward their prey.

Jim heaved himself over the ledge and onto the roof. Only a few cars were parked on the top, their owners having long since abandoned them. Exhausted and bleeding from a dozen different wounds, he stumbled forward, looking for the others and fleeing the birds.

A flock of crows is called a murder, he thought, *and that's what is about to happen. A murder . . .*

He cupped his hands to his mouth. "Danny?" There was no reason to think they would have climbed up to the top, but at this point he had nothing to lose. Maybe he'd survive long enough to search the garage for them.

A sparrow pecked at his hand, drawing blood.

The sonorous thrum of the helicopter echoed off the concrete. Jim glanced into the sky and saw two things. The first was the helicopter, its running lights off and its outline almost invisible against the night, hovering directly overhead. The second was the birds, suddenly dropping like stones, their bodies limp and unmoving.

In a flash, the temperature jumped. Jim felt warm, then hot. Sweat broke out on his forehead and his ears turned red. Pain pulsed through his brain, pressing on the inside of his skull. His ears felt like they would explode. He gripped his head and screamed—and just when he thought he couldn't take it anymore, the pressure increased.

The helicopter drew closer. The broken and battered birds rained down around him. The pain surged through his head again, and his eyes grew hot. Jim's ears began to bleed. He covered them with his hands and screamed again.

Jim kept screaming even after he collapsed.

The door banged open below them and a horde of zombies rushed up the stairs. Frankie, Don, and Danny barely heard them over the roar of the chopper, which was right over their heads. The garage shook, the concrete walls vibrated and the ceiling sounded like it was about to collapse. The noise of the rotors increased, making speech next to impossible.

Despite the cacophony, they could still hear Jim's screams.

"Daddy!"

Danny twisted free of Frankie's grip, pushed the door open, and ran outside onto the roof. Immediately, his small hands clenched the sides of his head. He collapsed, screaming.

Frankie and Don ran after him.

The zombies followed.

"Turn it off," Steve shouted. "For fuck's sake, Quinn, shut it off. You're killing them!"

"How do we know they ain't zombies?" the pilot answered. "Just because they aren't decaying yet doesn't mean they're not dead."

"The birds were attacking him, you asshole." He froze, staring in horror. "Jesus, Quinn—it's a little kid. Come on man, shut it off now."

"All right, all right already."

Quinn flipped a switch, and instantly, the man and

boy stopped squirming. Now a young black woman and a middle-aged Hispanic man stepped out onto the roof, rushing to their sides and staring up at the helicopter in panic. They were obviously wounded, limping and bleeding.

Steve grabbed the bullhorn.

"How do you work this?"

"Press the fucking button. Don't you Canucks know how to do anything? Why the hell did Bates stick me with your ass? Why did DiMassi have to go and get sick?"

"I'm here because I'm a pilot—just in case you don't make it back."

"You're an airline pilot, not a helicopter jockey."

The Canadian grinned. "Hey man, I can fly anything. Besides, I thought you didn't like DiMassi."

"I don't. He's a worthless, lazy, fat fuck."

"Him and Bates really went at it, huh?"

"Yeah. Can't say that I blame Bates. DiMassi took this baby up without clearance. If something had happened, we'd have been totally cut off."

Quinn grew quiet and concentrated on landing.

Steve pushed his headset microphone out of the way, turned on the bullhorn and raised it to his lips. He steadied himself and then leaned out the open door.

"ATTENTION. YOU ON THE ROOF. EVERYTHING IS GOING TO BE OKAY. GET DOWN AS LOW AS YOU CAN, AND WE'LL GET YOU TO SAFETY."

He shot a puzzled glance at Quinn.

"Why aren't they listening to me?"

Quinn sighed and shook his head.

"They think we're zombies. Happens all the time."

* * *

"Check on Jim," Frankie told Don as she bent over Danny. The boy was curled into a ball, his face contorted with pain. The helicopter drew closer.

Don dragged Jim's unconscious form away from the middle of the deck, afraid the zombies would land the helicopter on his friend, and brought him alongside Danny. He could barely make out two figures in the cockpit. The machine hovered directly over them.

"GET AS LOW AS YOU CAN," the voice repeated. "WE NEED TO DO THIS FAST."

Over the bullhorn, it was impossible to tell if they were undead or alive.

"Daddy?" Danny coughed, starting to awake.

"What happened to them?" Frankie asked.

Don shook his head.

"Daddy?"

"He's okay, sweetie. He's okay. Just lie still."

"Let's get them back inside," Don panted, pulling Jim toward the stairwell.

"Are you crazy?" Frankie shouted.

Don jabbed a finger at the helicopter. "How do we know those aren't zombies flying that thing?"

The stairwell door crashed open.

"We don't." Frankie clenched her teeth. "But they are."

Don spun around. The undead poured from the stairwell with weapons drawn, their pale and gray faces alive with glee. Then they saw the helicopter and stopped.

The voice on the bullhorn boomed.

"DROP!"

Frankie and Don ducked, shielding Jim and Danny with their bodies. Steve opened fire, strafing the zombies at head level. Craniums exploded like rotten vegetables. The remaining creatures fired back, then ducked inside the stairwell for cover.

"Guess that proves they're not zombies!" Frankie yelled. "Let's go!"

She pulled Danny toward the helicopter as it touched down on the roof in a cloud of dust. Don followed with Jim.

—

All four survivors were battered and bleeding, and for a second, Steve considered that they might actually be zombies. Then he saw the little boy gaze at the unconscious man, and knew better. Only a son could stare at his father with that much love. He helped the four aboard and got them situated.

Quinn sent the helicopter skyward just as the remaining zombies opened a second volley.

The thrum of the chopper's blades filled the cabin. Don and Frankie glanced around in confusion.

"Strap yourselves in," Quinn yelled, flipping up his visor. "It's gonna get bumpy."

He turned away from them and opened fire. The massive rounds shredded the zombies on the roof.

"Who are you people?" Don asked.

"My name is Luke Skywalker. I'm here to rescue you."

"What?"

The red-haired, freckle-faced pilot chuckled over his partner's gunfire and the roar of the rotors.

"Sorry. I always wanted to say that. My name is Quinn and this here is Steve."

"Where are you guys from? What's going on?"

"I'm from Brooklyn. He's from Canada. Like I said, we're here to rescue you."

"Clear," Steve said, and leaned back in his seat, breathless. He removed his helmet. "Whew—that was intense."

Lacking a headset, Don had to shout. "I don't understand any of this. How did you know where to find us?"

"For that matter," Frankie piped up, "how did you even know we were in trouble?"

"We didn't," Steve answered, reloading his rifle. "There was a big battle near the border of Pennsylvania and New Jersey earlier today. Near Hellertown."

Startled, Frankie jumped in her seat, but kept quiet.

"We were sent out to look for survivors. We were on our way back when we saw zombies converging on the garage. We figured with that much activity there must still be somebody alive on the ground. Lucky for you guys we decided to investigate. You folks weren't involved in that, were you?"

Don shook his head. Frankie kept quiet.

Steve reached out and shook Don's hand. Then he reached for Frankie's. She turned away.

"It's okay," Steve told her. "We're not gonna hurt you."

"She's had a bad day," Don said. "And she needs medical help."

"I understand." He smiled at Danny. "What's your name, little buddy?"

"Danny."

"Nice to meet you, Danny. I bet that guy there is your father, huh?"

"Yeah. How did you know that?"

"Because you look like him . . . and because you remind me of my little boy, back in Montreal."

"Why aren't you with him now?" Danny asked.

"I—I got stuck in New York when everything happened. I was there on business. I don't know if he's . . ." He trailed off and shook his head.

"You should go find him," Danny said. "My daddy came across five states looking for me."

"Five states, huh?"

"Yep." Danny counted them off on his fingers. "West Virginia, Virginia, Maryland, Pennsylvania, and New Jersey."

"Wow." Steve's face turned sad.

"My head hurts." Danny rubbed his temples.

"I've got a headache too," Don said.

"That's our fault," Quinn replied. "Sorry about that. Looks like it knocked your father out completely."

"What are you talking about?" Frankie asked.

"Shit." Don pointed ahead of them. "Look at that!"

A massive cloud of dead birds swarmed toward them.

Frankie gripped the seat. "Oh my God."

"No sweat." Quinn grinned. "Watch this."

He flicked a switch and the birds began to drop from the sky.

"What the hell is that?" Don whistled.

"U.B.R.D., or Ultrasonic Bird Repelling Device. I can't tell you how it works, but it's saved my ass more than once. That's why your heads hurt. Guarantee you the zombie's heads hurt worse, though."

"What's it do?" Frankie asked, kneading her scalp.

"Doc Stern can probably explain it," Steve said. "He's the one who retrofitted the chopper with it. He's a medical doctor, but he knows a lot about other stuff too. But basically, it turns their little brains into pudding."

Cold air hissed through the cabin. Frankie shivered, both from the temperature and shock.

Don reached out and squeezed her hand. Smiling weakly, Frankie squeezed back.

Quinn picked up the radio handset.

"Pale Horse, Pale Horse, this is Star Wormwood. Do you copy? Over."

There was a burst of static, and then a voice answered.

"This is Pale Horse. Go ahead, Wormwood. What's your status? Over."

"Pale Horse, be advised we are returning to base with four, I repeat, four live ones. Our ETA is fifteen minutes. Over."

"Ten-four. Understood Wormwood. We'll have a medical team on standby. Out."

"I still don't understand any of this," Don muttered.

Jim's eyes fluttered, and he moaned, "Danny?"

"I'm right here, Daddy."

Jim smiled.

"So five states." Steve turned in his seat. "Sounds like you people have quite a story to tell."

"First," Frankie replied, "tell us where we're going."

Quinn stared straight ahead as he answered her.

"New York City. Specifically Manhattan. Population eight million or so—ninety-nine point nine percent of which are now zombies. Except for a few of us."

He turned his eyes to the instrument panel.

"Even more specifically," Steve finished for him, "we're going to Ramsey Towers, the heart of the city—and possibly the site of humanity's last stand."

Don frowned. "That's a little melodramatic, isn't it?"

The Canadian shrugged.

"Doesn't sound very safe," Frankie said.

Steve lowered his head as he answered.

"Lady, nothing is safe anymore. We're just happy to live one more day."

EIGHT

When he couldn't find a functioning radio to contact his forces at the research facility in Hellertown, Ob sent a host of birds with messages tied to their feet instead. His orders were simple: LEAVE BEHIND SMALL CONTINGENCY FORCE TO ACT AS RESERVES—BRING EVERYTHING ELSE TO NEW YORK CITY—MAKE EXTREME HASTE—LEAVE NOTHING ALIVE IN YOUR WAKE—ADD TO OUR NUMBERS AS YOU GO.

He stood on the rooftop and watched them take flight into the pre-dawn sky, dead wings cutting through the air.

"Hurry," he called out to them. "I want the message delivered before the sun sets tonight!"

His black leather trench coat flapped in the wind. Earlier, he'd broken into a clothing boutique and dressed his new body, to help preserve its integrity and protect it from the elements longer. In addition to the coat, he wore a pair of black leather pants, and a simple black

T-shirt. On his feet, he wore a pair of silver-tipped cowboy boots.

A young zombie, once a boy of about six years of age, approached him and bowed. Its flesh was bloated and shiny, and the collar of its tattered T-shirt had sunk into the skin.

"My lord, Ob. It is a pleasure to serve you in this form."

Ob nodded impatiently. "Get on with it. Arise and speak."

"I bring tidings of your two brothers." A tooth dropped out of its mouth as it spoke.

"When did you see them?" Ob asked.

"Three days ago, I was in a place called Tibet. Our kind knew it of old, of course, but that land has changed since we last walked the Earth. Our forces were victorious—the humans were eradicated, as were the other forms of animal life. Nothing lives there now. The entire continent has fallen."

"So the humans in those lands are defeated, eh? That is good news. Their population was among the highest on the planet. Well done. Here, have an eyeball."

He held up a cardboard popcorn bucket, filled to the brim with eyeballs plucked from humans and animals. The zombie took a handful and chewed. Then it continued.

"Yes, lord. Their numbers were high. Especially in China. But those same numbers also aided us. There were so many of them, and their population was virtually unarmed. The resistance was disorganized and over quickly."

"And yet your body was dispatched?"

The undead boy appeared to grow nervous; Ob found the grimace to be an amusing effect on the decayed face. His teeth showed through one cheek. "I apologize, my lord. There was a battle in a monastery, and—"

"I care not." Ob held up his hand. "Finish with news of my brothers. What tidings from the Void? What did you hear of them while passing through on your way back here?"

"Your brothers grow impatient, especially now that all the flesh on that continent has been corrupted. The Elilum and Teraphim wish to escape the Void as we have. Your brothers ask that you make haste in freeing them from their eternal punishment."

"They know the rules," Ob grunted. "The Elilum cannot begin the corruption of the plants until the corruption of the flesh has been completed. Those are the rules, established long ago and written in sorcery and blood. We cannot change them. I understand their frustration. They are anxious to begin, for it will take some time. The Elilum travel through the roots, so their way is slower than ours. We have the advantage of going from the Void directly into these meat puppets. My brother's kind must go through a vast network."

The zombie nodded. "Yes, lord. To be fair, your brother Api is patient. He restrains the Elilum. But Ab's rage grows stronger by the day. He wishes for the Teraphim to be loosed upon the planet."

"No doubt." Ob sighed. "But he must be patient a while longer as well. We must all follow the rules as set forth after the Morningstar's fall or we risk destruction. Besides, the Elilum only destroy the Creator's plant life and poison the oceans. That is acceptable. We don't need those things in our struggle. But my brother Ab and his Teraphim will drown this planet in fire. It will burn with each step they take, until there is nothing left but cinders. I am not ready for that yet. There are still many of us to be freed and I have not yet sated my thirst for revenge. When we are done, when I have spat in the Creator's face, then my brother and his kind can turn this planet into an inferno. By then, we will be ready to move on to the next one."

The zombie grinned. "Indeed, lord."

Ob tossed a pebble off the roof and watched it fall. Then he turned back to the messenger.

"Come here. Step to the edge and look out upon our Necropolis. Is it not majestic?"

"It is wonderful, my lord Ob."

"I'm glad that you agree." Ob placed an arm around his shoulders. "Now, go and tell my brothers that they must wait a while longer."

The zombie flinched. "Me, lord? But I just got here. I've only been—"

Ob pushed him off the building and watched as he plummeted down, exploding across the pavement in a wet smear.

"I never got along with my brothers."

The sun rose over the city, peeking out from behind a curtain of gray clouds, reluctant to bear witness to the scene unfolding below.

"Hello, Ra, you old bastard." Ob smiled. "Like what you see? Run along and tell Daddy. He always liked you better anyway."

Laughing, Ob turned and walked inside. He summoned his lieutenants and ordered the city searched from top to bottom, beginning at the outskirts of the five boroughs and working inward. Nothing was to be left alive—no people, no livestock. The countdown to extinction had begun.

The sun did not return that day, lost beneath a layer of

haze. It saw what was happening, and stayed behind the dark and heavy clouds.

The heavens wept.

"Here comes the dawn," the doctor murmured, looking out the twentieth-story window, "but I don't think we'll see the sun today. Looks like rain."

A pretty young nurse with chestnut hair nodded, and then finished bandaging Jim's shoulder.

The doctor shined his light into Danny's eyes and then turned it off.

"Open your mouth for me, Danny."

Danny looked at his father for reassurance and Jim nodded, wincing as the stitches in his head pulled tight against his scalp. His shoulder had been re-stitched as well, and the pus-covered homemade sutures lay discarded in a plastic trashcan with a biohazard sticker.

"You must be feeling better now, Mr. Thurmond," Quinn said. He leaned against the back of the closed door. Except for the poster on the wall beside him—*Have you received your FLU SHOT yet? Remember: Ramsey Inc. Employees Receive Them For Free*—and the window, the examination room was featureless and sterile. After weeks of living with rot and decay, Jim found the change strangely disquieting.

"Not really. I still feel hot, and I'm weak as a kitten."

"That's the infection," Dr. Stern told him, staring down Danny's throat. "You've got a low-grade fever. It's really a wonder that it's not more serious. Luckily, you've got a strong constitution, Mr. Thurmond. I've seen people come in with half the damage you seem to have taken and be in far worse condition. What did you do before—this?"

"I was a construction worker down in West Virginia. Built new homes, mostly."

Stern pressed his fingers against Danny's throat, and then shined the light in the boy's ears.

"West Virginia, eh? I knew you must be from the South, by your accent. You're a long way from home."

"While you were passed out in the chopper, Danny said you came looking for him," Quinn said. "That true?"

"Yeah. But I didn't do it alone. I had some help. We traveled up through Virginia and Pennsylvania and into Jersey."

The pilot whistled. "That's pretty impressive. You're all lucky to be alive. Can't believe you made it."

"Not all of us did."

Jim nodded, his thoughts on Martin. He still couldn't believe that the old preacher was gone. He felt in his pocket for Martin's bible, reassuring himself that it was still there.

They were quiet while Stern checked Danny over. Then the doctor turned back to Jim.

"Do either of you have any medical conditions I need to know about?"

"Like what?"

"Epilepsy? Diabetes? Things like that? Allergies, perhaps?"

Jim thought the question was strange, but answered truthfully. "No. Danny's allergic to bee stings, but that's about it."

"How about drug allergies? Penicillin?"

"None that I know of."

Stern wrote the information down and placed it in a folder with Jim and Danny's names handwritten on them. Then he handed it to the nurse.

"Kelli, could you file these for me, and then check on Dr. Maynard?"

"Sure thing, Dr. Stern."

"What's that?" Jim asked.

"Your medical records," the doctor answered. "If you're going to be members of our little community, then I'll be your doctor."

"Oh." It seemed strange to Jim. Things like regular doctors visits and paying the bills and driving to the grocery store and watching football on Sunday seemed like dreams—a distant past. Life had become nothing but running from hiding place to hiding place, surrounded by the dead; a constant battle simply to stay alive. He struggled with the adjustment.

Kelli walked out of the room, files tucked under her arm. Quinn turned and watched her ass, smiling to himself.

Dr. Stern stepped back. "Well, Danny, you seem to be in fine shape, if a little dehydrated."

"What's that mean?" Danny asked.

"It means you need some water. And I bet you're hungry too."

The boy nodded.

"Well," the doctor reached into a drawer and pulled out a lollipop, "you can start with this, I suppose. In a few minutes, we'll show you gentlemen to your room. If your father is feeling up to it, we'll show him where the cafeteria is. Then you can get some real food. I bet you like pancakes, don't you?"

Danny's eyes lit up. "Yeah!"

"Then you'll like what we're having for breakfast. But I don't want you to eat too many of them, okay? You need to start out slow."

Smiling, he handed Danny the lollipop and then turned to Jim.

"Is he going to be okay?" Jim asked.

"He'll be fine." The doctor lowered his voice. "I don't think we need to run an IV, but we do need to get some fluids into him. And some food. But all in all, he'll be okay. There's no sign of reactive psychogenic shock."

"What's that?"

"It's something that happens when a human body is exposed to high levels of fear or stress. Your pulse increases but your blood pressure drops. Physically, your son is in good shape, all things considered. He has no infections or wounds. No physical damage, other than the slight dehydration. It's really quite remarkable, Mr. Thurmond. Things could have been a lot worse. Be thankful that you got to him when you did. How long was he alone?"

"A week."

The doctor's hushed tones became a whisper.

"I don't imagine his hair was turning that color when you last saw him either."

"No." Jim's voice cracked.

Stern placed a hand on Jim's good shoulder and squeezed. "Well, he's a resilient young man, much like his father. Frankly, I'm amazed. The Big Apple is rotting—literally. Just the biological threat from those things down there alone is enough to make you both sicker than you are—not to mention the wounds you've suffered. We know of a group that was hiding out in a publisher's building on Broadway. One zombie managed to get inside. They destroyed it before it could murder any of them, but the disease on the corpse killed them all within days."

Jim whistled. "I never even considered that, and I've had some pretty close contact with these things."

"You're very lucky. This other group wasn't."

"How did you stay in contact with them?"

"Radio," Quinn said. "Hell, they radioed us even after they were dead."

Stern put his pen back in his shirt pocket. "I think you'll both be okay, though I want to keep an eye on that shoulder of yours. I'm giving you some strong antibiotics to help with the infection, but both of you are to take it easy for at least a week. Everyone pulls their own weight here, and you'll have plenty to do soon, depending upon your skills—so think of this as a one-week vacation."

Jim nodded.

"Besides," Stern said softly, "I imagine you'd like to spend some time with your son."

Jim blinked the tears away. "You don't know how bad."

"Believe me, Mr. Thurmond, I do."

"If you guys don't mind," Quinn said, "I'm going to hit the sack. Been up for over twenty-four hours now and I'm pretty wiped out."

Jim stood up and shook the pilot's hand.

"I just want to thank you again for saving us. If you and your partner hadn't shown up when you did—well, let's just say I thought we were done for."

"Don't sweat it. Besides, we almost killed you ourselves with the U.B.R.D."

"What the hell is that thing anyway? My head still hurts from it."

"A remarkable device," Stern breathed. "Basically, it utilizes ultrasonic sound as a weapon."

"The doc can explain it better than me," Quinn said,

"so I'll let him take over. I'm sure we'll see each other around. This building is big, but it ain't that big. See ya, Danny!"

Danny waved. His fingers and mouth were stained red from the lollipop.

"Bye, Mr. Quinn! Thank you for helping us."

After he left, Jim turned to the doctor.

"So it's a weapon?"

"Oh, yes," Stern replied, "and a very useful one at that. The technology was a safety feature, used to keep birds away from aircraft, farms, buildings, and such. They are very sensitive to sound, you see, much more so than a human or even a dog. It's really quite extraordinary. They have a strong hearing ability. It assists them while hunting and helps them communicate with each other while in flight. Our device turns that strength into a weakness."

"You're telling me it gives them an ear ache?"

The doctor chuckled. "Not quite. It does much more than that. Ultrasonic sound creates extreme heat, and disrupts the nerves when played at a high frequency. It actually damages the living cells in a body. In the case of the birds, because of their sensitivity to sound, the mechanism's effects are greatly magnified. The stress forces them to flee. That's how it was used in commercial and military aviation. In our case, we simply cranked it up a notch, to use one of my grandson's favorite expressions. We broadcast at 1MHz, which virtually destroys a zombie bird's brain, and thus, destroys the zombie itself."

"But why?" Jim asked. "Why does it work on just the birds and not the other zombies? And I thought you said it only worked on living cells?"

"As for why it works on their brains even when the cells are dead—we can only speculate. These things, whatever they may be, seem to originate in their host's brain. It is my theory, and the theory of my associate, Dr. Maynard, who I'm sure you'll meet later, that deep within the host's brain, these entities may reactivate some of those dead cells and tissue. That's what gives them their mobility and reasoning capacity. The U.B.R.D. causes a loss of function in those reactivated cells inside a zombie bird's brain because of that sensitivity to sound, and because of the placement of their ears in relation to their brains."

Danny watched his father and the doctor talk. His eyes never left Jim.

"Going back to your first question," Stern continued, "we simply don't know. The effect is sporadic on the human zombies—it acts as a deterrent, but it doesn't incapacitate or destroy them. Probably because they don't have the same sound sensitivity that a bird's body does. It just isn't effective for a large-scale assault against any other creature."

"Seems like it would be," Jim mused. "I sure as hell felt it on that rooftop."

"We tried, of course. Both of our helicopters were outfitted with the devices. The first one flew over the city, using the U.B.R.D. in the streets below its flight path. The zombies did indeed fall back, and it even seemed to damage some of them, but not enough."

He paused.

"What happened exactly?" Jim asked.

Stern sighed. "The zombies had a rocket-propelled grenade launcher. They shot down the chopper while it was conducting the experiment. All onboard were killed. After that, Bates and Mr. Ramsey decided to limit its use to only the birds, since it proved effective on them."

Finished with his lollipop, Danny began to grow restless. He swung his legs back and forth beneath the examination table. The white paper covering it rustled.

"Who are Bates and Ramsey?" Jim asked.

The doctor arched an eyebrow. "Surely, you've heard of Darren Ramsey?"

"The billionaire developer?" Jim asked. "The one with his own board game and books and a reality series on TV?"

"That's him. He is our host. In fact, he designed this building. I'm sure you'll meet him soon."

"Wonderful," Jim drawled, his voice thick with sarcasm.

"I take it that you're not a fan?"

"Truthfully, doctor? I always thought he was a jerk. Just another rich yuppie with too much power and too much time on his hands." Jim immediately wished he hadn't said that, but he'd never been good at censoring himself when he was tired.

Stern smiled. "Well, he certainly has both. Especially now."

"So who's this Bates you mentioned?"

"Mr. Ramsey's personal assistant and bodyguard. A very good fellow to know—but a dangerous one as well. We all feel a lot safer with him in charge of security."

"This place is pretty secure? Even with all of those zombies out there?"

"According to Mr. Ramsey, it's impregnable, and I must say that I'm convinced. Those things outside have made numerous attempts to get inside, but so far they haven't succeeded. We're safe here—safer than anywhere else, at least."

"As long as we don't go outside?"

"We've no reason to. We have our own electricity and

our own air. There's plenty of food and water and medical supplies. We can withstand a long siege."

"Why don't they just burn it down?"

"They've tried." The doctor snorted. "They've also attempted grenade and rocket attacks, swarming us with birds and rats, scaling the walls, landing a helicopter on the roof. We've repelled every attack. Trust me, Mr. Thurmond. You and your boy are safe here. So are your friends."

"Don and Frankie!" Jim exclaimed, slapping his forehead with his palm. He winced—the action making his head throb again. "I'd almost forgotten about them. How are they?"

"Mr. De Santos suffered some contusions but otherwise, he's been given a clean bill of health."

"And Frankie?"

"My associate, Dr. Maynard, is examining her now. I imagine he'll start her on codeine or ibuprofen for the pain, and streptomycin or penicillin for the infection from her wounds. I'm sure your friend will come through just fine, as well."

Nurse Kelli dashed back in the room, breathless.

"You'd better come quick!"

"Maybe you didn't understand me the first time," Frankie spat, her hand wrapped around the fat doctor's throat. "I said you're not sticking me with any fucking needles!"

Dr. Maynard's eyes bulged and spittle flew from his lips.

"Young . . . lady . . . I . . . must . . . insist . . ."

"Frankie!" Don ran over to the hospital bed and grappled with her. "Frankie, stop it. You'll kill him."

"No shit, Don. That's what I'm trying to do."

"He's just wants to help you."

"He's not sticking me with that needle!"

"Can't . . . breathe . . ." Dr. Maynard turned purple and the veins bulged in his cheeks.

Don struggled to break her grip.

"Listen to me, Frankie."

"No! You don't understand." Her eyes were huge, her pupils dilated. Mucous ran from her nostrils as she trembled with shock.

The door opened. Don turned to see Jim, Danny, a nurse, and another doctor in a white lab coat staring in openmouthed astonishment.

"Get over here and help me," he grunted. "She's killing him!"

"Can't . . ." Maynard wheezed, "br . . ."

"Frankie!" Jim ran over to the bed and helped Don pull her off.

Dr. Maynard collapsed to the floor, gasping for breath. His fingers probed the bruises on his throat.

"She—she tried to kill me," he retched.

"Frankie, what the hell is wrong with you?" Jim asked.

"She just snapped," Don told him. "One minute she was fine. Then she saw that needle in his hand and all hell broke loose."

"Jim," Frankie panted, "don't let him stick me. No needles. Please? I helped you. Now I'm . . . I'm . . . asking . . ."

Her eyes rolled up into her head, and she collapsed back on to the bed, unconscious.

Don turned to Jim. "She doesn't like needles?"

"I guess not. I think—she may have had a problem with heroin at one point. There's track marks on her arms. Scars."

Danny watched from the doorway.

"Is Frankie going to be okay, Daddy?"

"I think so, squirt. She was just tired. That's all." He tried to sound casual and thought he did a pretty good job—but inwardly he felt disturbed that Danny had been exposed to the scene. Sure, this was nothing compared to everything else the boy had experienced, but that didn't make it right.

Dr. Stern helped Maynard to his feet.

"That *cunt,*" Maynard snarled. "I can't believe that she—"

Jim was in his face before he could finish.

"Mister, we appreciate all that you folks have done for us. But if I ever hear you call her that again, you'll be the one that gets knocked out. Do you understand me?"

Maynard blinked, and then mumbled an apology under his breath.

Don frowned. "Hell of a bedside manner you've got there, doc."

Stern tried to sooth them. "We're all under a bit of stress. Let's just calm down, shall we?"

"Yeah, sure," Jim grumbled. "Whatever."

Stern took Maynard by the arm. "Joseph, perhaps you should get some rest. You were up all night working in your lab again, weren't you? I'll take over here."

"Thank you, Carl." Maynard looked at Jim. "My apologies."

"Mine too. Kelli, can you give Joseph a hand?"

"Of course. Come on, Dr. Maynard."

Without another word, Maynard allowed Kelli to lead him from the room. As he passed by them, Jim and Don caught a whiff of something—rotten, like the man had rolled around in road kill. He noticed that the nurse was wincing too.

"Gentlemen," Dr. Stern said, "I'm going to ask you to

leave as well. I need to get her into surgery, and now I'm shorthanded. I'll let you know how she is as soon as I've finished."

He picked up the telephone on the desk and dialed an extension.

"Yes, can you send someone up to Examination Room B and have them give our new arrivals the tour? And have the rest of the standby nursing staff report to sick bay on the double. Thank you."

He hung up the phone.

"Somebody will be with you shortly. They'll show you to your living quarters and help you get assimilated."

"Sounds good," Jim replied, not liking the sound of assimilated. "I'm exhausted."

Distant thunder boomed outside, and both Don and Danny jumped.

Stern chuckled, sliding the needle into Frankie's arm.

"Relax," he told them. "You're all safe now."

The thunder rolled across the sky again and dark clouds blocked out the newly risen sun. Fat raindrops exploded against the window.

The doctor pulled out the needle and placed a cotton ball over the puncture.

"We're safe and sound. See?"

In her dream—because this time she knew it was a dream right away—Frankie stood on a street corner. Zombies bustled all around her: some in business suits with cell phones at their ears, others in blue jeans and T-shirts. One of them, obviously a tourist, gawked at the skyline. Its *I Love New York* T-shirt was crusted with dried juices. Some walked zombie dogs on leashes and others jogged, pieces of their bodies falling off in their wake. The streets were congested with zombies driving cars and pedaling bikes. A taxi driver leaned on his horn, cursing in a language that was old when the world was young. A bus flashed by her, and Frankie recoiled in disgust at the rotting faces staring back at her from the windows.

A zombie with a bloodstained beret perched atop its head stepped forward and said, "Hey baby, how much for a blow job?"

"Fuck off," Frankie snarled. "I don't do that anymore."

"You're standing on the street corner. How much? I've got money."

He pulled out a greasy wad of bills. His decaying fingers left splotches on the money. Then he produced a needle.

"Or maybe you'd like some of that old black tar instead?"

"Not interested," Frankie said. "I don't do that shit anymore either. Now get out of here."

The zombie stuffed the crumpled money back in its pocket and jammed the needle into its eye. Then it pulled down its zipper, releasing something that looked like a gray, bloated sausage. Insects swarmed over the rotting member. The pubic hair was matted with filth.

"Come on, sweetheart. How much to suck my cock?"

The corpse squeezed the shaft, and a maggot spurted from the hole at the end and fell to the sidewalk. The zombie's shriveled testicles squirmed from the inside with more maggot sperm.

"Get the fuck away from me." Frankie pushed the creature off the curb.

"Bitch," it mumbled, and stalked away.

Frankie took a deep breath, trying to decide what to do next.

A hand touched her shoulder.

"I told you to fuck off!"

She spun around.

Martin smiled sadly at her.

"Preacher-man," she gasped. "What are you doing here?"

The old man didn't reply.

"Hey, what the hell?"

Martin pointed over her shoulder.

"What is it?"

He pointed again, his face grim.

Frankie turned.

Ramsey Towers had turned into a giant tombstone, towering over the city. It was engraved with her name—and those of Jim, Danny, and Don. A sudden cold gust of wind tore down the street, and the sky grew dark.

"I don't get it," Frankie said. "What does it mean?"

She looked back to Martin for an explanation, but the preacher was gone. The zombies had disappeared too. She was alone in a city-sized graveyard. She thought of the graveyard they'd seen on the Garden State Parkway, just before arriving at Danny's house.

"Martin?"

No answer, except for the wind.

"Shit . . ."

She stared back up at the skyscraper-tombstone. The sky grew darker—obsidian.

Something rustled behind her.

Frankie turned around again and the entire undead population of New York City was standing behind her. Their clawlike hands shot forward.

She didn't even have time to scream.

NINE

"I'll bet you guys are hungry," Smokey said.

Jim's, Don's, and Danny's stomachs grumbled in agreement. After all they'd been through in the last twenty-four hours, food had been the furthest thing from their minds. But when they walked into the sprawling cafeteria, smelled the aroma of bacon and sausage and eggs and pancakes and fruit and coffee, heard the clank of silverware and glasses and serving trays—they were suddenly ravenous.

The room buzzed with conversation. About one hundred fifty people were gathered in the cafeteria, sitting at long tables, standing in line with trays, and standing around the coffee pots. Several of them looked up, appraising the new arrivals as Smokey led them into the room.

Smokey described himself as an ex-hippie. He was still in pretty good shape for a man in his sixties. A long, gray ponytail hung down over his flannel work shirt, and a matching gray mustache covered his upper lip. Friendly and talkative, he'd been assigned to show the three of them around.

"Where do you get the food for all these people?" Jim asked.

"The building had some restaurants and this cafeteria," Smokey answered. "All fully stocked. Plus, there were vending machines on most of the floors, as well as miscellaneous food items in the apartments and offices."

He leaned down, put his hands on his knees, and looked Danny in the eye.

"I bet you like blueberry pancakes, don't you, kiddo?"

"Yes sir."

"Good, because Etta and Leroy and their crew make the best darn blueberry pancakes you've ever eaten. Let's get in line."

Danny grinned in anticipation, and Jim began to relax. It felt strange after countless days spent on the run. His shoulders loosened a bit, his muscles relaxing. Maybe they would be all right after all. He thought back to his second wife, Carrie, and their unborn baby, both killed at the start of his quest. Then he thought about Baker and Martin, and all the others. Perhaps the deaths and the bad times were behind them for a while. He sighed.

"Feels good, doesn't it?" Smokey asked.

Jim nodded. "It does. It's—a community."

"That it is. About three hundred of us here, all told. Folks work in shifts, so you won't see everybody at once, unless we have a community meeting in the auditorium—and even then, there will still be folks on watch. The cafeteria is open twenty-four hours a day, to take care of folks on night shift and guard duty and what not. But we ration the food, and if you're not one of those folks, you won't get served when it's not your turn. People come here just to hang out, play cards, talk. Breakfast is when it's usually most crowded."

"I don't mind the crowd," Jim mused. "I'm just happy to be here. Feels like we've been on the run forever, going from one bad situation to the next. It's hard to believe I can let my guard down."

They got in line and each took a tray. Smokey joked and chatted with every person they passed. He seemed to know everybody. He introduced the three of them, but Jim and Don soon lost track of the names. Jim's wounded shoulder began to ache from all the hand shaking.

A young woman approached them and playfully pushed Smokey out of the way.

"Watch it, Val." He grinned. "Hey, meet Jim and Danny Thurmond and Don De Santos."

"Hi," Val said, flashing white teeth. "You're the group that Quinn and Steve brought in."

"We are," Jim replied. "How did you know that?"

"Val is one of our communication specialists," Smokey explained. "She's also eating for two."

"I'm pregnant," she confirmed. "Only two months, though, so I'm not showing yet."

Jim and Don congratulated her, and then she moved on.

"So what does everybody do around here, other than guard duty and radio monitoring?" Don asked.

"You name it, we've got it," Smokey answered. "Doctors and nurses. Scientists. Soldiers. Janitors. We've got a hydroponics lab and a greenhouse, so if you've got a green thumb, you could volunteer for that. Couple of teachers have started a school on the twentieth floor, so Danny here will be able to continue his learning."

"School?" Danny groaned. "Yuck."

Jim smiled at this. It felt good to hear Danny reacting like a kid to normal things—almost as if the zombies had been a bad dream.

"There's lots of other kids your age," Smokey told him. "You'll like it."

Danny considered this.

Smokey turned back to Jim and Don as the line moved forward.

"We've got janitors and cooks and a maintenance department," he said. "If you're good with plumbing or electricity or can hammer a nail straight, they'd be glad to have you. There's a full-sized movie theater and a pretty good library—not that I'm much for reading, mind you. We've got a group that puts on plays once a month, and an orchestra too—mostly musicians who banded together once they were inside here. They all use the auditorium. Hell, we've even got our own closed-circuit TV station. They don't show much: reruns of *Andy Griffith*, *Seinfeld*, *Deadwood*, and old game shows mostly."

A disheveled man tugged on Jim's shirtsleeve.

"Have you seen my cat?" His mouth held two good teeth, and his dirty hair was plastered to his head with what looked like motor oil. Jim reeled from the man's body odor. Along with the stink, the man smelled like he'd bathed in vodka.

"No, I'm afraid I haven't seen a cat."

"My cat smells like tuna fish," the man told him. "His name is God. He's omnipotent."

"Get out of here, Pigpen," Smokey barked. "Leave these people alone. They haven't seen your damned cat."

Pigpen turned to Don. "Can you spare a few bucks?"

Don's eyes widened in surprise.

"Go on now, Pigpen," Smokey insisted. "Get!"

The strange man wandered away. Don stared after him.

"What is it?" Jim asked. "He seemed pretty harmless."

"I know him," Don whispered.

"What?" Smokey and Jim said in unison.

"I swear I'm not pulling your legs. I know that guy. He was homeless. Used to stand outside my office every morning. We all called him Pigpen, because that's what he answered to. He was a fixture on Wall Street."

"You've got to be kidding me," Smokey exclaimed. "Pigpen really is his name?"

"I guess," Don said. "Too weird. It's the same guy, though. Even back then, he was looking for his cat. Sometimes he had it with him—a mangy old calico with a chunk missing from its ear."

"I feel sorry for the poor guy." Jim watched Pigpen cut through the crowd.

"Don't," Smokey said. "He's safe inside here. Same can't be said for everyone else out there."

"Unbelievable." Don shook his head. "A city the size of New York and the one person I know in this place, other than you guys, is the homeless person from where I worked."

"What did you guys do before the Rising started?"

"I was in construction," Jim answered.

"And I was a stockbroker," Don said.

"Construction." Smokey shuffled forward. "They'll probably put you on a maintenance crew, doing repairs and what have you. Stockbroker? Don't know much about that. Never followed the stock market myself. But I'm sure we'll have something for you."

"You think so?" Don asked.

"You can push a broom, can't you?" The old man

laughed and then stuck his tray out. Three strips of bacon were placed on it, followed by a scoop of scrambled eggs.

"Morning, Etta," he said to the large, hulking woman behind the counter. "Got a little boy here that traveled all the way from New Jersey just to try your blueberry pancakes." He introduced the three of them.

"Meetcha," the woman coughed, scowling. "Any fan of my pancakes is all right by me."

"Push a broom," Don muttered under his breath. "Yeah, I can push a broom."

"How about strip a weapon, reassemble it, and fire it with accuracy?" asked a low voice behind them.

Don and Jim both turned, while Danny thrust his tray out and salivated for the pancakes.

The speaker was impeccably dressed. A long, shiny black ponytail hung down his back, and several rings adorned his fingers. He was tall and lean and moved like a panther through the line. But it was his eyes that made them pause. There was something different about them. It took Jim a moment to realize what that was.

The man didn't blink.

"I'm Bates." He stuck out his hand and Don took it. "Head of security for Ramsey Towers."

"Don De Santos." The man's grip was firm. "This is Jim Thurmond and his son, Danny."

"You're the gentleman from West Virginia?" Bates asked.

Jim frowned. "Yes I am. Word must travel fast in here."

"It does. But yours is an incredible story, Mr. Thurmond, so it traveled even faster. After you've rested, we'd like to debrief you, if you don't mind. There's a lot you can probably tell us of what's going on in the rest of the world."

Jim shrugged. "I don't know how useful my information could be, Mr. Bates. All you've got to do is look out the window. It's pretty much that way everywhere."

"Indeed. Still, I hope you'll help us fill in some blanks? It really could prove helpful to our continued survival."

"Sure. Whatever I can do to help. I'd be happy to."

"Excellent." He turned back to Don. "So, you asked Smokey what you could do. Can you shoot a weapon? I'm assuming so, if you've stayed alive out there for this long."

Don's ears turned red. "I shot my wife after she became one of those things. I guess I can do all right."

"Then perhaps we can find a place for you on the security squad. I'll speak with you later, gentlemen. Welcome aboard."

He glided away through the crowd, filled a plastic travel mug with black coffee, nodded and spoke politely to those around him, and then left, eyes affixed to a clipboard.

Jim stared after Bates, watching the crowd part before him like Moses and the Red Sea.

"What are you thinking?" Don asked.

Jim glanced at Smokey, who was talking to Etta again.

"I'm thinking that I don't trust Bates," Jim whispered. "He reminds me of another guy that Martin and Frankie and I ran across down in Gettysburg. Fella' named Colonel Schow."

"And what happened to him?"

"A zombie named Ob shot him with a bazooka."

The rest of the morning was spent in orientation. After devouring their breakfasts, Smokey gave the three of them a tour of the building, starting on the third floor and working their way up. Jim and Don were amazed, and Danny kept commenting on how cool everything seemed. The interior of the skyscraper really was like a self-contained village. It was a wonderful place, but Jim had to wonder what the point of it all was—just to survive here forever? He hoped Ramsey and his staff were at work on a plan to take the world back.

"What's on the first and second floors?" Jim asked as they stepped into an elevator.

"A lot of guards on two," Smokey said. "When this all started, we dropped office furniture and stuff from the upper windows, to kind of make a barricade around the outside of the building. Heavy stuff, so they couldn't just move it all out of the way. The first floor, especially the lobby, is heavily barricaded on the inside too. We keep two guys on duty there, twenty-four seven. We've got it booby-trapped, and nobody is allowed down there without Bates's permission, other than the guards. Same with the parking garage and the basements levels. The two top floors are off limits too, so don't go up there either."

"Why's that?"

"That's the command-center—Ramsey's personal quarters and stuff like that. Nobody goes up there except for Mr. Ramsey and Bates."

"So what's Ramsey really like?" Don asked as they stepped out of the elevator. "I mean, I've seen him on TV and stuff, but what's he like in person?"

Smokey shrugged. "He's all right. Just a man, you know?"

"A very rich man." Don snorted. "He always topped the *Forbes* list. Fucking amazing, the way that guy could create wealth. Hell of a showman, too."

"Did all of the people here work for him before—this?" Jim asked.

"No. Bates and Forrest and some of the others did. A lot of these folks worked in the building, or lived here. Ramsey Towers had both office space and apartments. But the others were survivors, folks trapped in other parts of the city. The patrols found us and brought us back here."

"That what happened to you?"

Smokey tugged at his mustache. "Yeah. I'm from Michigan, originally. I was in Manhattan, visiting my daughter and son-in-law. They lived in a one-bedroom apartment on 34th and Lexington that went for three grand a month, but you could look out their window and see the Empire State Building. I was taking a nap when it happened. My daughter had gone out for a jog."

He paused, his Adam's apple bobbing.

"I never—I never did find out what happened to her, but when she came home, her bottom half was missing. She must have dragged herself up the steps and into the apartment. I woke up as she was crawling into the living room. There were—"

The old hippie looked away. His eyes were wet and when he spoke again, his voice cracked.

"One time, years ago, I accidentally ran over a nest of baby bunnies with the lawnmower. I didn't see them until it was too late. The yard was high, and the mother had hidden them pretty well, piled grass and her own fur over the nest. Didn't notice until I looked down and saw one of them crawling away across the yard. The blade had cut it in half. Its back end was missing and its guts were hanging out."

His fists clenched at his sides.

"That's what my daughter looked like when she came home that day."

Don and Jim looked at the floor, unable to meet his gaze. Danny's eyes were wide.

"I'm sorry, Mr. Smokey," he said, and took the old man's hand.

Smokey smiled, blinking away the tears, and patted the boy on his head.

"Thank you, Danny. Thank you very much."

He straightened up. "How about we find your rooms?"

"That'd be fine," Jim agreed. "And I apologize if we brought up bad memories."

"No." Smokey shrugged, regaining his composure. "It's okay. We've all got stories like that these days. But you asked about Ramsey. That's him. He saved us. Saved us all, gave us shelter from the storm."

"Why?" Jim asked.

"What do you mean?"

"I mean, he and his men have this secure building. Why jeopardize their safety by bringing in more refugees? And that light show we saw last night? Doesn't seem smart to me."

"You don't think he did it out of the goodness of his heart, Mr. Thurmond?"

"I don't know the man. You do. Did he?"

Smokey didn't respond. They walked down the hall and got into another elevator. Smokey pressed a button and the doors closed.

"All I know, Jim, is that we're better off in here than outside with those things. And anytime I start to doubt it, I think about the population of this city and how most of them are now like my daughter. Doesn't matter what I may think about Mr. Ramsey. Survival is all that's important."

The elevator rose in silence.

* * *

Their rooms were small but comfortable. They'd previously been office suites, converted now into living space, along with a kitchenette containing a sink and a small refrigerator, and a bathroom with toilet and shower. Jim and Danny were assigned a room, and Danny shouted in delight when they entered. Somebody had placed two action figures on his bed as a welcoming present.

Jim collapsed on the other bed and groaned with pleasure. Then he started to laugh.

"You've got no idea how good this feels."

"I bet I do." Smokey grinned. "We'll leave you two alone. If you're so inclined, Jim, a bunch of us get together every night and play cards in my room. You're welcome to stop by."

"We'll see. Thanks. I think Danny and I have some catching up to do, though. Don't we, squirt?"

"Yep!"

Smokey led Don to a door a short way down the hall from Jim and Danny's. He informed Don that he would be moving in with a member of the security team named Forrest.

"You'll like him," Smokey whispered as he knocked on the door. "Forrest is one of a kind."

The door opened and a large, muscular black man in a terrycloth bathrobe stared out at them.

"What's up, Smoke?"

"Heya, Forrest. Wanted to introduce you to your new roommate. This is Don De Santos."

Forrest opened the door the rest of the way and stuck out his hand. His grip was strong, and Don actually winced.

"Pleased to meet you," Don grunted. "Sorry to barge in like this."

"No problem," Forrest assured him. "They told me I was up next for a roommate, and when I heard they were bringing you folks in, I figured I'd get one of you."

"Well, I still feel weird about it. Seems like I'm being forced on you, and I haven't had a roommate, other than my wife, since college."

"Don't sweat it. I usually work the night shift, so it'll almost be like you've got the place to yourself. That's your bunk over there."

"Well, I'm gonna go take me a nap," Smokey said. "Let you two get acquainted. If you need anything, Don, be sure to let me know. Forrest, I'll see you for cards tonight, before you go on duty?"

"You know it. Hope you're ready to lose."

"All right, we'll see about that." Chuckling, he turned to leave.

"Hey, Smokey," Don called after him.

"Yeah?"

"You never did tell us. What's your job around here?"

Smokey laughed. "I just did it. I'm the welcome wagon."

After he'd left, Don wondered just how many people Ramsey was rescuing, to have Smokey in an official position like that.

Ob stared across the parking lot at the armory, then sat the binoculars aside and looked down at the rat.

"How many are inside?"

The undead vermin squeaked in an ancient language, and Ob listened carefully, and then repeated the information aloud.

"Six of them. Heavily armed. And they were not aware of your presence?"

More prolonged squealing. The rat's vocal cords hadn't been designed to speak Sumerian. Ob was patient.

"Very good. You have done well. Now, I want you and the others wearing rats and mice as host bodies to go back to Manhattan and do extensive surveillance on Ramsey Towers, from all angles; above and below. I don't care how you get in—just gain entrance. Do not alert them that you are there. Observe all and report back to me. I want to know their numbers, weaknesses, and defenses. Is that understood?"

The zombie rat twitched its scabbed tail in confirmation and scrabbled away.

Ob picked the binoculars back up, watched the armory, and spoke to one of his lieutenants.

"There are six humans holed up inside the armory. All but one are former police officers, so they'll probably be combat trained. After dispensing with them, we can loot the building. There is a stockpile of assault rifles, grenades, rocket launchers, urban assault vehicles, body armor, and more. We will add these to our weapons that we've found throughout the city, the ones we culled from former drug dealers, crime syndicates, terrorist cells, and of course, the ones the humans kept for home defense."

The zombie licked its lips. "Very good, lord Ob. We shall prepare to attack at once."

"The armory also has a fully functional ham radio unit and a gas-operated generator. Make sure that neither is damaged during the raid. After we restore the generator, I want to use the radio to contact our forces to the south, just in case our avian messengers didn't make it. We'll need those reinforcements before we launch an assault on the skyscraper."

"Understood. And lord Ob, if I may—this host body is deteriorating quickly. If it does not last the battle, it has been an honor to serve you in this form. I hope that my next possession takes place in a host body here beside you as well."

Ob waved his hand. "Good. Commence the attack. Send in the first squad."

The lieutenant keyed a handset and gave the order. The creature plucked a loose piece of skin from its thigh. It appraised the morsel, and then plopped it into its mouth. Rotted, broken teeth ground in delight.

Suddenly, there was a flurry of activity. Five zombie suicide bombers, each wearing a backpack loaded with explosives, charged toward the armory. One of them was gunned down before he reached it, the bullets eradicating the top of his head. The other four arrived unscathed, crossed the wires clutched in their cold, pale hands, and set off simultaneous explosions, shredding both their bodies and the armory's door and outer wall. Before the smoke had even cleared, Ob's forces poured into the building through the fiery, twisted hole. There were gunshots and screams—and then silence.

"That didn't take long," the zombie lieutenant mused.

Ob quipped, "In a New York minute."

When it was over, the zombie army grew by six more bodies and hundreds of weapons.

Still watching through the binoculars, Ob smiled.

TEN

Jim sighed in contentment, drained a bottle of cold spring water, popped his neck, and watched as Danny sprawled on the floor and played with his action figures. The boy was making sound effects and doing the dialogue.

"Take that, you! Ka-pow. Ka-pow."

Jim stifled a laugh, not wanting to make Danny feel self-conscious. It had been far too long since he'd watched Danny play, and the sight was joyous. He marveled at his son's resilience. Despite all that had happened to them, it appeared that he was adjusting fine to this new situation.

"So which superheroes are those?" Jim asked.

"The red guy is Daredevil," Danny said. "The one with the skeleton head and flames coming out of it is Ghost Rider. They're both from Marvel."

"I thought Ghost Rider was a good guy. Why is he fighting Daredevil?"

"He's good, but I'm pretending that he's bad, like the monster-people outside. They got into his body and made him bad."

"Oh."

Jim propped his feet up on the couch. The bathrobe felt soft against his skin. Clothes had been hung in the room's closet for both of them, not exactly form fitting or new, but clean and comfortable enough. Jim wondered who they belonged to before, and who had been responsible for assigning them to him and Danny.

"Daddy?"

"What, squirt?"

"Do you think it was Mr. Ramsey that left these toys for me?" He echoed his father's thoughts.

"I don't know. It could have been, I guess, though I'm inclined to think it was probably Smokey."

Danny thought about this, and then said, "He seems nice."

"Smokey? Yeah, he does. Nice old guy. I think he's sort of the welcome wagon around here. At least, that's the impression I got."

Guided by Danny's hands, Daredevil kicked Ghost Rider in the face. Ghost Rider fell over, complete with Danny's sound effects.

"I wonder if Mr. Ramsey is nice, too."

"I don't know, buddy. I guess so. He's helping all these people."

"Mommy used to watch him on TV."

"Did she?"

"Yeah. She liked him, but Dad—I mean Rick—said he was a pompous jerk."

Jim grimaced, trying not to react to his son's referral of his stepfather as Dad.

"Well, Rick was right, as far as I'm concerned. Guess Rick and I agreed on that."

"What does pompous mean, Daddy?"

"Pompous is when somebody thinks they are better than you. When they act stuck up."

"Kind of like Grandma used to act to you?"

Jim choked down the laughter that Danny's assessment of his ex-mother-in-law had inspired. Then he noticed that his son was grinning too.

"Yeah. I guess that's not a bad definition."

Jim snorted more laughter through his nose, and Danny followed suit. Within seconds, they were both laughing out loud.

"God, I missed you, squirt."

"I missed you too, Daddy."

Jim slid off the couch, crawled across the carpet to his son, and gave Danny a big hug. It lasted a full thirty seconds, but felt to Jim like it was over too soon. Then the two of them began to play Daredevil versus Ghost Rider. Daredevil, controlled by Danny, won every battle, but Jim didn't mind.

After a while, they stopped. A frown creased Danny's brow.

"What's wrong, squirt?"

"I'm thinking about Mommy."

Jim put an arm around his shoulders and held him tight.

"And Rick," Danny continued, his eyes filling with tears. "And Carrie and Mr. Martin and Mrs. De Santos and everybody else. Before Mr. De Santos saved us, Mr. Martin told me that when people die, they go to Heaven. Do you think that's true, Daddy?"

"I hope so."

"Do you think that's where Mommy went?"

Jim chose his words carefully.

"I think probably so. I know this—wherever your

Mom and stepdad and stepmom and all the others went, they are safe, just like we are. The monster people can't hurt them anymore."

Satisfied, Danny picked up his action figure and began to play again. He wiped away a tear and said, "I love you, Daddy."

"I love you too."

"Everything's going to be okay now, right?"

Jim nodded. "You know, Danny, I think it is. I really think it is."

Outside, the rain continued to fall, the fat drops pelting the building like missiles.

Father and son were oblivious.

Minutes later, something else fell from the sky, but their attention was on each other, and they missed its plummeting arc past their window.

Kilker lit a cigarette. "It's really coming down out there."

He looked out the window, watching the zombies milling about, oblivious to the downpour.

Carson nodded, and popped the tab on a can of soda. "Yeah, it is. Maybe we'll get lucky. Maybe a hurricane will blow through Manhattan and wash those ugly fucks off the streets."

Both were in their early twenties, and wore sneakers and baggy jeans with the waistband of their boxer shorts showing. A Yankees cap was perched atop Carson's head. Next to them, a battery-operated boom box played Hatebreed.

Carson set the soda down and played air guitar, growling along with the singer.

"Will you turn that shit down?" Kilker protested.

"Yeah." Carson sighed reluctantly. "I've heard this

one too many times anyway. There won't be any more Hatebreed discs, I guess."

"That's a shame." Kilker's voice dripped with sarcasm. "Don't know how you can stand that growly metal shit."

"Saw them in concert once. With Biohazard and Power Plant and Agnostic Front. Gave myself whiplash in the pit."

Kilker just shook his head.

Carson slurped the soda.

"Do you have to do that?" Kilker asked, clearly annoyed.

"Do what?"

"Drink like a fucking pig? It's disgusting."

"Jesus—I'm sorry, bro. Chill out."

They lapsed into silence. Carson checked his weapon, an Ingram MAC-11. It was light and compact for a submachine gun, not much bigger than an average pistol. A high-capacity forty-seven-round magazine sat next to it. He hadn't used it since joining the group inside the skyscraper. It had been assigned to him when he was put on the building's security team.

"What are you thinking about, dog? You're quiet today. What's up?"

Kilker stared out the window, watching the rain fall past on its way to the streets far below.

"They don't seem so scary from up here," he said dreamily. "They look like ants."

"Dead ants, maybe," Carson replied. Grinning, he started humming the *Pink Panther* theme. "Dead ant dead ant, dead ant, dead ant dead ant dead ant dead a—"

"Shut up!" Kilker snapped. "God, you're such a dick sometimes."

"Yo, what the fuck is your problem?"

Kilker jumped to his feet, his cigarette falling from his mouth.

"My problem? I'm sick of this shit. I'm sick of this fucking building and fucking guard duty and the fucking smell from those things down there. I'm fucking sick and tired of it, man. I'm not a soldier. I was a fucking fry-cook, for fuck's sake!"

"So tell Bates you want to be transferred to the cafeteria," Carson yawned. "I mean, shit, man, I worked in a convenience store. Never held a gun in my life until I came here. But I'm glad I've got one now. You should be too."

Kilker didn't respond.

Carson pointed to the smoldering cigarette. "You gonna finish that? It'd be a shame to let it go to waste."

Kilker didn't appear to have heard him. Mumbling and cursing, he walked toward the elevator and pressed the up button.

"Dude, where are you going? You can't just leave. We're on duty."

"Fuck this," Kilker hissed. "They can't get in and we can't get out. So why does it matter? What are we guarding against?"

"You never know, bro. They could figure out a way in. Get their hands on a bomb or something."

"We should be so lucky."

Carson picked up the still-lit butt, took a drag, and walked over to his friend.

"Seriously, Kilker. What is your malfunction? You're acting weird, man."

"Do you know what today is?"

Carson scratched his head. "Tuesday, I think. To be honest, dude, I don't really keep track anymore. Seems kind of pointless, you know?"

"Today would have been my father's birthday."

"Oh. Well, when we get off, we'll do a few shots of tequila in his honor. How does that sound?"

Kilker ignored him. His eyes were far away. In the silence, the gears hummed inside the elevator shaft. When he spoke again, his voice seemed far away.

"Did you get along with your father, Carson?"

"I did—until about tenth grade when he figured out that I was gay. After that, we weren't really on speaking terms, you know? My mom wigged out too. She always wanted a grandbaby. Guess she didn't think I could adopt."

"I loved my dad. He never judged me. Supported me in everything I ever did."

The elevator bell dinged, and the doors opened. Kilker stepped inside and they started to slide shut again.

Carson stuck a booted foot out and stopped them.

"Look, dog, I know you've been depressed lately, but what are you doing? You gonna quit or something?"

"I just need some air. Come with me?"

The pleading tone in his voice gave Carson goose bumps.

"Okay, man, but we can't be gone long. Five minutes, no more. Deal? I don't want Bates or Forrest kicking our ass."

Kilker smiled. "Deal."

Carson picked up his MAC-11 and then stepped in alongside Kilker. The doors hissed shut. Kilker pressed a button on the control panel, and the elevator began to rise.

"Yo, you hit the wrong button. That's Mr. Ramsey's floor. We can't go up there."

"We're not going to see, Mr. Ramsey," Kilker told him quietly. "We're going to get off the elevator and go to the fire escape."

"For what? To get in even deeper shit?"

"No. Trust me."

"Dude, you're whacked."

Kilker ignored the comment. "I never got the chance to say goodbye to my dad. Before those things took over the city, during the riots, while the phones still worked, I called home. I just wanted to talk to him, tell him that I loved him and that I was proud of him. So I called, and he answered."

"And you got to tell him? That's good, man. More than a lot of folks got."

Kilker shook his head. "No, I didn't get to tell him."

"But you said he answered?"

"He did—but it wasn't him." The young man's face clouded and he blinked back tears. "It wasn't him. It was one of those fucking things! Living inside of him."

"Shit."

"Yeah. I thought it was him at first, even though he sounded odd. But then it started saying these things—horrible things. And I knew."

"That's fucked up, dude. I'm sorry."

Kilker sniffed, wiping away tears.

The elevator stopped and the doors slid open. He stepped out.

"Kilker." Carson grabbed his arm. "Where are we going?"

"I told you," Kilker whispered, "the stairwell. You can get to the roof from the fire escape."

"The roof? Are you fucking crazy?"

"No." His voice cracked with grief. "Just tired. Sick and tired. If this is living, then I don't want to live anymore."

He pulled free and walked toward the red door to the

fire escape. Carson followed him, unsure of what to do. The plush carpeted hallway was silent. There was no sign of Ramsey or Bates.

"Hold up, dog. What—you want to be a fucking zombie?"

"No, I just don't want to live anymore. I'm tired, Carson."

He pushed the door open and started up the stairs.

Carson began to panic.

"Kilker. Hey, man, don't do this. Come on, fucking stop it. We can't go out there. The birds will tear us to pieces!"

They reached the top of the stairwell. Kilker pointed to the protective gear hanging on the wall. It looked like a cross between a beekeeper's outfit and the clothing worn by somebody working inside a nuclear reactor.

"Then put one of these on. That's what Quinn and DiMassi and Steve do when they go out to the helicopter. The birds can't get through them. I won't need one."

He put his hand against the door and closed his eyes. Then he took a deep breath, paused, and steadied himself.

Carson grabbed his shoulder.

"Don't."

"I have to. I can't do this anymore, man. It hurts too fucking much. Let me go?"

Carson stared into his friend's eyes, and saw that he meant it. Swallowing hard, Carson let go. Kilker turned back to the door and suddenly, Carson jumped him from behind.

"Mr. Bates," he shouted. "Mr. Ramsey! Help!"

"What are you doing?" Kilker grunted as Carson wrapped him in a bear hug.

"Well, I'm not letting you commit fucking suicide,

asshole. You're not thinking straight, Kilker. Something's wrong with you. You need to see Doc Stern."

"Get the fuck off of me, Carson!"

"Help! Bates? Anybody? Somebody come quick!"

Below them, a door slammed and footsteps echoed in the hall, running toward the stairwell.

Kilker slammed his head backward and Carson's nose exploded, spraying them both with blood. Screaming, Carson dropped to his knees, cradling his nose in his palms.

Kilker shoved the door open and ran out onto the roof.

Bates charged up the stairs.

"Carson, what the hell is going on? What are you doing up here?"

"It's Kilker, Mr. Bates!" Carson winced as blood poured through his fingers. "He's lost his fucking mind and went outside."

Bates ran to the door and looked out through the thick glass window in its center. Kilker ran across the wet roof, his body hidden beneath a swarm of undead birds. They covered every inch of him.

He didn't stop running until he disappeared over the ledge.

Bates sighed. His fist clenched until the nails dug into his palm.

Carson stumbled to his feet. "Is—is he . . ."

"He is."

"Fuck—Kilker . . ."

Bates nodded, then turned to the wounded man.

"Get down to sick bay and get your nose fixed up."

Carson hung his head. "Am I in trouble, Mr. Bates?"

"I don't know, yet." Bates shook his head. His voice was hushed. "I'm too tired at this point to decide anything. Just go get your nose taken care of, okay?"

"Yes, sir." Carson slumped down the stairs, dripping blood in his wake.

Bates looked back out at the roof and watched the rain. His conversation with Forrest ran through his mind.

"Something bad is coming."

"What's that, sir?" Carson called from the bottom of the stairwell.

Bates didn't reply.

Frankie awoke from the nightmare, opened her eyes, and looked around. She was in what appeared to be a hospital room. For one brief moment, she thought it might be another dream, but when she moved, the pain throughout her body proved it all too real.

She lay in a bed; white sheets with a pale yellow stain covering her legs and abdomen. Her street clothes were gone, replaced with a thin, open-backed hospital gown. An intravenous tube ran from her arm to a bottle dangling above her. A machine echoed her pulse, and another one whose purpose she didn't know, was silent.

She tried to sit up, and then sank back down. How had she gotten so weak? She felt as bad as she did when she'd gone cold turkey from heroin. She dimly remembered the doctor with the slaughterhouse body odor who'd tried to stick her. Apparently, he'd succeeded.

Clenching the bed rails, she tried again, forcing herself upright. She paused, exhausted from the effort. After a moments rest, she slid her legs over the side and rested her bare feet against the cold tile floor.

Her leg and arm ached. She studied her wounds. Somebody had fixed her up.

Then she remembered the dream. Martin had been there, and he'd showed her something. Something horrible.

"Gotta—gotta find . . . Jim and Danny. Have to tell them."

She yanked the tubes from her arm, and an alarm began to sound, soft but urgent.

Frankie stood up, swayed, and then regained her balance. She took one faltering step and then another.

"Got to . . . warn them . . ."

Dr. Maynard wiped gore on his lab coat, adjusted the tripod, and turned the camcorder on. It was pointed at the surgical table, on which the corpse of a once-pretty young blonde was tightly bound with Velcro straps. Her legs were parted wide and suspended in stirrups. The lips of her vagina were puffy and gray, and the hair around them had been recently shaved off. Her full breasts now sagged, and the nipples had turned black, as had her swollen tongue, dangling from her mouth like a piece of raw liver. She licked her peeling lips, revealing pale gums. Each of her teeth had been pulled. Her digestive track and major organs had been removed, and the open cavity was wet and glistening. A diamond wedding ring had sunk into her sausage-like finger.

Her name had been Cindy. She'd worked as a receptionist for one of the law firms with an office inside Ramsey Towers. She'd died a week before, after choking on a piece of hard candy. Rather than destroying her brain before she could be reanimated, they'd tied up her corpse to use as research.

At least, that was the ruse that Maynard had fed to Stern, Bates, and the others.

"More questions," she rasped, "or do you wish to fuck me again?"

Maynard glanced guiltily at the camera, turned it off, rewound the tape, and then began recording over it.

"Oh, I see. I guess that will be our little secret." The zombie laughed, writhing in its bonds. Its eyes and nose leaked gummy, yellow fluid.

Maynard raised his voice. "After death, the subject functions like a living being. The stomach and other digestive organs have been removed, yet it still seeks nourishment, specifically in the form of living flesh."

He illustrated this for the camera by pointing to the gaping hole in the creature's abdomen.

"I'm hungry," the zombie verified, as if on cue. "Just give me a little something."

Maynard cleared his throat. "The flesh that it eats does not pass through the digestive system. It is absorbed through an as yet unknown process."

"You're very observant," the creature snarled. "Now feed me! Or better yet, release me."

"None of that, I'm afraid," Maynard said.

"I'll make it worth your while, Doctor," the zombie purred, spreading her legs wider. "I'll let you do things to me—things you've never done with a living woman. We can get rough, if you like."

Maynard's cock stiffened, pressing against his soiled pants. The zombie saw it twitch and smiled.

"Like what you see? Isn't my swollen pussy pretty?"

He shot another nervous glance at the camcorder, and then continued.

"How does your kind convert food into energy?"

"Why should I tell you?"

"Because I'll feed you after you answer my questions."

"You wouldn't understand. It's done on a sub-cellular level."

"But how?"

"Magic. At least, that's what your kind would call it."

"I don't believe in magic."

"Of course you don't. You're a man of science and reason. Logic is your god. And that is why your kind will lose this war. Magic is the only way to stop us, and you have eradicated it from your lives. There are none among you who still remember the old ways. You thought that science would keep you safe from the dark, and as a result, you have lost the only weapons capable of destroying us."

"Nonsense," Maynard scoffed. "Science is the key to stopping your kind. Not some superstitious bullshit that our ancestors learned in a cave."

The creature stirred restlessly, parting her legs wider.

His hardening member jumped again. The zombie stared at the bulge in his crotch and licked her lips.

"I'm so hungry." She sighed, exhaling fetid air from unused, rotting lungs. "And I've answered your questions for days. Sooner or later, you will understand that your age has ended. We outnumber you. We are your inheritors now. Humanity's time is over."

"We'll see about that."

"Are we done for the day? Give me what I want."

He turned off the camera, adjusted his glasses, and reached into a stainless steel bowl that contained the zombie's own heart. Using a bloodstained scalpel, he sliced off a small piece and dangled it over the zombie's snapping jaws with his fingers.

"This is what you want."

"Yes," the zombie moaned. "Give it to me."

He dropped the slice of muscle down the creature's gullet.

"Oh, I'll give it to you all right."

Maynard considered locking the door, but he couldn't wait. The need was overpowering. His breathing thickened along with his rigid member. His hands trembled as he unzipped his fly and let his pants fall to his ankles. He wore no underwear. He stepped out of the pants, leaving them on the floor in a discarded heap, and reached into a drawer. He tore a condom packet open with his teeth, and slid it onto his cock. Then he applied lubricant and approached the squirming corpse.

He held his breath as he slipped inside, trying his best to ignore the stench wafting off the body beneath him. He took extra precaution to stay out of range of its toothless mouth and hands. Even bound, the zombie's fingernails could scratch him.

He shuddered, thrusting all the way into her. Her cunt was cold, but Maynard didn't care. The creature arched her back and hips, allowing him deeper access.

"You—you like this?" he gasped.

"Of course," the zombie panted. "This is an abomination in the eyes of the Creator—the cruel one. It hurts His eyes. So I like it very much."

"Can you achieve an orgasm?" Maynard asked, carefully keeping his distance with every perfunctory stroke.

"No, but you can. I want you to come. I want you to shout your orgasm, spill your seed, burn His ears!"

With one hand, Maynard squirted some more lubricant, and then quickened his pace. His cock threatened to burst.

"I want you to come," the zombie urged him.

"I—"

"Come for me. Come in defiance of Him!"

"I'm going to—"

Frankie burst through the door.

"They're coming," she whispered, her voice faint, her mouth parched. "You've got to tell—"

She froze, staring in horror and revulsion at the scene before her.

"Jesus Christ! I've seen . . . some freaks in my time, but you . . . take . . . the fucking cake . . ."

Then she collapsed.

"Shit!" Maynard pulled out, even as his engorged member began to spurt inside the condom. Without pausing, he ripped it off in mid-orgasm, pulled his pants on, and ran to the door. He cast a furtive glance out into the hall, but the coast was clear.

"You should have locked the door," the zombie tittered.

"Shut up!"

He ran his glazed hands through his receding hairline.

"What are you doing?"

"She saw me. I can't let her tell the others!"

He knelt beside the unconscious woman and checked her pulse. It was slow but steady. He lifted her eyelid and checked her dilated pupils.

Then he spat in her face.

"Told you I'd get even with you, you cunt."

He walked back over to the table, picked up the scalpel, and crossed back over to Frankie.

"It's a shame, really," he said, more to himself than to Frankie or his undead lover. "She would have been fun. Never had a black woman before. But I can always do her after she comes back."

He clenched her hair in his fist, pulled her head back, and placed the scalpel to her throat.

"At least with your throat cut, you won't be that damaged. I can wrap a handkerchief around it or something, once I get you tied up. Maybe sew it shut again."

He gripped the blade tighter and bent down to whisper in Frankie's ear.

"Goodbye."

"Yo, Doc, you in here? Kilker's dead and I need help."

Maynard looked up. Carson stood in the doorway, nose bloody and swollen, his weapon unslung and pointed at the doctor. He snapped a magazine into place. His eyes darted from Frankie and Maynard, to the zombie, to the discarded condom, and then back to the doctor.

"What the fuck are you doing, Doc?"

"This—this doesn't concern you, Carson. She's dead already. Complications from her wounds. I'm just incapacitating her before she can come back."

"By cutting her throat? I don't think so, dude. Last time I checked, that didn't stop them from coming back. Drop the scalpel and step away from her."

"Stay out of this, Carson. I'm warning you."

"No, I'm warning you. I ain't playing, dog. You drop that knife and step the fuck away from her, or so help me God, I'll shoot you."

Maynard hesitated, then dropped the scalpel and slowly stepped backward.

"You don't know what you're doing," he pleaded with the young man. "You're hurt. Not thinking clearly. She's dead. And unless you want her getting back up again, you need to shoot her—now!"

Carson wavered, unsure.

Frankie's arm twitched.

"Do it," Maynard hissed. "Destroy her before she gets back up."

Carson's finger tightened on the trigger.

Frankie moaned, and then her eyes fluttered open.

"Where . . . am I?"

"You're in the laboratory, ma'am," Carson answered.

"Where?"

"Ma'am," Carson stuttered, "are you—you, or are you one of them?"

Frankie didn't seem to understand the question. "Last

thing I remember is that fucker with the needle."

Carson fingered the trigger more.

"What happened?" Frankie asked groggily. She tried to sit up.

"That's what I'd like to know," Dr. Stern said from behind them.

He strode into the room, glancing around in bewilderment.

"Joseph, what's going on here? Carson, what are you doing with that weapon?"

"I—" the young soldier was unable to finish.

"She attacked me again!" Maynard shouted. "It was self-defense, Benjamin."

"Liar," the zombie mocked. "The female interrupted us while we were fucking. He was going to kill her. Go ahead and kill him now, so that one of our brothers may have the body."

"Shut up!" Maynard screamed.

Carson and Stern both stared at the used condom, leaking its contents onto the floor, and then at the zombie. Her insides still glistened with lubricant.

Stern grew pale. "My God, Joseph, what have you been doing?"

"Don't fret, boys," the zombie snickered, "there's enough of me to go around. Who wants sloppy seconds?"

Not taking his eyes off of his associate, Stern picked up the telephone.

"Who are you calling?" Maynard demanded.

Stern didn't reply.

"Who are you calling, Carl?"

"You need help, Joseph. I'm calling—"

Suddenly, Maynard leapt for the scalpel. Seizing it, he charged at the other doctor, screaming with incoherent rage. Stern dropped the phone and screamed along with him.

Carson fired three controlled bursts. The rounds slammed into Maynard's back, punching through his chest. His feet went out from under him and he fell to the floor. The scalpel slipped from his crusty fingers and slid across the bloody tiles. He did not move.

Calm and detached, Carson stood over the dead doctor and fired another round into the back of his head. Then he walked over to the zombie and placed the smoking barrel against her forehead.

"Go ahead," she hissed. "I'll be back, and so will my brothers. Our number is more than the stars. We are more than—"

Carson squeezed the trigger. Then he leaned over and threw up all over his boots.

Shouts echoed in the hallway, followed by the sound of running feet.

Stern picked up the telephone and redialed.

"Bates?" he said after a long pause. "This is Dr. Stern. I think you'd better come down to the lab. We have a situation here."

He had to speak up over the sounds of Carson's retching.

On the floor, Frankie moaned, "They're coming . . ."

ELEVEN

The sky continued to weep, and daylight's murk turned to darkness while the scouring of New York City continued. The living were flushed from their hiding places—basements and closets and the back rooms of stores—hunted down and slaughtered in the streets and alleyways and gutters. Whenever possible, the zombies avoided damaging limbs or large portions of the body, so that the new recruits would be more useful in the coming battle. The preferred method of slaying their prey was a blade to the throat or another major artery. The captives bled to death, relatively undamaged when one of the Siqqusim took over the corpse minutes later.

A large group was discovered hiding at the top of the Statue of Liberty, and each was flung screaming to their deaths, plunging into the frigid, polluted waters below. Killed on impact, they sank beneath the waves. Reanimated, they walked along the bottom till they reached the shore, and then joined the others.

The armory bustled with activity too, as the undead worked feverishly to carry out their orders. Ob moved among them, checking progress and barking out orders. One of his lieutenants followed along behind him, trailing intestines in its wake.

Scowling, Ob stalked over to a zombie kneeling in front of the radio.

"Do you have it working yet?"

"Yes, lord," the zombie rasped. "It is ready for broadcast."

"Good." He turned to his lieutenant. "First, contact our forces on the Pennsylvania and New Jersey border. I want an update on their progress, and an estimated time for their arrival. They should be here soon. Also, find one of our brothers who still sounds alive."

"Sire? I don't understand."

"Someone whose vocal cords haven't begun to decay, you idiot! Someone who sounds human—especially to other humans. Then, have them begin broadcasting a message over the radio, advising anyone left alive in the listening area that this part of New York City is safe. Urge people to make their way here."

The zombie's laughter sounded like a belch. Its arms and ribs had been completely stripped of their flesh, and the bones scraped against each other as it chuckled.

"They'll walk into a trap. Great idea, my lord."

"Of course it's a great idea—I thought of it. I want the message to be broadcast over and over. How are we doing on getting the streets cleared of vehicles?"

"Ahead of schedule, sire."

Ob reached into a bucket and pulled out a loop of intestines, munching them like they were sausage.

"Excellent," he said, gore leaking from the edges of his smacking lips. "I don't want our advance on the skyscraper slowed down when our forces arrive. Have another team locate a radio station. There, they should find a sound van—the kind with loudspeakers that are used during remote broadcasts. Then, I want them to drive around the city, announcing the same message we're sending over the airwaves. Make it sound official. That should speed up the hunt quite a bit, don't you think? As the humans creep out of their little hiding places, we will be there to welcome them."

He rose, and checked his body. It was still in good shape, but was starting to show hints of the decay to come. The sallow flesh had begun to swell.

"I need energy. These weren't nearly enough—just appetizers. Bring me some dinner."

A captive human was led before him, a Sikh taxi driver whom they'd found hiding inside a garbage Dumpster on Fifth Avenue. Ob frowned. Despite the fact that he was surrounded by the undead, the man was smiling.

"What's your malfunction?" Ob asked in English. "What is so funny?"

The man blinked, uncomprehending. His smile never faded. Ob tried several different languages, till he found one the man understood.

"Are you not afraid? Do you not fear me?"

"No, I do not fear you. This is all a dream. A very long dream."

The man was clearly insane. Ob rose and walked toward him.

"Can you smell me, son of Adam? Can you smell my brethren as these stinking meat wagons we use fall apart around us? Is that stench not real?"

The man did not reply. His grin grew wider.

Ob slid a yellowing fingernail lightly across the captive's throat, tracing a second grin beneath his smile. A thin line of blood welled from the cut.

"Can you feel that? Can you feel in a dream?"

"It is a dream," the man insisted. "None of this is real. The dead do not move around. Therefore, it is a dream."

"Oh, but the dead do move," Ob said, his smile matching the captive's. "Even when we don't possess you, the dead move. You move when the oxygen in your lungs is expelled from your body. The muscles in your corpse dry out and contract. The dead move."

Ob blew fetid air into the man's face. The prisoner's smile faded. Ob's did not.

"And so shall you."

He pressed his nail into the man's throat, slicing deeper into the flesh. The captive's jugular squirted blood, spraying Ob's face and shoulders. Ob licked his lips and then brought the dripping finger to his mouth and sucked on it. Then he feasted.

Minutes later, as promised, the dead man began to move.

"Tell me a bedtime story?" Danny asked, as Jim pulled the covers up around him.

"I reckon so. We don't have any books here, but I remember Teeny Tiny Tale by heart."

A shadow passed over Danny's face; memories of the thing in the parking garage.

"No. I don't want that one, Daddy. How about something else? Maybe *Green Eggs and Ham*?"

Jim had the Seuss memorized too, and he recited it word for word. Danny laughed, clapping his hands and wiggling beneath the covers with enjoyment. When Jim was finished, Danny asked for another.

Jim sat on the edge of the bed and thought for a moment. Then he said, "Once upon a time, there was a king and his son, the prince. One day, the prince went missing, and the king decided to search for him. Their kingdom had been overrun with monsters, but the king didn't care. All he cared about was the prince."

He paused. "What do you think so far?"

"It's the bomb," Danny replied with a grin.

Jim continued. "The king didn't have a horse, so he set out on foot, armed only with a sword. He fought the monsters with every step, and they almost had him, until he met a kind old friar who lived in the woods."

"What's a friar?"

"Sort of like a monk, I think. Like Friar Tuck in Robin Hood."

"Oh, okay."

"So the king and the friar set out to find the prince, and they—"

"Daddy?" Danny interrupted. "Can we call the friar Martin?"

"Sure," Jim swallowed. "I think Martin would have liked that."

"I think so too."

Jim opened his mouth to start again, but Danny interrupted a second time.

"Daddy, do you miss Mr. Martin?"

"Yeah, I do, squirt. I miss him a lot. He was a nice old guy, and a good friend."

"Do you think anybody else is going to die?"

The abruptness of the question shocked Jim, and he wasn't sure how to respond.

"Well, I mean—"

His son looked at him expectantly.

"Nobody else that we love is going to die," Jim answered. "Not for a long time."

He continued with the bedtime story. Within minutes, Danny yawned, blinking his eyes and fighting sleep.

"Why don't you go to sleep, now?"

"I don't want to, Daddy," he murmured. "What if something else happens?"

Jim kissed his forehead. "Nothing else is going to happen," he promised. "I'm gonna watch over you."

"Will you be here when I wake up?" Danny asked as his eyes closed.

"I'll be right here."

"Goodnight, Daddy."

"Goodnight, Danny."

Then Danny opened his eyes slightly, and said, "I love you more than Godzilla."

Jim smiled.

"Love you more than Spider-Man."

"Love you more than Hulk."

"Love you more than 'finity, Daddy."

"You too, buddy," Jim whispered. "I love you more than infinity."

Danny shut his eyes again, and within seconds, he was asleep.

Jim turned off the light and sat by his son's bedside, watching him, listening to him breathe. He sat there for a long time, not moving or even thinking, until there was a soft knock at the door.

Jim tiptoed over to the door and opened it. Don grinned at him.

"Everything okay?" Don asked.

"Sure." Jim nodded, stepping out into the hall. "Danny's sleeping. He just laid down."

"Good. He needs his rest. Hell, I guess we all do."

"Yeah," Jim replied. "So what's up?"

"Well, I wanted you to know that I checked on Frankie, and she's doing fine. She had a scare earlier in the day, though."

"What do you mean?" Jim frowned as he realized he didn't know exactly where Frankie was sleeping tonight—the infirmary, he assumed. Damn, they'd been here less than a day, and he'd already lost track of his friends.

"Apparently, she got out of bed and went looking for us. She was delirious. Doc Stern said she had enough sedatives in her to knock out an elephant, but still, she got up and was wandering around. Wound up in a bit of trouble."

"Maynard." Jim hissed. It wasn't a question.

"I think so," Don agreed. "Forrest and Stern wouldn't confirm or deny, but I'm sure Maynard was involved."

"I knew that guy was trouble. Is Frankie okay?"

"She's fine now, and she should be up and about in a few days."

"Good. That's a relief."

"Yeah." Don paused for a moment. "Listen, Jim—everything's gonna be all right now, isn't it? I mean—I'm sorry about Martin, and everything else that happened, but despite all of that, it's okay now, right? We made it. We're alive."

"I don't know, Don. What is it you want me to say? What do you want to hear?"

Don's voice was barely a whisper.

"I want to hear that it's going to be okay. That we'll win. That they can't beat us."

"They don't win until the last human being left on Earth is dead."

Don frowned. "Judging by the way things have been going, I don't find much comfort in that, Jim."

"Well, I'm not going anywhere anytime soon, and I can god-damned guarantee you that nothing is going to hurt my son. Not ever again. And I've got your back too. So does Frankie. How's that sound?"

De Santos grinned sheepishly. "It sounds good. Look, I'm sorry. It's just that—I haven't had anybody to talk to in what seems like forever. Not since everything started. First there was our dog, and then Myrna—and then nothing until you guys came along. I guess I was just lonely."

"Well," Jim clasped his shoulder, "you're not alone anymore. None of us are."

It was hard for Jim to believe that he'd met this man less than twenty-four hours ago; it felt like they were brothers.

"Yeah." Don sniffed. "You've got that right."

The two of them drifted apart, straightening their posture, secure in their manhood.

"Listen," Don said, "me and Smokey and some of the others are gonna play cards. You want to come?"

Jim cocked a thumb at the apartment door. "No, I appreciate the offer, but I'm gonna stay here with Danny."

"Of course. Enjoy it, Jim. He's a good kid."

"That he is."

"Okay, well, I'll see you later then. Breakfast sound good? Seven o'clock tomorrow morning?"

"You're on. We'll see you there."

"Goodnight."

"Goodnight, Don."

Jim watched him walk away down the hall. Then he went back inside and quietly closed the door. Danny was still sleeping, and there was a smile on his face.

It matched the smile on Jim's own.

He undressed, lied down in bed, and read Martin's Bible, finding comfort from both his lost friend—and those still with him.

* * *

Ramsey folded his hands and shook his head in reserved disbelief. Seated around the conference table with him were Bates, Forrest, and Stern.

"You're absolutely sure of this?" he asked.

"Yes, sir." Bates nodded. "Dr. Stern found the videotapes. Maynard had quite the library, it seems. He filmed himself in the act with the . . . He must have been doing this for quite some time. They were—"

"They were repulsive," Stern finished for him. "He was having sex with captive zombies—necrophilia in the absolute worst sense. I wouldn't have believed it if I hadn't seen it for myself. I don't know how any of this happened without our knowledge. Apparently, Joseph covered his tracks exceedingly well."

"How is the young man who shot him?"

"Carson? He's fine, aside from a broken nose."

"Which he sustained during a confrontation with another young man?"

"Yes, sir."

"Who leapt to his death?"

Bates nodded again.

"And the woman whom Maynard was about to kill—the new arrival? She's fine?"

"She came through surgery okay, but she's not out of the woods yet," Stern answered. "Kelli and I will continue monitoring her condition. She needs rest more than anything else."

"My children aren't happy," Ramsey whispered. "They are not content."

"Excuse me, sir?" Bates cast a wary glance at Forrest and Stern. They stared back at him in confusion.

"We need more people." Ramsey's tone was decisive. "That's why all of this is happening, Bates. Our people are lonely—they grow dissatisfied. They are beginning to turn on one another. We need more people for our community, so that it may grow. Send another patrol out to look for survivors, immediately."

Forrest opened his mouth to protest, but Bates cut him off.

"Begging your pardon, Mr. Ramsey," Bates paused, choosing his words carefully, "but DiMassi is still sick, and Quinn and Steve were out all night looking for survivors, and didn't get to bed until later today, after they'd briefed me. They need to rest and recuperate first."

"Then send out a ground force."

"A ground force?" The blood drained from Bates's face.

"Yes. You read me a list of our weaponry last night, so I know we have the capability. Arm them well and send them out. I want the city searched. We mustn't leave anybody out there, Bates. We must save each and every one of them. That is our calling. We must save as many as we can."

"Sir, it's nighttime. And even if it were daylight, they'd be slaughtered before they got three steps away from the building, no matter how well armed."

Ramsey stood up and waved his hand in disdain.

"Nonsense, Bates. You personally trained them all. They'll be fine. Now get it done. I'll expect a full report when they've returned."

He walked to the door, and then turned back to them.

"Have the patrol look for some yarn as well."

"Yarn, sir?" Bates was incredulous.

"Yes, yarn. I want to do some knitting. I'm going to knit a cake. And cucumbers. I've got a craving for fresh cucumbers. See if they can find some of those too."

"Knit a cake. Yes, sir." Bates felt a twinge of real, undiluted fear. "Anything else?"

"Have the tapes that Dr. Maynard recorded sent up to my room. I'll need to study them in detail."

Ramsey left the room, and the three men gaped at each other.

"Bates," Forrest said carefully, "I know he's the boss and all, and I know you've worked for him a long time—but that motherfucker has lost it, man. He's completely whacked. Over the fucking rainbow! Knit a fucking cake? What the hell is that about?"

"I concur," Stern agreed. "Obviously, Mr. Ramsey has suffered some form of mental breakdown. He's a danger both to himself and others. We need to do something."

Bates put his face in his hands and rubbed his tired eyes. Then he looked at them. His expression was grave. "Okay. Now you both know what I've been dealing with for the past few weeks. What do you suggest we do about it?"

"Confine him," Stern said. "We lock him up and you assume command, at least temporarily. We have several mental-health specialists in the building. They can work with him, diagnose the problem."

"I can diagnose the problem," Bates answered. "He's suffering from delusions of grandeur. He feels like it's his personal duty to save every living person still out there. He's got some kind of messiah complex."

"Well, I ain't drinking no purple Kool-Aid," Forrest vowed.

"Mr. Ramsey is only part of the problem," Bates said, ignoring the soldier. "We need to seriously start thinking about getting out of this city. We can't stay here much longer."

"Why not?" Stern asked. "We're relatively secure, aren't we?"

"Sure—until those things outside get their hands on a

tank or some artillery. They think and plan, Doctor. What happens when they find some fertilizer and cook up a truck bomb?"

"Supposedly, this building can withstand something like that."

"You want to wait around to find out if it really lives up to the engineer's hype?"

"But surely we can defend ourselves. We have guns. Weapons."

"So do they—and there are more of them than there are of us. It doesn't matter how many guns we have. We're outnumbered in any case."

Bates was quiet for a moment, and then continued.

"When you've been doing this for as long as I have, you learn to trust your gut, to honor your instincts. Right now, my gut is telling me that something really bad is about to happen."

"What?"

"I'm not sure. But whatever it is, it's getting closer."

"Then how the hell do we get out of here?" Forrest rapped his large knuckles on the table in frustration. "I mean, we can't fly everybody out. The chopper holds ten people, maximum, and that's with the pilot and co-pilot. We try sneaking ten of us out in the middle of the night, and those folks downstairs will string us up by our necks. And there's no way we could use the vehicles in the parking garage. They'd slaughter us as soon as we got outside."

"We could airlift people out slowly," the doctor suggested. "If we don't want to oppose Mr. Ramsey, tell him you're doing scouting and rescue missions, and secretly take a group of people out every time."

"And go where?" Bates shook his head. "Where do you suggest we take them? The mountains? That's no good, as long as the animals are reanimating too. There's also the small matter of our dwindling fuel supply for the chopper."

"Okay." Forrest's brow creased in thought. "The wilderness is out. We're close to Philly, Pittsburgh, and Baltimore. But they're no good either."

"If we go to a major metropolitan area, we'll be in the same situation we're in now," Bates agreed. "And most of the mid-Atlantic region is near a major metropolitan area. So what does that leave us?"

Stern raised his hand. "An island, perhaps?"

"No." Bates shook his head. "Same problem as the mountains, just on a smaller scale."

"A boat then."

"Again, you have to factor in the wildlife. A school of zombie sharks or an undead killer whale would destroy the type of boat we could safely get our hands on. Plus, there are the sea birds to think about. They'd massacre anybody that went topside. And how are you going to fit all of us on a boat?"

"So where would you go, Bates, if you could get out of here?" Forrest asked.

Bates creased his brow in deep thought. "If I could escape the city, and had the capability to fly anywhere, I'd go to the Arctic Circle or Antarctica. It seems to me that below-zero temperatures and the harsh environment would slow them down somewhat. They have no body heat, so maybe they'd freeze. And the wildlife there is sparse, compared to other wilderness areas."

"You'd live on a fucking iceberg?" Forrest snorted.

Bates nodded silently.

"Look," Forrest said after a long pause, "who says we got to take everybody with us? It would be a fucking logistical nightmare trying to sneak these folks from the building without Ramsey finding out about it."

"You're not suggesting we abandon all these people?" Stern asked.

"Not everybody, but maybe we get the three of us, and seven other people and we get the hell out of here in that helicopter. I mean, somebody has to survive, right?"

Bates rubbed his eyes. "That still doesn't solve the problem of where to go."

"I know where to go," slurred a voice from behind the podium in the corner.

All three of them jumped up in surprise. Forrest's chair fell over backward with a loud crash. Stern's hand flew to his chest.

Bates drew his pistol, crossed the room in three quick strides, and peered behind the podium. His eyes narrowed.

"Get out here, now!"

Pigpen crawled out of his hiding place, cradling a fat, calico cat in his arms. He petted the animal's fur, whispering to it soothingly.

"It's okay, God. That's Mr. Bates. He won't shoot us. He's a nice—"

"Shut up," Bates snapped. "What the hell are you doing in here, Pigpen? You know damn well that this floor is off limits to non-security personnel."

"I was looking for God. I found him behind the podium. Then we fell asleep. When I woke up, you guys were in here. I didn't want to interrupt. Sounded like you were talking about important stuff. God told me it wouldn't be polite."

"What's he talking about?" Stern whispered to Forrest.

"His cat," the soldier whispered. "Its name is God."

"Oh, that's right. I'd forgotten."

Bates motioned with his pistol and Pigpen scurried into one of the chairs, still clutching the cat to his chest.

"What did you hear us discussing, Pigpen?" Bates asked.

"Not much."

"What did you overhear? Tell me."

"Just enough to know that Mr. Ramsey sure is messed up. People say I'm crazy, but boy howdy, he's not right. He ain't playing with a full deck."

Bates clenched his jaw, and then turned back to the others.

"I'm open to suggestions as to what to do with him, too."

"Shoot him," Forrest said. "Put him out of commission before he can scare everybody by telling them that the Grand Poobah is off his rocker."

"Good Lord," Stern balked, rising to his feet. "You can't be serious!"

"He's not," Bates sighed, "but he is right. We can't let Pigpen tell the others. Not yet. Last thing this building needs right now is panic. Panic is infectious, and in a situation such as this, it will spread like wildfire."

Pigpen's rheumy eyes darted among the three of them. In his lap, God purred and then licked himself. The bum ducked his head low, putting his ear next to the cat.

"What's that, God?"

He raised his eyes and stared at Bates.

"God knows how we can get out of here. He says if you'll give me a drink, he'll tell us how."

Bates arched his eyebrows.

"Oh wonderful. I can't wait to hear this."

* * *

Val took a sip of coffee, even though it wasn't good for the baby inside her, and didn't notice when it burned her tongue. Her eyes were shut in concentration as she listened, totally absorbed in the voices coming from the radio. All around her, communication equipment beeped and hummed. An oscillating electric fan blew cool air on the units to keep them from overheating.

"I don't believe this," she muttered to herself. With the headphones over her ears, she didn't realize how loudly she was speaking.

Branson tapped her on the shoulder, and she jumped.

"Jesus fucking Christ, Branson! You scared the shit out of me."

The other radioman held up his hands in mock surrender. "Sorry, Val. Didn't mean to freak you out. What's going on? What you got?"

"Something really scary." She ripped the headphones off her head and handed them to him. "Listen to this. You wouldn't believe me if I told you."

"What is it? Another group of survivors?"

"No—just listen."

Branson place the headphones over his ears and adjusted his glasses. Suddenly, his eyes widened in surprise.

"This can't be real, can it?"

"I don't know," Val shrugged, her eyes serious, "but we better tell Bates right away."

"Shit," Branson breathed. "This is bad, Val. This is really bad."

Her hands darted protectively to her belly, and the unborn baby inside.

Branson picked up another radio to call Bates. His hands were shaking.

* * *

"I know you think I'm crazy," Pigpen said. "But I don't take offense. I guess I'd have to be crazy, living the way I did. But I ain't. Know what I did for a living before I was homeless?"

The other men shook their heads in unison.

"I worked for the city's department of public works. Down in the sewers. You know that people lived down there, right? Beneath the city. They lived down in the darkness and the stink, fucking and fighting and loving and dying in those tunnels just like we did up here. Children were born down there, spent their whole childhood down there."

"You're talking about the mole people," Bates responded.

"Mole people?" The derision was thick in Forrest's voice. "Give me a fucking break."

"It's true," Pigpen insisted. "They weren't mutants out of some horror movie. They were just folks like you or me, down on their luck and with no other place to go. When you're homeless, you live where you can; in alleyways or behind garbage Dumpsters, under railroad trestles, cardboard boxes, anywhere there's space. Down under, too. You'd be surprised at the people you find down there. Stockbrokers. Lawyers. Factory guys. Medical school dropouts and college graduates."

Bates thought to himself, *They banded together for safety in numbers, just like we've done.*

"I read several books about that," Stern said. "And I remember some prominent newspaper and online articles about it, too."

"Yeah, but that was just an urban legend," Forrest protested. "Like alligators in the sewers and all that other bullshit."

"It's true," Pigpen insisted. "I know it. I saw first hand, both before I was homeless and after. Shit, I lived it every day. And there *are* alligators down there, Forrest. Big albino fuckers with red eyes and white skin. I had a buddy named Wilbanks. He lost a damned leg to one."

"You lived underground?" Bates asked.

"Not at first, but I ended up down there. I came up to the streets during the day, panhandling and looking for cans to redeem and shit. But at night, I slept way seven stories beneath Grand Central Station, down where there was no trains or cops. We'd pick-axed a hole into the wall. Gave us access to an old service tunnel. There's all kinds of unused shit like that down there. Train stations and bomb shelters and stuff—just sitting there. It wasn't so bad. I had a place to sleep that was pretty dry, and we rigged some of the electric cables to give us power and light."

"Why'd you go underground, Pigpen?" Forrest prodded him.

"Didn't have nowhere else *to* go. I got sent to prison for a DUI charge. Got out and my old lady was running around on me, and I couldn't find a job. Pretty soon, I ended up below. It's that easy. I started living underneath the city, and that's when I found God."

"How did you survive?" Stern asked. "What did you eat?"

"There was a broken sprinkler pipe that we got water from. As for grub, handouts when we could get them, or else we'd go Dumpster diving. And lots and lots of track rabbits."

"Track rabbits?"

"Rats." Pigpen smiled. "We called them track rabbits. They're pretty good, believe it or not. Taste a little like chicken. We'd trap them, or just snatch the little fuckers by the tail and slam them against the wall. God was good at catching them, too, which is why nobody ever tried to eat him."

Shuddering, Stern made a disgusted face and turned away.

"Hey, Doc, you'd eat track rabbit too, if you were forced to do it. You'd be amazed what a fellow will do to survive."

Bates sighed in exasperation. "Get to the point, Pigpen. You're proposing we all hide out in the sewers?"

"Nope. The point is this. God says there's a way out of here."

"And?"

"If you've got somebody that can fly an airplane, there's a way to get from here to the airport."

"What the hell we gonna do at the airport?" Forrest kicked the cowering man's chair. "Come on, Bates. This crazy fuck doesn't know anything."

Stern said, "Even if we tried to get there, we wouldn't make it a block with those things outside. They'd tear us to shreds."

"We ain't going through the city. We're going underneath it. God says we'd go underground, through the sewers and the tunnels."

"Underground?" Bates looked Pigpen in the eyes. "Does God realize that there's a little thing called the East River between here and JFK?"

"There used to be." Pigpen winked. "But Mr. Ramsey built a tunnel underneath it. And there's other tunnels. The 63rd Street subway tunnel goes under the river. There's a whole bunch more. Stuff like the Long Island Railroad tracks go into Grand Central."

"The East Side Access project," Bates said, "but Mr. Ramsey didn't—"

"Mr. Ramsey," the vagrant interrupted, "spent six billion over the last five years building a private network of tunnels. Damn things run from beneath this building to JFK. He even had them install a concrete bomb shelter eight stories down. I know, man. We used to sneak in from our own tunnels at night and steal equipment and stuff that the construction workers left behind. And they hook up with all the other tunnels and shit down there."

"Something like that would have been in the news," Stern scoffed. "An undertaking of that size would have attracted all kinds of attention from the media and the public. There are zoning laws and permits to consider. Union requirements."

"Mr. Ramsey don't worry about zoning laws," Pigpen spat, his hand moving up and down God's spine. The cat purred, even when his master stroked him against the grain. "He's the richest guy in America. And unions? What the fuck—you think he had somebody other than Ramsey Construction building it?"

Stern and Forrest looked at Bates. He shrugged.

"If it does exist, I've never heard of it."

His previous night's conversation with Ramsey surfaced.

"Mr. Ramsey, we have to consider the possibility that sooner or later, no matter how well guarded, those things will breach our defenses."

"If that happens, then I have a contingency plan."

"Good. I can't tell you what a relief that is, sir. May I ask what it is?"

"No. As of now, that information is given out on a

need-to-know basis, and quite frankly, you don't need to know."

"Begging your pardon, Mr. Ramsey, but how am I supposed to protect us if I don't know?"

"Trust me, Bates. If and when the time comes, you'll be the first to know."

"So how do we gain access to this tunnel?" Bates asked Pigpen.

"Through the basement and then down into the sub-basement. God showed me before."

"And it will get us to the airport, without running into the zombies?"

"It will. God will lead us."

"You believe this shit?" Forrest asked.

Bates shrugged. "It might be worth checking into."

"You're serious?" Forrest asked.

"I am. At this point, I'll take any help I can get—even from God."

He reached down and scratched the cat's ears.

"Meanwhile, what do we do about Mr. Ramsey?" Stern asked.

"I'll handle him. It's my responsibility. You get a secure room ready, someplace where we can lock him up so he can't hurt himself or others."

"Bates," Stern arched his eyebrows. "Why didn't you tell us about Ramsey sooner?"

"At first, I thought it was just stress. Figured he was tired. It didn't get bad until a few days ago."

"Well, from here on out, the four of us need to trust each other implicitly. We're in this together."

"Agreed." Bates nodded. "Forrest, you keep an eye on Pigpen here. Don't let our fellow conspirator run his mouth. If I really am going to assume control of operations, I'm sure there will be some people who want to start trouble over it. We need to let those we trust know about it beforehand, so they can help quell any resistance. Something like that will just delay us longer. The two of you go wake up Steve."

Forrest frowned. "The Canuk? Why?"

"Because he's an airline pilot and we're not. If we *can* make it to the airport, I want to know exactly what would be required when we get there, how many people he thinks he can fly out, what type of plane he'll need—how feasible this whole thing is."

"You really do think there's a way out of here, don't you?" Forrest asked.

"Anything is better than sitting here, just waiting for those things outside to attack us."

Ob's ruse worked. By midnight, the undead forces encamped in New York City had netted over a hundred additional survivors, lured from safety by the phony broadcast. They were slaughtered as they crept from their basements and attics and storage rooms and everywhere else they'd hidden. One group was caught on the choked Long Island Expressway, driving an armored car. Another group emerged onto the rooftop of their Soho brownstone, saw what was happening, and began dropping cinder blocks on the corpses milling in the streets below. They were picked off by a combination of zombie snipers and undead birds. More humans came in during the night, from New Jersey and other parts of New York State. The dead welcomed them with open arms and flashing teeth. Their numbers swelled.

By the time the witching hour had passed, the only living creatures left in New York were sequestered inside Ramsey Towers.

On the outskirts of the city, a zombie with a can of spray paint tagged graffiti on the side of a building. It read:

WELCOME TO THE NECROPOLIS.

HAVE A NICE DAY

TWELVE

Bates was halfway to Ramsey's private quarters when his radio squawked. The burst of electronic static was like a gunshot in the silent corridor. He yanked it from his belt in frustration, and lowered his voice.

"This is Bates."

"Mr. Bates?" The speaker was Branson, a former meteorologist and now one of their communications specialists. "You'd better come down here to the communication center right away. We've got trouble."

"What kind of trouble?"

"You wouldn't believe it, sir."

"Try me. Quit speaking in riddles and just report what you have."

Branson's gulp was audible through the tiny speaker.

"The zombies, sir. They—well, they've taken over all the broadcast channels—ham, military, commercial, and even the marine frequencies. Everything."

"And what are they doing?"

"Announcing an all clear. Telling survivors in the listening area that it's okay to come out now. Telling them to come to Manhattan. They're saying the city's safe, and if they come here, they'll be protected and given food and shelter."

"And you're sure it's them?"

"Begging your pardon, Mr. Bates, but who else could it be? We know darn well that it's not safe outside. People are being led into a trap."

"Damn. That's clever." Despite his total loathing of the creatures surrounding the skyscraper, Bates had to respect their ingenuity.

"Sir? That's not all. We've picked up some transmissions from the south. There's a large force on the move, heavily armed. I'm talking tanks and heavy artillery."

"Human? A militia maybe?"

"Negative. They're zombies, sir."

"Any idea what their destination is?"

"Here."

Bates blood turned to ice water.

"I'll be down right away. Continue monitoring all channels."

Cursing under his breath, he stalked to the elevator.

Ramsey's door, which had been open a crack during the conversation, quietly shut again.

Darren Ramsey hadn't obtained his position in life by being stupid. Clever cunning, a keen sense of self-preservation, and a healthy dose of paranoia had served him well in his sixty-five years on Earth.

He drew upon those skills now.

He let the door slide shut and listened for the elevator doors to ding. When he was sure Bates had gone, he placed the loaded pistol on the desk and clicked his computer's mouse. The screensaver disappeared. Ramsey clicked again, and then typed in a password. This gave him access to the building's security system; something that even Bates was unaware was still fully operational. Ramsey had paid off the head of the maintenance crew with a box of cigars, a bottle of bourbon, and the promise of a million dollars when society was normal again, after the man had accidentally discovered the network. There were over one thousand carefully concealed, state-of-the-art surveillance cameras in the building, each with full audio and zoom capability. None was bigger than a pinhead.

Ramsey let his fingers glide over the keyboard, feeling like a pianist at a concert. Rapid-fire images flashed by on his monitor.

Smokey, Quinn, the mess-hall cooks Leroy and Etta, and one of the new arrivals, (De Santos—was that his name?—Ramsey couldn't remember) played a raucous game of poker, laughing and smoking and telling bawdy jokes.

FLASH

Carson had found comfort in the arms of another man. Though the room was dark, Ramsey could see the tears on the young man's face, trickling around his splinted nose. The old man wondered if the tears were for his suicidal friend, or for himself, or for them all.

FLASH

Kelli, the young nurse, lay on her bed, vigorously masturbating with one hand while the other caressed her breasts. Ramsey briefly turned up the sound, but soon lost interest. His penis remained flaccid. He wondered if the videos that Maynard had filmed before his death would interest him more.

FLASH

Steve, the Canadian airline pilot, lay sprawled on his bed, fully clothed and snoring. A half-empty bottle of

Knob Creek and a photo of the man's son sat on the dresser.

FLASH

On the roof, undead crows, pigeons, and sparrows strutted about or perched on the helicopter and the strobe lights, watching the door patiently.

FLASH

DiMassi, the sickened pilot, watched television, an old episode of *Hogan's Heroes* via the building's closed-circuit broadcast, and drank a can of warm beer. His room was littered with debris: crumpled cans and tissues, half-eaten pizza crusts and empty candy wrappers. Ramsey was filled with disgust, yet he considered the fat man's worth. DiMassi had recently had an altercation with Bates, and might yet come in handy.

FLASH

In the darkened lobby, all was silent, save for the distant curses of the zombies milling around outside the barricaded main entrance doors. A complicated nest of booby-traps and trip wires snaked through the lobby. Two guards (he was fairly certain their names were Cullen and Newman, but it was hard to keep track of everyone), sat behind the sandbagged receptionist desk-fortress, and listened to the undead outside. Ramsey could see the smoldering fear that they tried to hide from each other.

FLASH

Bates had entered the radio room, and was seated in front of a console, with Val and Branson flanking him. He knew that Val was pregnant. He didn't know much about Branson.

Ramsey turned up the sound and zoomed in on them.

". . . will be there to assist you. Message repeats. This is the Federal Emergency Management Agency, broadcasting to all who can hear this message. The United States Department of Homeland Security has determined that Manhattan and the other New York boroughs are now safe zones. The quarantine has been lifted. All civilian and military personnel are encouraged to make their way to the area immediately. Shelter and aid stations have been set up for your convenience, to provide food, water, and medical aid. Again, the threat alert for New York City has been lifted and the area is now designated as a safe zone. Make your way there for further assistance. Military and civilian authorities will be there to assist you. Message repeats . . ."

"Unbelievable," Val breathed.

"It's something, all right," Branson agreed. "What do you think, Mr. Bates?"

Bates lit a cigarette, and snapped his lighter shut.

"I think we're fucked."

"How so?"

Val wished he wouldn't smoke around her, but said nothing. Branson cleaned his glasses on his shirttail and waited for his superior's response.

Bates exhaled a line of smoke. "Why haven't they done this before? Why now, all of the sudden? They've got a leader—somebody new, telling them what to do."

"Do you . . ." Val paused, then continued. "Do you think any of our people will buy into it, try to go outside?"

"If they do, they'll be dead before they can get those lobby doors open. All lobby guards have standing orders to shoot anyone who tries. That's what these things want. Just a crack—enough to get their feet in the door."

The two young radio operators grew silent.

"Let me hear this other broadcast," Bates said.

Branson shuffled his feet. "They've gone silent again, sir."

"Did you manage to record any of it?"

Both shook their heads.

"Damn. Well, what did you hear? Don't leave out any details, no matter how trivial they may seem."

Val reported, "There's a large force of zombies heading this way from Pennsylvania. Estimated time of arrival was maybe four or five hours from now, right around dawn."

"Which doesn't make any sense," Branson interrupted, "because Hellertown is only about two hours from here."

"Usually, yes," Bates agreed. "But I'm sure the roads are clogged with abandoned vehicles. I've been meaning to speak with the Thurmond party, and get their assessment of the area outside our borders, especially the parts out of the range of our reconnaissance flights."

"How far did they travel?" Branson asked.

"From West Virginia."

"Holy shit. They managed to survive that long on the ground? Put a gun in their hands. They'd be good to have. Sound like some ass-kicking motherfuckers."

Bates nodded to Val. "So the zombie army will be here by morning."

Val's mouth was a thin, tight line.

"Continue," Bates encouraged her.

She took a deep breath. "The zombie army seems to mostly be made up of the military units we monitored in that same area, sir."

"I'd figured as much."

"It's a mobile force, consisting of several hundred vehicles, both military and civilian. The caravan has been reporting over the radio to somebody named Ob."

"Ob?"

"Yes. We've been unable to determine who or what he is, but we assume he's their leader. If so, then he's obviously one of them."

"And where is he based? Do we know this Ob's location?"

Val's face paled.

"Here, sir. He's here in the city. And from what we overheard, he knows about us too."

"Of course they do. That's why they've stayed camped outside this building day in and day out."

"But, Mr. Bates, there's more. This leader, Ob, told the other group that the way was being cleared, but that the tunnel might not be cleared in time. He gave them alternate directions from the bridge."

"Directions to where?"

"Here, sir."

"The city? You already told me that."

Val grew even paler.

"No, sir. Here. To Ramsey Towers."

Ramsey switched off the camera, and logged out of the security system. He sat back, bathed in the soft glow of his monitor's screensaver—the cover of his best-selling autobiography.

They were coming. Soon. He was nervous, but at the same time, he could barely contain his glee. This was the perfect opportunity to finally showcase how much damage his indestructible building could actually withstand. All doubts would be laid to rest, and more importantly, his flock would remain safe and secure within its walls. And when the failed assault was over, they would thank him. Praise him.

Worship him.

But was it enough to simply bask in their adoration? Ramsey was used to the public eye—indeed, he craved it. But he wanted more than just their accolades. He wanted—*needed*—to be their savior.

Bates could get in the way of that. Bates, Forrest, and Stern. They thought he was crazy. Him, Darren Ramsey! He'd listened in on their conversation after he left the conference room. Pigpen presented a problem as well. Ramsey wasn't surprised that the vagrant knew of the private tunnel. The foreman had reported several cases of vandalism and skirmishes with the homeless during its construction. But now this man had told the others, and it sounded like Bates was planning on leading his people—Ramsey's people—down into the network of tunnels beneath the city. Leading them from the safety of the building.

He couldn't allow that. He needed to maintain control. He needed to prove to them all that both the building, and himself, were indestructible. Bates lack of faith was regrettable. Ramsey had enjoyed working with the bodyguard.

But now he'd have to fire him.

Ramsey picked up the pistol.

"Shoot me now," Don muttered, "and put me out of my misery."

Quinn laughed as Don, Smokey, and Etta all folded, flinging their cards down onto the table. Then he raised and called. Leroy cursed, displayed his losing hand, and Quinn raked the pile of cash toward himself.

"That's another twenty-five grand for me."

"Don't know why you so happy," Etta grumbled, "That might as well be Monopoly money we're playing with."

"Yeah," Leroy chimed in, lighting a cigarette. "It ain't like you can go out and spend it, Quinn."

"It doesn't matter to me if it's useless or not," Quinn told them, pouring himself another glass of bourbon. "I just like to feel the cash between my fingers."

"Where did you guys get all this money anyway?" Don asked.

"The bank," Leroy grunted, "downstairs in the lobby."

"You—you just took it?"

"It's not like the customers will be needing it anytime soon. And besides, it gets old, playing for cigarettes."

"Shit," Etta groaned. "It gets old playing with this worthless cash too."

"You guys ever think about how much money is lying around out there? Not to mention diamonds and shit?" Smokey pointed to the window. A zombie bird hovered outside in the darkness. They ignored it.

Don did not. He shivered, and then turned back to the new hand that Smokey had just dealt him.

"Are you guys sure those things can't get inside the building?"

"Sure," Leroy said, and studied his cards.

"Absolutely," Quinn confirmed. "Aren't you?"

Don shrugged. "I guess I just feel like a passenger on the *Titanic*. It just seems so unrealistic. Nothing is totally impenetrable. Seems to me there should be a contingency plan of sorts."

The others were quiet. Finally, Smokey looked up from his cards, drained his glass, and spoke.

"We don't really like to think about it, Don. Not much we can do if they really tried, you know?"

"So you just sit in here and wait? Isn't that a bunker mentality?"

Quinn threw several thousand dollars into the pile in the middle of the table. Then he rolled up a hundred dollar bill, lit it, and then touched the flame to his cigarette. He stubbed the burning currency out in the ashtray.

"The world's gonna end anyway," he said. "Whether we're inside or out there on the streets. I prefer to wait in here and play cards and light my smokes with hundreds."

"We're gonna have to start rationing food," Etta said. "Leroy and I took stock of everything in the restaurant and the cafeteria's freezers and storage rooms. And we got all the stuff from the vending machines and such. But it won't last us more than a month. I don't know what we're gonna do after that."

"Maybe we can start eating zombies," Quinn joked.

Smokey gagged. "That's sick, man."

"Hey, why not?" Quinn scowled at his cards. "They eat us, right? I say we turn the tables and start eating them. Not the ripe kind, but think about this. Get one that's freshly dead and cook it up before the meat goes bad. Like if you drop dead of a heart attack tomorrow, Leroy cooks you up before you turn into a zombie."

"With the right amount of spice," Leroy grinned, "I can cook anything. Even zombie."

"That's just wrong." Etta's expression was sour. "You all are nasty."

There was a soft knock at the door. Smokey opened it and Forrest and Pigpen entered the room. God trailed along behind them, darting through Smokey's legs and jumping into Etta's lap.

"What the fuck's he doing in here?" Quinn frowned, fanning his nose.

"Joining the party," Forrest said. The big man looked uneasy.

"You play cards, Pigpen?" Leroy asked.

"No, God won't let me. But thanks anyway."

Forrest walked over to the window and stared out into the night. He clenched his fists so tightly that his knuckles popped.

"You want in?" Quinn asked him.

Forrest gave no indication that he'd heard him.

"Forrest? Forrest! Yo, big guy!"

He turned. His dark face was solemn.

Smokey poured another drink. "What's on your mind, Forrest?"

"Nothing." He tried to smile, but it looked forced. He turned to Don. "How they treating you, roomie?"

"They're robbing me blind," Don replied. "Of course, since I had no cash of my own, they were kind enough to let me use theirs, so I guess it doesn't matter."

Forrest's radio squawked. He picked it up and keyed the mike.

"Go ahead."

"Forrest." Bates sounded grim. "Where are you?

"At the evening card game. What's up?"

"Is Pigpen still with you?"

"Yeah. He's here, and so is his cat."

"Both of you meet me on the basement level."

"Now?"

"Now."

He grabbed Pigpen's arm and guided him from the room. The cat trailed along behind them.

Smokey sloshed his drink around in the glass. "I wonder what that was all about?"

Quinn grinned around his cigarette. "Probably just the end of the world again."

* * *

Jim woke up to the insistent urging of his bladder. Blearily, he crawled out of bed and tiptoed to the bathroom. He pissed, but did not flush so as not to wake Danny. As he washed his hands, he glanced at himself in the mirror. He'd aged ten years in the last two weeks. Carrie wouldn't recognize him now.

Thinking of his second wife brought a sudden pang of grief. Without warning, tears spilled from his eyes. Jim sat down on the toilet as sobs wracked his body. His emotions were a mixture of sadness and relief. He cried for Carrie and their unborn baby. He cried for Martin. He even wept for Tammy and Rick. He cried sad tears for what Danny had been through, and tears of joy that the boy was safe and with him now.

When he was finished, Jim turned off the bathroom light and slipped back into bed. He immediately fell asleep, emotionally and physically exhausted.

"The workers hadn't reached here yet," Pigpen told them as they stood in the sub-basement, "so we'll have to go about a mile through the sewers before we get to where they'd stopped."

Forrest's nose wrinkled in disgust.

God stood over a manhole cover in the corner of the sub-basement's cement floor and meowed. Then he twined between Pigpen's legs, purring.

"Down there?" Bates asked, skeptical.

"Yep, God says that's where we got to go."

"And you're absolutely positive you can lead us to the tunnel?"

Pigpen nodded. "And from there, it's a straight shot to the airport."

"And if they flank us?"

"Then I'll take us to the bomb shelter."

"Bates," Forrest asked, "how the hell are we gonna get all these people through that sewer entrance?"

"We're not, at least, not yet. We'll send a reconnaissance team, make sure this private tunnel of Ramsey's really exists. Get an idea of the challenges we're going to face. We'll go from there. But we'll need to send them soon."

"Why soon?" Forrest asked.

"Because there's an army on the way here."

"Ours?"

"Theirs."

God suddenly crouched down on all fours and hissed.

"What is it, God?" Pigpen reached down to scratch the cat, but it backed away, hissing.

The other two men ignored it. Bates studied the cover. "Let's pull it up and have a look."

He threaded a thin length of steel cable through two of the holes, and then he and Forrest squatted on either side and lifted, grunting with the effort. The manhole cover rose into the air with a grating sound. They dropped it onto the floor and stared down at the hole. The interior opening was dark, and all they could see was the top rungs of a service ladder.

Forrest fanned his nose. "Jesus, that stinks. Smells worse than a month-old zombie."

Bates produced a small flashlight from his pocket, crouched down, and shined the beam into the hole.

A pair of red eyes stared back.

"Shit!"

The undead rat launched itself from its perch on the ladder. Its claws raked across Bates's cheek, drawing thin ribbons of blood. Its teeth sank into the material of his shirt, ripping the fabric.

Shouting, Bates rolled backward and yanked the

squirming creature from his face. He tossed it across the room as more squeaking rats poured themselves from the sewer entrance.

Forrest freed his pistol from its holster, but before he could draw a bead, two of the rats swarmed him, climbing up his legs. He screamed, beating at them with his hands. Sharp, needle-like teeth bit into his palms and the soft flesh between his thumbs and index fingers.

Another rat raced toward Pigpen. The old man tripped and fell, sprawling on his back. Just as the rat darted for his groin, God leaped between them, seized the creature in his jaws, and shook it apart. Rotting limbs and clotted fur showered both man and feline.

Bates grabbed the cable and dragged the manhole cover back over the hole. Then he ran to help Forrest. The big man shook his leg, dislodging one of the rats. God pounced on it. Forrest clutched the other in his bare hand and smashed it against a steel support beam.

The rat that had attacked Bates skittered across the cement floor, making a beeline for the cat. Bates grabbed the zombie by its tail and swung it over his head. Then he let go. The rat sailed across the basement and splattered against the wall.

The three men stood gasping for breath. The cat licked its fur.

"How are your hands?" Bates asked Forrest.

"Fuckers bit the shit out of me, but I'll be okay."

"Go find Doc Stern and have him take care of those wounds. No telling what kind of diseases those things were carrying."

Forrest suddenly looked sick. "At least it ain't like in the movies, where if they bite you, your ass turns into one of them."

"I'm going to find Mr. Ramsey and take care of that

situation. When I'm finished, we're calling an emergency meeting."

"You're not still thinking about going down there?"

"Why not?"

"Bates, what the fuck just happened? Zombie rats, man! They were down there waiting for us."

"Consider this, Forrest. How many birds are waiting on that roof and outside our windows? For that matter, how many zombies are down in the street? All they need is an opening and then they'll break through."

"No shit. What's your point?"

"Only four rats came through that opening. There wasn't a large force waiting to rush us. Just those four."

"Yeah?"

"Yes. I think they were up to something else. I think they were sent to spy on us. To look for a way in."

"Spies? Bates, you're beginning to sound crazy too, man."

"We can send out a reconnaissance team. Why can't they?"

Forrest opened his mouth to reply, but just shook his head. He pulled off his shirt and wrapped it around one of his bleeding hands.

"Okay." He sighed. "But once we're down there, what's to stop us from being sitting ducks? What if this tunnel doesn't exist or if it don't go all the way to the airport?"

"Worst case scenario, we make for the bomb shelter. That much I know exists. There was an article about it in *Time* magazine. The city is riddled with them."

God rubbed against Bates's shoes. Bates scratched the purring feline behind its ears.

"I guess your cat came in handy after all, Pigpen."

The bum crossed his arms. "I told you, Mr. Bates. God will protect us."

Bates stared back down at the sewer entrance.

"He can take point if and when we go through there. And I'll be right behind him with a flamethrower."

"A flamethrower?"

"Yes. While I still think these zombies were an advance team, I have no doubt that there are plenty more down there. Between God and a flamethrower, I think we can even the odds."

Don stumbled back to his room just after two in the morning. He hadn't planned on staying awake so late, but he'd been reluctant to leave. It had felt so good to laugh again, to just hang out with people, talking and playing cards and just having fun. No walking corpses to shoot or flee from, no jumping from one peril to another. He hadn't realized how bad his cabin fever had been while he was sequestered inside the panic room—and finally, he felt alive again.

He hadn't thought of Myrna during the entire card game. He realized it as he slid his key into the door lock. At first, he felt guilty about it, but as he fumbled for the light switch, he decided that it was okay. In fact, it was probably healthy.

He slipped out of his shoes, leaned back on the bed, and looked around his new home. Forrest still wasn't back, and his bed was made, unused. Dimly, Don wondered where he was. He wondered if Jim, Danny, and Frankie were asleep. Then alcohol and fatigue got the best of him, and he passed out.

The zombie army rolled over the bridges and tunnels leading into Manhattan. Riding in armored tanks,

Humvees, and deuce-and-a-half trucks, they poured into the Necropolis, bringing ordnance and reinforcements. Tractor-trailers and civilian vehicles followed along behind them. The caravan rumbled through the streets, smashing aside the few remaining abandoned and wrecked vehicles that the New York forces hadn't cleared away. The concrete and steel canyons echoed with their thunder.

Ob ordered all of them to converge on his location, several blocks away from Ramsey Towers. Although the streets had been cleared of major blockages, barricades were constructed in the streets surrounding the skyscraper.

Watching the approaching forces through binoculars, Ob said, "Our forces arrive quicker than we predicted."

"Our brethren are anxious to begin, sire," said one of his lieutenants.

"Have our rat spies returned yet?"

"Not yet, lord Ob. They are overdue."

"Perhaps the humans discovered them. No matter. We have what we need from other sources."

Turning to the plotting table at his side, Ob resumed his study of the maps of the area, blueprints of the skyscraper and the sewers and tunnels that lay beneath it. He conferred with his generals and gathered his army together. They planned and plotted until dawn.

One of the sentries radioed Bates as he was on his way to search Ramsey's office, and private living quarters, along with Branson and Quinn, who was still drunk from the card game. The red-haired pilot sipped a mug of hot coffee, trying to sober up as quickly as possible. Bates had filled both men in on Ramsey's crumbling sanity. Bates then advised Quinn of the approaching zombie army, which Branson verified. Bates told them both about the possible escape route.

Bates answered the radio and told the sentry to go ahead.

"Sir, this is Cullen, down in the lobby."

"What is it, son?"

"There's—there's some kind of activity going on down here. Several trucks just pulled up, and it looks as if they're arming the zombies."

"Arming them?"

"Yes, sir. It's hard to tell for sure through our barricades, but it looks like they're handing out weapons and ammunition. And there's more zombies showing up too. A lot more than we normally have milling around outside. I think they're lighting the other buildings on fire."

Bates stopped in the middle of the hallway and exchanged wide-eyed looks with Branson and Quinn. "Are you sure?"

"Yes, sir. What should Newman and I do?"

"Stand fast, and keep me advised. I'll send some reinforcements down to you."

"This is getting fucking bad, man." Quinn moaned.

"We've got to alert everybody. I need the two of you to continue searching for Mr. Ramsey. I'll send you some help as soon as I can."

"What are you gonna do, sir?" Branson gulped.

"Call an emergency meeting."

The radio squawked again. Frustrated, Bates answered.

"This is Bates."

"It's Forrest."

"Did Doc Stern get you fixed up?"

"Yeah. Any sign of the old man?"

"None. Obviously, he's somewhere in the building. Wake up Carson and DiMassi. Apprise them of the situation and get them involved with the search too. Tell them to meet Branson and Quinn on the top floor."

"But DiMassi's still quarantined."

"Then he'll need to get better in a hurry. Meanwhile, have Val sound the alarm over the P. A. system. I want everybody in the building, with the exception of those on watch, to assemble in the auditorium in twenty minutes."

"Before that, there's something else you ought to see."

"What, Forrest? I don't have time for anything else."

"I'm down on the thirtieth floor."

"And?"

"There's a shitload of zombies out there. That army you were talking about? I think they just arrived."

"I know. I'll be right down."

Forrest stood at the end of the hall, looking out the thirtieth floor's big observation window. The way the building had been designed, it seemed as if he was standing overtop the street itself. Raising the binoculars, he studied the skyline and the burning city below.

"Jesus Christ."

His dark skin had gone ashen. He was still staring when Bates arrived. Both stood speechless.

The occupants of Ramsey Towers slept.

Entwined in the arms of his lover, Carson dreamed of Kilker. In the dream, Kilker teetered on the edge of the roof, his body blanketed by zombie birds. But when he went over the side, Kilker flew instead of falling, flapping his arms and cackling as he hovered above the helicopter pad. He swooped toward Carson, dead but alive, pleading with Carson to have sex with him, just as Maynard had done with the corpses. Carson ran back inside the building, and stood there panting, his back to the door. Kilker clawed on it from outside. Carson whimpered in his sleep.

After falling asleep in the comfortable throes of her masturbatory post-orgasm, Nurse Kelli had a nightmare as well. In it, she was walking down the halls of the Mount Sinai Hospital in Queens, where she'd worked before the world fell apart. The lights still worked, the rooms buzzed with the sounds of equipment, yet the hospital was deserted. Her heels echoed in the silent halls. Someone had painted the word *HORROR* on the walls in blood, over and over again. She touched one wall and her fingertips came away sticky. She was still wondering what it meant, when a zombie lurched out of the ICU and rasped, "I will show you horror, wench." Kelli woke screaming, and couldn't fall back asleep.

Steve dreamed of his son. They were in a field near their home in Ontario, and his son was flying a kite. Steve glanced up at the kite, watching it soar through the clear blue sky. The sunlight blinded him for a moment. When he looked back down, his son was gone. Frantic, Steve ran through the field, calling his son's name. Unfettered, the kite rose into the sky, disappearing behind the clouds. Tears ran down Steve's face as he slept. He moaned his son's name, and then rolled over, entangled in the sheets.

Don's dream was an alcohol-fueled exercise in surrealism. In it, he was back at his home in Bloomington. He opened the refrigerator to make a snack for himself and Myrna, and a bologna sandwich started talking to him in a language he didn't understand. Despite that obvious handicap, he continued trying to communicate with it, until Rocky padded into the kitchen, rose up on his hind legs, and wolfed down the intelligent sandwich in two bites.

Smokey thrashed, gripped in the throes of a nightmare. In it, he walked through Ramsey Towers's cafeteria. Etta and Leroy were serving their fellow occupants as dinner entrees. Alarmed, Smokey backed away. When he tried to run, the undead versions of his daughter and son-in-law blocked his way. Smokey's arm lashed out in his sleep, knocking the glass of water containing his false teeth from the nightstand.

Danny sighed happily. He and his father made a trip to the mall, where his daddy bought every comic book there was at the comic store, even the ones he wasn't allowed to read, like *Hellblazer* and *Preacher*. The two of them sat on the floor, eating potato chips, wiping their greasy fingers on their clothes, and reading the exploits of Hulk and Spider-Man and the Justice League of America. Then his mother and Rick walked in with even more comics. Carrie entered the room after them, carrying a stack of Godzilla movies. His new stepsister lay in the nook between her other arm and her chest. In the dream, all the grown-ups were getting along.

Jim did not dream. He slept the sleep of the dead, sound and still.

Frankie dreamed of Martin.

They stood in a forest. The lush greenery was aromatic and vibrant. Frankie could smell honeysuckle and maple and pine. A light breeze ruffled the leaves over their heads.

"You gonna talk this time, preacher-man?" Frankie asked.

"Yes."

"What is this place? Where are we?"

"Earth," Martin answered. "White Sulphur Springs, West Virginia, to be exact. This is where Jim and I met.

The town is down yonder through that hollow. And my old church, too."

"So what are we doing out here in the damn woods?"

"Waiting."

"For what?"

"For them."

The foliage parted, and a man, woman, and child emerged, cautiously looking around. The group of survivors crept past Frankie and Martin, seemingly unaware of their presence. Leaves rustled beneath their feet.

"Who are they?" Frankie asked.

"Survivors, like yourself. They haven't seen a zombie in over a week, so they think it's safe to come out."

"And is it?"

"No. As a matter of fact, it's even deadlier now."

"I guess so." Frankie smirked. "There's dead people walking around everywhere, not to mention the dead animals and shit."

"But that's just it, Frankie." Martin swept his hand around. "Do you see any zombies? Can you smell them?"

She sniffed the air and glanced around. She smelled pine and moss, but no decay or rot.

"No. Where are they? Waiting in hiding and planning on ambushing these folks? We should warn them if that's so."

"Let's follow them. I reckon you ought to see this for yourself. That's why I'm here. To show you what's to come."

"You're just as crazy now as you were when you were alive, Preacher."

Martin smiled. "Then you'll really think this is crazy. Look at them again."

She did, and stumbled from the shock. The man was Jim, the child was Danny, and the woman—

—the woman was herself.

"Fuck it." Frankie ducked beneath a branch, walking directly behind herself. "I'll play along. This is a dream anyway. At least there ain't no zombie babies in it."

"There are no zombies at all," Martin confirmed. "They're gone—moved on to the next world."

"So you gonna explain that? What happened? Did they all rot away to nothing or turn to dust or something?"

"The dead are not our true enemy. We named them zombies because we did not understand what they were. The creatures that possess the dead are demons called Siqqusim, and they are our true antagonists. They are older than man—far older. They were worshipped alongside Baal on the mountain of Peor, in the land of Moab."

"Moab? That anywhere near Baltimore?" Frankie quipped.

"Not quite. The Siqqusim held sway over the court of King Manasseh, and their cults sprang up in Assyrian, Sumero-Akkadian, Mesopotamian, and Ugaritic cultures. They were consulted by necromancers and soothsayers, before finally being banned. Secret worship of the Siqqusim continued into the Middle Ages, but by then, they'd been banished to the Void and were unable to hear their servant's entreaties."

"I don't understand a damn thing you just said. Get to the point, preacher-man."

"They wait until our souls have departed, and then they take up residence in the empty space left behind. Specifically—in our brains."

"Animals have souls too?"

Martin nodded. "Every living thing has a soul. And that energy leaves the body at death. All the Siqqusim have to do is wait in the Void for one of us to die, and then they move right in."

"And that means we're fucked," Frankie said. "Because sooner or later everything dies."

Martin smiled.

"Everything dies, Frankie. But not everything has an ending."

"Who are you? Obi freaking Kenobi? What the hell is that supposed to mean?"

"You'll understand in time. Meanwhile, let's get back to the zombies—or perhaps, more accurately, the demons. You're right. The odds look grim. The Siqqusim boast that their numbers are more than the stars, more than infinity. But the truth is something different. Although there are many more of them than there are us, they have a finite number, just like everything else. The only thing that's infinite is God. That's a fundamental rule of the universe, and even the stars bow to it. We only see the Siqqusim as infinite, because we cannot fathom their number. It's like trying to count the number of stars in the universe. Although they are finite, it would be impossible for us to do so."

"How do you know all this?"

Martin laughed. "I know many new things. There is great knowledge where I live now."

"Where you live now? In case nobody bothered to tell you, Martin, you're dead. You're fucking arm came off in that car crash. Jim split that gray old head of yours open like a watermelon when your corpse came back. Where you live, my ass. You don't live at all."

"But I do. I exist on a higher plane. That's what I'm

trying to get through to you, Frankie. Our bodies are just shells, casings made of flesh and blood to temporarily house our souls. When our souls move on, these things take over the shell. But with the exception of Ob and some of the other major demons, they have to wait their turn."

"Who the fuck is Ob? That's the one the scientist told you and Jim about?"

"He's the one, the leader of the Siqqusim. You, Jim, and I actually crossed paths with him, though we didn't know it at the time. When we were all at the government facility in Hellertown. Ob led that zombie army. And soon, you will all meet him again."

"Well that's just wonderful. Looking forward to it. You got any other cheery news for me?"

She noticed that the forest had grown dark. Clouds blocked out the sunlight filtering through the treetops.

"There are ancient laws, set forth by God before this planet ever existed. These are not laws of physics or science, but of magic—which is a force more powerful than any other. And a force that sadly, mankind has forgotten."

"You know something?" Frankie observed. "You look and sound like Martin, but you talk differently. Your words are different."

The preacher ignored her. "One of the laws is that once the Siqqusim have been freed from the Void, they reanimate the flesh and blood constructs of the planet they're on. But those host bodies have limits, and sooner or later, must give in to decay. Once the body is destroyed, the departed Siqqusim returns to the Void and awaits transference to a new host. The process begins anew. Finally, when they have destroyed the planet's life forms, they move on to somewhere else, just like locusts, and start all over again."

"So you're telling me that if we stay alive long enough, there's a chance these things will move on to another planet and not come back? That we can just wait for the zombies to rot apart and turn to dust and sooner or later, they'll leave us alone?"

"Yes and no."

"I'm gonna smack you, talking in riddles like that. And I guess you expect me to believe in little green men too?"

"There are a multitude of life forms out there, Frankie, and yes, some of them are green and others are what we would consider little. There are also life forms on other planes of existence, other realities. And Ob's kind has reign over them all. But I don't speak in riddles. The Siqqusim aren't the only demons awaiting release from the Void. There are other groups of creatures there; a second and third wave of demons that, according to magical law, cannot be released until a certain percentage of life has been destroyed. That is one of the reasons why the zombies are so intent on destroying us—so that this second wave of possessions can begin, and they themselves can move on to the next planet."

"How much? What percentage of the population has to die before this next wave begins?"

Martin shook his head. "I cannot tell you. It is forbidden. Look to your Bible. It is full of numerology. And there are other books too, tomes even older than the original Bible or Koran. Books like the *Daemonolateria*."

"Never heard of it."

"Some call it a spell book, but it is really nothing more than a book of laws. Everything, even demons, must obey the laws of the universe. There is a finite number of living beings on every planet, and once a percentage of those living beings have been corrupted, each new wave is free to attack."

"And I guess that new wave takes over the rest of us that are left alive?"

"No. The Siqqusim are given reign over mammals, birds, reptiles, and amphibians. But those aren't the only life forms on this planet, or on any other planet for that matter. Look around you."

Frankie paused.

"The plants. You're talking about the plants."

Martin nodded.

Around them, the greenery began to wither and turn brown. A leaf crumbled at her touch.

"Zombie plants, Martin? You've got to be kidding me."

"The plants, and the insect life that exists on this planet, which is neither mammal nor reptile nor amphibian. There are over two hundred million insects per each person on this planet. Both the plant and insect kingdoms are given to Ab and his kind."

"Ab?"

"Ob's brother and leader of the Elilum."

"Don't any of these creeps have normal names like Fred or Leon?"

"The Elilum possess the plant and insect kingdoms just as the Siqqusim do with mammals, amphibians, and reptiles."

"Fuck me running . . . How are we supposed to hide from bugs?"

Martin continued as if she hadn't spoken. "There is a third and final wave, and that one involves fire. The demons in that group have many names. In the Arab cultures, they are known as the Iffrit, but their true name is the Teraphim. Ob and Ab's brother, Api, leads them, and they are the most terrible of all. They are beings made of fire, and the earth burns with their every step. At the end of their reign, the entire planet is consumed."

"Well Jesus fucking Christ in a god-damned chicken basket, Martin! What kind of a chance does that give us? I mean, if all the plants die, then we've got no fucking oxygen, but that doesn't really matter anyway because everything gets burned up at the very end!"

As if in answer, the dead, brown plant life began to move. Desiccated vines snaked across the forest floor, slithering around her other self. A withered tree limb speared Jim through the chest. A giant Venus flytrap's jaws slammed shut on Danny, swallowing the boy whole. His muffled screams echoed from inside the plant.

"There are rules, Frankie. The third wave cannot leave the Void and begin until all life forms—all of them—are destroyed. The Elilum can run amok once the Siqqusim have destroyed a percentage of life. But the Teraphim cannot be loosed upon the planet until all the kingdoms of life are gone. Don't you see?"

"So what are you telling me? Go hide out in a greenhouse somewhere and make sure we keep enough of us alive, keep having babies and growing new trees and shit? Make sure we keep some animals and bugs alive too? That way we prevent the other attacks from happening? We're just supposed to wait it out, and then repopulate and reseed the fucking planet when the third wave doesn't happen? What is this Noah's ark bullshit, preacher-man?"

Martin didn't respond.

"Or are you telling me that it's hopeless—that we're gonna die? That we'll lose these bodies but go on to this other place where you went? That's it, isn't it, Martin?"

The old man was gone.

"Soon as people start getting eaten, you pull a Houdini. Am I allowed to wake up now?"

Remember, his voice whispered inside her head, *everything dies, but not everything has an ending.*

Around her, the forest continued to die. Then it started to come back to life again.

Frankie awoke in her hospital bed. Somewhere above her head, an alarm was shrieking.

THIRTEEN

"What is it, Daddy?" Danny sat up, startled awake by the blaring alarm. His eyes were sleepy but frightened. "What's going on?"

"I don't know, buddy. Hang on a second. I'll check."

Jim jumped out of bed and pulled on his jeans. There was some kind of commotion outside, people running down the hallway, clamoring voices. He opened the door, barefoot and shirtless, and shivered in the air-conditioning. The alarm continued to blare over the building's speaker system.

An overweight man ran past him. Jim grabbed his shoulder.

"Sir, can you tell me what's going on?"

The man scowled, out of breath. "Emergency meeting, buddy. Just like the drills. What rock you been sleeping under?"

"I'm new here. We just arrived . . ."

"Oh, sorry about that. Well, like I said, they're calling an emergency meeting. Everybody is supposed to meet in the auditorium right away. And they never do drills at this hour, so whatever's going on, it must be real. Best get down there."

The man pulled away, hurrying on before Jim could ask him how to get to the auditorium. He dimly recalled seeing it during Smokey's tour of the building, but he couldn't remember what floor it was on.

Jim ducked back inside and shut the door just as the alarm stopped.

Danny was sitting up in bed, looking small and frail. "Is there trouble, Daddy? Are the monster-people coming?"

"I don't know, squirt. I'm sure it's okay. Probably just a drill."

Danny looked confused. "You mean like a fire drill? We had those in school. They were kind of fun."

"You know what? Why don't you get dressed and we'll see what's happening?"

"Okay."

Danny clambered out of bed, his hair mussed and his face creased from the pillow. He slipped out of his pajamas and into some clothes that Jim laid out for him. While he dressed, Jim slipped into his shirt, socks, and work boots. It felt strange to be wearing the steel-toed boots again, the same dusty, weather-beaten boots that had carried him from West Virginia to here. Once again, he thought of Martin. And Frankie.

Frankie . . .

Jim wondered if they should check on her. If there was trouble, they needed to make sure she'd be safe, and aware of what was happening. He felt a sudden twinge of unidentifiable dread.

"Daddy?"

"What, Danny?"

"I'm worried about Frankie."

Danny felt it too, whatever it was.

"So am I."

"Maybe we should go check on her," Danny suggested. "Make sure she's getting better."

"I think that's a good idea. Let's go."

Jim locked the door behind them. The hallways were crowded with people, and they elbowed their way through the throng. Danny clutched Jim's hand so they wouldn't get separated.

It took ten minutes to get an elevator that wasn't heading downstairs. They stepped inside and the elevator lurched upward. While they waited, Jim's apprehension grew worse.

Danny squeezed his hand.

Jim smiled, trying to be brave for his son. He felt anything but.

DiMassi belched, and said, "What's up, fellas?"

Branson nodded, but said nothing. He continued to watch the corridor.

"I thought you had tuberculosis or some shit," Carson said. "What the hell are you doing here?"

"Nah, I'm fine." DiMassi coughed. "Forrest told me to get up here on the double. What the fuck is going on? This better be important. I was asleep."

Branson shrugged, stifling a yawn. Carson just glared at the overweight pilot.

"Listen up," Quinn whispered. "Ramsey's gone off the deep end."

"Say what?" The fat pilot's belly hung over his belt, wiggling as he laughed. He stank of sweat and cigarette smoke.

"I'm serious," Quinn insisted. "The whole building's

getting cabin fever or something. Everybody's going crazy. Maynard and Kilker snapped today too."

Carson's face darkened at the mention of both.

"Sorry man," Quinn apologized, and then turned back to DiMassi. "Maynard tried to kill Carson and Doc Stern, and Kilker jumped off the roof this morning."

DiMassi turned to Carson. "That true, faggot?"

"Yeah." The young soldier nodded in affirmation. "And I told you before, you fat fuck. Don't call me a faggot."

"Both of you knock it off," Quinn bristled. "We don't have time for that shit. Mr. Ramsey's lost it, too. He's no longer fit for command, and apparently, something big is getting ready to go down. Bates wants us to take him."

"Kill him?" DiMassi asked.

Quinn shook his head. "No, we're just supposed to arrest him. Doc Stern's got a safe room set aside to restrain him in."

"What's this big thing that's supposed to happen?" Carson asked.

Branson stiffened, and glanced at Quinn. The red-haired pilot shrugged.

"There's an army on the way here," Branson told them while cleaning his glasses on his shirt. "A zombie army. They've got heavy armament—tanks, Bradleys, the works."

"Shit," Carson breathed. "What's their ETA?"

"Anytime now."

DiMassi sneered. "Fuck. I'm out of commission for a few days and this whole place goes crazy. What's big bad Bates's plan for this army?"

"I don't know," Quinn admitted. "All I know is we've got our orders."

"This doesn't seem right," DiMassi grumbled, "arresting Mr. Ramsey. I mean, he's Darren fucking Ramsey. The guy's a celebrity. A billionaire. Maybe Bates is mistaken. You guys ever consider that?"

The other men didn't respond. Weapons drawn, they crept down the hallway. Quinn produced a key card that Bates had given him, and slid it into the office door. The door opened silently. Inside, the office was pitch black. The air-conditioning hummed quietly.

Quinn fell back as Carson and Branson rushed in. Quinn charged in behind them, ducking low. DiMassi brought up the rear, and flicked on the lights. It looked like a hurricane had blown through the office. The computer monitor lay smashed on the floor, and the tower casing was dented. Shredded paperwork lay strewn like confetti. The desk's contents were scattered across the carpet. Chairs and lamps had been knocked over, and soil from the potted palm tree covered everything.

Quinn pointed at Branson and indicated the private restroom door, then motioned for Carson to check the closet.

"It's clear, dog," Carson confirmed.

"He's not in here either," Branson called.

"Why would Mr. Ramsey do this to his own office?" DiMassi asked.

"Because," Quinn said, ruffling through some paperwork, "I told you. He's suffered some kind of breakdown."

"How do we know Bates didn't do this? Maybe him and Forrest are gonna pull a coup."

The other three looked at him with distaste.

"Come off it, DiMassi," Branson grumbled. "You really think Bates would lie about this?"

"Wouldn't surprise me one bit. Makes more sense than this cock-and-bull story about Mr. Ramsey going insane."

"That's crap and you know it," Carson snapped. "You're just pissed off because Bates reprimanded you last month for taking the chopper out without clearance."

"Shut up, Carson," DiMassi warned.

"Why should I? It's true. You took that blond schoolteacher for a ride, just so you could get laid."

"Least I got laid by a woman, you fucking faggot."

Carson ran across the room, fists clenched. His eyes shone with anger.

Quinn stepped between them.

"Knock it off, both of you! We've got a job to do. DiMassi, you stay here in case Ramsey comes back."

"But I—"

"Carson. Branson. You guys come with me. We'll check out the rest of the floor."

"Quinn," DiMassi argued, "this is bullshit! If there's a fucking army getting ready to attack us, we should be doing something about it, not looking for the old man."

The two pilots squared off. Quinn stepped closer, his face inches away from DiMassi's. The fat pilot's breath reeked, and drops of sweat beaded on his forehead. Quinn's nose wrinkled in disgust.

"I told you," he hissed, "that Bates has it under control. Now unless you want to face disciplinary action when this is all over and done with, I suggest you do as you're told. We don't need you, DiMassi. In case you've forgotten, Steve and I can fly that fucking chopper too. You dig?"

DiMassi stepped back. "Yeah, man. I'm cool. Shit, Quinn, you don't have to bite my head off."

Ignoring him, Quinn stalked out of the office. Carson and Branson followed. On his way out, Carson blew DiMassi a kiss and curtsied.

"Call me a faggot when this is all over, you fat fuck."

A pencil snapped beneath DiMassi's boot. He sat Ramsey's leather chair upright, and then plopped down in it. The springs creaked beneath his weight. He laid his pistol on the desk and cracked his knuckles. His shoulders slumped, and after a moment, he closed his eyes and rested.

He opened them again a few minutes later, when he felt the cold barrel of a gun pressed against the back of his head.

"Mr. DiMassi," Ramsey whispered, "I would appreciate it if you did not move. My office is already a mess. It would be a shame to add the interior of your cranium to it."

Yawning and bewildered, Don stared around in confusion, trying to find a seat in the crowded auditorium. The rows were full, and more people stood in the back and in the aisles. He got his first sense of just how many people occupied the skyscraper. They milled around, half-awake like himself, wondering what was going on. The sounds of rustling papers and nervous babbling filled the room.

Don searched the crowd, looking for a familiar face. There was no sign of Jim or Danny, and he wondered where they were. He thought of Frankie, wondered if she was okay, and then pushed it from his mind. His head pounded. He'd woken with a hangover and then realized just how little sleep he'd gotten before the alarm sounded.

"Don! Hey, Don!"

Smokey waved to him from the front. Don weaved his way down the aisle and then cut through the row, excusing himself to each person that he slid by. He took a seat between Smokey and Etta, who still had in her curlers. Leroy sat next to her, his eyes half-open, his face cloudy.

"Where are your friends?" Smokey asked.

"Frankie's still in sick bay, I guess. I don't know where Jim and Danny are. What's going on?"

"Emergency meeting."

"This better not be another god-damned drill," Leroy grumbled.

"I don't think it is," Smokey muttered. "Didn't you guys notice how troubled Forrest was acting tonight, when he stopped by the card game? Something's up."

"Any idea what?" Don asked.

"Looks like we're about to find out," Etta said, nodding to the front.

Bates walked out onto the stage, flanked by Forrest and Stern. There were scattered cheers, some brief applause, and a few shrill whistles; but for the most part, the audience was subdued. Without pausing, Bates strolled up to the podium and spoke into the microphone.

"Good morning."

There was an electronic squeal of feedback. He paused, and then repeated himself.

"Good morning. I know that it's very early, and I want to thank you all for your promptness. I assure you that this is not a drill."

A rumble of concern rippled through the crowd.

"At approximately 0100 hours—"

"Wait a minute," Etta interrupted. "Aren't we forgetting something?"

Bates paused, and bowed his head.

"Of course," he apologized. "Thank you, Etta. Forrest, will you lead us?"

The crowd rose to their feet and a hush fell over them. Forrest stepped to the podium and sang the first line of the National Anthem.

"Oh, say can you see . . ."

Don stared in amazement. Forrest sounded like an angel. It was like Marvin Gaye had been reincarnated in the body of this hulking soldier. Goose bumps broke out along Don's arms as he joined in. The crowd's voices swelled as one, buffeting against him like waves. Many people were holding hands and many more were crying.

When it ended, Forrest launched right into another song, one that Don didn't recognize.

"In times of wounded hearts, when souls are torn apart . . ."

Next to him, Smokey, Etta and Leroy sang along. Don listened to the words.

"We need to let them heal, and time it will reveal. For all the things that we believe in—freedom in our time, for all the people in the world. I know that we will rise."

Don shivered.

"I know that we will rise . . ."

When the song was over, Don leaned over to Smokey and whispered, "What was that?"

"It's a song called 'Our Dream,' by a musician named Fiz."

"The pop star? He was from New York, right?"

"Yeah. He wrote it about the first terrorist attack on the city, but now we've adopted it."

"What happened to him? He was huge!"

Smokey shrugged. "Probably got eaten—or ate somebody else."

"Thank you all, again," Bates said.

The crowd returned to their seats, quieting down once more, with the exception of some sniffling and one woman's sobs.

"At approximately 0100 hours, our communications center detected a large, mobile zombie force. We determined that they were heading here, to Ramsey Towers."

Shocked gasps, and even a muffled scream, met this statement.

"They are heavily armed. We've verified both through continued monitoring and through visual confirmation that they are now within the city limits. Their intent is to launch an assault on this building. We must assume that this attack could come at any moment, so I'll be brief."

"What are we so concerned about?" a man yelled from the back. "This building is supposed to be able to withstand anything."

There were shouts of agreement. Bates cleared his throat and the room got quiet again.

"Indeed, Mr. Ramsey has repeatedly assured us that this building could withstand any attack. However, he designed it with terrorism and natural disasters in mind. It is my opinion, and the opinion of others in our command structure, that it will not hold up to the sheer amount of firepower we expect to be launched at us."

"They've attacked us before," another man hollered. "What makes it different this time?"

"This is a full-scale military attack. They didn't have tanks and artillery before, and they didn't have a leader."

Don thought about something that Jim had mentioned to him; that there had been a zombie named Ob who led the others. But Bates couldn't be talking about the same creature, could he?

"His name is Ob," Bates continued, "and though we don't know much about him yet, it's clear that he seeks our destruction. So we must fight. Every able-bodied man and woman will be given a weapon immediately after we adjourn. You will join those already on sentry duty. This is not open for debate. I expect each and every one of you to defend yourselves and your fellow man—because we cannot do it for you. Forrest will be in charge of the lower floors and I will be in command of the upper stories of the building. If you refuse to help protect this building, you will be put out onto the streets."

An old man rose to his feet. "You can't do that!"

"Try me. I'm not playing around here, people."

"What about Mr. Ramsey?" a woman called out. "Why isn't he in charge?"

Dr. Stern stepped forward and took the microphone. "Mr. Ramsey is ill and unable to assume command. It's not life-threatening. But he gave express orders that Mr. Bates was to lead this battle."

Bates shouted down another question. "We must prepare immediately. None of us could have ever conceived what has happened to our world. It's like something out of a horror movie. But it's real, and it's coming for us all. There's no more time for debate."

He paused, gripping the podium. When he spoke again, his voice cracked.

"I know that it looks hopeless. Believe me. We ask ourselves, late at night, what the point of all this is. For all we know, we might be the last people left alive in the world. Those things are everywhere, and there are more every day. All they have to do is wait for us to die. So why bother?"

Some murmured ascension and nodding heads greeted his question. Bates continued.

"Because this is our last stand. Think about everything humanity has accomplished throughout history. Do we really want it all to mean nothing in the end? Should our achievements be worthless—appreciated and enjoyed only by those things outside? We stand at the brink of total extinction, but I will not go without a fight."

Scattered applause broke out amongst the crowd, but many more people remained quiet, still unsure.

"Maybe you're thinking this sounds hokey or stilted. You're probably right. I'm not a public speaker. I'm a warrior. I don't have a lot of oratory skill, and it's not easy for me to inspire people through speech. Believe me, I've been in situations where I've had men looking at me for inspiration. I gave it to them through leadership. I inspired by example. Hopefully, I can do that for you too. But let me tell you of another example. A few days ago, our scouts brought in a father and his son."

Don sat up straight, listening.

"The father, Jim Thurmond, traveled from the mountains of West Virginia all they way up the coast to New Jersey. He and his companions faced unimaginable horrors with every step of his journey—things that we haven't even considered, clustered away here in our stronghold. Mr. Thurmond did this for one reason and one reason only. The love he had for his son. That's what powered him, what kept him going.

"I ask you to look around. Is there someone here whom you love? Will you lay down your life so that they have a chance to continue to live? Perhaps your loved ones aren't here. Maybe they're outside, their bodies corrupted by those things. Maybe our enemies have turned the one you love into a perverse mockery of who they were before. How many of you saw your loved ones turn into a zombie? Don't you want an opportunity to set things right? This may be the last chance any of us will get. It's us versus them. I say we reintroduce these things to death. Show them what it really means to die. Show them just what humanity is capable of when its back is against the wall! Will you fight?"

Thunderous applause filled the auditorium. The crowd rose to their feet, cheering wildly. Bates held his fist in the air and pumped it a few times, eliciting more shouts.

"Report to the armory," he shouted. "Each of you will be assigned a weapon and get a crash course in how to use it. From there, you'll be directed to where we need you. Let's show them that we are not afraid to die, that we reject their promise of what comes after death. Let's show them that we will not go quietly! Let's reclaim our bodies—and our lives!"

Bates strode off the stage. Forrest and Stern followed him. All three were already talking into their radios.

"Well," Leroy quipped, "I guess it wasn't a drill after all."

As they filed out, Don's legs felt numb, as if they'd fallen asleep. Fear gripped him, but at the same time, he felt determined—and proud. He wondered again what had happened to Jim and Danny, and how Frankie was—if she was aware of what was going on. Then he fell in with the crowd and was swept away.

DiMassi's pistol was tucked in the waist of Ramsey's tailored slacks. Ramsey clutched his own pistol in a liver-spotted hand, pointing it directly at DiMassi's chest.

"I assure you, Mr. DiMassi, that I am not crazy. I'm just trying to save us."

"Begging your pardon, sir, but then why do you have that gun pointed at me?"

"Bates is drunk on power," Ramsey said, his voice calm and assured. "He's attempting a coup, and he's involved Dr. Stern and Forrest as well. Think about it, DiMassi. We are about to come under attack. Does this seem like the most opportune time to arrest me?"

DiMassi agreed that it seemed odd.

"They've killed Dr. Maynard and poor Kilker, because both of them tried to warn me of their plans."

"But are we really going to be attacked, sir?"

"Look out the window," Ramsey told him. "Go ahead. Look and see for yourself."

DiMassi pressed his face against the glass and looked down upon the city. The streets were blazed with thousands of pinpoints of light. Ant-sized vehicles and miniscule zombies surrounded the building, and more were on the way. Barricades had been constructed, sealing off the block. As he watched, the creatures began to set the neighboring buildings on fire.

"Holy shit," DiMassi breathed. "There must be thousands of them!"

"Indeed," Ramsey nodded. "Now do you see? Bates is out of control, and you've been tricked into following along with him."

"Okay," DiMassi nodded, unable to tear his eyes away from the scene unfolding far below. "I believe you. Hell, I always did. Used to watch you on TV, had stock in your company."

Ramsey smiled, and lowered his gun.

"The question," DiMassi continued, "is what are we going to do about it?"

"We must flee," Ramsey said. "We can't remain here any longer."

"But, I thought the building could—"

"This tower can take anything those creatures throw at it. But that is not my concern. There is simply no way Bates will let either of us live now. He's absolutely mad. He may very well be in league with the zombies. It pains me to say this, but our only chance for survival—indeed, humanity's only chance, is to flee immediately."

"But to where? Quinn and I have been all over. The fucking zombies are everywhere."

"Leave that to me."

"We should stop off and grab one of those M-60's. Happiness is a belt-fed weapon, after all. If we're going on foot, we'll need a lot more firepower."

"We're not traveling by foot. There was a subway tunnel under construction beneath this building, but sadly, it was never completed. And obviously, we can't go out into the streets."

"The helicopter?" DiMassi looked up, as if he could see it through the ceiling.

"The helicopter. How far can it fly?"

"Depends on how much fuel is in it. Quinn and the Canuck were the last ones to take it out. I don't know if they refueled."

"Could we make it as far as the Haverstraw marina?"

"Up near Brackard's Point? Sure—even on fumes. But the airstrip in Brackard's Point is overrun."

"But you could land us near the marina, yes?"

"Yeah. Not much there. Blue-collar folks' boats, mostly."

"You'd be surprised." Ramsey winked. "I keep one there myself, away from the media's prying eyes."

"Why not just steal a boat here in the city? Maybe one of those armored Harbor Patrol boats or something?"

"You've seen the situation below. Do you really think

our enemies wouldn't have anticipated that, and taken the appropriate counter-measures?"

"I guess not."

"You will fly us to Haverstraw, and from there, we shall begin the second leg of our journey."

"We gonna go to an island?"

"Something like that." Ramsey's smile faded. "I have many strongholds. One is directly beneath this building, far below the tunnels and sewers and pipes and layers of fiber optic cables. But I fear we'd never reach it, especially not as a group."

"A group?" DiMassi glanced around, verifying that it was just the two of them.

"We'll need others, of course. A woman, at the very least, for breeding. Two of them, if possible. We have to keep the human race alive."

DiMassi nodded in agreement, half listening. He watched the burning buildings below, watched the zombies as they swarmed around the skyscraper. His mind was still on the boat, wondering how dangerous a journey on the open water would be. Then he looked back outside and decided it couldn't be as perilous as staying here.

"A woman would be good," he said.

"Perhaps the young woman under Dr. Stern's care?" Ramsey suggested. "She is strong and beautiful—fierce. She was brought in two days ago."

"Sure. Haven't seen her myself, since I was quarantined, but I'll take your word for it."

A red light pierced the darkness outside the window. Both men turned.

"They're shooting flares," DiMassi gasped. "What the hell are they up to?"

"A signal of some kind, I should imagine. Perhaps we'd best be going. I think our time grows short."

"Maybe we should just forget the broad," DiMassi said. "Get the hell out now."

"Nonsense. It has fallen to us to save the human race. How are we to do that if we can't procreate?"

The pilot shrugged and retrieved his pistol from the desk.

"Go into the hall and see if the coast is clear," Ramsey commanded.

DiMassi peeked outside. There was no sign of Quinn or the others.

"We're good," he said.

"Excellent. Let us proceed."

The two men hurried for the elevators.

The wailing siren echoed inside Frankie's head even after it stopped.

"H-hello?" Her throat felt like sandpaper, and her voice rasped as she tried again. Her head throbbed.

"Is anybody there?"

There was no response. The equipment around her bed beeped and hummed in the silence. The room smelled of antiseptic.

"Anyone?"

When her queries went unanswered, she sat up and took several deep breaths, slowly regaining her strength. The weakness in her limbs melted away after a few minutes. Other than the headache, thirst, and an insistent urge to pee, she felt fine. Better than she had since kicking heroin. Her stitches itched, but the flesh around them was a healthy pink, rather than the vicious red of the day before.

"Got to hand it to them," she said aloud. "They really fixed me up."

She slipped out of the bed, swallowed several times to

wet her throat, and padded to the bathroom. She sat down on the cold toilet seat, shivering in relief.

As she sat there, Frankie considered her options. She could get back into bed and wait for the doctor or nurse to show up. Or, she could find her clothes, get dressed, and track down Jim, Danny, and Don.

Deciding on the second option, she pulled her panties back up and flushed. Something was obviously happening, unless the alarm had been a drill. And the absence of the medical staff concerned her as well.

When she walked out of the bathroom, a man was standing next to the bed, pointing a gun at her. She recognized him from television—Darren Ramsey, the billionaire developer. Except that without a team of makeup artists and public relations handlers, he looked old. Sick. Frankie also recognized the look in his eyes. She'd seen it before, in the gaze of certain johns. Ramsey was insane. Next to him was a fat, greasy, nervous-looking man.

"Please," Ramsey said, "don't be alarmed. We won't harm you."

"You planning on lowering that pistol anytime soon? That would go a long way toward helping me relax."

"Of course." He smiled, and dropped it to his side. "You must excuse me. We weren't sure who, or what, was coming out of the bathroom."

The fat man's eyes crawled over her, resting on her breasts and the triangle of hair between her legs, peeking out below her hem. Frankie pulled the gown down as far as it would go and glared at him.

"Anything more than a look costs you twenty," she quipped.

His face turned a dark, angry scarlet.

Ramsey opened his mouth. "My name is—"

"I know who you are," Frankie interrupted. "Seen

you on television a bunch of times. You're Darren Ramsey. Who's this?"

"Frank DiMassi," the fat man grumbled, then turned to Ramsey. "We've got to get going, sir."

The old man nodded impatiently.

"You'll have to excuse us—I'm sorry, I didn't catch your name?"

"Frankie."

"You'll have to excuse us, Frankie. The building is about to come under attack."

"What?"

"I'm afraid so. We're completely surrounded. The zombies have gathered an army like nothing I've ever seen. Mr. DiMassi and myself are leaving for a safe location. We'd be honored to have you accompany us."

Frankie's eyes darted to the gun and then back up to his face. His smile faltered a bit under the scrutiny, and his upper lip and forehead were beaded with sweat.

"Thanks," she said, side-stepping past him, "but I've got friends that came in with me. I need to check on them, make sure they're all right."

"I assure you, Frankie, if your companions are on the floors below, their fate is sealed. It would be better—safer—if you came with us."

Frankie edged farther away, but doing so put her closer to DiMassi. The fat man licked his lips, gawking at her legs.

"Thanks anyway," Frankie said, "but if it's all the same to you guys, I'll take my chances finding them."

Ramsey raised the pistol again.

"I'm afraid I must insist. I'd hoped it wouldn't come to this, but you are essential to my plan for repopulating the planet. DiMassi, if you would, please?"

The fat man lunged, crushing her beneath his weight.

* * *

Ramsey Towers rose into New York's gray pre-dawn sky, already half-obscured by the smoke pouring from the burning buildings around it. Beyond the reach of the flames, thousands of zombies formed ranks, surrounding the block.

Ob gazed out at the undead force, reveling in the sheer size of his army. Then he turned his attention back to the skyscraper.

Inside, humans took position at the windows, or scurried back and forth behind them like frightened mice. Mounds of splintered, broken furniture lay strewn around the building's exterior plaza and sidewalks, forming a crude but effective barricade. The exterior doors and the windows on the first five floors, including the large plate-glass windows in the lobby, had been boarded over.

One of his lieutenants approached him. Its intestines hung loose, swaying with each step. Flies clung to the strands.

Ob turned to him. "I take it that the last flare signals everything is in order?"

"Everything is in position, my lord. Our forces are ready."

"Excellent," Ob hissed, exhaling fetid air. "Let's finish this, so that our remaining brothers can be free of the Void once and for all. Commence the attack."

The zombie lieutenant barked orders back to the line. Minutes later, a box-truck cruised down the street, rolling to a stop in front of the skyscraper. The zombie behind the wheel gunned the engine, revving it to a frenetic crescendo. Then the truck shot forward. It crashed up over the curb, racing along the sidewalk.

Above, windows opened and the humans fired at the

vehicle. Undead birds immediately swarmed the snipers. The humans reeled backward, screaming and clawing as the birds poured themselves through the open windows. A shotgun plummeted to the ground, clattering on the pavement. A zombie darted forth from the lines and snatched it, but fell sprawling as a bullet obliterated his head.

Another zombie stepped forward and pulled the pin on a grenade. Before he could throw it, a round tore into his wrist, severing his hand. The hand fell to the ground at his feet, still clutching the grenade. A second later, the explosion tore the creature apart.

"Now that's what I call a hand grenade," Ob quipped. "That's what he gets for not following orders."

His lieutenant said nothing.

The truck continued to pick up speed, rocketing toward the building. It crashed through the barricades and roared toward the lobby entrance.

"This is going to be good," the lieutenant gloated.

Ob agreed. "Let's knock and see if anybody is home."

Cullen and Newman both hated the midnight watch, but they hated lobby duty even more. Normally, they would have been relieved at dawn, when the next shift took over. But now, with the attack underway, Bates had ordered them to hold their position. He'd promised that reinforcements were on the way down.

Neither man had been a soldier before the rising. Newman had worked in a recording studio, and Cullen had been an attorney. Now, they were volunteers in Ramsey Towers's security squad. Never had they regretted that duty more than they did now. The lobby stank, not just from the constant stench of the rotting flesh outside, but from the smoke as well. It seeped into the building from various cracks in the windows, and through the ventilation system.

"What's happening?" Cullen hissed from behind the sandbagged receptionist desk. He remained crouched, not wanting Newman to see him shaking.

"I can't see much because of the smoke." Newman peered through a peephole. "The fuckers are burning everything down though, man."

"Figures," Cullen snorted. "The rain stops just when we need it."

"Yeah," Newman agreed. "Guess it don't matter. I don't think we're going to see the sunrise today."

"Hope the reinforcements get here soon," Cullen said. "I'm fucking tired, man. We've been up all night."

"Dude, we're about to be attacked. You really think you're going to get some sleep?"

"No," Cullen admitted, "but I thought maybe I'd track down Rebecca."

"Who's that? The nurse?"

"No, that's Kelli. Rebecca works in the greenhouse up on the fifteenth floor. Met her a few days ago in the gym. I'm worried about her."

"Better worry about yourself instead, man. Stay focused on what's happening."

The elevator dinged and its doors slid open. Ten more heavily armed men stepped out of it and hurried toward them, taking positions. Their gear clanked as they ran.

"What's the situation?" one of them barked.

"We're not sure," Newman responded.

"How many are out there?"

Suddenly, Newman gasped in alarm. He backed away

from the peephole as headlights raced toward the blockaded doors.

"Oh sh—"

A second later, they saw the sunrise after all.

It burst inside the lobby.

FOURTEEN

The fertilizer bomb exploded as the truck crashed through the barriers, the massive concussion rocking the building. Fire and smoke ripped through the first floor. Shards of metal, chunks of concrete, and shattered glass hurtled into the air. The lobby and all inside it were instantly vaporized. Then, the billowing smoke cleared, revealing twisted steel girders and tongues of orange, flickering flame.

Amazingly, the building stood firm.

Ob watched through the binoculars. His gray lips pulled back in a grimace.

"The bomb didn't work as well as I'd hoped. That blast should have taken out the first five stories. Instead, it only destroyed a portion of the first floor and the parking garage. The building was touted as being indestructible. The designer was a bit of a gadfly, given to hype and self-grandeur. Perhaps it wasn't hype after all. No matter. Ready the artillery and the mortars. Take out the section where the building's generator is housed. I want the power out immediately. Also, bring the tanks forward and have them create some more entrances. And send in the first wave of foot soldiers."

As the column of tanks rumbled toward the skyscraper, a horde of zombies charged across the plaza toward the gaping hole created by the truck bomb. Heedless of the damage to their bodies, they strode through the flames. Their burning corpses emerged on the other side. Not slowing, they clambered through the wreckage. Moments later, they burst into the stairwells in search of more prey. When the stairs became crowded, they even climbed up the elevator shafts, using the service ladders and cables.

Then the screaming began.

The elevator doors slid open. Danny squeezed Jim's hand tighter as they stepped out.

"Was that thunder, Daddy?"

"Sure sounded like it. It rained most of the night, I think. But you're not scared of a little thunder and lightning, are you?"

Danny shook his head. "No, but Frankie might be."

"Why do you say that?"

"Because she's a girl."

"You might be surprised," Jim chuckled. "Frankie's pretty tough. Girls can do just about anything boys can do—Frankie especially. I bet she'll be happy to see us."

They started down the corridor. Despite the alarm, Jim was surprised that none of the medical staff was present. The entire floor was eerily silent. His boots echoed on the tiles.

"Do you like Frankie, Daddy?"

"Sure I like her. She helped me find you."

"Are you going to marry her now that Mommy and Carrie are dead?"

The question stopped Jim in his tracks.

"Now where did that come from?" he asked.

Danny shrugged. "I think she's pretty."

She is pretty, Jim thought to himself. *But with everything that's been happening, I guess that I never really thought about it until now.*

"I think we've got more important things to worry about right now," Jim said, hoping Danny would change the subject.

But the boy refused to be diverted. "I think she'd make a good mommy."

They approached Frankie's recovery room. Jim considered explaining to his son that Frankie had been a mommy, and what had happened to her child. But he decided against it. Danny had seen enough horror and lived through enough traumatic events. He deserved some time to be a kid again, free of violence and terror.

"Daddy?"

"What, buddy?"

"I smell smoke. Something's burning."

Before Jim could respond, the door to the recovery room opened and a man stepped out. He wore wrinkled gray trousers and a sweat-stained white dress shirt. His right hand clutched a pistol. Despite his disheveled look, Jim recognized him immediately. It was Darren Ramsey.

A large, unkempt man followed, pushing Frankie in a wheelchair. She'd been gagged, and bound to the wheelchair's armrests with rubber surgical tubing. A thin line of blood dribbled from her nose. Her eyes widened in surprise as she spotted Jim and Danny.

"Frankie!"

"Stay where you are," Ramsey ordered. "We mean you no harm. I'm Darren Ramsey."

"I know who you are," Jim said, pulling Danny

close. "That's my friend you have tied down in that wheelchair."

"I can assure you, it is for the young lady's own good. Her welfare—indeed, the welfare of us all—is my utmost concern."

"Is that why her nose is bleeding?"

"She became unruly. Her behavior has been quite erratic. I'm sure you know that the building has come under attack. We are simply restraining her so that we can move her to safety."

Frankie grunted, straining against the gag. The fat man's grip tightened on the wheelchair.

"Attack?" Jim stepped in front of Danny and slowly walked toward them. "I know there was an alarm, but I haven't heard anything about an attack. Where are you taking her?"

"To salvation. She will be the new Eve."

"I think you'd better let her decide that."

"That's far enough, Mr. Thurmond." Ramsey brought the pistol up.

"How do you know my name?"

"I know everything about my children, even when they are disruptive and disrespectful, as Bates is now behaving. I'm sure he's told you that he thinks I'm insane?"

"Listen," Jim held his hands up, "I don't know what you're talking about. If you and Bates have a problem, then that's something the two of you need to work out. All I know is that you've got my friend tied to that wheelchair, and she's hurt. Why don't you go ahead and untie her, and then we'll be on our way and let you fellows go do whatever it is you're doing."

"We are attempting to save her." Ramsey sighed. "And you are trying my patience, Mr. Thurmond. I offer you and your son the same salvation. Come with us. DiMassi and I intend to leave this place. Ramsey Towers could have withstood this attack, but with Bates in charge, its defenses will weaken. Our time here is over."

Beaming, he offered his free hand. The other hand tightened on the pistol grip.

Beside him, Frankie grunted again. "Ungh umnh!"

"No chance," Jim said, and stood his ground.

"Then you leave me no choice." Ramsey pointed the gun at his chest. "You are standing between us and the elevator to the roof. Get out of our way, Mr. Thurmond, or I can guarantee that you and your son will join the undead."

"Fuck this, Mr. Ramsey," DiMassi grunted. "Let's just use the stairwell on the other end of the hallway."

Jim clenched his fists and whispered, "Danny, run back to the elevators and get help."

Instead, Danny stepped forward, his own small hands balled into fists like his father's.

"You leave my Daddy alone, and let Frankie go!"

Ramsey laughed. "That is exactly the kind of spirit the next generation of humanity will need to survive. You will definitely be an asset, young man. You may come with us."

Danny darted forward and kicked Ramsey in the shin. Before Jim could move, DiMassi seized Danny. He twisted the boy's arm behind his back, and used Danny as a shield. Danny cried out.

"Don't move, Thurmond," Ramsey shouted. "Do as I say, and I give you my word that your son will live. Disobey me, and I will kill you all, starting with him."

"That will be the last thing you ever do, you son of a bitch. Leave him alone."

"This is not the time for bravado, Mr. Thurmond. I know your story. You traveled hundreds of miles to save your son. You won't let him die now."

Jim bit his lip. Blood filled his mouth.

Ramsey motioned with the pistol. "Get down on the floor, now."

Jim hesitated. He saw his own fear reflected in Danny and Frankie's eyes. Then, reluctantly, he sagged to his knees.

Ramsey grabbed Danny's ear and twisted it between his fingers.

"Let me go!"

"Quiet, you ungrateful little brat. You will do as I say, or I will kill your father."

Frankie struggled against her bonds.

Ramsey pinched Danny's ear harder. "Lay down on the floor, Thurmond, and put your hands over your head. DiMassi, bring the woman. We're leaving."

"The only way you're getting out of here with my son," Jim said, "is to go through me."

"Indeed?"

"Over my dead body." Jim drew himself up, ready to spring.

Ramsey cocked his head and smiled.

"Very well then. If you insist."

The gunshot echoed through the corridor.

The zombies swarmed onto the second floor, pouring from the stairwells and spilling out of the elevator shafts. The men and women defending the entrances had no time to scream, let alone impede their progress. Like a tidal wave, the zombies washed over them, slaughtering everything in their path.

Nurse Kelli was on the third floor, on her way back to

the medical wing to watch over Frankie and the quarantined family with tuberculosis, when the explosion occurred. The force of the blast knocked her to her feet, and ceiling tiles and insulation rained down on her. She lay there breathless, waiting to see if it would occur again.

She'd been assigned a small .22 semi-automatic pistol, which she knew how to use. Kelli's father and brothers had been avid target shooters and she'd received a marksman rating from the National Rifle Association years before. She'd been able to shoot a grouping of three tight enough to cover them with a quarter. Nailing a zombie in the head would be easy enough.

Picking herself back up and retrieving the pistol, Kelli ran for the stairwell. The gun made her feel safer. She wondered where Dr. Stern was, and hoped that he was okay.

Two men and a woman stood by the elevator doors, repeatedly jabbing the buttons.

"Don't take the elevators," Kelli cautioned. "That was an explosion."

"Are you sure?" one of the men asked. The others stared at her blankly.

"I think so, yes."

"Bates didn't say anything about explosions. What should we do?"

"Fight back."

"How?" one of the women asked. "There's nothing here to fight. They're all outside."

The man nodded. His voice was frantic, pleading. "Mr. Ramsey said they couldn't get in. He promised."

"Mr. Ramsey was full of shit," Kelli said.

The woman gasped. "You shouldn't talk like that! Mr. Ramsey saved us all."

Not bothering to respond, Kelli hurried on. She rounded the corner, and spotted an exit sign at the end of the hall. Just as she reached for the door, it slammed into her, shoved from the other side.

Zombies swarmed through the doorway and opened fire.

The first bullet caught her in the stomach. The second punched the breath and blood from her lungs in mid-scream. Kelli had time to see a butcher knife flashing downward and then her severed artery squirted blood into her eyes, blinding her. She slipped to the floor, crushed beneath their stomping feet.

She thought, *I never got to fire the pistol . . .*

Then a zombie was kneeling over her.

"You're still alive," it rasped. "Good. I will show you horror, wench."

She remembered her nightmare.

The zombie slid a razor blade across her breast, parting both cloth and flesh.

The fire alarm began to wail, drowning out her screams.

The first round of artillery explosions rolled across the city, sounding like thunder. The building shook. Lights swayed back and forth and furniture collapsed. Screams and gunfire echoed through the corridors. Above it all, the fire alarms shrieked.

Steve and Bates ran down the hall and ducked behind some sandbags.

"Is it an earthquake?" Steve shouted.

"No," Bates yelled. "They're shelling us!"

"But—but that doesn't make sense. They use us for food; possess us when they're done. They can't do either of those things if they blow us up."

"They aren't trying to blow us up," Bates grunted. "This is calculated. Think about it. In order to kill us, they have to get inside. The artillery barrage is creating entrances for them."

A second wave of explosions shook the skyscraper. Suddenly, the lights went out and the fire alarm faded. The emergency lights came on, but their illumination was faint.

"Shit." Bates grabbed for his radio. "They've knocked out the power."

The radio squawked. Forrest sounded frantic.

"We've lost contact with the lobby," he shouted. "I think they used a truck bomb, Bates. A fucking truck bomb! We've got zombies on the second and third floors. Two and three are breached. We're holding them off on four, but we need reinforcements."

Another voice broke in on the channel. "Sir, we've got birds on six and seven! They're coming in through the windows! We opened them to shoot at— They—"

The report was interrupted by one long, wailing scream. It went on and on, turning into a high-pitched shriek before finally tapering off.

"Forrest?"

"I'm here!" The sounds of gunfire erupted in the background. "Hard to see from all this smoke. They won't stop coming. There's just more and more of them!"

"Forrest, get your people out of there," Bates ordered. "You've got hostiles above and below your location. You've got to fight your way to the basement!"

The response was more gunfire, and muffled screams.

"Forrest, do you copy?"

Silence.

"Forrest?"

The channel went dead.

"The basement?" Steve checked his weapon. "What's in the basement?"

"A way out of here," Bates said. "It might be our only chance."

"But if they blew up the lobby, won't that have taken out the basement levels too?"

"I hope not. If the sprinkler system is still functioning, it should have been activated down there by now. That will help curtail the fires, along with the fireproofing between the floors. And the building's design features should keep the concussion damage confined to the lobby itself."

"What if you're wrong, Bates?"

"Then I'm wrong and we're dead. But to tell you the truth, Steve, we're probably dead anyway."

"But your speech—"

"Was designed to give these people false hope," Bates lowered his voice. "Look at the odds. Look at what we're facing. We can't win this fight, Steve. But I'll be damned if I'm sending these people to their deaths without seeing them put up a fight. It's how I was trained."

"So why the charade? Why not just tell everybody about this escape route?"

"Because there are too many of us. Believe me, I'd like to save everybody, but we can't. The more we take, the better the chance that we attract attention. Then we all die."

Steve was quiet for a moment. Another scream drifted from the radio, and then it went silent again. The hallway slowly filled with smoke.

"That's harsh, Bates—but I guess that's the kind of thinking that will enable us to survive. So what's the plan?"

"You're going to fly us out of here."

"What?"

"Pigpen says there's a tunnel that goes under the river and leads to the airport. You can still fly a jet, can't you?"

"I've flown commercial and experimental aircraft all of my life. I can fly anything. But that's not the point. You're trusting Pigpen? Come on, man. He thinks his cat is God, for crying out loud. How do we know JFK is safe? Even if we can find a plane, we've got to fuel it and—"

Bates held up his hand.

"Let's just worry about getting out of here first. Quinn and some of the others are busy looking for Mr. Ramsey. I'm going to tell them to cancel the search and meet us downstairs."

"Do I have time to go to my room?"

"For what?"

"I'd like to get the picture of my son."

"I'm sorry, Steve." Bates shook his head. "I really am. But there's no time, and I need you to stay with me. You're too important to lose."

He tried reaching Quinn on the radio, but there was no answer. The building shook again, and somewhere on their floor, people began to scream.

Bates sniffed the air. The stench of rotting flesh overpowered the smoke.

"They're here."

Frankie and Danny stared in horror, the gunshot still ringing in their ears. Blood splattered across Jim's face, chest and arms, bright against his pale skin.

Darren Ramsey's blood.

The pistol clattered onto the floor, and Ramsey followed it. He clawed at the hole in his chest, his face a mask of confusion.

"I don't understand . . ." he gasped.

Three men ran down the corridor behind Frankie, Danny, and DiMassi. Jim recognized one of them as Quinn, the helicopter pilot that had rescued them. He didn't know the other two.

DiMassi whirled, keeping Danny in front of him and a knife at the boy's throat.

Quinn and the other two soldiers slid to a halt, their machine guns raised.

"Let the kid go, DiMassi," Quinn shouted. "It's over!"

"Hey man," DiMassi protested. "I ain't involved with this."

"Bullshit," one of the younger soldiers said. "We heard you when we came down the stairwell, you fat fuck. Heard everything you and the old man were saying."

"Fuck you, Carson. Ramsey had me at gunpoint! What was I supposed to do?"

A radio clipped to Quinn's belt emitted a burst of static. Jim heard Bates's voice calling the pilot.

Quinn ignored it, his eyes not moving from DiMassi's.

"Come on, man, let the kid go. Hasn't he been through enough? Haven't we all?"

"And let you shoot me, the way you did Mr. Ramsey? I don't think so, Quinn."

On the floor, Ramsey groaned. Something gray and wet slipped from his belly. He tried to stuff it back in, but it flopped back out again.

With DiMassi's attention distracted, Jim inched toward Danny and Frankie.

The other young solider spoke up. "DiMassi, the zombies are inside the fucking building. It's only a matter of time before they make it up here. Let's figure this shit out together. Let the kid go. He hasn't done anything to you."

"You're lying, Branson," DiMassi said, but sounded uncertain. "If they were in the building already, we'd be dead."

"We will be soon, you idiot," Quinn snapped. "Jesus—can't you smell the smoke? Hear those fire alarms going off?"

"The building's fireproofed. It can't spread between floors."

"Didn't you hear the fucking explosions or feel the building sway? They're shelling us, you asshole! Fires are breaking out all over."

At that moment, the lights in the hallway flickered, and then vanished. The emergency lighting kicked in, casting an eerie red glow.

Jim took another step toward DiMassi.

Shoulders sagging, DiMassi let go of the boy. Carson and Quinn covered him with their rifles.

Danny ran to his father. Jim hugged him tight and made sure he was unharmed.

"Looks like you've saved us twice now, Quinn. Thanks."

"Thank me later, Jim. We've still got to get out of this building."

"Is it really as bad as you said?" Jim asked, removing Frankie's gag.

"Probably worse," Branson quipped.

Quinn nodded at Ramsey's unmoving body. "Check him out, Branson. I got him in the gut. Finish him off."

Jim undid Frankie's bonds. "You okay? Your nose is bleeding."

"Fat bastard kneed me in it when I was going for his balls, but yeah, I'm okay."

"Thank God. I was worried we'd lost you, just like Martin."

At the mention of his name, Frankie started to tell Jim about her dreams. But before she could, he turned to DiMassi.

"You think you're a big man, beating up on women and children?"

"Hey," Frankie protested, "he sucker punched me, or else I could have taken him myself."

"I was just following orders," DiMassi defended himself. "That's all."

Jim's voice was like ice. "Following orders? We've seen what happens when men like you follow orders. You shouldn't have touched my boy, you son of a bitch."

Quinn slid between them. "Jim, let me handle this. And Branson, hurry up with Ramsey, before he gets back up."

Branson prodded Ramsey with the barrel of his rifle. When there was no response, he cautiously knelt down beside him. The old man's eyes stared sightlessly.

"Be a shame to let this gold Rolex go to waste. Can I have it, Quinn?"

Ramsey's eyes blinked.

Before Quinn could answer, Ramsey's corpse sat up and knocked the rifle aside. His intestines boiled from the hole in his stomach, splattering onto the floor. His teeth sank into Branson's wrist. The young soldier screamed.

Using the distraction, DiMassi shoved Jim and Quinn out of the way and bolted for the stairwell.

"Carson," Quinn shouted, "Get him. Shoot him if you have to!" Then he grabbed Branson's shirt collar and pulled him backward. A hunk of Branson's flesh disappeared down the zombie's throat. Blood dripped from the ugly wound in Branson's arm.

"I have come to join my brothers," the thing that had

been Ramsey hissed. "As shall you all. We are undefeatable!"

The rifle kicked against Quinn's shoulder, and the zombie's head exploded. Ramsey fell to the floor a second time.

"Your building was supposed to be undefeatable too, you son of a bitch."

Carson took off down the hall in pursuit of DiMassi.

Quinn pulled out a pocketknife and cut a strip of cloth from Ramsey's pants leg. Then he tied the cloth around Branson's wound.

"You okay to move?"

Branson nodded. His face was pale and sweaty.

"I'm not going to be able to shoot for shit, but I'll live. Don't—think I'm gonna go into shock or anything."

"Just make sure you keep this tourniquet tight," Quinn told him. "Can't have you bleeding all over the place. That would be like leaving a trail of breadcrumbs."

Jim stepped forward. "I'll take your gun, if you don't mind."

Branson shrugged. "Sure."

Jim gave Ramsey's pistol to Frankie and then picked up the rifle for himself.

"You guys know how to use those?" Quinn asked.

"We didn't make it this far shooting spitballs," Frankie said. She got out of the wheelchair with a wince, and made a show of slapping her clip in and out of the semiautomatic pistol's handle.

Danny frowned. "How come I don't get a gun?"

"Doc Stern kept an aluminum baseball bat in that storage room over there," Quinn pointed. "He and Maynard used to hit the ball down the hallway. How would that be?"

Danny's face lit up. "Can I carry the bat, Daddy?"

"I guess." Jim sighed. "But if we come across any zombies, I want you to promise that you'll stay behind me and Frankie. Okay?"

Danny promised and then rooted through the storage closet. He came back out with the bat, and swung it like a sword.

"If they try to get us, I'll hit them in the nuts."

"Danny," Jim warned.

"Try their head instead," Frankie whispered, giving him a playful punch on the shoulder.

Quinn checked the tourniquet and then disappeared into one of the offices. He came back out with a bottle of painkillers and made Branson swallow four. Then he turned to the others.

"Let's go."

"What's the plan?" Frankie asked.

"We've got to catch up with Carson, and stop DiMassi before he gets to the helicopter. Then I'll radio Bates and see what our status is."

"And if Bates is dead?"

"I'll fly us out of here the same way I flew us in. The chopper will hold us."

"Where will we go?" Frankie said.

"Anywhere but here."

FIFTEEN

Don's hands shook, and the rifle jerked up and down. He fought to calm himself. His handkerchief, tied around his mouth and nose to block out the smoke, was drenched with sweat, and his muffled breathing sounded very loud in his ears. Don wondered if the zombies could hear it too. He sighted on the first corpse as it rounded the corner, and squeezed the trigger. The hollow-point punched through the creature's throat. The second drilled into its head, painting the wall behind it. More zombies emerged, blocking the corridor, and the glow of the emergency lights. Don poured bullets into them, readjusted his fire, and watched them drop with the second group of shots.

Smokey, Leroy, Etta, and a man who'd introduced himself to Don as Fulci, all had time to squeeze off shots as well, and then the zombies returned fire. They ducked behind their makeshift barricade of desks and filing cabinets.

Leroy dug in his pocket for more ammunition. "Anybody hit?"

"I'm okay." Smokey confirmed. Don and Etta murmured assurances as well. Fulci said nothing, because his lower jaw and most of his throat were now a ragged, wet hole. Air whistled through it.

"Better finish him off, Etta." Leroy quickly reloaded. "Don't need any more of those things in here."

Etta slid a screwdriver into Fulci's ear, shoving it through his brain. Blood trickled down the side of his mangled face.

"He ain't getting up again."

Don shuddered.

Another barrage slammed into the barricade, and all four ducked lower, hugging the floor. Smokey fired three wild shots, and the zombies laughed.

"What the hell do we do now?" Don asked, trying to eject the magazine.

"You're doing that wrong," Leroy told him, then took the weapon and did it for him. He handed it back to Don.

"There's two more stairwells on this floor," Smokey said. "One of them is behind us. The other, the fire-escape route, is on the other side of the building."

"I say we make for that," Etta said. "Get up to the roof and the helicopter."

"Who the hell is gonna fly it?" Leroy scoffed. "Ain't none of us know how to pilot that thing."

More bullets chewed up the barricade.

"Well, we can't stay here," Don yelled. "Let's go."

Still crouched down, he turned to run and then froze. Four more zombies were creeping up behind them. None of the creatures were armed with ranged weapons, but each carried a knife or club.

"They flanked us!"

With a triumphant cry, the zombies to their front charged. A second later, an explosion went off in their midst. Shrapnel and bits of pulped flesh showered down upon the group. Leroy cried out, hands flailing as a hot fragment of metal scorched his forearm. The stench of his burned flesh filled the air. The zombies to their rear pulled back, hesitating.

"Make a hole, motherfuckers," Forrest shouted. He clutched another grenade in one beefy hand. The other held an M-16.

Pigpen stepped out from behind him and drove an axe through the forehead of a zombie crawling across the floor. God poked his furry head out of a backpack slung over the vagrant's shoulders.

Smokey and Don took advantage of the four remaining creatures' hesitation and gunned them down. Then they stood up.

"God damn, it's good to see you, Forrest!" Leroy grasped his hand, and then winced, favoring his forearm.

"Good to see you guys alive too. Now let's move."

Etta grabbed Leroy's arm, her face concerned. "You gonna be okay?"

"It hurts like a bitch, but I'm fine."

"No time to talk," Forrest insisted. "They're all over the place. We need to go, now."

"Where?" Don asked.

"The back fire stairs, and then the sub-basement."

"And then," Pigpen grinned, "God will lead us out of here."

Val finally left her post in the communications center. The radio traffic was becoming ominous—more attack orders from zombies than humans—and she figured it was time to bolt. Naval radio operators went down with the ship, but not her.

She crept down the corridor, wondering where Branson had gone, when a zombie bird slammed into her face. Screaming, she grabbed the creature and flung it away. It smashed against the wall and crumpled to the floor. Val stomped it, feeling the bones snap beneath her feet.

The elevator doors at the end of the hallway stood open, revealing an empty shaft. The darkness inside the gaping hole wasn't just black, it was solid. From somewhere far below her, she heard muffled gunshots and explosions. A drought of warm air drifted from the empty shaft, brushing against her face. With it came smoke.

"Shit. Guess I can't go that way."

Val retraced her steps down the darkened hallway. Something fluttered behind her. She turned around and stared at the shaft. The noise repeated itself, a dry, rustling sound.

"What the—"

Without warning, a dozen undead pigeons flew out of the dark hole, soaring down the hallway toward her. Val ran, fleeing their terrible, squawking cries. She felt claws rake at the back of her neck, and beat them away. Another bird snagged her hair, pulling out a clump by the roots. She pumped her legs faster, lengthening the distance between herself and her attackers. Her hand instinctively covered her abdomen, protecting her unborn baby.

She rounded a corner and slid to a halt. At the far end of the hall dozens of zombies were searching room to room. They hadn't noticed her. Quickly, she tried the first door to her left. It was unlocked.

Val heaved herself into the room. Two birds made it through before she could slam the door shut. One launched itself at her face, and its razored beak clamped onto her eyelid and flew away. Val shrieked as it tore loose. The second bird darted for her lidless eyeball, plucking it from its socket.

Half-blind, Val grabbed a lamp from the table and swung it, clubbing the first bird to the floor. Still screaming, she smashed the other one against the wall. Both the lamp and the pigeon exploded. The first bird rose from the carpet and speared her other eye. The last thing she saw was the pointed beak. Then, everything vanished in a red cloud of pain. She clutched at the bird, feeling the gore-matted feathers, her fingers tracing over her own eyeball before she squeezed both it and the bird into a pulp.

Doubled over with agony, Val crashed around the room, blindly searching for the door handle. She found it, and stumbled out into the hall. Blood streamed from her empty eye sockets. Part of her brain warned her that there were still zombies in the corridor, but she didn't care. Something flared inside her head. Hands held out in front of her, she weaved down the hallway, one shoulder sliding along the wall.

"Can somebody help me?" she sobbed.

The air stank of smoke and cordite—and rot. She smelled the creature before it spoke.

"Where are you going, bitch?"

"Please . . ."

"Come here, little mouse."

"Somebody help me!"

"One blind mouse. See how it runs . . ."

"Leave me alone!"

Val turned in the darkness, seeking only to escape the stench and that horrible, grating voice. She ran, hearing the unmistakable sound of a racking shotgun. She fled, sightless and crippled from the pain and shock.

"Please," she sobbed. "Somebody—"

Still running, she tumbled down the open elevator shaft.

Ob and his lieutenants strolled through the burned-out lobby, stepping over the smoldering ruins and surveying the damage. Above them, the slaughter continued.

Relentless, the undead hordes pressed forward, murdering every living creature in their path—humans hiding in apartments and offices, cowering in bathroom stalls and ventilation ducts, and making a stand in the hallways and stairwells. For the most part, the killings were quick and efficient, but some of the Siqqusim who had remained trapped in the Void for a lengthier time than their brothers stopped to feed, relishing the moment.

The residents of Ramsey Towers fought back; cab drivers and models and clerical assistants and telemarketers—all turned warriors in the face of their own extinction. Both the living and the dead suffered heavy casualties, and pieces of human wreckage littered the building. But for every walking corpse that was destroyed, four more rose up to take its place. The bodies of the recently dead returned, hunting down their former friends, family members, and lovers. Methodically, the creatures swept through each floor of the building, choking the passageways with their presence and leaving abominations in their wake. Slowly, they worked their way to the top.

Bates and Steve emerged from the armory, each carrying a flamethrower. Their backs were strapped with lightweight canisters full of jellied gasoline. Bates had used one in Iraq, and had seen the liquid fire melt skin and bones.

They ran down the hall and straight into a massacre. Thirty feet away from them, ten zombies stood in a circle, feasting upon the gored remains of three adults and two children that lay in a dismembered pile between them. Absorbed in their meal, the creatures didn't notice their approach. Quickly, the men ducked out of sight, and watched, deciding what to do next.

"We should move on," one of the creatures grunted around a mouthful of liver.

"I'm hungry," another moaned, carving a layer of yellow fat from one of the children. "Let's finish eating first. I haven't had man flesh for three days."

A third elbowed its companion out of the way, and wrenched the heart from another body.

"We must continue," the first one insisted. "We can enjoy these spoils later."

"Not until we replenish ourselves. I waited longer than you for release from the Void. I will eat my fill!"

Another zombie held up one of the children's arms like it was a chicken leg, and greedily bit into the bicep.

"Try this first." It smacked its lips, nudging the first one. "The children are much more succulent than the adults. Have a bite before we move on."

"Ob's orders were to—"

Bates and Steve leapt out, and pulled their triggers at the same time. The flames whipped toward the clustered zombies, incinerating them in mid-feast. They howled, not in pain, but in enraged confusion. Two of the corpses stumbled forward, scorching the floor with every halting step. Bates directed the flame toward them, and they crumbled. Nothing remained but burning meat.

Steve turned away and retched. In the ceiling above them, the sprinkler system kicked in, drenching them both.

"Bates," Steve gasped. "I can't take this anymore, man. I can't . . ."

"With luck, it will all be over soon."

"You think so? Because I sure don't see it."

Without a word, Bates flicked his wet hair from his face and led Steve toward the stairwell.

Dr. Stern was inside an elevator between the twenty-seventh and twenty-eighth floors when the power went out. He froze, terrified that the car would plummet to the bottom of the shaft. When he realized it was still suspended safely by its cables, he breathed a sigh of relief.

He pressed the emergency call button, not expecting results and not receiving any. He tried the radio clipped to his belt, but there was no response. Then he waited, wondering what to do next. He studied his M-16, refamiliarizing himself with the weapon. He recited from memory the crash course that Forrest had given him. He listened, hoping to hear voices, footsteps, anything that would indicate that somebody was aware of his predicament.

Nobody came.

The air inside the elevator grew hot. Stern removed his shirt and mopped his brow, trying not to panic. His throat felt dry and scratchy. His eyes seemed to swell, as did his hands and fingers. His ears burned and it was suddenly hard to breathe.

My blood pressure is up, he thought. *Need to calm down, think rationally, and get the hell out of here.*

He tried the radio again. There was a burst of static, and then a garbled voice. He listened carefully, but couldn't make out what the other person was saying.

"Bates? This is Stern. Do you copy?"

Something unintelligible.

"This is Dr. Stern. I'm trapped in an elevator. Can anyone hear me?"

Static, and then, "My dick . . ."

"Say again?"

"Dick . . . it's gone. They . . . took it . . ."

"Who is this? I need help. I'm stuck inside one of the elevators."

"They're everywhere, man . . . Thousands of them . . . They . . ."

"Who is this? Can you hear me?"

"It's c-cold. Savini's missing. George is dead . . . So is . . . Ken. Ripped his arms out . . . Joe and Gary . . . They shot them both before I could do a-anything. And then . . . and then they . . ."

"Go ahead, son. I'm listening."

"They turned on me. They tore my pants off . . . and . . ."

Stern drew in a breath and held it.

"They . . . cut it off and ate it . . . and then they just . . . they just left me here."

Stern was speechless. The elevator suddenly seemed to spin. He closed his eyes against the vertigo. His stomach churned.

The man on the other end began to sob.

"They left me here to . . . to bleed out and die. They cut my fucking dick off!"

"It—it's going to be okay," Stern said, feeling foolish. "Can you tell me your name?"

"I don't want to be like them," the man wailed. "Not like that! I don't want to come back."

"Please," Stern whispered. "Tell me your name."

"I don't want to come back."

"Please? Can you tell me who you are? Where you are?"

"Hail Mary, full of grace . . ."

There was a gunshot, and then silence. Stern turned the radio off, wrestling with a wave of nausea. After a moment, it passed.

The air inside the elevator grew hotter, stifling. After a moment, he sat the rifle aside, stood up, and studied the doors. He experimented with them, sliding his fingers in between the crack. Grunting, Stern pulled. The doors didn't budge.

"Damn it."

He strained again, pulling with all his might. The doors slid a half-inch, then an inch, and then stopped. He let go and caught his breath.

"It never looked this hard in the movies."

He put his eye to the crack and peered through. The wall of the shaft stared back at him. Two feet above his head, he saw the bottom half of another pair of doors. He realized that the elevator was stuck between floors. If he could force these doors open, and wedge the others apart as well, he could climb through.

He set to work again, and with a final heave, the doors slid open all the way. Warm air brushed his face. He smelled smoke.

"Well, that's half of it," he panted.

He laid the radio on the floor next to the rifle and his shirt, stood at the edge of the elevator, and reached up. His fingers just reached the outer doors, but he had no leverage to pry them open.

"Where's the ladder? In the movies, there's always a ladder inside the shaft."

Cursing, he slammed his hand against the shaft in frustration.

An answering knock came from the other side of the doors.

"Hello," he called, "Is somebody out there?"

The knock sounded again, along with muffled voices.

"I'm in here!" Stern pounded on the shaft wall. "Can you get me out? I'm stuck."

They called back to him. Stern wasn't sure what they said, but it sounded like "Hang tight."

So he did. He waited, listening to the activity on the other side. Within moments, the doors slid open, bathing the shaft with the soft glow of emergency lights. A flashlight clicked on, and one of his rescuers shined the beam into his face.

"Thank God," Stern gasped, squinting against the light. Several figures stood illuminated in the open doorway, but the beam blinded him and he couldn't make out who they were. "I wasn't sure how I was going to get out of here."

There was no response.

"Could you kill that light, please?"

"Sure," came the reply. "Right after we kill you."

The zombies reached down and grabbed his hair and shoulders, yanking him upward. Screaming, the doctor thrashed and kicked, as they pulled him out. They threw him to the floor, holding him down as they tore into him with their bare hands. They clawed open his abdomen and reached inside, pushing and prodding. One of the creatures gripped a fistful of his intestines and pulled them out, running its tongue along the glistening offal. Another grabbed a fistful of his lung, pulping the organ between its fingers.

Stern tried to scream, but no sound came out. His lips moved silently as a zombie thrust its hand inside him, wrenched something loose, and then held it up for him to see.

He stared at his own spleen, and minutes later when he came back, he ate some of it himself.

* * *

DiMassi slipped through the fire door and ran up the last flight of stairs. His heart hammered in his chest, and his lungs burned. Gasping, he stopped at the door leading out onto the roof, and looked through the window.

The roof was gone. Presumably, it was still there, but he couldn't see it beneath all the undead birds. Even the massive strobe lights were buried.

"Holy shit."

Hands shaking, he pulled a bright yellow protective suit from its hook on the wall and put it on. When he was a boy, DiMassi's father had been a beekeeper, and the outfit reminded him of that. Heavy mesh Kevlar covered him from head to toe, including a hard plastic visor, sewn into the hood to cover his face. Movement was laborious while wearing the protective suits, but they kept the birds from tearing the pilots to shreds on their way to the helicopter.

His muffled panting sounded loud inside the covered hood, and his breath fogged the face shield. He pulled on the thick gloves and waited for the fog to clear. Outside, the zombie birds stared back at him through the window.

Footsteps pounded in the hallway below, and Carson crashed through the door.

"End of the line, fat boy."

DiMassi flung the door open and stepped outside. The birds took flight, moving as one toward him. Crows, pigeons, finches, sparrows, robins—dead wings beat the air. Their deafening cries sounded like children screaming, and the sky was black with their bodies. They slammed into the pilot, crushing him with their numbers. More creatures soared through the open door.

DiMassi stumbled, falling to his knees in the middle of the roof. His back, legs and arms felt heavy from the weight of the birds. Their beaks and claws pecked and tore at his protective suit, but the material held up. He collapsed into a ball and rolled around, crushing them beneath him. DiMassi struggled to his feet. Slowly, methodically, he plodded across the roof to the helicopter. The birds were so thick that it was like walking underwater. He yanked the door open but the birds crashed against it, forcing it shut again. A large crow pecked at his visor hard enough to crack the plastic. Another managed to wedge its beak in the seam between his glove and wrist, drawing blood.

Screaming, DiMassi pulled the cockpit door open again, and lunged inside. He pulled the door shut, smashing the birds that had made it inside with his gloved hands.

"Fuck you, Carson! You fucking faggot! Fuck you too, birds!" He tossed the gloves and hood into the seat next to him, and raised his middle finger to the stairwell door. But the door had vanished inside a cloud of rotting, feathery bodies.

"I did it. Son of a bitch—I made it!"

Laughing, DiMassi crossed his fingers and started the helicopter. The engines whined to life and he laughed louder.

Carson was halfway up the stairs when the air turned black. He managed to let out a short, strangled cry and then they fell upon him, smashing into him like torpedoes. Razored beaks jabbed at every inch of his exposed flesh. His ears and cheeks were sliced to ribbons. His eyeballs were plucked from their sockets, and his nose was ripped from his face. His weapon slipped from his bleeding hands, clattered down the stairs, and discharged. The explosion was lost in the din of the screeching zombies and Carson's tortured shrieks. He screamed as something clawed and pecked its way into his stomach. The bird took wing again, a curd of fat hanging in its beak. Agony erupted in his groin. His throat was flayed open.

Carson collapsed, tumbling down the stairs and rolling to a stop against the closed door. The birds swarmed down, tearing his clothes to pieces. Then they dug into the rest of him, turning the young soldier into a quivering mass of bloody meat and exposed nerve endings. Despite the pain and blood loss, Carson remained conscious through it all.

It took him a very long time to die.

Jim, Quinn, Frankie, and the others arrived at the stairwell in time to hear Carson's screams. Branson turned white and Danny shrank away, covering his ears with his hands.

"We've got to get him out of there." Branson reached for the doorknob with his uninjured arm. "They'll tear him to pieces!"

"Don't open that door," Quinn cautioned. "You'll let them in here!"

"But Quinn, we can't—"

The rest was drowned out by Carson's shrieks.

"There's nothing we can do." Quinn steadied himself, trying to remain calm. "If we open that door, those things will be on us in a second."

"He's right," Jim said. "Frankie and I have both seen what a flock of those birds can do. We won't stand a chance."

"But it's Carson . . ."

"And it will be us next if you don't listen to me." Quinn seized his shoulders and shook him. Branson winced, and the wound in his forearm began to bleed again.

"But, Quinn—"

Something slammed against the door. Then another. The door rattled in its frame.

"They're trying to break it down," Frankie said.

"Can they?" Quinn asked.

"Damn straight they can. How many birds are in New York City?"

Quinn shrugged. "Millions. Why?"

Jim spoke. "I reckon all of them are on the other side of that door."

The thudding continued. Jim was reminded of the sound of hammers falling. More birds hurtled themselves into the door, heedless of the damage to themselves. The metal began to buckle.

Suddenly, the grille on the air duct above them snapped open, swinging on its hinges. An undead child dropped from the ductwork, landing in a crouched position behind them. Giggling, it lurched forward.

Quinn raised his rifle and squeezed the trigger. The zombie's head was sheared off. It took two more faltering steps and then toppled over. Danny slugged it with the bat.

The pounding continued on the other side of the door.

"Come on," Frankie urged. She ran inside Ramsey's office. Jim and Danny followed her.

"Get your shit together, Branson," Quinn said, and then pushed him out of the way. He pressed his back against the door and braced his legs. A second later, Branson joined him. The weight on the other side of the door was immense.

Quinn's radio crackled. He grabbed it with one hand, keeping up the pressure with his legs and other arm.

"Quinn."

"It's Bates. What's your situation?"

"Situation normal. All fucked up."

"Say again?"

"We're on the top floor. Ramsey and Carson are both dead. DiMassi's either dead or fleeing in the helicopter."

"How many are in your party?"

Quinn paused, counting in his head. "Five. There's me, Branson, Thurmond, his kid, and the woman, Frankie."

"Can you move?"

"We'd love to. Anything's better than where we're at now."

"Good. Remember where we caught you getting head from that hooker the first week here?"

"The sub-basement? Yeah, I—"

"Don't say it out loud. This channel may not be secure."

"Okay," Quinn coughed. The door started to slide, and he pushed harder. "Put your back into it, Branson."

"Quinn," Bates barked. "Do you copy?"

"Copy! I'm a little preoccupied here, Bates. How the hell do we get down there? Aren't those things thick by now?"

"Be advised, they are everywhere. You'll have to fight your way down. But it's our only chance, Quinn. Meet us there, and hurry."

"What's going on? Why there?"

"I'm not saying anything else over the radio. They might be listening. Just do it. We've got a situation here, too. Got to go. Out."

The door slowly began to slide open again. Quinn and Branson gritted their teeth, shoving against it.

"Hurry up," Quinn yelled. "We can't hold them much longer!"

The door inched open, and a small bird darted through the crack and fluttered into the air. The two men shoved the door closed again, smashing feathered heads and wings.

Frankie and Jim lugged Ramsey's heavy, oak desk out into the hall. The bird darted forward and pecked at Jim's cheek. His hands slipped off the desk and it dropped on Frankie's toes. She yelped, letting loose with a string of curses. Jim ducked as the bird swooped toward him a second time, but suddenly, Danny stepped forward.

"Leave my Daddy alone!" He swung the bat, and the bird exploded like a rotten tomato.

"Nice shot, kiddo," Frankie said. "Now tell your daddy to get this frigging desk off my foot."

Jim smiled with pride. They picked the desk up again and shoved it against the door, blocking it. Carson's screams echoed from the other side. Jim turned back to thank Danny and froze, stunned.

Danny was savagely beating the bird's corpse into a red smear. Gore and feathers splattered both the walls and stuck to the bat. His lips were pulled back in a grimace.

"I—told—you—to—leave—my—daddy—alone!" Each syllable was punctuated by another swing.

Jim's mind flashed back to the car crash, and the look on Danny's face when he saw his father beating the zombie with a rock. And now . . .

My God, what effect is this way of life having on my son?

"Danny? Danny, stop."

The boy's grunts faded. He looked up at his father, and his face was pale and tired.

"Danny. It's okay now. Stop. It's dead."

"I know, Daddy."

Jim put an arm around his shoulders. "That was very brave and I'm proud of you, but—"

"It was hurting you, Daddy."

"I know. But you need—"

Carson mewled on the other side of the door.

"Oh, Christ," Branson shouted, horrified. "He's not dead yet!"

Quinn interrupted Jim and Danny's embrace. "We need to move."

"Never mind," Jim whispered. "We'll talk about it later."

"I love you, Daddy."

"Love you too."

They ran for the rear utility stairs, and Carson's fading screams followed along behind them.

The helicopter rose into the air, blades and rotors chewing up the zombies hovering around it. DiMassi activated the U.B.R.D. and the remaining birds dropped from the sky like stones. Still laughing, he swerved to the left and soared out over the city, high above Madison Avenue.

"Sayonara, suckers."

He checked the fuel gauge, and considered his destination options. Getting far away from New York City was his top priority, but eventually, he'd need to refuel, and find food and shelter. He decided to head northwest, toward Buffalo. There were lots of mountains and forests between here and there, some with airstrips or flat areas where he could land safely and take off from again. Perhaps the wilderness would be more hospitable—or at least less populated.

DiMassi eyed the dials, making sure everything was functioning properly. Slowly, he relaxed, the tension melting from his limbs. The gray, sunless sky opened before him, promising more rain.

He was still going over the instruments when a zombie on the ground raised an RPG, locked onto him, and squeezed the trigger. DiMassi saw a brief flash out of the corner of his eye, and then it was too late.

The helicopter exploded in the skies over 35th Street, looking very much like the second sunrise of the day. Twisted metal and burning fuel rained down into the streets. The smoke from the explosion mixed with the black cloud rising from Ramsey Towers and the burning buildings around it.

Inside the structure, the massacre continued.

SIXTEEN

Jim, Frankie, Danny, Quinn, and Branson began the long trek down the fire stairs. Quinn took point and Frankie brought up the rear.

"I can go last if you want me to," Branson offered.

"You're hurt," Frankie reminded him, "And the back of this hospital gown doesn't tie completely. I don't want you checking out my ass."

Blushing, Branson turned away. Frankie grinned.

They zigzagged downward, their footsteps echoing around them. The stairwell was quiet, save for their heavy breathing and the metallic clink of their weapons. The sounds of carnage drifted from behind closed doors with every level they passed: screams of fright, pain and dying; cruel, guttural laughter; gunshots and crackling flames.

"It's hot in here," Danny complained. "How far down is it?"

"A long way," Jim told him, his voice concerned. "You okay?"

Danny nodded. "Just sweaty and tired. My feet hurt."

"I'd carry you, squirt, but if the zombies come after us we may have to fight, and I can't do that with you on my shoulders."

"It's okay, Daddy. I'm a big boy. I can do it."

They continued down, pausing occasionally to listen for sounds of pursuit.

Branson wiped sweat from his forehead. "Kid's right, though. It is getting hotter in here. I'm sweating like a motherfucker."

"Probably the fires," Quinn mused. "But I don't think we have to worry."

"Why's that?" Jim asked.

"If I remember correctly, these stairwells were designed to act as a deterrent to fires. I don't know the engineering specifics, but they built them with the World Trade Center disaster in mind."

"So they're fireproof?"

Quinn nodded. "I think so."

"I hope so," Frankie added.

"How can the fire jump floors?" Branson asked. "I thought each floor had fireproofing materials in it to prevent that."

"Don't know," Quinn admitted. "But I'm guessing that the zombies are starting fires on each floor. Either that, or the shelling started several small fires, and they're out of control."

"So what's the plan?" Jim asked.

The pilot stopped, listening. He brought a finger to his lips. The others halted behind him. After a moment, he relaxed and continued on.

Frankie stared back up the stairs. "What was that about?"

"Thought I heard something above us, but I guess it was just our shoes. Sound is funny in here."

He led them forward. "Anyway, about the plan. I talked to Bates on the radio while you guys were getting the desk. He wants us to meet him in the sub-basement."

"Why?"

"He wouldn't say, in case the zombies were monitoring our communications. I'd guess we're going to escape through the sewers. Or try to at least."

Frankie halted, remembering her journey through Baltimore's sewer system: the darkness, the stench, the overwhelming sense of claustrophobia—and the rats. Especially the rats. It hadn't helped matters that she was withdrawing from heroin at the time.

Jim touched her arm. "You okay?"

She nodded, her mouth a thin, grim line.

Quinn noticed her demeanor too.

"What is it?" he asked.

"Had a bad experience inside the sewers back in Baltimore. That's all. If we get out of here, I'll tell you about it. But don't sweat it. I'll be okay."

They walked on, footsteps still bouncing off the walls.

"So where do we go once we're underground?" Jim asked.

"I don't know," Quinn said. "Bates couldn't talk long. Sounded like they were in a firefight. He said to hurry. If they get there before we do, they won't wait for us."

Their descent continued for another fifteen minutes before the group stopped to rest. They were exhausted and thirsty. Branson's arm dripped blood, and Danny's eyes had black circles under them. They debated sneaking onto one of the floors and raiding a soft drink machine, but decided against it.

"Can't believe we haven't run across any of them

yet," Branson said. "Hell, do you realize just how many of those things must be in the building?"

"Don't jinx it," Quinn replied. "Let's just hope our luck continues."

Frankie pulled Jim aside.

"I need to ask you something."

"Sure. What's up?"

"Have you been having weird dreams?"

"Not really," he said. "In fact, I've only dreamed once since Martin and I left West Virginia, at least as far as I can remember. Why?"

Frankie shrugged. "I don't know. I—I've been dreaming about Martin."

"About how he died?"

"No. About the present, and the future. He shows me things. It's like he's a fucking ghost or something. He's been warning me."

"Warning you about what?"

Before she could answer, a door squeaked open several floors above them. For a moment, the booming sounds of battle grew louder. Then the door swung shut again, muffling them.

They froze, staring upward in silence. Footsteps padded down the stairs.

Quinn put a finger to his lips and readied his weapon. Frankie and Jim did the same. They could smell the zombie as it drew closer. Not rot or decay, but blood. The air was thick with blood.

"I know you're down there, little piggy," the corpse chuckled. "You left a trail of breadcrumbs."

Horrified, they glanced down at their feet. Dime-sized drops of Branson's blood had dripped from his wrist, spattering every other step on their way down.

"Shit." He cradled his wound to his chest.

"Helloooo," the zombie called. "Why not go easy on yourself? I'll make it quick and painless, and I promise only to eat a little bit of you."

They shrank away from the railing, their backs against the wall. The zombie continued its descent. Suddenly, they heard another door open, several landings below them. They were surrounded, cut off on both ends.

Danny and Branson exchanged frightened looks. Quinn signaled Frankie and Jim to deal with the zombie above them, and then slowly crept forward, inching his way down the stairs toward the second group.

The footsteps grew louder, as did the stench. The zombie was on the landing above them. Jim could see its shadow in the glow of the emergency lights. Then they heard something else: the racking of a shotgun.

"Ready or not," the zombie chuckled. "Here I come."

Frankie and Jim pointed their rifles back up the stairs, waiting. Unnoticed, a blued shotgun barrel was lowered between the handrails on their level and the level above them. The explosion was deafening, and rocked them all.

Frankie ran halfway up the stairs, spun around, and dropped to her knees. Her eyes widened in surprise. Dr. Stern's dead face split in a wide grin. His abdomen had been emptied; his ribs pried apart and sticking out of his flesh like porcupine quills.

Frankie squeezed off three wild shots and then ducked down again, crab-walking back to the wall. One bullet plowed into the wall, and the others ricocheted through the stairwell.

"Did you hit it?" Jim asked.

"I don't think so."

"Now that's not very nice," Stern taunted. "After I took such good care of you when you were hurt."

"No," Frankie said, "I guess not."

The thing began talking in a language that Stern had never known. *"Enga keeriost mathos du abapan rentare."*

Several landings below them, Quinn's M-16 rumbled a staccato beat. Distracted by the sudden gunfire, Frankie and Jim didn't notice the zombie. Stern rounded the corner and charged down the stairs, shotgun pointed directly at them. When the thing that had been Stern saw that he was outgunned, he pulled the trigger and then turned to run.

The shotgun pellets peppered Branson's face. Blinded, he slammed into the handrail and tipped over the side, teetering for a moment like a seesaw before he fell. His screams ended in a sickening thud from far, far below. More cries drifted up to them from Quinn's location.

Frankie and Jim simultaneously returned fire. The barrage ripped into Stern, severing one arm and splattering his brains all over the stairs.

Jim whirled. "Danny, are you okay?"

Staring in horror, Danny pointed at the handrail. His bottom lip quivered.

"Daddy—Mr. Branson fell . . ."

Jim rushed to Danny's side and pulled him close, whispering in his ear and smoothing his hair.

"And that nice doctor turned into one of the monster-people. He was all opened up."

"I know," Jim soothed. "I know. It's okay. There was nothing we could do."

Frankie stepped past them and looked over the handrail.

"Quinn?" she called. Her voice bounced back to her. "Quinn? Are you okay?"

"Come quick," he shouted. "Get down here. We've got trouble!"

Another voice followed his, one that sounded familiar. "You're a god damned idiot, Quinn."

"Who the hell is that?" Jim asked. "Is somebody down there with him?"

"Couldn't see. They're too far down. It sounded like Steve."

"Who?"

"The pilot that was with Quinn when they rescued us. The guy from Canada."

Danny wiped his nose with his sleeve.

"Come on," Frankie urged. "Let's go."

They ran down four more flights of stairs. Steve and Quinn were crouched over a body. They saw black combat boots and black leather pants. The legs beneath the pants trembled in pain and shock. A white shirt, soaked with blood, and more blood spreading onto the stairs in a widening pool. The blood, the shirt, the pants and the boots all belonged to Bates.

"Oh shit," Jim muttered.

"Understatement . . . of the . . . year, Mr. Thurmond," Bates hissed through clenched teeth. His face was chalk white.

"I'm fucking sorry, Bates," Quinn sobbed, clenching the wounded man's hand.

"This is Bates?" Frankie whispered. Jim nodded.

"And you must . . . must be Frankie. Nice . . . to make . . . your acquaintance."

"Does it hurt?" Quinn asked.

"Shock . . . is starting to . . . set in."

"We need to move," Steve said. "The zombies must have heard the gunshots. They'll be here any second."

"What happened?" Jim asked.

"Bates and I entered the stairwell," Steve said. "We heard you guys above us. Before we could call out, the fighting erupted. That was when genius here shot Bates in the stomach."

Jim caught a glimpse of the wound, and turned away.

"It was an accident," Quinn insisted. "I thought he was a fucking zombie!"

"Get . . . out of . . . here," Bates coughed, spraying bloody spittle. "Steve's right. They'll be . . . on us any second. I'll hold them . . . off."

"Bullshit," Steve told him. "Jim, strap on his flamethrower. You can carry that and sling your rifle at the same time. You're covering our rear. Frankie, you've got point. Quinn, give me a hand."

Quinn and Steve used the straps from the rifles to hold Bates's guts in, wrapping them around his waist. Their wadded up T-shirts covered the exit and entrance wounds. They cinched the straps tight, and Bates grew even paler.

They hoisted him to his feet, and he moaned, clutching at his stomach.

"Put your arms around our shoulders," Steve told him. "I know it hurts, but you're not gonna die. It takes a long time for somebody to die from a gut shot. We'll get you out of here and fixed up in no time."

Bates tossed his head, trying to see past the long hair plastered to his face.

"Steve," he rasped, "whom . . . did you have . . . in mind to . . . fix me up? Where are they . . . going to operate—in the sewers? Just . . . shoot me in the head and . . . leave me here."

"Stop that," the Canadian pilot answered. "Just stop that talk. You'll be fine."

"I'm so sorry, man," Quinn apologized again.

"Shut up, Quinn."

"How do I work this thing?" Jim asked, strapping the flamethrower's tanks to his back.

Steve gave him a quick lesson and then they started down the stairs again, Frankie in the lead, Steve and Quinn supporting Bates, Danny behind them, and Jim bringing up the rear.

They only made it three more floors before the zombies poured into the stairwell above them. The creatures opened fire, and the air rang with the soft pop of .22 rifles, the thunder of a .45, and the concussive blasts of a Browning sub-machine gun. Jim unleashed a stream of liquid fire, torching the creatures in mid-run. The descent became a running battle. Frankie shot the creatures below them and Jim incinerated anything to the rear. The stairway echoed with gunfire and reeked of burning hair and flesh. The smoke grew thick, and they had to put their clothing over their mouths and noses to filter the air they breathed. Their eyes stung, and their ears rang from the constant explosions.

A zombie on the next landing shimmied up the handrail and clutched Steve's foot. He tried to shake it off without jostling Bates, and the wounded man groaned. Dirty fingernails clawed at Steve's ankle, slicing into his flesh. The pilot screamed as the nails burrowed deeper.

Danny swung the baseball bat. He brought it down again, shattering the creature's wrist. The hand pulled away. A second later, Frankie shot the zombie from its perch.

Eventually, the pursuit dwindled, and then died. Still, they kept running, moving as fast as they could without jostling Bates or losing Danny, who was having trouble keeping up.

Then they found Branson. His body had plummeted more than twenty stories before coming to rest on one of the landings. His back was snapped. His legs and arms hung askew, splintered and broken, and his head had split open like a melon.

"Guess he won't be coming back again," Quinn said. "Lucky bastard."

Bates croaked, "We should . . . all be so . . . lucky."

Frankie checked her magazines and reloaded. Steve and Quinn caught their breath, grateful for the stop. Danny snuggled close to Jim, hugging him tightly. None of them spoke.

Footsteps pounded after them from far above.

They ran on.

Carson's body wasn't recognizable as a human being, yet the red, raw mass struggled to its feet, controlled by another. His hand had only two remaining fingers and a thumb, but he managed to turn the doorknob. With the combined weight of the birds slamming against it, the door exploded outward, shoving the desk out of the way.

The zombies flew down the hallway, darting through open doorways and soaring down the empty elevator shafts and open stairwells. The thing that had been Carson stumbled along behind them, shedding pieces of meat.

The hallway was quiet, and there were no humans in sight. It wondered where its host's friends had gone. The creature searched Carson's memory, and then traced Branson's trail of blood down the corridor. Eventually, it found its way to the utility door, and opened it. The birds followed him, pouring into the stairwell. With each floor they passed, more zombies joined in the chase.

The stairway filled with dead bodies, all hurtling downward in pursuit of the living.

SEVENTEEN

"Forrest, how much longer are we going to wait?" Smokey whispered.

The sub-basement was dark, cold, and dank, reeking of smoke from the fires above them. Their only sources of illumination came from a flashlight that Pigpen found on a tool bench, and a battery-operated lantern. The concrete floor was piled high with boxes and storage bins. Workbenches were heaped with tools and scraps of pipe and wiring. Spider-webs dangled from the air ducts.

Forrest shifted his weight from foot to foot, guarding one of the doors.

"As long as we have to. We ain't leaving without them."

Etta found some clean rags in one of the boxes and changed the bandages on Leroy's burned forearm. God brushed up against her side, purring loudly, and she shooed him away.

"Get this damn cat out of here," she snapped at Pigpen. "Leroy don't need his arm getting infected."

Leroy pushed himself up. "I'm fine. It's just burned. Quit your fussing, woman. You cluck more than a chicken."

"Don't you talk to me like that, Leroy Piper," Etta's head darted back and forth like a snake's, "or that burn on your arm will be the last of your worries!"

"Etta," Forrest snapped. "Keep your voice down! For God's sake, why don't you just walk upstairs and let those things know we're down here?"

She opened her mouth to reply, but saw the storm brewing behind the big man's eyes, and shut it again.

Forrest glanced at his wristwatch, and chewed his lip. He looked around the basement again. There were four entrances: a service elevator, two regular stairways—both of which led to the destroyed parking garage, and the fire stairs. Don guarded one stairwell, and he kept watch on the other.

"Smokey," he grunted, "get over there and watch that fire door. Pigpen, shut that damn cat up. He's meowing as loud as Etta."

"Hey," the big women protested.

"Sshh!"

Forrest's radio hissed static. He snapped it up.

"Forrest?" It was Quinn. "You copy, big guy?"

"Here. Where you at?"

"We're . . ." There was a moment of silence, and Forrest heard somebody else in the background. "We're on our way to the location you and Bates agreed on."

"He with you?" The relief in Forrest's voice was unmistakable.

"Yeah. So are Steve and the Thurmond party."

Don looked up, the grin on his face infectious, spreading to the faces of Leroy, Smokey, and Etta.

"Where are you?" Quinn asked. He sounded out of breath. "And who's with you?"

"We're waiting on you," Forrest said. "I got Smokey, Leroy and Etta, Pigpen, and Don De Santos."

"And God," Pigpen added. "Don't forget God."

The cat rolled over onto its back and Pigpen scratched its belly.

"Which way are you guys coming down?" Forrest asked. "We'll clear a path."

There was another pause, and then Quinn said, "Bates says not to tell you over the radio. Just be ready for us. If we don't run into anything else, we should be there in about five minutes."

"Copy that. We'll be ready."

"And Forrest?"

"Yeah?"

"See if you can find some clean linens, alcohol, maybe even some duct tape."

Forrest translated the list in his mind. Bandages, disinfectant, and sutures. Battlefield medicine. A poor man's triage. That meant someone was injured.

"Who's hurt?" he asked.

"Bates."

"Is it bad?"

"Yeah. Yeah, man, it is."

"Shit."

Forrest started to ask what had happened, but a gunshot cut him off.

"Got to go, man," Quinn shouted. "They're on our ass again!"

More gunfire crackled from the speaker, and then Quinn was gone.

Forrest clipped the radio back onto his belt and looked at his companions. Their faces were grim.

"They better get a move on," Leroy grumbled.

Etta got to her feet. "If those things is chasing them, won't they lead them down here?"

Nobody replied. Smokey, Don, and Forrest turned back to their posts. Pigpen began searching through boxes and storage bins, looking for anything that could be used to treat Bates. God trailed along behind him.

Suddenly, the door in front of Don burst open. He brightened, expecting to see Jim, Frankie, and Danny walk through. Instead, it was a lone zombie, dressed in a dirty, tattered delivery uniform. Before it could even step through the doorway, Don dropped it with a single shot to the head. Terrified, he checked the stairwell for more.

"Clear?" Forrest asked.

Don nodded, shuddering. He grabbed the creature's feet and dragged it out of the way so that the door would close again.

"Forrest," Etta pleaded, "we've got to go. If that one found us, then you can bet your ass there's more coming. They must have heard that gunshot."

"We're not leaving without Bates."

"And I'm not leaving without my friends," Don said.

"We don't even know if they're alive!"

"Of course they are," Don argued. "We just heard from them."

"Yeah, and they was in the middle of a fire-fight. They're probably dead now. I say we go."

"Etta." Smokey tried to reason with her, turning his back on the fire door. "Why don't you just sit back down and rest?"

"Smokey," Forrest warned, "watch the door."

At that moment, the door opened. Smokey turned and Don and Forrest raised their weapons. Then they lowered them in relief.

Frankie ran into the basement, followed by the two pilots, supporting Bates between them. Jim and Danny entered last.

They gaped at Bates's wound. Smokey tore his eyes away. He shut the door and began stacking boxes in front of it as a crude blockade.

Don exchanged hugs with Frankie, Danny, and Jim. "I was worried about you guys. Everybody okay?"

"We're all right." Jim nodded. "How about you."

"What happened?" Forrest helped lower Bates to the floor.

"Quinn fucking shot him in the stomach," Steve said.

"You what?" Forrest's eyes bulged.

"It was an accident! We were under attack. I thought he was a zombie."

Bates reached up and clutched Forrest's arm with one weak hand.

"Got . . . your . . . pistol?"

"Never leave home without it." He tried to smile, but it looked more like a grimace.

"Give . . ." Blood dribbled from his mouth. "Give . . . to me."

Forrest lifted up his shirt and pulled the weapon from its holster.

"Pigpen," he called, "you find anything?"

"Some sheets, and a roll of duct tape. Found a bottle of water too. Ain't been opened. No alcohol though."

"Bring them here."

Steve and Forrest poured the water over the wound to clean it. Bates clenched his teeth and writhed with pain.

"Do we have anything to cut the sheet up with?" Forrest asked.

"D-don't worry . . . about it," Bates gasped. "Just . . . g—"

"Lie still, Bates. It's gonna be okay."

"No." Bates grabbed his hand. "Get them . . . out of . . . here."

"But—"

Bates squeezed harder, and Forrest flinched, surprised by the wounded man's strength.

"Listen . . . to me. We're all . . . that's left. Get . . . them out . . . I'm going to . . . die."

"You're not going to die, god damn it!"

"Yes . . . I am." Bates coughed. "And . . . we both . . . k-know it."

Forrest's eyes were wet. His lips quivered. The big man tried to speak, but the only thing that came out of his throat was a choking sound.

"Pig . . . pen," Bates groaned. "You . . . ready to . . . lead them?"

"Yes, sir," he whispered.

Bates stared up into Forrest's face. "Go."

Forrest swallowed hard.

"Quinn, Don. Get that manhole cover up. Jim, have that flamethrower ready, just in case there's anything down there. The rest of you stand back."

"Danny." Jim pushed him backward. "Stay here with Frankie."

Quinn and Don set their weapons aside and gripped the cable that Forrest and Bates had threaded through the cover earlier. Jim stood next to them, the flamethrower at the ready. They counted to three and pulled. The manhole lid inched upward, revealing darkness. Forrest and Pigpen tensed, coiled and ready, remembering the dead rats that had poured out of the hole earlier. Don and Quinn eased down on the cable, setting the cover to the side. The shaft was empty, the ladder rungs disappearing into the dark. All of them breathed a sigh of relief.

"Block the doors," Forrest ordered. "Boxes, crates, anything heavy."

Steve, Don, Jim, and Frankie began stacking things in front of them.

"Bates?" Quinn turned back to him. "We can't just leave you behind."

"You . . ." Bates couldn't finish. He broke into a fit of violent coughing. Blood sprayed from his mouth and oozed from the gunshot wound.

"Bates made his decision," Forrest grunted. "And he's right. We can't waste any more time."

"But he's our friend."

"You think I don't fucking know that, Quinn?" Forrest exploded. "There isn't anything we can do! Now move!"

They finished with the blockades. Frankie found a pair of ratty old work boots that fit her feet, and changed out of her hospital slippers.

God sniffed the open shaft and meowed.

"I found some glow sticks on that workbench over there," Pigpen said. "Figure they'll come in handy."

Nobody responded.

Suddenly, the stairwells thundered with sound, the doors vibrating on their hinges.

"Here they come!" Etta screamed.

"How many?" Forrest asked.

Frankie pointed her weapon at the door. "All of them. And this barricaded door ain't gonna stop them for long."

"Go," Bates urged them. "I'll . . . hold them off when . . ."

They gathered around him, unsure of what to say. Pigpen broke the silence.

"Thanks."

Bates nodded, clenching his fists in pain.

Pigpen clicked on the flashlight and quickly started down the ladder. God perched on his shoulders, entwining around his neck. Leroy and Etta said their goodbyes and climbed along behind him. Smokey went next, followed by Frankie. Danny climbed down after her, and Jim prepared to follow.

The approaching din grew louder.

"Mr. Thurmond?" Bates wheezed.

Jim stopped, his head and shoulders sticking out of the shaft.

"I . . . hope it turns out . . . okay . . . for you and your . . . son. Your story is . . . an inspiration."

Jim nodded sadly. "Thank you, Bates."

He vanished from sight.

Steve, Quinn, and Forrest stood over their dying leader.

"No time . . . for . . . regrets. Just go. Hurry . . ."

Steve and Quinn walked away, leaving Forrest and Bates alone. They didn't look back.

The zombies began pounding on the door.

Forrest knelt down and wrapped Bates's fingers around the butt of the pistol. He held them firm, and stared into his friend's clouding eyes.

"You've got six shots in there. Don't forget to save one for yourself."

"Got . . . it . . ."

Tears ran freely from Forrest's eyes.

"Been a pleasure to serve with you, Bates."

Bates smiled. "The honor . . . was mine."

"Semper fi."

"Ooo rah . . ."

Forrest swung his legs over the shaft and climbed

down the ladder. With one hand, he grabbed the cable threaded through the manhole cover and pulled it shut behind him. The last thing he saw was his friend, lying in a pool of blood, eyes half-closed. Forrest let go of the rungs and dropped the last six feet, his boots thudding on the cement.

They crowded together in the tunnel. The impenetrable darkness increased their anxiety. Pigpen handed each of them a glow stick, and fastened another one to God's collar.

"This way," Pigpen said, pointing the flashlight beam into the blackness. God ran ahead, his tiny paws splashing through a pool of water. They followed.

After they'd disappeared around the corner, other tiny paws trailed along behind them, scurrying in the darkness.

Bates struggled to sit up, his back against a steel support pillar. The zombies battered at the doors. The racket was horrendous, and their cries were terrible. Something skittered through the air ducts over his head, searching for a way in.

Bates had known fear in his life. When he was eight and he'd almost stepped on a copperhead while walking through the woods behind his home. When he was sixteen, asking Amy Schrum to the prom. He'd been frightened during his first night in boot camp—lying there on his rack in the dark barracks, and listening to the guy below him sobbing. In Iraq, as they advanced north toward Baghdad with winds whipping at fifty miles-per-hour, burying everything under a fine coat of sand. That was the first time Bates had seen combat, and he'd been terrified. And more recently, when he'd first seen the hints that his employer, Darren Ramsey, was slowly going insane from what was happening in the world around them.

Bates was no stranger to fear. Yet now, as the zombies smashed through the doors, he did not feel it. A strange sense of calm washed over him. Nothing mattered, not even as the creatures descended upon him, surrounding him with their rotting forms.

Smiling, Bates tried to raise the pistol and found that he couldn't. He suddenly felt weak and cold. His stomach hurt. He tried to lift the pistol to his head again, but it clattered from his numb fingers. Bates closed his eyes as the zombies drew closer.

He didn't feel the blade of the handsaw as it ripped across his throat.

"It is finished, lord Ob. The humans are defeated."

"None left alive in the building?"

"Our forces have just slain the last one, sire. We are victorious."

Ob looked up at the burning building, a funeral pyre towering into the sky. The clouds spat rain, but still the fires roared, engulfing floor after floor. The buildings surrounding Ramsey Towers were also ablaze, and the smoking wreckage of the helicopter lay scattered in the streets.

"Well, if there are any left inside, cowering in some dark corner, they won't be for long. Gather our forces. Have them regroup. And set the rest of the necropolis alight."

"But lord Ob, is this place not to be our base of operations?"

"If all the humans are destroyed, then our time here is

done. We'll have no need of this city. It will be our kindred's turn, and we shall move on to conquer other worlds. The second wave can begin."

A zombie stepped from the ruins, dressed in black leather pants and a bloodstained white shirt. Long, dark hair spilled down its back. The corpse was fresh. Its throat had been sawed open from ear to ear. It walked toward them.

"Lord Ob!"

"Yes?"

The thing inside Bates struggled to speak through its damaged vocal cords. "I just took possession of this body mere moments ago. I have searched my host's memories."

"And?"

"A number of the humans still live. They've escaped."

"Where?" Ob growled.

"Under the city, my lord. Directly beneath our feet."

"How many?"

"Ten of them, sire. Several of them are formidable warriors."

"How so?"

"Three are trained soldiers. And one of them traveled several hundred miles in search of his son. His example rallies the others—gives them hope."

"In search of his son?" Ob thought back to his previous host, the scientist, Baker. He'd had two companions: Jim, the father searching for his son, and Martin, the elderly holy man.

"This father—what is his name?"

"Jim. Jim Thurmond."

Ob clenched his fist so hard that the fingernails punched through his palms.

"Was one of them an old black preacher?"

The Bates-thing shook its head. "There are two black males, sire, but neither is a preacher. One is named Leroy, and the other, Forrest."

"What is it, lord Ob?" the lieutenant asked.

"Unfinished business," Ob said. "Associates of one of my former hosts. They escaped me in Hellertown. It's a trivial matter. Not really worth wasting time over. But still—it would be beautiful to destroy this father and son after everything they've been through. The irony, the violation, would burn the Creator's ears and eyes."

"How shall we proceed?" The lieutenant stood ready.

"We didn't do all of this just to let ten of these creatures slip through our net. Order all of our forces into the tunnels beneath this city."

"All of them, sire?"

"All of them."

The rain drenched them all, spilling onto the streets and into the gutters. It swirled down the drains and sewer grates, into the tunnels below.

The zombies followed.

EIGHTEEN

They followed Pigpen in single file, while God darted ahead of them, exploring the shadows. The glow stick in the cat's collar flashed neon green in the darkness. The cat stopped occasionally, licking his paws until they caught up. Each step took them deeper and deeper into the network of tunnels spreading like veins beneath the city. The silence and darkness were overwhelming—the quiet broken only by the faint sound of dripping water. The dampness seeped through their clothing.

Frankie shivered, wishing she had something more than the hospital gown to wear. The thin cloth barely covered her, and her ass was an ice cube. She decided she'd conserved her glow stick long enough and snapped it on, activating the chemicals inside the plastic cylinder. The darkness surrounded the light, as if trying to extinguish it. She slogged forward, her fingers trailing along the wall to her left, and then yanked them away. Slimy moisture dripped from her fingertips. Wincing at the thick, unmistakable reek of raw sewage, Frankie wiped her hand on her leg and buried her nose in the neckline of the gown.

"Maybe we should have stayed upstairs," she joked.

The ceiling rose and sank like a roller coaster. They walked farther along the tunnel, alternately ducking under pipes and stepping over puddles. Jim gripped Danny's hand, making sure they stayed close in the darkness.

A small arch led into another tunnel, reeking of hydrogen sulfate. A pipe in the wall dripped black sludge. It felt like the weight of the city was crushing down on them.

Pigpen and God led them on, emerging into a new passageway. They stepped over a jumbled mound of cinder blocks and a discarded roll of copper tubing. The floor was dry, and the darkness wasn't as thick. Thin beams of light from the burning buildings in the streets above filtered down through overhead grates.

Frankie caught a whiff of burning flesh from the streets above, and wished for the darkness again. A roach the size of a half-dollar popped beneath her heel. She thought back to her dream in the hospital, of the plants and the insects becoming reanimated after humanity and the other life forms were destroyed. She opened her mouth to mention it to Jim and Don, but then decided against it. No sense alarming the others because of a dream.

Pigpen stopped, tilting his head and listening.

"What is it?" Forrest whispered.

"God heard something," the vagrant breathed. "His hackles are up."

They peered into the darkness, but saw nothing.

Danny squeezed Jim's hand, and clenched the bat tighter in his other fist.

"Daddy, I'm scared."

"It's okay. None of us are going to let anything get you. The cat probably just smelled a mouse or something."

"But what if the mouse is one of them?"

God prowled ahead, and Pigpen followed. The rest of the group plodded along behind them.

"So how far does this tunnel run?" Forrest asked, whispering now.

"Almost the whole way," Pigpen answered. "They ain't finished building it, but it's sturdy enough. We'll pass a few rough spots, places under construction. We used to sleep near one of them sometimes, when we couldn't get below Grand Central. There's a bomb shelter a few stories below our feet too."

"A bomb shelter?" Smokey was puzzled. "Who built that?"

"Mr. Ramsey. There's bunches of them under the city, and I know where a few of them are located. Most of them got built during the Cold War, and they've sat empty since then. But folks live in them now. Last time I checked, Ramsey's was vacant, but it's got food and stuff inside."

"Well shit," Leroy grumbled, "why don't we just make for that? Hole up inside, barricade ourselves? Might be easier than going to the airport and stealing a plane."

Forrest snapped a glow stick and wedged it into his belt. "If we do that, and the zombies found us, then we'd be trapped. I say we stick with the original plan. I don't want to spend the rest of my days holed up in a bunker."

"You've got that right," Jim said. He thought back to how this whole thing had started—trapped in a backyard bunker while the dead raged above him. He didn't want it to end that way as well.

They continued down the tunnel. Minutes later, they passed a manhole shaft. Shelves made from pallet boards and scrap wood hung over the ladder rungs, along with soiled sleeping bags. Needles, crack vials, broken bottles, and shriveled condoms lay scattered on the floor. The darkness grew thicker again, enveloping them all. The temperature dropped, and they could see their breath reflected in the soft light of the glow sticks.

"It's getting colder," Etta whispered.

"That's because we're getting farther away from the fires," Pigpen explained.

Frankie shivered again, and pulled the hospital gown closer.

They came to a section where muddy water dripped from the ceiling, forming a pool on the floor. A layer of scummy film floated atop it. It stank worse than the corpses in the city streets above them. More cockroaches scuttled through the detritus. But that was it. No humans or rats, undead or otherwise. They skirted the pool and moved on.

They continued in silence, with only the sloshing of their wet shoes and the sound of their breath as company. The network seemed endless, each tunnel vanishing into the distance, beyond the reach of the flashlight. But Pigpen and God crept on with unerring assurance, tirelessly guiding them through the twisting, graffiti-covered catacombs. Eventually, they arrived at a crossroads where several tunnels merged into an open area.

"What was this gonna be?" Forrest asked.

Pigpen shrugged. "I don't know."

"It looks like some sort of hub," Don whispered. "Service tunnels maybe?"

Quinn lit a cigarette. "Well, one thing's for sure. It'll never get finished now."

They crept on through a large, round tunnel, which emptied out into an uncompleted subway station, deserted except for a skid piled with new turnstiles, and an abandoned lunchbox and thermos. The flashlight beam reflected something in the darkness, and Steve stepped closer to investigate. A decapitated head stared back at him; a *Ramsey Construction* hardhat perched on its scalp. The skin on its face looked like wax—greasy and swollen. The lips moved silently, and the eyes darted back and forth, tracking his movements.

"Ugh!" Steve lashed out with his foot, kicking it down several flights of stairs to the lowest platform. The head rolled off the platform and bounced onto the tracks, coming to rest against the third rail. He held his breath, waiting for the crack and sizzle of electricity, but there was no power. Instead, the head just lay there, cursing him without vocal cords.

"Touchdown." Quinn smirked. "Hell, Steve. You could have played for the Giants."

They continued on; Pigpen and God in the lead, Steve and Quinn bringing up the rear, and the rest of the group sandwiched between them. When the glow sticks began to fade, they cast them aside and activated new ones.

"Pick those up," Leroy suggested, pointing at the discarded glow sticks. "No sense in leaving a trail for them to follow."

They put the discarded sticks in their pockets and kept walking.

Jim took hold of Danny's hand again.

"Daddy?"

"What, squirt?"

"Do you think they'll ever make a new Godzilla movie?"

Jim stifled a laugh. The question surprised him, so unexpected and removed from their surroundings.

"I doubt it, Danny. I think Hollywood and Tokyo are probably just like everywhere else now."

"That sucks," the boy pouted. "I'll miss Godzilla. And Spider-Man and Dragonball Z. Maybe when I grow up, I'll make new ones."

"Maybe we can find you some comic books somewhere along the way, after we get to where we're going."

Danny's face brightened at the prospect. "I miss my comics. They were all back at Mommy's house. Now they're probably burned up, or else the monster-people are reading them."

"You know what I missed?" Jim asked him.

"What?"

"I missed you." He gave Danny's hand a squeeze.

"But what do you miss now, Daddy?"

Jim thought about it. "Your stepmom. And West Virginia. My friends back home. Watching the Mountaineers play, even if they're losing. And Martin."

"You know what I miss?" Quinn spoke up from the rear. "An ice-cold beer. God, I'd kill for a beer right now. And a big, juicy steak, cooked rare with a baked potato on the side."

"I miss *Days of Our Lives*," Etta said.

"You and those damn soaps," Leroy grunted. "That's all you ever watched."

"I watched it ever since I was a little girl. Last I saw, Abe and Lexie was getting back together, but Stefano was gonna stop it. Now I don't guess I'll ever find out what happens next."

"You won't be missing much." Leroy shook his head in frustration. "I miss my car. I swear, my damn feet got blisters from all this walking."

"What about you, Steve?" Quinn asked.

"My son."

They grew quiet. In the darkness, Steve sniffed.

"Yeah," Don finally broke the silence. "I miss my wife, Myrna."

Pigpen's eyes were far away. "I miss that Italian place on 24th. They used to give me a meatball hoagie every day. God and I would share one, and eat it outside on the sidewalk bench. Boy, those were good. Didn't last long, though."

"You mean God didn't turn the sandwich into more, like Jesus with the bread and fish?" Quinn teased him.

"God's just a cat, Mr. Quinn."

They all laughed at this. In the darkness, Quinn's ears got as red as his hair.

"What about you, Forrest?" Don asked. "What do you miss most?"

"Honestly? This will sound weird. I was a news junkie. Growing up in Harlem, my momma made me watch the news every day. Stuck with me when I became an adult. Always started the morning with a cup of coffee and *The Daily News*. Then I'd watch Fox or CNN in the evening. I miss the news—I miss feeling connected to the world. I don't feel like I'm a part of it anymore."

"You might not want to be a part of it," Frankie said. "It belongs to those things now."

"I miss my home," Smokey mumbled. "And my dog. He was a good dog—kind and gentle, scared of his own shadow. Followed me around the house all day. I boarded him in a kennel when I came here to visit my daughter. I wish I knew what happened to him."

"Maybe it's better that you don't," Leroy said.

Frankie didn't speak her desire aloud. She missed her baby—her stillborn child. She squeezed her eyes shut and tired to force the image from her mind. She could still hear the nurse's screams when the infant had come back to life.

Danny murmured, "I miss Mommy."

Jim put an arm around his shoulders and squeezed.

They all fell silent again, each lost in their own thoughts.

Soon, the sounds of running water echoed from ahead. They emerged into a wide space filled with tools and construction equipment. A seamless curtain of water poured from a broken pipe fifteen feet over their heads. To their right, there was a hole in the cement wall. It looked like something or somebody had chiseled it out. Pigpen shined the flashlight beam into the hole.

Etta and Smokey both screamed.

Rats had eaten half of the zombie's face—whether before or after it had died they didn't know. The eyes were scratched out, and the tongue had been chewed away. An ear was missing; the other was a ragged lump of gnawed cartilage. When it sat up, the creature's empty eye sockets swarmed with wriggling maggots and a plump, white worm dropped from its nose.

The blind creature slumped out of the hole and crawled toward them, guided by their screaming. God reared up, hissing, and Pigpen dropped the flashlight. He bent, fumbling for it, as the monster crept closer.

Forrest raised his rifle to his shoulder, carefully lined up the crosshairs of his scope, and squeezed the trigger. The stock bucked against his shoulder and the zombie's rotting head exploded, splattering the wall with gore and maggots.

Pigpen snatched up the flashlight and gasped for breath.

Behind them, a thin figure separated itself from the

darkness and glided toward the group. They didn't see it until it's yellow, broken teeth sank into Leroy's neck. Flesh and tendons tore, and blood gushed from the hole. Leroy's scream became a long, drawn out wail. He beat at the creature with his hands, but the jaws clamped down on the wound again. The zombie shook its head back and forth like a dog, burrowing deeper into his neck and shoulder. Its pus-covered fingers dug into the burn wound on his arm, popping the blisters and peeling his skin back.

"Get it off me! Oh God . . ."

"I can't get a shot," Quinn yelled. "Steve! Nail it!"

Steve ran forward, clubbing the creature with the butt of his rifle. He smashed the stock against its face a second time, and the zombie reared backward, taking another mouthful of Leroy's neck with it.

The wounded man collapsed next to the zombie on the tunnel floor. He tried to scream, but blood shot from his throat rather than sound. He inhaled, the air whistling in his chest. The zombie reared up on its hands and knees and gnashed its teeth.

"Leroy!" Etta screamed.

She ran to his side and the zombie lunged for her. Steve swung the rifle over his head and slammed it down a third time. There was a sickening thud, and then blood and other fluids gushed from the cracked skull. Steve clubbed it again. The corpse went limp, sprawling in a puddle of sewage.

The others checked the perimeter, but there were no more zombies. They gathered around Leroy and Etta.

Leroy held his hands up to his face and saw the blood on them. His eyes widened in panic and he grasped his throat. Etta sobbed, begging him not to die. He tried to speak one more time, and then his lips stopped moving.

"No," Etta cried. "This ain't happening. You come back, Leroy. You come back to me right now, god damn it!"

Forrest's voice was gentle, but firm. "Etta, you know what we've got to do."

"He ain't gonna rise. Not Leroy. He ain't gonna come back."

Smokey knelt down beside her and clasped her hands. "Etta, you know that's not true."

Don sniffed the air. "You guys smell something?"

"Just the sewer," Frankie quipped.

Suddenly, God howled. The cat paced back and forth in front of the large tunnel, hissing and spitting with rage. He peered into the darkness and then backed away.

"Listen," Quinn gasped. "What the hell is that?"

"Whatever it is," Frankie whispered, "the cat doesn't like it."

Then they all heard it, racing down the tunnel toward them—the whispered scurrying of rats. Hundreds of beady red eyes reflected back at them from the darkness.

"Oh, God," Quinn whispered. "We are so fucked . . ."

Frankie shoved him. "Run!"

"Jim," Quinn shouted, "Get that flamethrower back here! Toast the fuckers!"

"No," Forrest yelled. "Those are gas mains over our heads. You light up and you'll kill us all. Move, people!"

Jim glanced upward and spotted the gas pipes hugging the ceiling. Small, furry shapes darted along the top of them.

The undead rats rushed down the tunnel like a brown wave. They made no sound, save the clicking of their claws. As they drew closer, they began to squeal. The sound was like fingernails on a chalkboard.

God was the first to run, followed by Pigpen, Frankie,

Don, and Smokey. Jim scooped Danny into his arms and raced down the tunnel after them. Quinn, Forrest, and Steve brought up the rear. All three fired into the scurrying mass, but it had no effect.

Etta never had a chance. The undead vermin swept over her as she struggled to get to her feet, crushing her back to the floor. Her body was completely obscured. They stripped the flesh from her bones in minutes, and then did the same to Leroy. The rest chased after the group.

Ob stared down the shaft in the sub-basement's floor.

"They went down there? You are sure of it?"

The gash in Bates's throat opened and closed as he talked. "Yes, lord. It is all here in my host's mind. They could not have gotten very far."

Ob turned to his lieutenant. "I want our forces to enter through every manhole cover and subway station within a twelve-block radius. Hunt them down and eradicate them. I would be done with this. Also, have a group dispatched for the airport, just in case they slip through our net."

The zombie nodded, and then lurched off to convey the orders.

Ob realized that his right pinkie finger was loose and dangling by a thread of sinew. He hadn't noticed until this moment. Perhaps he'd cut it on a piece of wreckage, or maybe the body was deteriorating faster than he'd expected.

He ripped the half-severed digit from his hand and dropped it down the hole.

"I don't like loose ends."

Ob climbed down the shaft. His forces followed.

NINETEEN

They ran down the tunnel, their breath burning in their lungs. The rats bounded after them, unstoppable, closing the gap.

Smokey tripped over the rail and fell, sprawling across the tracks. Forrest bent to help him. The others kept running, not looking back or stopping until a sudden hail of gunfire from in front of them brought them to an abrupt halt.

The human zombies surged forward, blocking their escape. Frankie and Don dropped to their knees and returned fire, aiming for the muzzle flashes. Jim dove to the floor, sheltering Danny beneath him. Steve and Quinn fired into the rats, still bearing down from the rear.

"We're cut off," Forrest shouted. "Defensive positions!"

"Defensive my ass," Quinn wheezed. "This is gonna be a massacre."

"Jim," Steve hollered, "Get back here with that flame thrower."

"What about the gas lines?" Jim shouted back.

Quinn clamped his tongue between his teeth and squeezed off another shot. "The hell with the gas lines! I'd rather get blown up than eaten."

"I'm not leaving Danny!"

"God damn it, Jim! Get your ass back here or we're dead!"

Thin, rusty ladders climbed up the sheer cement walls on each side of the passageway, providing access to two small service tunnels. God scurried up the one to their left, and Pigpen followed him. The vagrant wrenched the steel door open and turned back to the group.

"This way," he called. "Hurry!"

Jim lifted Danny into Pigpen's waiting arms and then scrambled up the ladder behind him.

"Go," Frankie urged Smokey and Don. "I'll cover you."

Smokey stood up and ran for the wall. The guns sang out, and the air buzzed with lead. A bullet plowed into him, and his heart exploded through the front of his shirt. Smokey collapsed back onto the tracks, eyes staring sightlessly.

"Fuck!" Don returned fire. "I can't see what I'm shooting at. It's too dark!"

Frankie's weapon clicked empty. She cast it aside and grabbed Smokey's.

"Is he dead?" Don asked.

"What do you think? You see the size of that hole in his chest?"

"I can't see shit. That's the problem!"

Another explosion rang out and more muzzle flashes erupted in the darkness.

"I'm hit," Steve cried out. "Oh shit, that fucking hurts!"

Frankie returned fire, aiming for the muzzle flashes.

Steve writhed on the tunnel floor, blood streaming from his leg. Quinn and Forrest knelt over him, and fired into the wave of dead rats.

"Get out of here," Forrest told Frankie and Don. "That's an order!"

"We don't work for you," Frankie shouted. "You can't hold them yourselves."

"Go, god damn it!"

A bullet pinged off the concrete next to Frankie, and fragments of stone pelted her skin.

Don tugged her arm. "Come on. We need to move, now!"

Crouching and firing at the same time, they reached the ladder. Frankie tossed Jim her weapon and climbed up while Don and Jim laid down cover fire. Then Don hoisted himself up, while Jim and Frankie held the zombies at bay.

Pigpen, Danny, and God watched from inside the service tunnel. Jim, Frankie, and Don remained on the ledge, turning back to the others. The zombies had the men pinned down, and the rats were less than twenty yards away, and closing fast.

"Get out of there!" Don yelled.

Forrest reloaded and unleashed another barrage into the moving wall of vermin, then spun and fired into the midst of the other zombies.

"You guys go," Steve groaned. "I'll hold them off."

"Bullshit," Quinn snapped. "We ain't leaving you behind the way we did Bates. He was mortally wounded. You're just shot in the fucking leg."

"And I'll slow you down," Steve insisted, clenching his teeth. "No way I can run from those rats."

Forrest kept firing. "Help him to his feet, Quinn."

"Damn straight. We'll carry him if we have to."

"No," Forrest said, wincing as hot shells bounced off his forearms. "Steve is right. He'll just slow us down. Help him to his feet and give him a gun."

Quinn gaped in disbelief. "You cold hearted—"

"You heard the man," Steve grunted.

"Oh fuck," Quinn moaned. "Fuck, fuck, fuck! This isn't right, man! What about the airplane? Who's gonna fly it?"

"Use your head, Quinn. There's no way you guys will make it to the airport now!"

"This isn't right."

Steve grabbed his hand and squeezed it tight as another bullet ricocheted off the rail.

"Listen to me. We don't have time to argue. I'll never see my son alive again. But maybe, if there is an afterlife—and God, I fucking hope there is—just maybe, I'll see him there. I want to find out. The only thing that matters right now is that little boy up on that ledge, and his daddy. You want to do something for me? Get them out of here. Now!"

Slowly, Quinn nodded. "Okay, man."

The rats drew closer, their stench thick and cloying.

"Kick some ass, Canuck," Forrest said.

"You know it." Steve wobbled, shifting his weight onto his uninjured leg.

Quinn hesitated, eyeing the rats. "I still—"

"Don't. Just go . . ."

Forrest handed Steve an extra magazine and then shoved Quinn forward. They were halfway to the ladder when Smokey's corpse sat up and grinned at them.

"Hey guys," it slurred. "Who's up for a game of cards?"

The zombies opened fire again. Bullets slammed into the ledge where Jim, Don, and Frankie were standing. The three of them ducked inside the tunnel.

Quinn frantically reloaded. "We're cut off."

"This way!" Forrest lunged for the other ladder. He climbed to the top, and then helped Quinn clamber up behind him.

The others stared across the tunnel in dismay.

"Where you going, Forrest?" Smokey's corpse called.

"You guys go ahead," Forrest shouted to the others. "We'll catch up, if we can!"

Jim flashed him a thumbs up and shut the door.

"Hurry up!" Steve shouted.

Forrest and Quinn spared Steve one last glance, and then they disappeared into the second service tunnel.

Steve cracked his neck from side to side, and planted his legs as firmly as he could, wincing from the pain. His leg felt cold, and the blood had run down into his shoe, soaking his sock and pants leg.

Smokey stumbled to his feet and pointed at the rats. "Say hello to my little friends, Steve."

"Never figured you for a Pacino fan," Steve grunted.

The zombie ran toward him, blood still dripping from the hole in his chest. Steve opened fire. The bullet shattered the zombie's sternum. The pilot readjusted his aim and the second one drilled into the creature's forehead. Smokey tottered forward over the tracks and lay still.

"Come on," Steve shouted, turning back to the rats. "Let's see what you've got!"

His machine gun roared. Brass jackets rained down, and the air became thick with smoke. The weapon grew hot in his hands.

As the rats bore down on him, Steve realized that he had never felt more alive.

He smiled, hoping that his son would be waiting on the other side.

Pigpen turned the flashlight back on, and they gathered around him.

"What about the others?" Frankie asked.

"Cut off," Jim said. "Forrest said they'd try to catch up."

"How? They got a map?"

Jim shrugged.

Don wiped the mud and gore from his face. "What now? They've blocked our way to the airport. And even if we could, going there would be useless without our pilots."

God meowed, twining himself between Danny's feet. The boy reached down and petted him.

"The bomb shelter," Pigpen said.

"Ramsey's?" Jim asked. "But we're cut off from that too."

Pigpen shook his head. "I told you—there's lots of them down here. I know of one nearby. Last time I was there, it was still stocked. Ain't been used in years. Government built it and then forgot about it when the Russians became our friends."

"Surely there are people in it now," Don said.

"No, I don't think so. Only folks that knew about it were me and God, and my buddies Fran and Seiber. Fran got killed at a soup kitchen in the East Village. A zombie shoved his head into a vat of boiling stew. And Seiber was shot by five-oh, down on Madison Avenue during the riots. They caught him looting a jewelry store."

"How far is it?" Jim asked.

"Eight stories down and a little to the south."

"And you know the way?" Frankie whispered, not at all convinced.

"Yeah." Pigpen started forward, then stopped and turned back to them.

"And if I don't, God will deliver us instead."

The cat sprang out from between Danny's feet and ran ahead, green eyes glinting in the darkness.

Quinn stopped when he heard the gunshots. Steve yelled something unintelligible, muted by the concrete between them.

"Forrest? Maybe we ought to go back. We can't just leave him. Abandoning Bates was bad enough."

There was no reply. The big man had been swallowed up by the darkness.

"Forrest?"

More gunfire echoed.

"Forrest, quit fucking around!"

Quinn crawled on his hands and knees. The tunnel was tall enough for him to stand up in, but it was pitch-black, and the feeble light of his glow stick only made the darkness worse.

He crept forward, cautiously feeling his way. Then the floor disappeared beneath his hands, replaced by a hole. The chasm ran from wall to wall, completely blocking his progress. The edges of the crevice were jagged, and the masonry crumbled beneath his fingertips. Cold air brushed his face.

"Forrest?"

His voice echoed back to him from below.

"Oh shit."

The big man had obviously fallen down the hole.

Quinn called again, but there was no answer. He had no way of knowing if Forrest could even hear him. How far down was it? Maybe he was unconscious. Or dead.

Behind him, more distant now, Steve continued shooting.

Carefully, Quinn turned around and started crawling back to him.

"I'm not leaving you, man. We've lost enough people today."

The shots were sporadic now.

"I'm coming, Steve! Just hold on!"

He made it back to the doorway and put his ear against the cold steel. The gunshots had stopped, both Steve's and the zombie's. All he could hear was a high-pitched squealing.

Slowly, he opened the door. The rusty hinges creaked.

Quinn gasped, horrified at what lay before him.

The squealing didn't belong to the rats. It was coming from Steve. The tunnel was flooded with wriggling, rotting vermin. The brown, furry creatures were almost six feet deep in places. If he weren't seeing it, he would have never believed there were this many rats in the world, let alone New York. They crawled overtop one another to reach the ledge. The human zombies waded through them, toward the doorway that Jim and the others had disappeared into.

Steve's arm jutted from the sea of rats, like a buoy in the middle of the ocean. The rest of him was buried beneath the squirming mass. Incredibly, his fingers were still twitching, his fist clenching and unclenching.

"Steve!"

Quinn crouched on the edge of the service ledge, and reached for Steve's hand.

"Get off him, you little fuckers!"

The rats chattered angrily, and Quinn was sure he could hear words—formed by creatures that lacked the necessary equipment for speech. Attracted by his outburst, the human zombies turned, and raised their weapons.

Quinn grabbed Steve's hand. Steve's fingers curled around his. Quinn pulled. His friend didn't budge. He jerked harder, and suddenly, the arm came free. Quinn stumbled backward, knocking his head against the concrete wall. Steve's arm came with him, their hands still clenched together.

The rest of Steve stayed with the rats.

Gibbering, Quinn tossed the severed arm aside and turned to run. A rifle cracked. The first shot caught him in the leg, but he felt no pain. The second round punched the breath from him, and brought a muted burning sensation. Teetering, he fell backward, landing on top of the writhing masses. Hundreds of razor sharp teeth and claws ripped at his flesh. It felt like thousands of tiny needles piercing his skin.

Quinn opened his mouth to scream and a small rat scrabbled inside it, stretching his cheeks as it forced its body farther into the orifice. Its nails slashed at his tongue. Blood welled in his mouth. He was unable to spit it out because the rat blocked his airway. He tried to move his arms and legs, but the creatures' combined weight kept them pinned. His lungs pounded, desperate for air. The last thing he saw was a large rat's misshapen, decaying head, darting for his eyes. Then there was a bright flash of pain, and then he saw no more.

Quinn sank to the bottom of the pile.

Forrest awoke in the dark, soaked to the bone. When he opened his eyes, the darkness did not dissipate. He grimaced, tasting blood, and spat. Gingerly, he explored his mouth with his tongue, and found a gaping hole where a tooth had been.

He was half-submerged in a pool of warm, stinking liquid. He shuddered to think what it was. Slowly, he rose to his feet, sloshing out of the foulness, and checked the rest of his body for injuries. No broken bones, but he was bleeding from at least a dozen different cuts and abrasions.

He stood there in the darkness, shivering and dripping with slime, and tried to get his bearings. He'd been crawling along the tunnel, feeling his way, when suddenly, the floor had disappeared beneath him. He remembered falling, so surprised that he hadn't even had time to shout a warning to Quinn—and then he remembered no more.

"Must have blacked out," he said aloud, and immediately wished he hadn't. His voice echoed off unseen walls, sounding strange and alien to him. When the noise faded, the silence was deafening.

He knelt, feeling around beneath the pool's surface for his weapons, but came up empty. He checked his belt and was relieved to find that he still had an unused glow stick and his knife. He grasped the hilt and pulled it from the sheath. The feel of the blade in his hands was comforting.

Forrest stood still as stone, snapped the glow stick, and waited for his eyes to adjust. The liquid came halfway up to his knees, clinging to him. He wondered again what it was. Finally, he dipped a finger into the pool and brought it to his lips, tasting it. Water—brackish and foul, but only water.

At least it isn't shit, he thought. *Even so—I'm in a world of shit anyway.*

He cocked his head, listening for anything that would indicate his location and whether or not he was alone. Water dripped, but other than that, the silence was as solid as the blackness around him. There were no shouts or footsteps or even gunfire, nothing that meant the others—or the zombies—were nearby.

When he could see, he edged forward. He was in an old, unused tunnel, left over from an earlier era. The walls were circular, and lined with crumbling, red bricks. Lichen and mold clung to the cracks, and a thin stream of brown water trickled along the floor.

He debated whether to call out for Quinn, or to remain silent. If there were zombies nearby, he didn't want to alert them to his presence. But what if Quinn had tumbled down after him, and was hurt or unconscious? He couldn't just leave him here.

"Quinn?"

The darkness didn't respond.

"Yo, Quinn! Speak up if you're there."

His voice taunted him, transforming into something unfamiliar.

Forrest crept slowly forward, his body coiled and ready for anything. The tunnel sloped downward at a steady decline, and he picked his steps carefully, not wanting to slip on the slime-covered bricks.

"Hello?" he called again, and thought he heard something rustle behind him.

Forrest turned and his feet shot out from under him. He landed on his back, his jaws slamming shut. His knife skittered away, and he slithered down the tunnel, desperately grasping for a handhold.

Then the tunnel disappeared, and suddenly, he was falling again. He splashed into a large pool of water, and sank beneath the surface. His feet touched bottom and he kicked for the top. He emerged, choking and gasping for breath.

Something brushed against his leg. Forrest jumped, and slapped at his thigh. He glanced down to see a small, white flash darting away beneath the surface—some kind of albino fish.

Treading water, he swam across the pool to a circular concrete platform. He pulled himself up and collapsed, gasping for breath. He wished for his knife, and glanced back down at the pool. Albino fish teemed in the water by the dozens. Forrest wondered if they were some type of deformed goldfish, flushed down here long ago.

He tried to figure out what to do next. Climbing back up the shaft was impossible, yet he didn't see any other tunnels to escape through. He considered the possibility that the exit might be underwater, and surveyed the pool. The ripples had ceased, and the dark surface was still again. Something white jutted up from the center; a pipe or possibly a piece of wood, bleached from years of floating in this chemical soup.

He bent down and peered over the edge, studying the fish closer. One of them swam up to the concrete island, and Forrest froze.

Its left eye was missing.

"Dead. They're fucking dead."

The piece of wood began to move, slowly coming toward him. Something glinted in the darkness. Teeth. Rows of long, pointed teeth.

"Oh my God . . ."

His conversation with Pigpen, when he'd scoffed at the bum's tales of what lay beneath the city, came back to him.

And there are alligators down there, Forrest. Big al-

bino fuckers with red eyes and white skin. I had a buddy named Wilbanks. He lost a leg to one.

A baleful red eye glared at him, and then the alligator clambered up onto the platform. Pustulent, open sores covered its scaly hide, and its snout was a raw, red wound. Vertebrae poked out of the creature's side, and a chunk of flesh was missing from its massive tail.

Forrest backed away. The alligator lumbered after him. It opened its mouth and hissed. The stench of its foul breath was overpowering.

Exhausted and weaponless, his back to the wall, Forrest could only scream.

The zombie nosed his legs with its decaying snout. Forrest kicked it hard. The jaws snapped shut on his leg, and the darkness erupted with hot points of light. The alligator tugged hard, dragging him toward the water.

Forrest slammed his head against the concrete, desperately trying to crack his own skull open before the creature could kill him.

The creature severed his leg at the knee with a loud crunch. Forrest struck his head against the platform again and again, and felt warm wetness on the back of his scalp. But it was too late to kill himself. The alligator rushed forward and opened its mouth.

"Headfirst, you motherfucker. Headfirst! I ain't coming back!"

He leaped into the gaping jaws, and they crunched down on his shoulders.

His last thought was, *Choke on it . . .*

Minutes later, Forrest's severed head opened its eyes inside the alligator's stomach.

TWENTY

They ran, not caring now if the creatures heard their flight. Caution and their sense of self-preservation had given way to sheer terror. Their feet pounded down the tunnel, the echoes pursuing them. God leaped through a hole in the wall and they jumped through after him.

Pigpen slid to a stop and opened a circular hatch in the floor, revealing a narrow shaft. They started down it, Jim assisting Danny with the climb. Don brought up the rear and closed the hatch behind them. The shaft continued downward for thirty feet, and the rungs were cold and slippery. Jim's flamethrower tanks kept getting stuck as they descended, and he had to struggle the whole way down.

They reached the bottom and Pigpen glanced around them, seemingly unsure of which direction to go. The tunnel ran north and south, and he stared into the darkness in both directions.

"Which way?" Don gasped, breathing hard.

"I'm not sure," Pigpen admitted. "This way, I think." He pointed with the flashlight beam.

"You think?"

"Been a while." He looked down at the cat. "What do you think, God?"

Without hesitation, the cat headed north. They stumbled along behind it.

"I don't believe this shit," Frankie muttered.

"What?" Don asked.

"We're following a fucking cat named God, and trusting it to lead us to safety."

Don chuckled. "Would you prefer a burning bush?"

They continued onward, their wet shoes rubbing against their feet. They climbed down another shaft, and exited into a tubular passage. Gas mains and fiber optic lines ran along the top.

"We're close." Pigpen sighed, sounding relieved.

Don stopped and knelt to tie his shoe. Danny, Jim, and Frankie passed him.

"You okay?" Jim asked.

"Yeah," Don said. "Just don't want to trip down here in the dark. Knowing my luck, I'd break my neck or something."

Danny squeezed his father's hand.

"How about you, squirt?"

"I'm scared," Danny whispered. His voice was weary. "It's quiet down here."

"Maybe that means we've lost them."

"We'll be safe now?" Danny stared up into his father's face.

"I won't let anything hurt you, Danny. I promise."

"Anybody else smell something?" Frankie asked.

Pigpen's nose wrinkled. "You mean besides the sewers?"

She shrugged. "Good point. Forget it."

Jim rubbed his hands together for warmth. "Boy, what I wouldn't give for a pair of gloves right now."

Frankie shivered in the darkness. "I hope there's something to wear inside this shelter. I'm freezing my ass off."

Pigpen shrugged. "I don't know. There's food. Freeze-dried stuff. And cases of bottled water. I'm not sure if there's clothing, but it is warm inside."

The flashlight beam flickered. Pigpen smacked it against his palm.

"Batteries are starting to die. I think I saw some of those in the shelter too. Hopefully they're still good."

"So what's this thing like?" Frankie asked, her teeth chattering.

"Kind of like a big boiler," Pigpen told her. "It's made out of steel, and the door is a hatch, like on a ship or a submarine. It's divided into two big rooms. The government stocked it up and then forgot about it. Your tax dollars at work."

"Lucky for us," Jim said.

"You can lock the door from the inside," Pigpen continued. "So that nobody else can get in. We used to do that, to keep the other homeless out. It's warm and dry. We'll be okay there. Hell, you could set off a bomb right next to it and that steel wouldn't buckle. It's stronger than anything Ramsey ever built."

Frankie's brow creased in thought. "Is there more than one exit? I'd hate to get trapped inside."

"There's a door on each side," Pigpen said. "We can lock both of them from the inside."

Jim thought again of how things had started. Then, he'd been alone, and left the safety of the bunker to find his son. Now, Danny would be with him, along with Frankie, Don, Pigpen, and God.

"God is with us," he whispered, quietly so that the others didn't hear him. He thought that Martin would have found it funny.

"Not much farther now," Pigpen reported. "I bet your feet are tired."

Frankie, Jim, and Danny all groaned in agreement. Don didn't reply.

"You okay, Don?" Jim asked. "You're awfully quiet back there."

"I'm fine," the zombie answered, and leaped onto his back.

Jim and Don tumbled to the floor. Don clawed at his face, his fingers seeking to rip open Jim's cheeks. Jim rolled, crushing Don beneath him. He sat up and punched the zombie in the face.

Danny and Pigpen screamed, and God hissed. Frankie grabbed Don's hair in her fist and yanked his head back.

His throat had been cut. Something had slipped up behind Don and slashed it in the darkness.

How long was he dead? Frankie wondered. *How long has he been following us?*

Pigpen shined the flashlight beam back the way they had come.

Zombies filled the tunnel.

He turned and ran. God raced along behind him.

"Run!" Frankie shrieked.

Jim jumped to his feet, kicked Don in the jaw, and grabbed Danny's hand, dragging the terrified boy along with him.

"Mr. De Santos," Danny screamed. "Daddy, Mr. De Santos is a monster-person!"

Jim swept his son into his arms and rocketed down the tunnel. Frankie pounded along behind him.

Enraged, the zombies pursued them. One of them

worked the bolt on its rifle, aimed, and fired. Jim cried out, and sprawled across the tunnel floor. Danny fell with him.

Pigpen, Frankie, and God rounded a corner and skidded to a halt. The tunnel ended at the fallout shelter, the exterior steel wall of which blocked their way. Pigpen flung himself at the hatch and grasped the wheel-like door handle. He grunted, straining to turn it. Frankie latched on and helped him. Slowly, the wheel began to turn, squeaking in protest.

There was an explosion behind them, and a bullet ricocheted off the shelter's outer wall.

"Danny," Don called, "want to come back to Bloomington with me? We can play with Rocky."

"Leave us alone," Danny shrieked. "You're not Mr. De Santos! You're not!"

"Come on, Danny. I'll take you back to your home. Don't you want to see your mommy? We'll find your comic books."

Tears coursed down Danny's cheeks. "Daddy, make him go away!"

The zombie tittered, "You can join us, Danny. You can be just like your mother and your stepfather and Mrs. De Santos. It only takes a second . . ."

Jim clenched his leg, trying to stop the flow of blood. It ran between his fingers, staining them red.

"Danny," he grunted, "Listen to me. Go with Frankie."

"What about you, Daddy?"

Don rounded the corner and Jim leapt to his feet, yelling in pain and rage. Blood streamed from the wound in his leg. He gripped the side of Don's head, and slammed it against the wall. Blood and teeth exploded from the zombie's mouth. The gun slipped from the creature's fingers. Jim smashed its head against the wall again. Screaming, he released the zombie and dug his fingers into the neck wound, pulling the flesh apart. The gash widened, and he thrust his hands inside the hole.

"Leave my son alone, you bastard!"

Pigpen flung the hatch open and God darted inside. More zombies appeared. Jim and Don struggled between them and the others.

Frankie grabbed Danny's arm. "Come on, Danny! Get inside!"

"Daddy!"

"Danny," Frankie shouted. "Get inside the shelter! Now!"

"I'm not leaving you!"

One of the zombies raised its rifle, peered through the scope, and squeezed the trigger. Pigpen cried out, and slumped against the wall, holding a hand to his chest. He stumbled through the open doorway, leaving a bright trail of blood behind him.

"Danny," Frankie urged, "come on!"

"Daddy!" the boy screamed again, turning back to his father.

Don's head lolled to the side, dangling over his shoulder. Jim had ripped it halfway off. He flung the corpse aside, pointed the flamethrower at the zombies, and backed away. Another bullet slammed into his leg. Jim bit his lip to keep from screaming. His head swam.

"Don't shoot him again," one of the zombies warned. "Hit those tanks and we all go up."

"So? What does it matter? We can get new bodies. This one is falling apart anyway."

"Lord Ob said to wait. He wants to deal with these humans himself."

"Where is he then?"

"Here," said a new voice, deeper and more powerful than the others.

Jim wobbled to a halt. "Frankie, get Danny inside and shut the door."

"What? Jim, you—"

"Do it. Please?"

"Daddy?"

The group of zombies parted, and one of them stepped forward. Jim didn't recognize the corpse, but he instinctively knew who resided inside it.

"Ob."

"Nice to meet you." Ob grinned. "We were never formally introduced, but Baker's memories told me so much about you. I see that you found your boy. That's touching. Now you can die together."

Jim's eyes didn't leave Ob. "Danny, I love you."

"Daddy!"

Jim's vision blurred as shock set in. He felt weak from blood loss, and the pain traveling up his leg was excruciating. He turned toward Danny.

"I'm very proud of you, and I love you."

"DADDY! NO!"

"I love you more than infinity."

He turned back to Ob.

Weeping, Frankie pulled the screaming little boy inside the shelter, and slammed the door shut. The clanging steel echoed in the sudden silence.

Hell, Pigpen had said, *you could set off a bomb right next to it and that steel wouldn't buckle.*

Jim hoped the old vagrant was right. He'd started out on this quest to save his son.

He'd succeeded.

He thought back to what he'd told Martin inside Don's garage.

I'll sacrifice myself before I'll let those things get my son.

Ob kept smiling.

Jim grinned back, even as the pain surged through him and his blood continued to flow.

The zombie craned his neck upward, studying the reinforced steel walls. The other zombies closed ranks again, gathering around him. They pointed their weapons at Jim. Their stench was masked by the smell of the sewers, and Jim guessed that was how they'd snuck up on them. Don's corpse leaned against the tunnel wall, the head dangling at an impossible angle.

"Did you think you'd be safe inside that tin can?" Ob asked. "You humans amaze me. So determined to survive, when the alternative would be much easier."

Jim fingered the trigger, stroking it slowly. "What alternative?"

"Having the good grace to die, and quickly. What do you live for? What is there to look forward to? Cancer? War? Famine? We offer a much better choice, don't you think?"

"No thanks."

"It doesn't matter where you hide. Did you really think you could escape us underground?"

"I started this underground. I reckon I'll finish it underground too."

Ob laughed. "You aren't the first. The slaves in Egypt and Rome lived and died in the mines. I remember the Sumerian priests, who lived in underground dwellings, and used tunnels to visit one another. Poor bastards weren't allowed to see the daylight, and only ventured to the surface after dark. The Crimeans hid underground during the Tartar invasions. You are no better than a lowly worm. Your kind always cowers beneath the earth, Jim Thurmond."

"My boss and my fourth-grade teacher called me Thurmond. Everybody else called me Jim. You don't know me, so don't call me either."

"But of course I know you. Your friend Baker's memories are my own. I know all about you and Martin. Where is he—inside with the others? No matter. You escaped me once, but it ends here. I'm going to enjoy killing you, but I think I'll keep you alive long enough to watch as I pull your son's intestines from his stomach and feed them to him."

Jim's eyes flicked up to the ceiling and then back to Ob. Ob noticed the movement and looked up as well. He laughed, and then stepped closer.

"Praying to your God? He can't help you now, Jim. All He can do is watch. And when we've killed the rest of you, and my brothers are freed from the Void, His screams will be like thunder and His tears will be like rain. And then, when the second wave is over, we will drown His creation in fire."

Jim rocked backward on his heels. "Well, you're half right."

"What do you mean?"

Jim tilted the flamethrower upward and squeezed the trigger. Orange fire erupted from the nozzle and engulfed the gas mains in the ceiling above them. There was a bright flash of light. Jim closed his eyes as the heat blasted against his face.

"More than infinity, Danny . . ."

On the streets above them, the earth moved.

The rain had stopped.

EPILOGUE

The motherless child and the childless mother awoke in the darkness. The cat lay between them, purring and twitching in its sleep. Frankie turned on the flashlight, thankful that the shelter had included batteries among the stockpiled supplies.

She rose, and checked the door. Remarkably, the reinforced steel had withstood the blast, but the door had twisted in its frame. The second night, undead rats had burrowed through the wreckage and tried to squeeze in through the crack. She'd fought them off, and then used a tube of silicone sealant and some boards to seal it off. She'd found both in a storage locker. It wasn't a marvel of engineering, but it was enough to keep the smaller zombies out.

So far . . .

She made her way across the room, and rummaged through a cardboard box, producing a package of freeze-dried corn. She tore the wrapper open with her teeth.

"You hungry, Danny?"

"No." His voice was hoarse.

She emptied the package into a container, and poured a bottle of water over it. They had no way to heat the food up, so she set it aside, waiting for the water to be absorbed.

"You've got to eat, kiddo."

"I don't want to eat. I want Daddy."

Frankie fought back the tears. In the corner, Pigpen's blood still stained the floor. He'd died of his gunshot wound shortly after the explosion. Frankie cracked his skull with an iron bedpost before he could get back up again, and disposed of the corpse out the rear exit. The front entrance was blocked, buried in tons of rubble, but the back door was clear. She'd briefly opened the hatch since getting rid of Pigpen, just to empty the coffee can they were using for a toilet.

She crossed back over to their cots and sat down next to Danny. He snuggled tight against her and she held him close, smoothing his hair and stroking his back with her fingernails. She breathed in his scent and closed her eyes.

Danny tried to speak, but his voice was cut off by a sob. His entire body trembled.

Frankie wasn't sure how long they stayed that way, but eventually, Danny sat up and wiped his nose on his hand.

"Maybe I am a little hungry," he said.

"Good. I'll get the corn."

She got up and spooned the corn into two bowls.

"Frankie? What will we do next?"

"I don't know, Danny. We're okay for now, but eventually, we'll have to leave this place. We've got enough food and water to last for a while, but we can't stay down here forever."

"But where will we go?"

She didn't respond.

They ate in silence. Danny let God lick his bowl clean while Frankie used the coffee can. When she came back out of the spare room, Danny was looking at her with an odd expression.

"What's wrong?" she asked.

"You'll think I'm making it up."

"No, I won't. What is it?"

He paused before continuing. "While we were asleep, I dreamed about Daddy. He said he was in a better place now, and that I shouldn't be sad. He said we would see him soon. Him and Mr. Martin and Mr. De Santos and everybody else that died."

Frankie's breath caught in her throat.

"Do you believe me, Frankie?"

Slowly, she nodded. "Yeah. Yeah, Danny, I do. I dream about the preacher-man, and he says the same thing."

Danny reached down and scratched God behind the ears. The cat raised its face to him and closed its eyes in contentment.

"Maybe they're not dead. Maybe the monster-people are the only ones that are really dead."

"Maybe," Frankie agreed.

Still exhausted, they lay back down on their cots. Frankie turned the flashlight off. Soon, the sound of Danny's soft breathing filled the room.

Maybe death isn't the end, she thought. *I still don't know if I believe in Heaven, but hell is right outside that door. Maybe Danny is right. Maybe death is just the beginning for us, and maybe it gives us an escape from those things. Maybe that's why they are here—so that we don't have to deal with them in the place we go to next. So that it's free of their kind . . .*

Frankie pulled the sleeping boy to her womb and closed her eyes.

What was it Martin had told her?

Everything dies, but not everything has an ending.

In the darkness, God watched over them while they slept. Eventually, the cat curled into a ball and drifted off as well.

The three of them slept like the dead.

When the rats finally chewed through the wood and silicone that blocked the hole in the door and poured into the shelter, Frankie, Danny, and God never woke up.

When they did, their loved ones were there to greet them.

In the streets of the Necropolis, silence reigned once more. Far above the empty skyscrapers and concrete canyons, the newly risen moon shined down upon the world, staring at a mirror image of its cold, dead self.

In Central Park, a broad, gnarled oak tree began to move its branches, stretching the massive limbs with a deep rumble. Individual blades of grass began to sway.

The moonlight disappeared, and the city was engulfed in darkness.

Thunder crashed in the sky, and the heavens wept one final time.

GET FREE BOOKS!

You can have the best fiction delivered to your door for less than what you'd pay in a bookstore or online. Sign up for one of our book clubs today, and we'll send you *FREE* BOOKS* just for trying it out...**with no obligation to buy, ever!**

As a member of the Leisure Horror Book Club, you'll receive books by authors such as

RICHARD LAYMON, JACK KETCHUM, JOHN SKIPP, BRIAN KEENE and many more.

As a book club member you also receive the following special benefits:

- **30% off all orders!**
- **Exclusive access to special discounts!**
- **Convenient home delivery and 10 days to return any books you don't want to keep.**

Visit www.dorchesterpub.com or call 1-800-481-9191

There is no minimum number of books to buy, and you may cancel membership at any time.

*Please include $2.00 for shipping and handling.